HelenKay Dimon is a divorce lawyer turned full-time author. Her bestselling and award-winning books have been showcased in numerous venues, including *The Washington Post* and *Cosmopolitan*. She is an RT Reviewers' Choice Best Book Award winner and has been a finalist for the Romance Writers of America RITA® Award multiple times.

USA TODAY bestselling author **Kat Cantrell** read her first Mills & Boon novel in third grade and has been scribbling in notebooks since she learned to spell. She's a Harlequin So You Think You Can Write winner and a Romance Writers of America Golden Heart® Award finalist. Kat, her husband and their two boys live in north Texas.

D0042758

Also by HelenKay Dimon

Pregnant by the CEO
Reunion with Benefits

Also by Kat Cantrell

Marriage with Benefits
The Things She Says
The Baby Deal
Best Friend Bride
One Night Stand Bride
Contract Bride
Wrong Brother, Right Man

Discover more at millsandboon.co.uk

THE RELUCTANT HEIR

HELENKAY DIMON

PLAYING MR RIGHT

KAT CANTRELL

MILLS & BOON

First Published in Great Britain 2018
by Mills & Boon, an imprint of HarperCollinsPublishers,
1 London Bridge Street, London, SE1 9GF

The Reluctant Heir © 2018 HelenKay Dimon
Playing Mr Right © 2018 Kat Cantrell

ISBN: 978-0-263-93619-3

0918

MIX
Paper from
responsible sources
FSC® C007454

This book is produced from independently certified FSC™ paper to ensure responsible forest management.

For more information visit: www.harpercollins.co.uk/green

Printed and bound in Spain
by CPI, Barcelona

THE
RELUCTANT
HEIR

HELENKAY DIMON

One

This could not be happening.

Hanna Wilde disconnected the call with the dry cleaner next door and stared at her cell phone.

He was here, in Milton. Many miles and a few states away from his big fancy home—make that *homes*—in the Washington, D.C. area.

Not *that* he. Not the one who'd tracked her and tried to scare her months ago. Not the one who'd threatened and lied. No, the man in her building, on his way up to her apartment, was the son, not the horrible father.

Carter Jameson. Youngest heir to a vast real estate fortune. Grandson of a disgraced congressman. The boy whose family had employed hers back when they were kids.

Her unwanted teen crush.

Amazing how the last name Jameson could start a shake running through her that rattled right down to her bones. Her reaction arose out of anger, not fear. Though, if she were being honest, she'd have to admit to a mix of both.

His visit here meant his family had hunted her down and found her again. The last round of contacts started with letters from Carter's father, Eldrick, then from his attorneys, all insisting she come in for a meeting. When she ignored those, the unwanted visits started. But she'd done what Eldrick ordered. She stayed away from Virginia and Carter and kept her mouth shut.

She'd already lost so much to the Jamesons—her father, her sister, her peace of mind. Now it looked like they were coming around again for one more shot.

She slipped her cell phone into her back jeans pocket and headed for the one closet in her studio apartment. It held her clothes, her cleaning supplies and, well, that just about constituted the entire list of what she owned. That and the photo album. If they were going to hound her it was easier to leave town for a while then go through it all again. She didn't have any real connections here anyway, but the album was coming with her. It was all she had left of the past she tried so often to forget.

The knocking started as soon as she dropped to her knees. The rickety closet door with the broken slats screeched to a halt on the tracks. She usually shoved and pushed, half lifted the thing, to get it to open the whole way. But that would make noise and require her to move, and she seemed to be frozen in place.

Her heartbeat thundered in her ears. It was the only sound in the silent room.

Then the knocking started again.

"Hello?" A deep male voice, all silky and smooth, floated through the door.

She refused to fall for that sexy sound a second time. She wasn't a teenage anymore. She knew better now…in theory. "What?"

"Hanna?"

He acted like he knew her but that had been years ago. Another time, almost another life.

"She's not here." She winced as she made the nonsensical remark.

For a second there was no response. Hanna scrambled to her feet and tiptoed to the door. She saw the shadow of Carter's feet at the bottom. So, he still stood there, quiet now.

"Are you sure you don't want to try another answer, Hanna Wilde? Maybe one a bit more believable?"

She couldn't insist he had the wrong apartment. He remembered her name and he still had the same smiling lilt to his voice. This, the guy she'd been warned to stay away from was now hanging out in the hallway. Maybe he wanted to take a turn telling her not to disclose the misdeeds of his past. Either way, she refused to be blamed for being near him when he was the one who found her.

Taking a deep breath, she threw open the front door. Almost slammed it right into her own face but had the good sense to step back in the nick of time.

Her words cut off at the sight of him. A smile lit up his stupidly handsome face. He was tall, probably six-one or so, looming over her by inches even though there was nothing tiny or petite about her.

A billionaire born into a family of extreme privilege, the type of people who did whatever they wanted, without consequence. A long line of Virginia landowners who considered themselves Southern gentlemen, a bloodline that had been broken only by a Japanese grandmother—or so said the nasty whispers of their fellow rich people. The same grandmother who had gifted Carter with the striking combination of glossy black hair and near black eyes.

Carter was the youngest of the Jameson sons. The playboy with the carefree reputation. The one not defined by the rules as much as his older brothers because no one expected or demanded anything of him. He was the "extra" child, or that was the joke his father used to describe him. She knew about the nickname because she'd watched interviews with Carter's old man, hating him as much on-screen as she had in person.

Carter had been living in California for almost a year now—after he'd breezed through her sister's life…and destroyed it.

"It's been so long." He sounded genuinely happy to see her.

Hanna ignored whatever traitorous emotion started jumping around in her stomach at the sound of his voice. "What do you want?"

"That's an interesting welcome."

She could have sworn his eyes actually sparkled. She glanced at the ceiling, figuring it had to be a trick from the hallway lighting. But no, the dude's eyes looked sunny and warm and welcoming.

This guy, the one who wined and dined her sister, made promises then left town, now acted as if nothing had happened. As if he'd lost touch with Hanna by accident, not because his father cut off all contact. He'd never really noticed her before, certainly not when she was younger and desperate for his attention, which still haunted her, but now he pretended to.

"Why are you here?" Her fingers dug into the wooden door. She held on to it like a shield, positioning her body half behind it, ready to slam it shut if he moved even an inch.

Later she would assess why just seeing him touched off a spinning inside her. Why, after all this time, her heart still sped up when he shot her an inviting look. The reaction struck her as self-destructive and wrong but realizing that didn't make it stop. It also made her wonder if she'd really overcome those feelings of not being good enough as she'd hoped.

The longer they stood there, the more those sparkly eyes dimmed. They started to narrow a bit. "Hanna? Do you remember me?"

She snorted. Little did he know she used to dream about him. "Of course."

His gaze wandered over her head, into the studio behind her. "Are you okay?"

"I was up until three minutes ago."

He let out a long, labored exhale. The kind that telegraphed a this-woman-is-working-on-my-nerves vibe. "Let's start over. My father sent me."

The memory of her youthful crush vanished. Her stomach squeezed and twisted until she had to fight the urge to yell. "To tell me to stay away? Well, I did that. If he's ticked off it's his own fault, or yours, because you came hunting me."

"What are you talking about?"

"Whatever he wants this time, the answer is no." She gave in and shoved the door. Put her weight behind it and let it fly.

Carter grabbed the edge before it crashed into his shoulder. "Whoa. What do you mean by *this time*? I have no idea what you're talking about."

Yep, his reflexes were just as solid as the rest of him. All muscle and long legs and perfect cheekbones... Man, she hated the Jameson family and their hot-male genes.

"You need to go." She'd said it in a few ways now. Maybe this time would sink in.

"What did he do? My father. Your reaction is...telling."

Carter could not be this clueless. It wasn't just his father. It was him, too. He'd created a mess and had his big ol' rich daddy sweep the problem away.

That was almost a year ago. Now Carter showed up, taking the never-happened part a bit too far. "Oh, please."

"Hanna." This time there was a bit more *oomph* behind his tone when he said her name. "We haven't seen each other in, what, ten years?"

True, and it managed to feel like both forever ago and like yesterday. "Your point?"

"Normally, I need to see a woman more often for her to be this angry with me." One eyebrow lifted. "Or can I assume my father is responsible for your mood?"

Oh, this younger Jameson was a smooth one. Calm, standing there in his slim black pants with his hands in his pockets. A short gray winter coat highlighted his trim waist and likely cost more than her beat-up car with its side view mirror held on with electrical tape.

He rocked back on his heels, as if they were having a friendly chat. She had to give him credit. Carter Jameson had never tripped through that typical gawky preteen stage. Nope, he went from young and cute back then to all grown-up and hot now. Confidence pounded off him. The mix of perfect genes and I-know-my-place-in-the-world control proved pretty compelling.

Too bad he was a lying sack of garbage.

"The threats." She stared at him, watching confusion sweep through his eyes. *Yeah, nice try.* "The baby."

The color left Carter's face. Drained away, leaving him pale and listing to one side. "Oh, damn. Please tell me you didn't date my father and get pregnant."

She almost gagged. *"What?"*

"Look…" Carter held up both hands. "He's… I don't know, charming? At least that's what women have said. I don't get it at all but—"

"Stop talking." She grabbed a handful of his jacket when her nosy neighbor from across the hall opened his door. After a quick wave to send the guy scurrying away, she pulled Carter into her apartment and shut the door, trapping them inside. Together. Which was her nightmare.

"I did not sleep with your father." She practically hissed the words at him.

"Good." Carter visibly blew out another breath as a bit

of color returned to his cheeks. "You said something about a baby?"

She shouldn't have mentioned it. She refused to travel down that heartbreaking road. "How did your father find me?"

"Uh…" Carter closed one eye as if he were trying to reason something out in his head. "Were you lost?"

She didn't buy the act. This errand had a purpose and Carter was the only one of the two of them who knew what it was. "Skip to the part where you explain how and why you're here."

"Okay." His frown came and went. By the time he made eye contact again he seemed to have gotten control of whatever emotions were churning inside him. His expression morphed into a blank and unreadable one. "It's a long story, but suffice it to say, my father asked me to come and see you. Specifically, to give this to you."

He held out an envelope. Another envelope just like the ones his father had handed her and sent to her with messengers before. The idea of being told to stay away when she already had done just that didn't make any sense. But the idea of reading through more correspondence from Eldrick Jameson exhausted her. She refused to do it. She would not give him or Carter the satisfaction of ordering her around and getting their way a second time.

The envelope might as well have been on fire because there was no way she was touching it. Never again. "Put that away."

He flipped it around in the air a few times. "You don't want it?"

He sounded stunned at the thought. She almost laughed at the reaction. It was as if he didn't know his father and the old man's schemes at all. There were always strings when it came to dealing with a Jameson.

"Save us both some time and just tell me what it says."

Carter shrugged. "How should I know?"

"You're telling me you didn't open it? You flew here or took a million-dollar taxi ride or whatever and you never gave in to the itch to crack open the seal?" That seemed to defy human nature.

"Gotta say it sounds like *you* want to know what's inside." When she didn't say anything, his hand dropped. "He left the envelope for you and said he wanted you to have it. My job was to deliver it."

"Why?"

"I figured you knew."

Anger whooshed out of her, but frustration quickly settled in its place. She had no idea what was happening. From the apologetic sound of his voice, she wondered if he did either. "Are you serious? You really don't know what this assignment your father gave you is about?"

"Unfortunately, no." Carter moved around the small space, careful to dodge the corner of her dresser and the edge of her bed, to stand by the window. "I'm not sure how to ask this, so I'm just going to blurt it out. I apologize in advance for the delivery."

"That sounds ominous and—"

"Did you have a thing with my father? Maybe not sexual but…something?"

The question sounded just as horrifying the second time. The words had changed but the idea still screeched in her brain. "I don't want anything to do with your father. Never did."

"That's new."

"Meaning?"

Carter shook his head. "Well, he's been married four times and had a series of mistresses and girlfriends, so I guess some women like him."

She shivered. "I don't get that."

"On that, we agree." A smile tugged on the corner of

Carter's mouth as he took a few steps around her small space.

That cocky walk, the self-assurance. The way he stepped into a room and owned it. He was older now, more attractive in the way age and life experience molded and changed a person. Defined his features. That firm chin. The sexy smile.

The teenaged version of her had suffered from a debilitating crush that made her stammer and stare at her feet during the few times he'd talked to her. The grown-up version of her, the one who had experienced nothing but grief and anguish at the hands of the Jameson family, appreciated the way he looked but was smart enough to be wary. To not get reeled in.

"So, your father's sole instructions were to find me and give me that."

"Yes." He held the envelope out again.

None of this made sense. She'd never said anything. Never tried to see Carter. Ripped up the damn check his father had given her as a payoff, but there's no way the elder and famously impulsive Mr. Jameson had waited all these months to send Carter to try to pay her off again. Something else was happening here.

A terrible thought floated through her mind, freezing her to the spot by the door. "Is he with you?"

"My father?" Carter shook his head. "He's not even in the country, as far as I know. He and the new wife live in Tortola. Since I haven't heard from him in a few weeks, I'm assuming he's back there."

She noticed Carter didn't sound upset about living that many miles apart. The family dysfunction was his business, but she did have a few seconds of silent celebration at the thought of being some distance away from Carter's father. "Good."

Carter eyed her, his gaze assessing her, as he leaned

against the wall next to the window. "I'm guessing whatever happened between you two was bad."

"The good news is you've done your duty. Daddy asked you to visit me and you did. Mission accomplished." It was time for Carter to leave. She needed to make plans, figure out where she went from here.

"I still have the envelope, so I'm not convinced we've resolved anything."

"The reality is I'm not related to the man, so I don't have to do what he wants."

Carter made a noise that sounded a bit like *huh* before he started talking. "Any chance you're going to fill in the blanks and tell me what all of this is about?"

No way would she give up her small advantage by sharing anything she knew. "Hey, stud. You came to see me."

"I guess shy little Hanna is all grown-up now."

She reached out and opened the door. "And she's done with this conversation."

He pushed off from the wall and took the few steps that put him in front of her. "You know this isn't over, right?"

Her hand tightened on the doorknob. "Sure feels like it."

His smile returned as he nodded. "Goodbye for now, Hanna."

Then he was in the hall and she slammed the door behind him. Her heart hammered in her chest as she tried to drag in enough air to breathe. She gulped and panted as she fell against the door, letting her back slide down when her knees gave out and she fell to the floor in a boneless heap.

"Now what?"

Carter walked out of the lobby and stepped into the cold upstate New York evening. Winter fell early and heavy here. There was talk of snow in the forecast and he wanted to be long gone before it arrived.

It was a little after five. The sun had set and clouds filled the darkening sky. He zipped his jacket to block some of the biting October wind. He glanced up at Hanna's window and saw a peek of light behind the drawn curtains blocking his view inside.

She might not want to reminisce with him, but he possessed some vivid memories of her. Shy and pretty. She'd been a teenager on his family's Virginia estate and had hidden behind her older, more outgoing sister. The Wilde girls. Back then he'd thought of himself and Hanna as friends. It wasn't until he was older that he'd realized he'd held the sisters at a distance. He'd all but ignored Hanna, treating her as the child of the "help" and nothing more, just as his father insisted.

Carter shook his head, hating the reminder of his past and who he'd once been. The same history he'd run from and gotten dragged back into when his brother called him home, asking for help. Now Carter was the one who needed assistance. At the very least, a little information. He couldn't do much more without that.

He grabbed his cell phone out of his jacket pocket and called Jackson Richards, the real hub of information at Jameson Industries and one of the few people in the world Carter actually liked and trusted.

"Hey, I need your help."

"Nothing new there. You still working on your top-secret mission for your dad?"

Carter decided to ignore the question as he listened to Jackson typing in the background. "Ready for the list?"

"Wait, don't you have an assistant?"

"I don't actually work at the company. I'm happy staying on the Virginia property, far away from the family business."

Carter's preference for the Virginia countryside was a fact his father had once used to drive a wedge between Carter and his brothers. They were the business-minded ones. He was the disappointment. Carter had heard the refrain so often it rang in his ears even now.

He'd come back to the D.C. area expecting to check in on his brothers and help out with their ongoing fight with their dad about governing interest in the business, then go again. When that didn't happen he'd settled in to the Virginia estate. It was a small act of defiance against his father, who had kicked him out of that same property almost a year ago and told him never to come back.

But now he needed some intel. "No one is as good at this stuff as you are."

"Flattery won't work." Jackson cleared his throat. "For the record, expensive liquor will."

"Done. As soon as I get back, I'll come by with a bottle." Carter moved out of the glare of the streetlight and leaned against the brick wall of Hanna's apartment building. Cars buzzed by and people moved around him on the sidewalk, likely on their way to the bars and restaurants two blocks over. "I need all the information you can get me on Hanna and Gena Wilde. Sisters. Their dad used to work for our family at our Virginia estate."

"Do you know what you sound like when you say *estate* like that?"

"I have an idea." Carter glanced at his watch and made a quick decision. "You have three hours to gather intel."

The typing stopped. "What the hell? I do have a real job, you know."

A fair argument but a strange anxious feeling settled inside Carter. He sensed if he didn't talk to Hanna again soon, this time armed with information, she'd slip away. And he didn't want to go another ten years without seeing her again.

The wary blue eyes, almost baby blue. That wavy, shoulder-length, deep auburn hair that he ached to run his fingers through. The way her jeans balanced on her hips, giving him the tiniest glimpse of bare pale stomach as the edge of her long-sleeve T-shirt shifted around. He wanted to know more. To talk with her. To dig and see what had her on edge.

He guessed he'd trace most of her problems right back to his father. Carter had no idea what had her spooked or what game his father was playing, but something bigger than an envelope was happening here.

Carter took it out and studied it. No writing or clue to the contents. It was killing him not to rip it open. If he didn't have an answer in a few days, he would. Until then, he could respect her privacy…but barely.

Jackson sighed into the phone. "Does this have something to do with your highly problematic father?"

"Doesn't everything? Talk to you soon."

Carter hung up before Jackson could complain or swear. He glanced up at Hanna's studio a second time. "It looks like I'm not going anywhere just yet."

Two

Hanna decided to get away. Not forever. Just long enough for the Jamesons to find another target. Her job was a temporary solution anyway. She cleaned houses and businesses. Worked part-time in the coffee shop. She could take time off but she had to do it without pay, which sucked. That choice would be a financial struggle but going round and round with the Jamesons could cost her the equilibrium she'd been fighting to gain ever since her sister's death.

For the hundredth time, Hanna wondered if she should have just taken the money Eldrick offered her months ago to stay away from Carter. She'd tried to find Carter back then, and then the stay-away letters started. Then came the bribe.

The cash would have made rebuilding her life much easier. Saying no just made Eldrick double down on the threats of attorneys and lawsuits if she came near his family or talked about them with anyone. He thought it was her job to keep his family secrets.

Man, she hated the Jamesons and how they turned everything upside down. Irrational or not, that hate extended to all Jamesons…even, admittedly to a lesser degree, to the one she used to stare at as he played football on the lawn with his brothers. The one who turned her into a babbling fool every time he smiled at her.

Back then, of course. She was wiser now.

She dunked the mop in the murky water with a bit too much force. The wheels under the bucket spun around. Before she could catch it, the bucket tumbled and smacked into the coffee counter, sending the dirty water spilling over the sides.

Apparently, it was going to be that kind of day.

She sighed as she balanced the mop handle against the edge of the counter and wiped her hands on her faded blue jeans. A tingle at the base of her neck had her glancing up and turning around. The shadow moved in the glass front door of Morning Grind, the coffee shop she cleaned to offset part of the cost of her rent upstairs. Her breath hitched as the face came into view.

Carter.

Of course it was.

It was five in the morning and still dark outside, but she could see every inch of that amazing face. Watch his shoulders lift as he shifted his weight from foot to foot, likely trying to fight off the punishing cold that had settled in early this year, or so the locals told her.

She should let him freeze. Let him form a big Jameson ice cube right there on the sidewalk.

So tempting. But that would just give his father a reason to breeze into town, blaming and threatening her about something new.

She wiped her hands on her jeans again. This time not to dry them off but to beat down the nerves jumping around inside her. A strange mix of wariness and excitement hit her the second Carter pinned her with a crooked smile.

No wonder her sister had gotten reeled in. If the gossip

site stories about him were true, a lot of women had trouble saying no to the guy.

Maybe the whole turning-otherwise-smart-women-into-giant-puddles-of-goo thing was an inherited skill. A family trait of some sort. If so, she needed to get over the affliction and fast.

Her hand shook as she turned the lock and opened the door a fraction. "What?"

"You need to work on your welcoming tone." He grumbled something under his breath before talking at normal volume again. "I was hoping you'd be a bit happier to see me this morning."

"Since you seem determined to stalk me, no. For the record, I'm not into that." Or being unsure or off-kilter or vulnerable. None of those feelings worked for her, even though they all raced through her now as she tried not to notice how the wind brought a sexy rush of color to his cheeks.

"I wanted to apologize for just dropping in on you last night."

Sure he did. "By dropping in on me this morning."

The corner of his mouth lifted even higher, showing off that arresting smile. "Now that you mention it, I guess this visit wasn't all that well thought-out either."

She studied him, letting her gaze wander over that mouth before giving him full-on eye contact. The cute, self-deprecating act held a certain charm, but she knew it was just an act. No longer a carefree boy, he was a man who possessed power and money. In her experience, the Jamesons used both of those as a weapon against others.

Then there was the more obvious problem. "How did you know where to find me at this time of the morning?"

His mouth opened and closed twice.

She cleared her throat. "I'm waiting."

"Yeah, I can see that."

She knew stalling when she heard it. Heck, she excelled

at that sort of thing. He couldn't fool her. "Feel free to use words."

He made a strangled noise that sounded like *hmm*. "I'm going to be honest with you."

"That would be nice." Not that she'd believe whatever he said, but it would be interesting to see what subterfuge he tried to use on her.

He unzipped his coat, just enough for her to see the V-neck of the blue sweater underneath. "I had a friend back at the Jameson office look into you."

Look into? Creative word choice. "You mean, investigate me."

"I didn't say that."

That was kind of her point. "So, you had one of your employees *not* investigate me."

"I don't actually work for Jameson Industries."

"Uh-huh." It was as if he didn't know his own last name or for some reason thought the verbal gymnastics would work on her. Either way, she wasn't buying it. "I often call up places where I don't work and get people to scurry around, looking stuff up for me in the middle of the night."

"It does seem to lack credibility when you say it that way."

"Is there another way to say it?"

She hated to admit that she was enjoying this steady back-and-forth that had her mind clicking.

After months of reeling and mourning, she still kept to herself, not letting anyone she met move past the acquaintance stage and into the friend stage. Not dating. She blamed her time away from the friendship and dating pool as the reason for the adrenaline surging through her now.

Not a new round of attraction. Nope, that could not happen.

"I called in a favor, but that's not the point." He held up a hand when she started to respond. "Initially, I assumed coming here and handing you an envelope would get the job done. When it became clear that wasn't going to happen, I decided I needed to know more about you."

She folded her arms in front of her. "Because that's not heavy-handed at all."

"I *wanted* to know more about you. About who you are now." With that, his eyes wandered—not far and not too obvious—but he did give her a quick once-over.

She hated that her stomach tumbled in response. She vowed to ignore the effect seeing him after all this time still had on her. The weird bubbling giddiness, the feeling of not being good enough or pretty enough. All those sensations she'd felt as a teen still battled inside her, which she found truly ridiculous. Getting older should have made her immune to him and all those stupid insecurities.

Guilt swamped her. He'd abandoned her sister and her own failure to stick up for Gena, to hold the line and not feel anything for him, was nothing short of a betrayal to her sister. Gena had talked about Carter leaving and his father sniffing around, trying to figure out what Carter had meant to her. She'd warned Hanna to be careful and not trust them.

Hanna tried to hold on to all of that advice and mistrust, to funnel what had been her sister's pain and her own frustration, into a defensive shield against Carter. To question every word he said and bury that leftover attraction down deep, but it kept bubbling back to the surface.

Some of the lightness left his face. "You've changed."

The words and his seemingly innocent delivery had her anger spiking. Heat raged through her. After all those years of ignoring her, he pretended he had some insight into her then and now. "Did we know each other well enough for you to make that assessment?"

"I remember the Hanna who would run around the Virginia property and get into everything. Climbing fences and trying to play on the equipment." He shoved his hands in his dark gray jeans pockets and focused that intense stare on her.

She didn't flinch. "You mean the same Virginia property I wasn't allowed to visit after my dad died?"

His eyes narrowed. "What?"

Years before Hanna lost her sister, she lost her father. Her parents had long been divorced but her mom had been listed as her father's heir and tried to go to the cottage he lived in on the Jameson estate. Her mother never talked about what happened during the visit, but she came back with clothes and a few personal items and that was all.

Hanna knew more existed. Her father had kept a journal. He'd been a faithful employee at the estate for decades. He'd built a life there, had friends and people who worked for him and respected him.

He died on the job at that stupid Virginia estate and her mother had gotten excuses and two duffel bags filled with dirty shirts.

Carter shrugged. "Okay. Visit Virginia now."

He seemed as surprised to have said the words as she'd been to hear them. "Sure, I'll just use the key I don't have and go into the house I'm not allowed to visit in the state I don't live in."

"Maybe the envelope is an invitation to visit."

"You think after all this time your father is willing to hand over my father's property and wrote to tell me?"

"I can't explain my father's actions, but I can offer to help now. If you don't want anything to do with him or the envelope, then deal with me. Come back to Virginia and get whatever you need."

Temptation tugged at her. She could go to the property and maybe get some answers to all those questions about her father's death. About how a man so skilled could fall off a ladder and die. But that meant trusting Carter and possibly running in to Eldrick. It meant owing them, and she'd vowed never to do that.

Breaking eye contact, Carter glanced around. His gaze moved over the tables with the chairs stacked on the tops, and the shelves of merchandise. It hesitated on the espresso machine. "You must have vacation days."

If he'd looked into her background, he already knew the answer. But, fine. They could play this game.

"I'm not a full-time employee." She lifted her chin because she was not going to hide who she was or what she did to earn a living. "I clean houses and buildings. It's what I do so that I can eat."

"Sure. Okay."

"Sometimes I also take shifts here, usually nights and weekends when the college kids who work here would rather go out."

He shrugged again. "Makes sense."

The casual acceptance threw her off. He came from inconceivable wealth. Growing up he only ran with other kids from the same background. He'd segregated himself as if money did matter. Went to a private boys' school, then off to an expensive college. Spent the last year playing in California. She knew because his photo showed up on gossip sites now and then with this beautiful woman or that one on his arm. And it always pricked at her.

"I'm not ashamed of what I do." She wanted to be absolutely clear about that.

"You shouldn't be."

Okay, he said that but nothing in his past or looking at him now suggested he actually believed it. "I work hard. I don't get to play much, and I certainly can't just hop off to Virginia."

"Then open the envelope."

He made it sound so simple, but it wasn't.

"Your father is trying to manipulate me. He's done it

before. Sends letters and expects me to jump to his commands." And she had…sort of. When she'd emerged from the fog surrounding her sister's death she'd made a promise. She would never again let Eldrick intimidate or scare her. That meant not letting him in to her life. Not letting him in her door or reading his letters.

Carter sighed. "Tell me why and I can try to help."

"No." Part of her still believed Carter knew and this was some sort of game. He was the one who had a relationship with Gena. He'd lured her in with promises of a future then left. Everything that came after—the threats and bribery attempts by Eldrick— related back to Carter. How could he not know?

But that expression seemed so genuine. The offer of coming to Virginia opened a door she'd thought she'd closed. The possibilities whirled around in her head until she had to lean against one of the tables.

"I'm staying at the Virginia estate, so I can pack up whatever may belong to your dad and get it to you. Or, hear me out." Carter held up a hand. "Come to Virginia yourself. Get whatever property, whatever closure, you need."

She snorted. It came out before she could stop it. "Because you know so much about closure."

"I've been hunting for it for years where my father is concerned. If I can't find it for me, maybe I can at least hope you get it." A new emotion moved into his eyes. Behind that determination something else lingered. A note of sadness, maybe. "My father isn't in the country. My brothers don't go to our estate except for special events. I'm there, but I'll stay out of your way."

The idea of taking a look at her father's possessions, of figuring out once and for all if something else happened that sunny afternoon when he died, tugged and pulled at her. But the offer also tripped the silent alarm in her head. The internal warning wail almost had her wincing.

"I can't just walk away from my responsibilities." *Like some people*.

"You're not the only one who is sick of my father's constant maneuvering." Carter hesitated for a few seconds before continuing. "I can help you with whatever he wants from you, but if you don't want that I still can make sure you get access to the house you once lived in. Stay a few days and do what you need."

Common sense battled with curiosity. She'd never bought the story about her dad's death. Being there might let her take a peek and move on…or she could uncover the truth, and she owed her dad that.

But there was still the problem of the newest envelope and whatever Eldrick intended to threaten her about now. "What makes you think your father wants something? I know why I think it, but what do you know?"

"The man doesn't make a move without an ulterior motive." Carter shook his head. "Look, the easiest thing to do would be to open the envelope. But it's your life, not mine. You want to keep your secrets? Fine."

He actually sounded like he *did* get it. That eased some of the tension zipping through her.

"I don't want to be manipulated by my father either. Honestly, I'm only here because my brother, you probably remember Derrick, only gets the family business if certain conditions are met. My brothers have a list of things we must do for that inheritance to happen and this is what I have to do."

She didn't like that at all. "You mean me. I'm your 'thing to do.' How flattering."

Carter frowned. "I don't really understand why or what any of this means or how you fit in, which is likely how my dad wanted it."

He didn't exactly speak about his father with love and respect. That piqued her interest, made her want to ask questions, but she refrained. Getting sucked into a big Jameson family mess was not on her agenda today...or ever. "So, you need me to open the envelope."

"I don't need anything. My brother does. But if Derrick had seen the look of panic on your face last night when I mentioned Dad, Derrick would have torn up the envelope and told you to never worry about any of us again."

If true, she liked Derrick way more now than she did when she was a kid and was kind of afraid of him. "And you?"

"We both know you and my dad have unfinished business of some sort." When she started to deny it, he interrupted her again. "I'm not asking what it is, but I'm giving you a chance to do some exploring on your own, without his knowledge or interference. To come back to his home turf of Virginia and figure it all out, then decide if you want to confront my dad."

She never wanted to see the man again. She'd tucked away in this corner of New York, far away from the bribery and warnings specifically to avoid having to see him. "What do you get out of all of this?"

"Honestly?" He winced. "The idea of going behind my dad's back and letting you on the property where he didn't want you to be gives me an odd satisfaction. Plus, I liked your dad. You deserve to go through his things and visit the place you stayed one last time."

"You sort of sound reasonable." Which immediately made her skeptical.

Carter took in a long, deep breath. "My offer is for housing and food, if you want it."

So smooth. He knew exactly what to say to get her thinking. There was no way he could have guessed from his investigation into her background that there were doubts swirling in her head about that Virginia estate and what really happened to her father there. This offer might be her one chance to look around without a bunch of people following her or chasing her off the property. She might be able to uncover the truth.

The only problem? Nothing ever turned out to be free.

"Who did you say would be at the property?" Not that she was conceding. This was all part of a big plan Carter's dad had worked out. She was sure of it and equally determined not to be a pawn. But if she could get the upper hand, then maybe…

"I'll be in the main house. I'm living and working there."

Her stupid heart jumped. She had no idea why that deep voice affected her. She should know better, learn from her sister's mistakes. "I thought you didn't work for the family."

His head dipped to the side for a second. "It's a complicated story."

"It always is." Because there was nothing easy about the Jameson family.

"Does this mean you're coming back with me?"

He looked far too satisfied with himself. That didn't sit right with her at all. She had the sense that once Carter thought he'd won, he would become impossible.

"I didn't say that."

He smiled. "You kind of did."

That look. His face. It was so handsome it bordered on annoying. "You leave and I'll think about the offer."

"Not exactly a people person, are you?"

Not the first time she'd heard that. She'd been tagged as the quiet sister. Not as pretty or outgoing or charismatic but steady. She got a little tired of playing the role of forgotten sister.

She'd grown up and grown apart from Gena. Hanna moved away and worked as an administrative assistant. Had a good job. Friends. A life. When Gena's world came crashing down after Carter, she'd begged for help and Hanna came rushing in. She pushed aside the mix of jealousy and hurt that swamped her at the idea of Gena and Carter together when Gena had known all about the old crush. But she'd arrived too late to save her sister. Even now as she tried to rebuild her life and find a job to replace the one she'd lost, the guilt over not doing enough or the right thing still beat down on her every day.

He rocked back on his heels. "You do know I'm not getting anything out of this, right?"

No way did she believe that. "You poor thing."

His gaze slipped back to the espresso machine. "I'd settle for something with caffeine in it."

"You could open a bag and suck on a bean."

He laughed and the rich, genuine sound washed over her. He moved and it mesmerized her. He spoke and her brain replayed every word.

"I would have been disappointed if you'd offered to make me coffee," he said.

"I'm happy we understand each other." She glanced at the clock and dread pummeled her. Employees would start showing up in about fifteen minutes and she still had to deal with that puddle on the floor. "I need to get back to work."

"Here." Without another word, Carter went over the counter and grabbed the mop. "I can take care of the spill."

She would have been less surprised if he'd made a cup of coffee magically appear in his hand. "You're going to clean something? You…?"

"I have skills."

She could feel her mouth drop open and her eyes bulge. "With a mop?"

"I'm not my father, Hanna."

The words shook her out of her stupor because she was starting to believe him. "That's the only reason you're still standing here."

That and his eyes. And those impressive shoulders. That

cool voice. Okay, she might have let him inside the shop to look at him for a while. She hadn't expected him to offer a way for her to settle the past.

No, Carter Jameson was not what she expected at all. Problem was she didn't have a defense against this Carter and that made him potentially more dangerous to her than Eldrick.

Three

Carter walked into Jackson's Jameson Industries office two days later without knocking. Since he carried sandwiches and everything else they needed for lunch, Carter doubted Jackson would mind the unscheduled intrusion.

He'd volunteered to pick up the food because he needed a distraction from his phone and its lack of messages.

There was exactly one reason for his frustration: Hanna. She still hadn't gotten in touch with him. No call. No message. No text. He'd made a point of giving her his contact information after making his big come-to-Virginia offer, convinced she wouldn't refuse…and yet, nothing.

The hours ticked by and he tried to forget her and their odd meeting, write off her apparent mix of disdain and disinterest. Not dwell on the secrets she hid and her relationship, whatever it was, to his father. Not think about how she'd grown up, about her legs or the gentle sway of her hips as she'd tried to rush him out her door. That face. Those curves.

Yeah, he definitely needed to find something else to think about.

Carter glanced up as he shut the office door behind him. Jackson sat at his desk, studying the contents of the file with such extreme concentration that it looked as if he expected to be tested on the details. Carter got three steps across the room before Jackson started talking. He didn't lift his head but his voice rang out loud and clear.

"Are you ever going to tell me why you needed the information?" Jackson asked while flipping pages.

Carter froze in midstep. "Did we start a conversation before I entered the room? Because I have no idea what you're talking about."

With a long, exaggerated sigh, Jackson finally lifted his head. After a quick look up and down, he frowned. It was the kind of once-over Jackson did before he launched into a Jamesons-are-impossible speech. The same kind of look that made Carter self-conscious, and he was rarely that.

After the prolonged visual inspection, Jackson rested his elbows on the desk in front of him. "The Wilde sisters."

"Oh, right." Knowing this topic could lead to trouble, Carter tried to deflect. A shrug usually worked, so he went with that. "That was nothing."

"Uh-huh." Jackson closed the file almost in slow-motion before lounging back in his big leather seat. "I've worked for this family for years. I've investigated many people and businesses. It's never *nothing* and it usually causes trouble that rolls downhill to my desk to fix."

Carter started to shrug a second time, then stopped because Jackson would notice multiple shrugs and take it as a sign of…something. "I just wondered what happened to them."

"Right. So, your dad sends you on this errand. You go and while you're there you just happen to need emergency intel on the daughters of the man who used to be the caretaker of your family's Virginia property. A man who died on the job, though you know that part."

Carter dropped the bag filled with food on the edge of the desk and sat down across from Jackson. "See? Perfectly reasonable."

"That's not a word I would ever use to describe your family."

The bag rustled, making a crinkling sound, as Carter unloaded the sandwiches and what looked to him like two child-sized bags of chips. "Do people really only eat seven chips at a meal?"

He threw one of the bags in Jackson's general direction. Instead of catching it, Jackson stayed still. The chips crunched as they landed on his keyboard. The only reaction he gave was the slight lift of an eyebrow. Carter took that to mean Jackson was not ready for a new topic.

"So, when you asked me about Hanna and Gena—and yes, I remember their names because I remember everything—that was just a coincidence?" Jackson asked.

"I sense you're not going to let this go."

"Want me to give you a list of all of the other people who worked at the Virginia property?" Jackson ripped open the bag of chips and shoved two in his mouth.

The room filled with the sounds of munching, shuffling and sandwich unwrapping. But Carter knew it was only a brief reprieve. Jackson had an annoying habit of holding on to a question and unloading it later, just when Carter relaxed his guard. "It's kind of freaky how much you know about our family."

"I like to be ready."

"For?"

Jackson handed over one of the two water bottles sitting by his phone. "Anything. It's a good trait in an employee, so feel free to give me a raise."

"If I had that power, I would." Hell, he'd sign over part of his interest in the company and bolt. The day-to-day monotony of desk work didn't appeal to him. And being here reminded him that his father thought he wasn't worthy to even have an office.

If Derrick didn't need him and if his sister-in-law-to-be Ellie's pregnancy eased into a safer rhythm, he might. Of course, then he'd miss seeing what would happen as his other brother, Spence, tried to negotiate a new stage of his relationship with his fiancée, Abby. And that was just too funny to miss.

Poor Spence had it bad and Abby was not the type to make it easy for him. Carter loved her for that. Loved both of the women his brothers managed to convince to date them. They were smart, beautiful and strong. Very different from each other, but perfect for Derrick and Spence.

Which for some reason got Carter thinking about Hanna. She had the smart, beautiful and strong combination down. She also looked at him like she wanted to backhand him with a mop handle, so it was good he wasn't interested. Not in anything permanent anyway. There was no way to have a few private, discreet hookups just for fun with his family nearby. Someone always seemed to be watching. And sometimes it was the guy sitting right in front of him.

Jackson. Friend, invaluable asset to Jameson Industries and all-around smart-ass.

"Stop acting like you're not management." Jackson finished unwrapping the sandwich and crumpled the paper underneath it. "You could write me a check tomorrow. In fact, you should. You know, just because."

Carter knew Jackson was kidding but he'd hit on a sore spot. One Carter couldn't exactly laugh off since it guided everything he'd done for the last year. "My father ran me out of the family and the business a year ago, remember? No power to do anything here."

Jackson swallowed the bite he'd been chewing. "When did you get so dramatic?"

"You weren't here, but he did." Carter grabbed for his

food. He fiddled with the paper, trying to untuck the edge, but finally gave in and ripped it open. The smell of tuna fish salad hit him a second later.

"I missed the actual office fight between you two, but I do remember the fallout. You refused to talk. Derrick was pissed because your dad refused to listen to your ideas about what to do with the Virginia property." Jackson shook his head as he whistled. "It was a hell of a welcome back from my vacation."

"I believe the exact phrase Dad used was that my ideas were *beneath the Jameson name*." The dismissive tone echoed in Carter's brain. No matter how he tried to write off his father and erase the memory, it kicked up every now and then. "He pointed out that I was an embarrassment and should go out and prove myself or not bother to step in his office again."

"That is some interesting Jameson tough love." Jackson took another bite, almost devouring half the sandwich in only a few minutes.

Carter glanced at the tuna fish, then to his unopened bag of chips. The idea of food suddenly didn't appeal to him. He blamed the office and the city. Being this close to what his father viewed as the center of his power made Carter want to be anywhere else. To not be a Jameson or have to deal with the steady stream of disappointing everyone. It was easier to be away and just be Carter, not the rich kid who didn't live up to the family standard.

He dropped the sandwich and then pushed the paper away from him. "He deactivated my key card to the building and told security to kick me out that afternoon. Derrick undid the orders, or so he said when he called and asked me to come back, but I was done by then."

"Eldrick couldn't make a phone call without having three people help him." Jackson swore under his breath. Not that he was quiet about it or tried to hide his anger at Eldrick.

"But yeah, that will teach me to take three days of vacation. By the time I got back you were driving across the country and the office had descended into chaos."

Jackson's controlled outburst eased some of the frustration coursing through Carter. There was something comforting about having Jackson on his side that made talking about his father tolerable. "Your timing was terrible. You take three days off a year and you picked *those* days."

Jackson did what he often did when talking about family business: he shook his head. "All kidding aside, your father is an ass."

Among other things. "Very true."

"You have a second chance, you know." Jackson made a show of taking a drink and wiping his hands on his napkin. Drew out the suspense but didn't deliver a punch line.

Carter didn't shy away from asking. "Meaning?"

"Derrick liked your ideas about converting the Virginia property. He had me look into the legalities of changing the property's legal use and run some numbers on the financial feasibility of trying your solution."

For the business retreat and possible private club and party event facility? That was news to Carter. *"What?"*

"Like you, Derrick doesn't often agree with your father. He has always been pretty clear that his memories of living at the estate as a kid weren't great."

"It was fine, if you liked yelling." Carter thought about the big redbrick mansion, stately with the columns surrounded by acres of rolling hills. The pool, the pond, the outbuildings. As much as he loved the house and the outdoors and the open space, it was hard to ignore the bad memories that lingered over every inch of the land.

He'd been a teenager when his mother got cancer. Only a few months older than that when she went into the hospital, then to hospice to live out her final days, where Dad served her with divorce papers. Eldrick couldn't allow her the simple dignity of dying in peace. No, he thought his girlfriend was pregnant and he needed to move on. His girlfriend wasn't and now he was on wife number four and Carter doubted the man was one ounce more faithful to this one than he had been to Carter's mother.

Before his mother's death and the shock and the ripping sensation of having all his safety nets stripped away, life hadn't been so great either. Dad used his wife and sons as public props while bouncing between ignoring them and screaming at them in private. He was demanding and difficult and manipulative. He liked to pit Derrick and Spence against each other. It was a miracle the brothers managed to maintain any meaningful sibling relationship, let alone establish the strong one they had.

As soon as he graduated, Carter escaped and shuffled off to college, only visiting when ordered home, which amounted to little more than once a year at the holidays. Even when Derrick had moved back home with the thought of taking over the family business, he'd skipped the mansion and moved to D.C. Insisted the commute to the office would be prohibitive, which was true but not really the reason he avoided the place.

As the years rolled by, the brothers rarely used the space for weekend getaways or events. For the most part, the big house and the grounds stood empty. Eldrick lived there on and off, depending on whether his then girlfriend or wife, or whomever he was sleeping with at the time, had any interest in the country.

A skeleton staff ran the place. The only event Carter could remember attending there in the last few years was Derrick and Ellie's engagement party. Ellie had insisted the party would replace some of the bad memories of growing up there with good memories. It was a nice thought, but Carter didn't think it had worked.

"Which is why you should repurpose the house and

grounds." Jackson tipped the small bag and dumped the remaining chips and crumbs on his desk blotter. "Talk to Derrick. Of course, all of this depends on if you intend to stick around."

The tone. Jackson might not be related to them, but he shared Derrick's ability to convey a get-your-act-together message with a few words.

"Are you trying to lure me back into the family?" For the first time in a long time, Carter entertained the idea and it was all due to his brothers. The idea of fitting in, of being a part of something that didn't depend on his father's whims, appealed to him even though he was not a set-down-roots kind of guy. But maybe he could let something matter to him. Maybe.

Jackson picked up a chip and pointed it at Carter. "Forget your dad. You and your brothers support each other. I understand how that works because it's how it is with me and Zoe."

"Ah, yes." Carter smiled at the thought of Jackson's fraternal twin. She looked like him with brown hair and blue eyes, only female and much prettier. Petite and fiery. She was one of the most determined people Carter had ever met. "Your baby sister. You are eight minutes older, right?"

Jackson's mouth flatlined. "Pretend I don't have a sister."

"But I love her." Like the sister he never had, but Carter didn't say that part out loud. Not when he enjoyed Jackson's reaction to the joke of potentially tying him even more tightly to the Jamesons through his sister's dating choices.

"Get over it," Jackson said in his most grumbly voice.

The fact was, they all viewed Jackson and Zoe as family. And some days, when his resistance was down, Jackson admitted that the feeling was mutual. Well, one time he had. He'd gotten drunk one New Year's Eve and let that slip. Now he denied it.

Carter decided to take pity on Jackson. "You do know if I made a pass Zoe would kick me in the balls, right?"

Jackson snorted. "Who do you think taught her that move?"

"Figures."

Jackson grabbed the chip bag in front of Carter and opened it, dipping his fingers inside. "But back to the Virginia house. I'm telling you that when Derrick is in charge—and I'm hoping that happens soon because I dread the idea of Eldrick dropping back into the office again—you should run it by him. You might be surprised by how much support you get."

"Is there anything you don't know about this family and the business?"

"Nope." Jackson popped one of Carter's chips in his mouth.

"We're lucky to have you."

Jackson stopped chewing long enough to smile. "That's what I keep telling you all."

She should run and keep running.

That thought raced through Hanna's mind as she stepped out of the cab she really couldn't afford in front of a gate meant to keep her out. She stared up at the high wall that circled and protected the Jamesons' expansive Virginia property. This was how rich people lived—cut off from others, safe from having to touch or talk with anyone but their own.

For years, on and off, she'd lived behind that wall when she visited her father during those weekends, school holidays and a handful of weeks in the summer when he had visitation. During those times, she'd slip through the gate. Not this one, of course. The one around the side meant for staff. Never really welcome or accepted inside, her presence had been tolerated so long as she stayed quiet and knew her place.

Despite all the rules, her father insisted he enjoyed working here because he was part of something. That living at the estate, having the responsibility of managing the grounds, gave him purpose. He'd felt at home there.

He'd also died there.

That's why she'd taken Carter's suggestion and showed up. Before they talked, she'd convinced herself she needed to move on and rebuild. Not look to the past. But now the need for answers gnawed at her. Real ones, not the ones passed through Eldrick's fancy lawyers years ago. For the first time since she lost Gena, Hanna felt like she might be able to control some part of her life.

Her mother had collected the death benefit check along with Eldrick's short explanation. After years of fighting over custody schedules with her father, when it came to his death, her mother mourned. She also never believed the Jameson line about Dad falling off a ladder. Neither did Hanna.

Standing there, lost in a haze of memories, she heard the rumble and crunch of tires. She watched a dark sedan slow down as it drove by. The driver stared at her, and at the scuffed duffel bag with the broken strap sitting at her feet. She stared right back, watching until the car turned a corner and headed for one of the other estates that dotted the hillside.

"I hate being here." She mumbled the truth to herself as she slipped her cell out of her front jeans pocket. Her finger hesitated over Carter's number just as it had every time she started to call over the last few days.

She'd shown up unannounced, but she first called the Jameson office in D.C. pretending to be a business contact looking for him. The person who answered said he wasn't there, so she took a shot that he'd been telling the truth when he said he lived and worked at the estate now.

It was just one of many chances she was taking. Carter didn't refer to his dad in glowing terms. They seemed to share a distrust of the older man, but family was family and she still had a tangled past with Carter that made her wonder how far he'd come from the entitled boy who once caught her watching him work out in the gym at the estate and laughed at her interest.

Being near him now was such a risk. She'd tried to move on, not think of herself as the second-best Wilde sister, but memories of Carter and the attraction that still seemed to beat inside her had the power to flip her back to that inse-cure mental place.

She stared at the screen until the numbers blurred. Shift-ing and typing again, she started texting.

I agree to the terms we discussed. I stay in the cottage and you leave me alone.

She winced at the tense tone but hit Send anyway.

Carter shot back a text response almost immediately.

How could I say no to that charming agreement?

"They were your terms, but fine," she grumbled as she thought about what to write next. She couldn't exactly admit she thought his family had something to do with her dad's death. That would shut down all access, and this access onto the property only just opened for her thanks to Cart-er's offhand suggestion.

Before she could come up with the right response, an-other text popped up from Carter.

When are you coming so I can be ready?

She wished *she* could be ready.

Why, are you going to change the sheets for me?

She bit her lip as the Sent notification appeared on her screen. Then a wave of panic hit her. She didn't mean to sound flirty or interested or even happy about any of this…even though she kind of was. The whole trip over she thought about Carter and that sexy smile when she should have been thinking about her dad and Gena and how good it would feel to finally beat the Jamesons at their own game.

And bed? Why did she mention a bed?

I thought we established that I know how to clean. I actually have many skills.

She absolutely did not remember conceding that point. And the skills comment could not be flirting. If they started a game of mutual flirting her control would fizzle. But he had looked cute with that mop in his hands…

You used a mop without hurting yourself.
Congratulations.

I'm sighing at you right now.

She could almost hear him and the idea made her laugh. She smothered the sound as soon as it escaped her. But she didn't type fast enough. Another text flashed across her screen.

Trying again…when are you coming?

This time she switched to calling because, really, she wanted to hear his voice for this one. The element of surprise was on her side. She intended to enjoy that.

He picked up on the first ring. His deep, rich voice filled the line. "Hello, there."

The whole shivering in her stomach thing hit her again.

It was unnecessary. She needed her reaction to Carter to stay…flat because she needed to keep her defenses strong against him and remember what happened to Gena when she didn't. She struggled to find that tone when she responded.

"I'm here now. Unlock the gate." When he gasped, she hung up.

This round to her.

Four

Carter refused to admit he jogged to the gate. It was a quick walk and he only picked up the speed to avoid being rude. He couldn't just leave Hanna hanging out front. He wasn't a complete jerk, after all.

As he walked down the long drive, he spotted her peeking between the bars of the electric front gate. She wore jeans and a purple Henley, both formfitting to the point where his brain power kept blinking out.

The temperature was cool but not cold like it had been at their last meeting in New York. A bag and what looked like a rolled-up jacket sat at her feet. That's all she had. A few things in an oversize duffel. Carter had no idea if that was a statement on how little she owned or on how short of a time she planned to stay. Either way, his brain had turned traitor on him because he was stupidly excited to see her. He could feel his mouth curl into a smile as his gaze wandered over her hair and that ponytail. The second he recognized the unwanted excitement racing through him, he tried to tamp it down.

At his worst in those days after his father kicked him

out, he'd run into Gena and they spent a weekend together. It had been fun but meaningless for both of them. Flirty but nothing more.

He hadn't felt a shot to the gut when he saw Gena like he did when he saw Hanna again, which had a weird vibe both because they were sisters and because Gena was dead.

He smiled, trying to forget the twisted road that brought them to this place. "You're here."

She watched his hands as he punched in the code and the electric gate rumbled open. "You don't sound surprised."

"You have to admit I offered you a pretty good deal." He let the gate roll past him, then gestured for her to step inside. "Free housing and food with no expectations in return."

He felt the need to say that. To be clear he wasn't his father. He'd been trying to make that distinction with people his whole life.

"You're a prince."

"I'll take that as a thank-you." Because he was pretty sure that was as close as he'd ever get to gratitude.

"Should I be coming in this way?"

It had taken her less than ten minutes to lose him in conversation. "Huh?"

"I've always used the door on the side gate."

"The..." Right, the service entrance thing. His father had always been very clear on separating *the help*—his words—from those the family invited for a visit. "You can use whatever entrance you want."

"That's an interesting change."

"Is it?"

She shook her head as she reached down and grabbed her bag and jacket. "Never mind."

Without saying a word, he took the bag out of her hand and balanced the strap on his shoulder. It didn't weigh much, which renewed his curiosity about what she'd packed. "I know it's strange to come back to a place you used to think of as home. It took my sister-in-law-to-be's high-risk pregnancy to lure me back to the area. Little else would have worked."

For a second Hanna didn't say anything. She gnawed on her bottom lip as she eyed her bag, but then she seemed to snap out of the haze surrounding her. "I read about that. Derrick's fiancée, right?"

Finally, a topic Carter could handle without trouble. He stepped back, closer to the house, and Hanna followed. He waited until she was out of striking range, then hit the button to close the gate behind her.

It rattled to a close as he guided them toward the main house. "Things have evened out a bit with her health but the pregnancy is still risky. Derrick is an embarrassing wreck. He's driving Ellie, that's his fiancée, and us, right to the edge. It's taking all I have not to order him to stay home from work, but Ellie would kill me because then she'd be stuck with him."

"I don't remember that much about Derrick. He seemed pretty disconnected from the house by the time I started visiting."

"He was mostly away at college by that point. He's five years older than me." Carter was thirty and Hanna a year younger. Carter knew most of the basics about her because Jackson had included those in the file, including the truth about Gena's car accident. The police and medical examiner had termed it a suicide. Hanna never contested the finding, which made Carter think it must have been right. A finding that had crashed through him on a rush of guilt and sadness when he'd read it.

Carter needed to talk with Hanna about all of it, but he didn't want to scare her off. There were so many secrets hovering between them and as much as Carter pretended not to care about what his father did or said these days, that unopened envelope sat on his dresser, taunting him. While it was true he'd offered her the chance to come and fight whatever demons she had, he'd also wanted her to come for him. Bigger than that, he wanted her to confide in him. He wasn't sure why that suddenly mattered, but it did.

Something in her called out to him. She seemed lost and a bit broken. He understood exactly how that felt and wanted to help.

The curiosity about whatever secret bound her to his father also drove him. The need to know the answer grew each day. Nothing in the background search on her provided a hint, and Carter would never ask his father. Doing so might bring him back to Virginia, and he didn't want to deal with his father at all.

Gravel crunched under their feet as they walked. Without any warning, she stopped and stared at him. "I'm not staying in the main house."

He balanced his foot on the bottom step leading up to the front porch that spanned the front of the house. "I remember, but—"

"No."

He blew out a long breath, trying not to let frustration overwhelm him. "Maybe you could let me finish a sentence."

She nodded. Almost looked like she smiled, too, but if she did it flashed then was gone just as quickly. "Fair enough."

"Until ten seconds ago I wasn't sure you were coming because, clearly, you are unfamiliar with how a phone works." When she started to interrupt, he held up a hand to stop her. "My point being, if I had known I would have had the cottage cleaned and aired out. Since your arrival is a surprise, and a welcome one so don't get all grumpy on me, I thought we could wait in the house while I have the place readied for you."

"First, I did call you."

She had to be kidding. "Ten minutes ago, from the front gate, but go on."

"Do you want me to text you a message right now?"

That tone. She was messing with him. No question.

"I can imagine what that message would say." But it was tempting to let her try. Everything she did and said intrigued him, made him want to know more.

That time she did smile. Even let it linger. "Second, I clean for a living. I can handle the cottage… I *want* to handle it."

Maybe it would make her feel closer to her father's memory, but the idea still struck him as wrong. He wasn't hiring her. He was trying to help her, though it was pretty clear she planned to fight him with every ounce of life inside her. "You're not here to work."

"I actually am."

Damn, she was exasperating and he kind of loved that about her. Not many people outside of his family challenged him. Most bought into the supposed power behind the Jameson name, which was why he sometimes used a fake last name. He wanted people to know him for him, and that included her. "I mean, for me. You don't work for me."

"You gave me the speech about how no one would bother me. I don't want people skulking around the cottage."

He wasn't the type to be knocked speechless but he didn't have a comeback for that one. "Skulking?"

She shrugged, looking disinterested…except for the way she twisted her coat in her hands. If she tightened that death grip even a fraction she'd likely rip the material. He found her reaction interesting. Here she was, all cool and annoyed on the surface. Underneath it looked like something very different was happening. Maybe it was the stress of being back or that stupid envelope. Part of him hoped she was fighting off the same attraction that threatened to overwhelm him.

She was a puzzle he wanted to solve. Hot with all those curves and those big eyes. Her looks caught his attention, but something about her made him want to dig deeper. She wasn't the little girl he'd once known. She'd grown up, gotten strong, acquired an attitude and that shyness, if it still existed, was firmly banked. The whole package worked for him. Which probably said something about him. Something not great about being attracted to a woman who looked at all times as if she were ready to punch him.

The argument in his head about having people who could clean for her died in his throat. "You win."

She smiled again. This one was big and sunny and for a few seconds she dropped the assessing I'm-watching-you stare she'd perfected. "I'm shocked you conceded so quickly."

That made two of them. "I'm not unreasonable."

"We'll see."

The way she pushed, her refusal to back down…so sexy. It was a shame so many secrets stood between them. So much history. "Then we should head to the cottage."

"I know where it is."

That stubbornness could also be annoying. He made a vow to remember that, to focus on how much she seemed to dislike him, even without knowing he slept with her dead sister.

"Right." He held up the key. "But I have this. I'll escort you, run through some of the cottage's issues, like a sticky window we'll get fixed as soon as possible."

"I think I can handle it."

He dropped his arm to his side. "Indulge me."

"I already am."

He'd stayed away for a full day.

Hanna was almost impressed by Carter's restraint. He'd left her to herself in the cottage the first night, even though she had the sense he wanted to stay and oversee everything she did.

But looking out the window now she saw him crossing the lawn, heading in her direction. Her reprieve had ended.

Not that the time alone had amounted to much. She'd been determined to search the place. It was a long shot, even though the cottage had sat unused after her father passed, but since she hadn't uncovered a new angle in the decade since his death, she didn't have anything to lose by being here.

But she'd been sidetracked yesterday when everything touched off a memory. The blue curtains Gena insisted they hang for privacy. The beige couch with the flat cushion on the left side because that's where her dad always sat. Then she'd found a stack of boxes in the hall closet filled with Dad's long-sleeve shirts and baseball hats. With photographs and cancelled checks.

At least looking through things helped her to not dwell on Carter. Getting sucked in by his charm felt like a betrayal to her mom and to her sister. The Jamesons had landed so many blows on her family and now here she was, watching Carter stalk across the lawn and not being able to look away. Those confident strides. The way his jeans sat low on his hips, highlighting his fit body. She never wanted anyone to be different from the perception she had in her head as much as she wanted that for Carter.

Hanna sighed when she heard the knock. Since Carter owned the property, it's not as if she had a choice about opening the door. "Hello."

"You haven't left the cottage since you walked in here yesterday morning." He held up a white bag and shook it. "So, I brought this." Then he held up a brown bag with the logo from a local grocery chain. "And this. Nothing much. Just the basics."

Her stomach growled in response. Food. Man, that

sounded good and the fact he thought to do it set off a tingling in her stomach. She'd eaten two breakfast bars in twenty-four hours. She might be able to eat the bag at this point.

"The place was filthy. Not years-without-a-basic-cleaning dirty, but not good." It also qualified as a bit more than a cottage. It was an eight-hundred-square-foot house with an open kitchen and a family room, one big bedroom and a loft, where she used to sleep with her sister. Tiny compared to the main house but then so were some hotels.

His eyebrow lifted. "Whose fault is that?"

"Well, I haven't been here for about a decade, so not mine." She took the bag out of his hands, leaving him with the groceries. "What's in here?"

"Does this mean I can come in?"

"Kind of depends on your answer."

She saw him smile as he stepped inside and closed the door behind him. His face was turned away from her, but she picked up that sunny open charm that seemed innate to him.

"Chicken and a salad." He shrugged. "I don't know. Fruit?"

She closed the top of the bag and stared at him. "Are you asking me? Shouldn't you know?"

"I didn't make any of it."

He sounded horrified at the thought of cooking, which made her wonder exactly how he survived in California for all those months without his usual staff of helpers. "Who did?"

"Lynette."

The fact he thought that was a full response almost made her laugh. "Who is she?"

"She works at the house."

He seemed to be dancing around the answer and that

made Hanna want to keep poking. "Was that so hard to admit?"

"Since you're judging everything I say? Yes."

She had to admit she was. Sure, he had all the trappings of a rich guy. When he was younger, he had played the wealthy-boy role pretty well. Then there was the issue of her sister and what happened between them and all the strong-arming by his father. But when she dealt with Carter one-on-one she didn't see any of that. He was charming. He didn't make demands or act like he was better than her. He'd picked up a mop and actually seemed to know how to use it.

But it all could be a carefully crafted act. His father excelled at games and forcing people to do what he wanted. It wasn't hard to believe Carter learned his skills at home. Still, a nagging voice in her brain kept saying that Carter was not his father.

Another day with him and she'd have a serious case of whiplash.

"That's likely fair." She nodded toward the kitchen. "Come on."

She dropped the bag on the counter and went in search of plates. It was a good thing a few of the hours she'd cleaned had been dedicated to the kitchen. Her plan for the afternoon was to figure out where to go grocery shopping. She'd do that after she saw what he'd brought with him and ate a bunch of chicken, because it sure smelled good.

She turned around with plates in hand and there he was, sitting on one of the bar stools at the counter. He wasn't waiting to be served. No, he had dived right into the bag and started unpacking. She liked a man who prioritized food over everything else. And she was sure there was something else. He seemed distracted, as if he wanted to talk with her.

No, thanks.

Verbally sparring with him, though invigorating, would bump her off track. She could not afford to spend the day thinking about him or that face or that sexy walk of his. She needed to settle in somewhere and restart, which was the plan even before she saw him again, but she had to try this first.

"I'm sorry." He mumbled the words as he placed a piece of chicken on each of their plates.

Her hand froze on the lid to what looked like homemade potato salad. "For?"

"Your sister."

Her whole body went numb. "What?"

"I know she…died."

Hanna couldn't say anything, couldn't even choke out a word. Her mouth had gone dry and the words refused to form in her brain.

She'd tried to push thoughts of Gena away because being here, on the property with him, trusting him at all, was a slam against Gena. It had been six months and Hanna no longer cried every day, but she thought about her sister all the time. Her pain. Her fear. How desperate she must have felt at the end. How lost.

And Carter had caused Gena's confusion. At least some of it. So, to drop a stale apology at the table while munching on chicken struck her as an insult. One she couldn't process.

Maybe it was the silence or the suffocating tension that suddenly filled the room, but Carter looked up. "Hanna?"

"What exactly are you sorry for?" Her voice shook as she asked the question. That shaking was nothing compared to her muscles. They strained until she had to grab on to the edge of the counter to keep from falling down.

"The accident." He slowly lowered the piece of chicken to his plate. "I remember her from years ago and from…"

"When?"

His shoulders seemed to slump. "We saw each other more recently."

Saw each other. Heat raced through her body. The rage-filled-throw-things kind.

"That's a pretty neutral statement." She dropped the potato salad container on the counter with a thud. "You didn't come back from California after she died."

He'd committed so many sins when it came to Gena. There was so much fault and blame. Since the second she saw him, that reality did battle with the need he touched off in her. The same need she tried to stomp out but it refused to extinguish.

His eyes narrowed as he stared at her. "I didn't know she passed until just recently."

"I tried to contact you." And his father showed up instead. First, in writing. Then in person. Gena was barely in the ground before Eldrick demanded that Carter's name not be associated with Gena's in any way. There was only one way Eldrick would know about Gena and Carter—Carter had told him. Only one reason for his visit—to fix Carter's mess.

"I didn't find out until after I came to your apartment in New York," Carter said.

She shook her head, trying to decipher what he was saying. Gena died months ago, not days ago.

There was only one explanation. He was playing some sort of game with her and it made her feel queasy and sad. "You should leave."

His eyes narrowed but he didn't hop off the bar stool. "What just happened?"

"Please, just go." Or she would. Maybe she shouldn't have tried this at all. The offer had sounded too good to be true, and clearly it was.

"You know this is my house, right?" The edge in his tone was there. As if he had a right to be ticked off. No way.

"Then I'll go." Because she couldn't sit there and try to rationalize away his lies. That sexy drawl of his, the self-assurance, even the subtle charm and little jokes…they had reeled her in. Made her lower her defenses but now reality came back and slapped her in the face.

He wasn't two different people, which meant the guy she'd spun teen dreams about in her head and whose voice echoed through her even now was the same guy standing in front of her, lying. This was her nightmare. He actually was just like his father.

She hadn't unpacked her duffel. It sat on the coffee table in the living area. She snagged the strap and threw it over her shoulder. Took a quick look around but, honestly, whatever she left here didn't matter. She never got attached to anything, which made it easy to walk away.

Turning around, she ran right into him. Her hand went to his chest to steady her balance. The firmness registered first. The hard muscles under her palm… Despite everything, how much she still ached to explore every inch of him. Then she dropped it, not wanting one extra second of contact with him.

"Hold on." He reached for her but stopped when she flinched. His hands went into the air as if he were surrendering. "Okay, I get it. You're upset, so I'll go."

She wrapped her fingers around the bag's strap. Tightened until her palms ached.

"We're going to talk about this." Backing away from her, he nodded as he headed toward the door. "You can't keep running me off."

She absolutely could. So much of her life had been swallowed up by the Jamesons. Her sister. Her father. Even her mother was collateral damage. She could not invite them into her life again. "I don't think you want to hear the truth."

He couldn't miss her message. It's not as if she was trying to be subtle.

A nerve ticked in his cheek as he stood there. It took another minute before his jaw unclenched and he blew out a long breath. "Fine, you want space, you got it."

She waved in the direction of the counter. "You can take the food."

But he was already headed for the door. "Keep it."

"I don't need your charity."

He stopped with his hand on the doorknob and turned back around to face her. "One of these days you're going to realize I'm not my father."

"Don't count on it."

Five

Carter tried to block out the memory of yesterday's lunch fiasco with Hanna. He worked in the library, went for a run, but none of it helped. His gaze kept wandering to the cottage. His thoughts centered on how her mood had flipped. She'd been guarded since he'd first knocked on her apartment door in New York, but yesterday had been different. She'd shut down and he still wasn't sure why.

He'd been raised to be quiet, seen and not heard. He'd learned to tiptoe through disappointment and difficult situations by using a mix of acting like he didn't care and humor. He kept most of his relationships pleasant but shallow. Shallow was safe.

All of that practice meant he could charm his way out of most situations. He'd smile and engage in unimportant chatter. His brothers joked that he was the perfect party host. He kept the conversation flowing. And for the first month after his dad kicked him out, he'd spent a lot of time partying. The alcohol flowed freely, which had allowed him to capitalize on the whole life-of-the-party thing, getting sucked in deeper and deeper.

He'd stopped cold turkey after he blacked out. It only took that one time, that complete loss of control, to scare him. He'd realized he preferred the warm heat of scotch rolling down his throat to being with people…to doing anything. The realization was enough to turn him around.

He refused to give his father the satisfaction of breaking him, so he'd stopped drinking. But he had the very real sense he'd been on the verge of a full-blown addiction that would have dropped him to his knees.

But all of that was his secret and in the past. He'd refused alcohol since he'd been back home, but neither of his brothers were big drinkers, so they didn't seem to notice. But now, looking around the small conference room table just outside Jackson's office, Carter was tempted to dive in and tell them everything.

His brothers and Jackson were in fine form, joking as they reviewed plans for some new commercial building project that would bring in millions of dollars. It sounded fine to him but wasn't really his expertise. Which was why it didn't make sense for them to have called him in from Virginia this morning. But he'd come willingly, relieved to be away from the temptation of Hanna and his plans to confront her.

The building talk died down and Derrick spun his chair around at the head of the table so that he faced Carter head-on. "So…"

One of the walls was all glass and faced the hallway and the desks and offices beyond. Still, Carter suddenly felt trapped. Spence, Derrick and Jackson all stared at him. Tension pressed in on him and he didn't care for the suffocating sensation one bit.

He also knew he needed to stop whatever nonsense was headed his way before it could start. "No. To whatever you're going to say. The answer is no."

"It doesn't work that way." Derrick took a long sip of

coffee, leaving a charged silence in his wake. "I'm oldest. I get to be bossiest."

Jackson nodded. "We should put that on your business cards."

Derrick kept his attention on Carter. "Where have you been hiding and why?"

Carter looked across the table at Spence, then to his right to Jackson. They all paid attention now. None of them looked at files or paperwork or reached for the fruit and bagels sitting in the middle of the table.

Carter sensed a setup and decided to play it off. "I drove in, then tried to steal Jackson's coffee—"

Jackson cleared his throat. "In related news, I'd like a lock on my office door."

"I'm surprised it took you this long to come up with that idea." Spence laughed as he swooped in for the bagel closest to him.

Derrick being Derrick, he did not get knocked off stride by the chaos swirling around him. He hopped right back into the conversation where he left off. "Not this morning. I mean that you ran off to do Dad's dirty work and then—"

Spence made a strangled noise. "Please rephrase that."

"Then you came back to town and subsequently disappeared for a few days." Derrick leaned back in his big office chair as he continued to talk to Carter. "Now you're here, with that blank look on your face."

"Blank?" He did not need this today, not when he'd spent the entire morning trying to decipher Hanna and the mystery of the envelope and gauge how to read her fluctuating moods. But turning the conversation away from wherever Derrick was heading could only be a good thing. So, Carter grabbed a mug and then the coffee pot. Skipped the sugar and went for black. A shot of caffeine might do him some good. "Sounds to me like you're not getting enough sleep."

"Nice try, but you're wearing your I'm-trying-to-come-up-with-a-lie face." Spence laughed at his own joke as he turned to Jackson. "Carter has been using that ever since he could walk."

Jackson shook his head. "I forgot how fun it was to deal with all of you in the same room."

"Consider yourself an adopted Jameson," Spence said as he spun the plate in the middle of the table and grabbed the cream cheese.

Jackson caught the spinning tray before items started to fly off. "No, thanks."

Derrick exhaled louder than necessary. He also scowled and generally looked annoyed. He'd perfected that look. "Let's circle back to the original question." Derrick aimed all of his focus on Carter. "What's up with you?"

Admitting he had Hanna hidden at the Virginia estate would only invite questions. Sure, he could insist she deserved closure and they owed it to her after what happened to her father on their property. But the truth was his reasons for inviting her were far more complex and confusing. He did it for her, but he also did it because, after years away from her, he didn't want the time with her to end. He was the guy who moved on but when she tried to make him do that, to leave her house, all he wanted was to stay.

He didn't get it. He couldn't explain it. He really didn't even want to analyze his reaction to her all that closely.

He took his time twisting off the cap on the water bottle. "You guys were all busy with your women—"

Spence whistled. "I dare you to say it that way to them."

"He's stalling and saying provocative things in the hope of throwing us off track. He thinks it's charming or something." Derrick's gaze hadn't wavered. It stayed locked on Carter as the conversation swirled. "Which makes me wonder… Do you have a woman of your own you're hiding somewhere, like maybe in a big house in Virginia?"

Derrick made the comment just as Carter swallowed, or

tried to. The water came rushing back up his throat and he started coughing.

Spence snorted. "Well, well."

"That's telling," Jackson said at the same time.

Then, for once, and not when Carter wanted them to, they all stopped talking. Their joint attention focused on him until he had to fight the urge to squirm. Calling up all of his life-of-the-party reserve, he aimed for calm and nonchalance. "I've been doing some work on the Virginia property."

Spence dropped his bagel without taking a bite. "I don't know how you can stand being there."

"Not all the memories are bad." Carter said that more as an automatic reaction than with genuine feeling. He'd programmed his brain to downplay the dysfunction. To ignore his playboy father, his dying mother, and every snide comment about being a failure and a disappointment.

His father had been harsh and cold. He'd thought nothing of throwing them to the ground or pitting brother against brother in both emotional warfare and actual physical fighting. Dear ol' Dad insisted that behavior made them strong. Made them ready to take over the business. The same business he nearly bankrupted with his questionable under-the-table deals and lying.

"You held your engagement party there. We can all agree that was nice," Carter said as the most obvious escape from the conversation popped into his head. He'd walked in on something interesting at the party, complete with Spence and Abby fidgeting and adjusting their clothes and looking as if they'd been caught if not in the act, then right after it. "Spence seemed to have enjoyed himself. Want to talk about that, Spence?"

Spence just smiled. "Not when we're still talking about you."

Well, damn. That didn't work.

"Look." Derrick set his mug down. "We just want to make sure you're okay. That you're not…"

Carter almost hated to ask but he had to know what thought or word had Derrick, his usually practical and reserved oldest brother, glancing around the room and avoiding eye contact. "What?"

Derrick grimaced. "Lonely."

"Do we really care about that?" Spence asked, the sarcasm obvious in his voice.

"You don't have to stay at the estate. You can live with me." Derrick shook his head. "Ellie is upset you're not at our place already."

Carter couldn't figure out if Derrick was using his fiancée as an excuse or not. But he did know the soon-to-be parents deserved some privacy. "Thanks, but now that Spence moved in with Abby, you should take a break from housing wayward brothers for a month or so."

Derrick pointed at his second-in-command and friend to all of them. "Then live with Jackson."

"Wait…what?"

Carter debated saying yes just to see Jackson sputter some more.

"Answer this question." The squeak from Derrick's chair echoed through the room as he sat forward and balanced his elbows on the edge of the table. "Are you thinking about leaving again?"

For a second, Carter's brain scrambled as he rushed to figure out what Derrick was talking about. Then he remembered the scene a year ago when Derrick begged him to stay and promised a united front against their father. Carter had kept on walking, a move he regretted because it sent a message to his brothers that he'd never meant to send.

This was a conversation they'd all avoided since he'd been back, as if by silent agreement. Carter didn't want to broach it now, but he didn't want Derrick to worry either. "Why would you think that?"

"You delivered the letter to Hanna Wilde as Dad insisted, right?" Derrick stared at Carter until he nodded. "That means there's nothing holding you here. I get that you want to move on, but I was hoping… I'd like you to stay. At least until the baby is born."

Derrick was one of the smartest, toughest people Carter knew and here he was, sounding like he was begging his baby brother to stick around for a few more months. Carter hated that his tendency to leave difficult situations—the family, any state where their father lived—meant Derrick felt he had to plead. He'd definitely screwed up with the way he'd handled leaving a year ago and this was the result.

"I'm not going anywhere." Carter pulled back from saying more before he made a promise he couldn't keep. "I mean, I know I'm not one to stick around, but as long as Dad isn't here, I'm here."

Jackson cleared his throat. "Is there anything else you want to talk about?"

The sentence was cryptic, but Carter understood Jackson was referencing Carter's ideas about the future of the estate. Now was not the time. Carter still wasn't sure those ideas were even the right ones for the business or for him. "No."

Spence looked at Jackson. "What's this about?"

Jackson looked at Carter an extra beat before turning back to Spence. "Nothing."

"So, you're hanging out in Virginia. You plan to stick around, at least for now." Derrick smiled as he spoke. "Got it. But what about the woman part?"

Carter should have seen that turn coming, but he didn't. It took his brain a second to unscramble. "We aren't talking about my love life."

"Actually, he was talking about fun. Some dating. A little

sex." Spence pointed at Carter. "You're the one who mentioned love, which is not something any of us will forget."

"I'd like to," Jackson mumbled under his breath.

"And with that, I'll be heading back to Virginia." Carter stood up. He'd walk there if he had to, just to get out of this conversation.

"Hey." Derrick didn't raise his voice. If anything, he grew quieter. "Thanks."

"I'm here because I want to be here." Carter needed to make that point. His brothers could count on him even though he'd failed to show that to them in the past.

"Just let us know if that changes," Spence said.

"Done."

Carter didn't get very far before Jackson caught up with him. In silent agreement, they both stopped walking and stood in the busy hall with phones ringing at desks all around them and the low rumble of voices filtering through the melee.

"I'm trying to figure out how brothers who are so good at loyalty and business, despite their idiot father's meddling, can stink at interpersonal stuff." Jackson shook his head. "Your ideas for the property, Carter. That was a perfect opening to talk it over."

"Not yet." He still hadn't fulfilled his part of the agreement—a fact he knew because he still had that damn letter, but his brothers didn't know yet. And without the three of them completing all of Dad's tasks, their father wouldn't officially turn the business over. He still held controlling interest.

Since Carter had vowed not to get into business with his father, that meant waiting until Derrick was officially in charge before moving forward with anything involving the Virginia property.

Jackson shifted his weight to the side to let two women from accounting pass by them. "Because?"

"I'm not ready." He hated being unsure of his place in the family business, but that's where they were. Jackson's frown suggested he knew that. "And you can stop looking at me that way."

"Is it possible you don't want to talk about the proposal because if you do, and Derrick wants to pursue it, then you're stuck here?"

Maybe that was another part of it. Settling in, creating roots, being a part of something. Not having the freedom to pick up and run to California for a few months. A part of him wondered if he'd ever be able to make the commitment to stay and rebuild his life here.

Another part knew the answer was no, not with all the memories chasing him.

"Did you get a psychology degree while I was away for a year?"

Jackson snorted. "I need one to deal with your family."

That probably wasn't far from the truth. Their dad had hired Jackson a few years ago. At first, Derrick had been skeptical but it hadn't taken long for all of them to realize he was competent and not reporting back to Dad. Jackson moved from business associate to friend almost immediately. "You love us."

"Some of you…" Jackson smiled. "But only sometimes."

Six

Guilt gnawed at Hanna as she walked the fence line closest to the main house. The red and orange leaves blanketing the lawn provided a nice change of scenery compared to her morning of dismantling and searching the cottage.

If anyone had seen her through the cottage windows, they would have thought she was cleaning. But the real goal was to find her father's journal, hoping it would provide some insight into how and why he really died. But nothing so far, so she went out for some air.

She walked, letting the cool breeze catch the loose hem of her sweater and billow up inside. The lawn was awash in color as the trees dropped their leaves. The fresh air recharged her. She'd spent the hours, the whole night, really, since kicking Carter out of his own cottage trying to think of a better way to handle her unwanted feelings for him and how guilty she felt for having them.

Her father had died. Her sister had died. Gena's baby had never been born. With that much loss came a load of distrust. Hanna had aimed it all at Carter when his father was her true target.

Not that Carter remained blameless. He'd taken a back seat when it came to dealing with Gena and he'd let his father handle everything. That made him weak, not evil. Only, the pieces didn't fit together for her. The man who'd hunted her down didn't seem like the type to evade responsibility.

But her sister's warnings still rang in her ears.

Don't trust the Jamesons. Carter ran away. He will do anything to hide his mistakes.

She heard the crunch of dying leaves before she saw him. Looking up, she watched as Carter walked toward her with his hands stuffed in his pockets. One thought filtered through her memories: no one looked better in faded jeans and a plain black jacket than he did. From the broad shoulders to that trim waist to those long legs, he had the body of an athlete, which he had been at one time.

He stopped a few feet away from her as if he wasn't sure if he was welcome to come closer. "You're outside."

Words backed up in her throat. "Yes."

He blew out a long breath. "I see you're sticking with curt responses."

She hated that these feelings welled up inside her and spilled over. She wasn't this person. She didn't usually snap and act like a jerk. Life had taken an unexpected left turn on her, but she tried to stay positive. The only thing guaranteed to throw her off stride was the name Jameson.

The inner battle between wanting Carter to be the man he appeared to be and the memories of his father showing up unannounced, waving around Gena's bills from the health-care clinic, caused a mental clash. Bills he shouldn't have had. The same ones that referenced her pregnancy. Carter hadn't mentioned that part when he'd spoken of Gena. He'd acted as if he didn't know.

Why did she have to keep convincing herself that was just an act?

But there was one truth she could share without trouble. "About yesterday… Let's just say I'm protective when it comes to Gena."

"I have brothers. I get it." He nodded. "And I knew her, Hanna."

That did it. She could almost hear the door creak open. She debated rushing through it, peppering him with questions. Once she started, she knew she wouldn't stop, but maybe she could peek in. "How?"

He frowned. "What?"

"What was she to you?"

His shoulders stiffened along with his jaw. "The way you're asking makes me think you know."

"I want to hear your definition." She inhaled and walked through, even as dread settled over her, creeping in until she could barely hear. "Dating? Using her? Sleeping around?"

"Is this why you're ticked off at me?"

"Your family…" What did she even say next? She had no idea how to start a conversation that ended with *you ignited an emotional firestorm that swallowed my sister.* "Forget it. I'm here, at the estate, for one thing."

"Which is what exactly?"

Answers. Closure. Revenge.

"I thought you were going to give me space and not ask questions."

"Hey." He reached out and took a step toward her but stopped when she pivoted away from his hand. "Okay. No touching. I get it."

Something about the easy way he waded through this conversation set her off. This wasn't about her old crush or the attraction that kept sparking even though she would give anything for it not to. This was about the pain she'd tried to lock away and her imperfect sister, who deserved better. "You think you can just swoop in and take whatever you want. That people's feelings don't matter."

His head jerked back. "Where did that come from?"

"Gena was my sister. We talked about what was happening in our lives. About who was in them." The rest threatened to spill out of her. Every horrible fact.

"Wait a second." His hands were in the air and every movement seemed careful, as if he expected her to blow and he was trying to manage the situation. "Gena and I had a fling. A meaningless fling."

With that, Hanna's mind went blank. For a second she couldn't say anything. Her mouth dropped open and it took all of her strength to close it again. "You're such a man."

"Which I'm assuming is a really bad thing in this scenario." His hands dropped to his sides.

"It's not good."

A lawn mower started in the distance. The motor drowned out the sound of the gentle swish of the trees. Looking up at the house, she saw a woman open the balcony door on the second floor and then scurry back inside. It all felt so ordinary when this conversation was anything but.

"What do you think happened between me and Gena?" he asked.

If he wanted to do this, fine. She'd heard the story from Gena. Well, *a* story. Gena had a habit of embellishing, but she always started with a truth and that's the part Hanna couldn't forget. "You found her, took what you wanted and then blew her off."

"That's not true. Not any of it."

"Oh, please." The fact that he out-and-out lied crushed something inside her. She'd hoped he would... She didn't even know what.

He shook his head. "We had an agreement. We were clear—it was fun only."

Fun? He had to be kidding. "Do you know how she died?"

"Car accident."

That would have been terrible but the truth was so much

worse. "She ran the car off a bridge. No brake marks. No other vehicles. It was on purpose. She was lost and alone and wanted to die."

All of the color drained from his face. "I'd heard the rumors, but are you sure?"

A new pang of guilt settled in her chest. Before Gena showed up at the door, Hanna hadn't seen her sister for a few months. "I was with her after you left. She came to me broken and distraught."

"Hanna, I'm not sure what you're thinking here, but your sister and I spent exactly one weekend together."

That couldn't be right. "No."

"Three days." He held up three fingers as if to emphasize his point. "That's it."

Gena's story unraveled in Hanna's head. She talked about Carter looking her up and all the dinners and gifts…then he was gone without warning. She'd talked in terms of months, not days. "That's not… You're downplaying the relationship to make yourself feel better about what happened to her."

"I can give you the exact dates if you need them, but that was it. This wasn't a big love affair for either of us." He never broke eye contact. Didn't fidget or stumble over his words. He spoke as if he believed what he was saying.

"She and I specifically talked about what you meant to her." It had killed Hanna. After all those years of admiring him from afar. All those computer searches she did as a grown-up just because she wanted to see what he looked like now.

"A weekend, Hanna."

The words refused to settle in Hanna's brain. His explanation didn't match anything she'd been told.

He took another step, closing the gap between them but not making any move to touch her this time. "Are you saying she drove the car off the bridge six months after our weekend together because of me?"

His voice shook. The stunned horror was right there on his face, in his words. He looked pale and unsure, his usual confidence gone. Nothing about his expression or the way he stood there fit with a man who didn't care that the mother of his child was dead.

She'd stoked her anger at him and painted him as one type of guy in her head because it was easier to heap the blame on him. She was self-aware enough to realize that. But only one person had been in the car that night. The police had been clear about that.

Gena had struggled her entire life with mood swings and those few months pushed her too far. Finding out she was pregnant, something she hadn't even realized until she felt sick, pushed her right to the edge. Carter's choices played a part in that, but only a part.

She couldn't blame him for Gena's choices no matter how much easier that would be. "No. That's not… I'm not arguing cause and effect."

"Then what are you saying, Hanna?"

Too much. Not enough. Tension gripped her until she thought she would shatter. He hadn't mentioned the baby or his father's insistence that every fact surrounding Gena's relationship with Carter be kept quiet, so she held back. Then there were all the other secrets about his family. So many things she suspected and now wasn't sure he knew.

She had no idea how or if she should spill it all. There just was no way for her to win. "Nothing. Forget it."

"How do you expect me to do that?"

"I'm sure you'll be fine." He would always be fine because he had the Jameson name to fall back on. That was the point.

She couldn't breathe. It was as if a tight fist had closed around her chest. She fought off the need to gasp. The cottage. Quiet. She needed both.

She spun around, intending to go back to the cottage but

she lost her balance. Carter's hand shot out. He caught her, then let go as soon as he steadied her.

He started talking as soon as they separated again. "Why do you think we were together longer than a few days?"

"You were bored. You, handsome and rich, this guy she knew as untouchable growing up, breezed into her life." That made sense to Hanna. It fit with his lifestyle and all that money. Everywhere she looked right now was a reminder of his great big piles of it. That, alone, should make her write him off but every time she tried she'd think up a new excuse for how his confusion might be real. "She really didn't stand a chance."

He zipped and unzipped his jacket. "She picked me up in a bar. Everything that happened was mutual."

"I didn't say it wasn't."

"I was a mess when I was with your sister. Not because of her. Because of everything else happening. I was wild and out of control, which she knew. Drinking too much and making bad choices. She said we could be wild together, then move on." A harsh sound escaped his throat. "Did she tell you that part?"

None of that fit. The drinking and bad choices sounded like Gena. She'd spun out of control after their dad died and never regained her balance. But the rest was so different from what Gena described. For a second Hanna wondered if her sister made up the relationship story because of her fears over being pregnant. She had been so shaky there at the end.

As soon as Hanna thought it, a new wave of guilt smacked into her. Was she just trying to think of ways to excuse Carter's behavior?

The lawn mower moved closer. The guy riding on it wore earphones. When he saw them, he did a double take. All it took was a raise of Carter's hand and a shake of his head to have the guy turning the machine around and heading off to mow another section of the land.

Carter waited until the noise quieted down and they were alone on that stretch of lawn to talk again. "I'd had a falling-out with my father. He kicked me out of the family, Hanna."

"But how serious could that have been? You were able to tap into your checking account to roam all over California. You're here now, so you're clearly welcome again." Because that story fit with how she needed to see him to keep some distance from him. If he'd really been pushed out then another piece of her defense against wanting to spend time with him would fall.

"Do you really want to talk about my finances?"

She didn't want to know anything. She didn't want to fight or to feel anything. All she needed was for him to see that what happened might not have been as simple as he thought. "You don't think, maybe, that you used her? That she was convenient and when she stopped being convenient, you left. After…however long."

Every one of his muscles visibly stiffened. "I told you how long. Three days."

"Right." She could not wrap her head around that or how broken her sister really must have been to make the relationship sound so much bigger than it was.

"We used each other."

"But she's the only one who's dead."

The words sat between them. They echoed in her head as tension wrapped around her and Carter. She couldn't draw in enough air, couldn't figure out how to call back her sharp response.

She hated who she was when she talked about Gena. Her death cast this harsh darkness over everything. Hanna thought she wanted to hurt Carter, to make him feel half of the pain that pulsed inside her, but looking at him now, seeing the shock and hurt in his eyes, she didn't feel one ounce of peace. Just dizzy and tired. If this is what revenge led to, she didn't want any part of it.

His chest rose and fell on heavy breaths. "If you're going to blame me for Gena's suicide, then have the guts to say it. Don't dance around the accusation."

She couldn't form the words. She wanted to blame him, but the pieces were all mixed up in her mind now. "There were…things that happened after. It wasn't just you. It was the aftermath."

His mouth dropped open. "I have no idea what that means."

Her mind went to the baby. For the first time, she saw the threats Carter's father made in a different light. She'd always assumed that he'd demanded she stay quiet because Carter wanted to hide from the truth. Now she wondered if Eldrick really wanted to hide the truth from Carter.

She had no idea what to do with that possibility or how to tell him such a crushing thing. "Do you know your father came to see her?"

Carter took a step back. Actually looked like he lost his balance and stumbled. "When?"

"After your supposed weekend together."

He made a grumbling sound. "Stop saying it that way."

"I didn't mean to… Once you were gone."

"Why?"

The confusion in his voice added to her own confusion. "I thought you sent him to find her. To fix your mess. Is that not true?"

"He kicked me out, Hanna. I didn't see or talk to my father until Derrick and Ellie's engagement party a few months ago. Even then, we spoke for less than fifteen minutes and there was nothing friendly about it." All of the confidence, those charming smiles and the carefree attitude he carried around had vanished. "And that was well after Gena's death."

"But he's your father. He still cleans up after you."

Carter's stunned expression morphed into something else. Frustration pulsed off him. "I'm a grown man. I don't need *Daddy* to fix anything for me. And, honestly, he's the last person I would ask for help."

That fit with how her father used to talk about Eldrick, but not with anything else. "You're saying you didn't send him to see Gena."

"Of course not." Carter sounded appalled at the idea. "For what?"

"I wasn't there."

She wished she had been. If she had stuck around and continued to live with her sister she would have seen the relationship between Gena and Carter and she would have been there when Carter's father came knocking and making threats. She'd lived through her own version of his intimidation when he tried to bribe her after Gena died, but she hadn't been alone and afraid. Hanna couldn't imagine how scary that must have been for her sister.

Carter crossed his arms over his chest. "But you know what he said to her."

"To stay away from you." It was a sanitized version but good enough.

"That doesn't make any sense. I was already in California. And I never told Dad that I spent a weekend with Gena."

"Because you were ashamed of it?"

"Because in addition to the fact my sex life is private, I go out of my way not to tell him anything." The longer Carter spoke, the more his voice rose.

Every possible comeback froze in her head. Every word he said changed every fact she thought she knew. The ground kept shifting under her until she didn't know what to believe or think. "Fine."

"Fine? You basically accused me of lying and, worse, of driving your sister to her death."

That's not... "I didn't."

"You think I'm some spoiled rich kid, running to Daddy."

She fought off a wince. "Look around you, Carter. Do you blame me? A house the size of an elementary school is standing behind you. The pool, the guesthouse. All these acres so close to Washington, D.C."

And the estate was only a small part of the Jameson empire. She'd read the business articles. They owned commercial and residential buildings throughout the area and down as far as North Carolina. The business. The other houses. That didn't even touch the cars, the money, the stocks and whatever else they had acquired.

He nodded. "For what you're suggesting? Yeah, I do blame you."

"We knew each other as kids. Maybe we weren't friends but I remember you from back then. You didn't act ashamed of the money or the family name." He'd been cocky and proud. The guy most likely to do anything. He partied and brought girls home when his father was away on business.

"Do you want to be judged by things you did years ago?"

She hated that he made her sound unfair, made her feel that way. "I guess that depends on if I have anything to hide."

His shoulders fell as he let out a long exhale. "You are dead wrong about me."

"Possibly." She stood there, trying to hold on to her preconceived notions of who she thought he was, but they no longer fit him as cleanly as she thought they once did.

"I'm not sure what I did to *you* to invite your distrust or what my father was doing six months ago, but I am sorry about Gena." Carter unwound his arms and let them fall motionless to his sides. "I really am."

A lump formed in her throat. She couldn't swallow it or clear it away because she believed him. She forced a word out over it. "Okay."

"That's all you're going to say to me?"

Her mind spun. She tried to think of what to say and explain how she'd viewed him through this specific lens because it was easier for her to tag him as spoiled than deal with the actual man. And now her defenses and biases were crashing at her feet and the vulnerability left her shaky and uncertain.

When she didn't say anything, he did a quick look around, then nodded. "Enjoy your walk."

Then he was gone.

She didn't see him the rest of the day but his words, that pained expression on his face, kept running through her mind. She'd accused him and then tried to ignore every response he offered. It had been the only way to hold on to that wall of anger she'd built. Letting that go meant leaving room for the pain and grief to sweep in.

It was easier to hate Carter and his father than to deal with her sister's death. She'd constructed this scenario where Carter refused to take responsibility, and that had started crumbling. But maybe she wanted it to crumble because then her attraction would make sense and be okay. The guilt would evaporate.

She could no longer tell the difference between how she wanted to see him and how she needed to see him for self-protection.

As she lay on the bedroom floor, sprawled on the fluffy carpet she'd just vacuumed for the third time, she had to admit she wasn't that great at responsibility either. She'd walked away from her sister when Gena refused to ease up on the partying. She'd seen Gena spinning out of control and tried to help, but then hadn't stuck around for the last round. And now her sister was dead.

An ache started low in her stomach, then it traveled. It seeped through her veins and landed in her chest. The weight had her rubbing the heel of her hand against her breastbone in the hope of wiping it out.

She took one last look under the bed, just to see if her father had hidden anything there. He had been the type to squirrel away money, in random coffee mugs, tucked in an envelope on the underside of his sock drawer, curled up in a small bag and rammed into an old boot at the bottom of his closet. She'd found all of those hiding places, but money was not her target.

Dad said his journal didn't have anything but everyday ramblings inside and that he only kept it to drive away the loneliness that settled in at night. But she still wanted to find it. It was a long shot, but if the journal still existed she wanted to read it. Just to see if there were any hints about a falling-out with Carter's father or problems at the house that could explain her father's sudden death.

That's why she was there, but Carter wouldn't leave her thoughts.

She needed him to be a jerk. That fit the story she had in her head. If he was a jerk, then she could roll her eyes over her stupid teen crush and move on. She could forget him and be satisfied that she'd ripped up the bribery check his father had offered in return for her never contacting Carter and never talking to him about the baby.

She could still hear the steady beat of Eldrick Jameson's words, how insistent he'd been back then. In her mind she remembered it as fury about the baby and Carter's choices, which she assumed Eldrick thought were beneath his son. Now she wondered if that tone really signaled desperation over something bigger.

She glanced up at the ceiling and the dark beams that gave the cottage a cozy chalet feel. Her gaze followed the one in the middle, then moved to the next. The old wood had a certain charm. A bit ragged and…discolored. Not all of it. Just a swath at the far edge of one beam. A square facing away from the main part of the room, as if someone tried to patch it and used the wrong stain.

She sat up, squinting and moving her head as if either would give her a better angle. When those attempts didn't work, she got up. Climbed on the armrest of the couch and reached up, but her fingers only grazed the wood. She needed something higher. With a quick look around, she spied the bar stool. It would be wobbly and not smart, so of course she was going to use it as a makeshift ladder.

After a quick run to the kitchen to fetch the hammer, she grabbed the bar stool. She didn't know if either item would help, but the off-color piece of beam would bug her all night if she didn't get a closer look.

As predicted, the bar stool shimmied when she put one foot on it. Balancing a hand on a couch armrest, she tried to find her equilibrium, silently cursing herself for not paying more attention to all that "core" talk in the free Pilates class she'd attended. After a few more seconds, she let go and stood up. One hand grabbed the beam, anchoring her a bit.

She ran her fingers over the scarred wood and felt a ridge. With a tug, she pulled open a door she didn't even know was there and felt around inside what she now assumed was some sort of lockbox without any lock. A small metal box came out in her hand. Lowering it as she stepped off the stool, she peeked inside and shuffled through the contents. A folded-up birth certificate—her father's—and a passport, which had expired more than a decade ago. Two coins she couldn't identify and a photo of her parents.

They were young and smiling, so different from how she remembered them. They weren't the joking-around type. Mostly, she remembered the fighting and all those debates about visitation days and who got the kids for Thanksgiving each year. But looking now she could almost hear her father's deep laugh as she brushed her fingertip over the photo of his face.

She hadn't known she wanted to find something like this until she held it in her hand. Memories flooded her. Grilling hamburgers with him outside this cottage. They'd had to stay close to the house and not make too much noise or Dad's boss, Carter's father, would get angry. It was like this undercover game that ended with food and laughter.

She smiled as she reached for the last item in the box. A small journal, maybe six inches long, rolled up and secured with a rubber band.

Finally.

Seven

"You're smart to be inside," Jackson said as he walked into the Virginia estate's library. He shook his head and beads of water splashed to the floor. More ran off his raincoat. He shifted his weight as he looked down. "Crap. I didn't realize—"

"It's fine." Carter sat up and his back muscles groaned in relief. He glanced at the clock and realized he'd been sitting there for three hours without moving.

He blamed Hanna. He could not get her out of his head. Her face, that wary expression, the mix of pain and fire in her eyes as she talked about Gena. He didn't understand the accusations or how she came to her conclusions. He had no idea how she could stand to be in the same room with him believing what she did.

But her doubts fueled him. Ever since their rough conversation yesterday afternoon, he'd been on a quest to piece together his schedule and show Hanna how short a time he'd been around and with her sister.

It was a ridiculous task. Totally unnecessary. He was a grown man and his sex life wasn't Hanna Wilde's business. But the idea of Gena committing suicide made him sick. The thought that he might have done something or said something to push her there left him feeling raw and hollow. She was funny and irreverent and the idea of her taking her own life left him feeling numb.

He hadn't lied to Hanna. He and Gena had been nothing more than a quick hookup. When Hanna had suggested otherwise, he'd been desperate to clear his name. Still was. It was as if he needed her to believe in him. He hated the idea that he'd spent most of his time since seeing her again wanting to kiss her, touch her, all while she viewed him as an ass.

Jackson dumped his raincoat over the back of a chair and ran a hand through his hair. He nodded in the direction of the wall of files, papers and books stacked around Carter like a fort. "What exactly are you doing?"

"Working."

Bookshelves filled with everything from nonfiction to thrillers lined the room. The desk sat away from the wall by the windows. The dark wood club-like room sat on the second floor with a shaded patio just outside the double French doors.

Jackson dropped into the chair across the desk from Carter. "I thought you didn't work for your family."

Carter silently cursed Jackson's poor timing in showing up for a visit now. "There are other jobs, you know."

"Uh-huh." Jackson tapped his fingers on the chair's armrest. "But you don't have one of those either."

"True."

The fragile wooden chair creaked as Jackson leaned forward and picked a piece of paper off the stack closest to him. He frowned as he scanned it. "Your credit card bill?"

Carter reached out and grabbed it. "When did you get so nosy?"

"Since I volunteered to come out here and see what you're really doing, I can't deny the claim." Jackson leaned back again, setting off a new round of creaking as the chair strained under his weight. "I'm here to poke around."

"My brothers sent you?" That should have been obvious from the beginning. They'd both texted earlier. Now he knew they were checking to make sure he'd be there when Jackson arrived.

"You know what *volunteered* means. We were sitting around, talking about how weird and secretive you've gotten. Then we drew cards to see who got to come out here and bug you."

The explanation sounded so odd that Carter knew it was true. "And you lost."

Jackson snorted. "I won."

Footsteps sounded in the hall. The person coming to visit was not trying to hide the entrance. Hanna stepped into the doorway perfectly dry but without an umbrella or raincoat. Carter guessed she'd dropped them downstairs, which left the question of how she knew where to find him.

"Lynette said I could come up." Hanna's steps faltered as her gaze landed on Jackson's back. "Oh, man. I'm sorry."

Jackson turned around as the chair tilted slightly to one side. "I'm not."

Hanna winced as she started to back out of the room again. "I had no idea you had company."

"It's fine." Carter watched her, looking for signs that she wanted to pick up where they left off yesterday. Her unreadable expression didn't give anything away. "He's more like family than company."

"Please stop saying that." Jackson got up and in a few steps stood in front of Hanna with his hand out. "Jackson Richards."

Her hand froze in the middle of lifting it. "Jackson?"

"You don't like the name?" Jackson glanced over his shoulder at Carter. "Or have you been talking about me?"

"Not really." But Carter had to admit the reaction was

bizarre. She'd stopped moving and seemed to be stuck in some sort of haze. She looked at Jackson, her gaze searching his face as she frowned. "Hanna?"

That snapped her out of whatever emotion had her in its grip. She cleared her throat as she started shuffling again. "I'm sorry. I can come back."

The confusion and uncertainty surprised Carter. All of yesterday's anger had vanished but she came off as shaky and unsure. He didn't know what that meant, but he cared. Of course he did. He couldn't seem to stop caring about what she was thinking and feeling.

"From where?" Jackson asked.

She slammed to a halt. "What?"

"You're already on the grounds and in the house. That's not an easy feat, by the way. That gate out there is no joke. I have a key and a security code and you move around easier than I do." Jackson kept his voice low and soothing. The tone carried a hint of welcome and amusement. "My point is that it seems easy for you to get in and out, which I assume means you're staying nearby. Possibly *very* nearby."

Carter wanted her closer. In the house, with him, touching him. Needs he'd hidden as he tried to figure her out. "Um…"

"It's not…" She bit her lower lip. "Yeah."

Her voice, that stumble. Suddenly, Carter didn't feel so alone in the battle with his attraction for her. They had so much to talk about and think through, but all of that fell away as he watched the slight blush cover her cheeks. Maybe what they both needed had nothing to do with the past and other people.

Jackson looked back and forth between Carter and Hanna. "For the record, you two are not good at this."

"What?" she asked.

Jackson waved a hand in front of him. "Whatever this is."

Silence filled the room. Hanna did a lot of staring—at

Jackson, at the hardwood floor and the expensive Oriental rug covering it, at the antique cherry desk Carter sat behind, at the bookshelf on the opposite wall. Finally, she focused on Carter. "Do you trust him?"

Carter appreciated the easy question because everything else between them had gotten so complex. "Completely."

Jackson let out a long, labored breath. "I can hardly wait to hear what comes next."

"I'm Hanna Wilde." She stepped fully into the room and this time shook Jackson's hand.

Now it was Jackson's turn to freeze. It only lasted a second. Carter doubted Hanna even noticed. But Jackson wasn't one to get knocked off stride and that extra beat of hesitation meant he wasn't expecting to hear that name.

Carter couldn't help but smile at the idea of Hanna getting the upper hand on Jackson.

"Oh, you're the one…" Jackson nodded. "Yes, hello."

She glanced at Carter and he didn't even try to hide the fact that her name would have clued him in. "He knows my father wanted me to find you."

Carter expected anger or frustration, maybe some yelling. Instead, she let out what sounded like a resigned sigh before turning back to Jackson.

"Then I can shortcut this." She stepped closer to the desk. "Carter's dad wanted me to have this envelope, but I don't want anything to do with the man or his games. Since my father used to live and work here, Carter offered that I come back to say a final goodbye and collect some of his things. I thought maybe I could also figure out what Eldrick wants without ever having to deal with him again."

Jackson's eye widened. "You said it all in one breath."

"That was impressive." And Carter meant that.

"Especially since I didn't expect to say it at all." Hanna walked over to the chair Jackson had abandoned and sat down. "Me being here is a secret."

"Okay, I'll play along. From whom?" Jackson asked.

She shrugged. "You, I guess. And Carter's brothers."

"I'm lost," Jackson said as he leaned against the bookcase next to Hanna's chair.

Carter empathized. "It's your turn. I've been in that state since I tracked her down."

She frowned at him. "Like your mental state is my fault."

Lately it was. Being this close to her, even with Jackson there, sent a spike of energy buzzing through the room. "Well…"

"Okay, let's go back to the Eldrick part." Carter braced his hands on the bookshelf behind him. "You don't know what he wants?"

She shook her head. "No."

Jackson looked from Hanna to Carter and back again. "Here's a suggestion, and I admit this may lack finesse, but why don't you just *open the envelope*?"

"She doesn't want to be manipulated." Carter understood that much.

"The Eldrick piece is only part of it. I also wanted to take care of my dad's belongings, the stuff Eldrick never turned over."

Jackson looked more confused, not less. "It's like you two are talking in code."

"Bottom line?" Hanna shifted until she faced Jackson. "I don't trust Carter's father."

Carter understood that. It was the part where she didn't trust him either that kicked him in the gut. He sat there wanting her, spent the night dreaming about her, and he'd bet she could walk away from him and not look back. He hated that. Hated that she refused to confide in him. But he really hated that he cared this much.

"You're smart to stay away from Eldrick. The guy has a tendency to destroy the people he touches," Jackson said.

Her eyebrow lifted. "Don't you work for him?"

Jackson made a humming sound, the same noise he tended to make as he thought through what he wanted to say. "I prefer to think that I work for Derrick."

Hanna glanced at Carter. "Does he?"

"Yes. We're hoping that soon Dad will fully retire, hand over the reins and everyone will work for Derrick."

Carter vowed to do whatever he had to do to make that happen. Unfortunately, the very stubborn, very hot and utterly compelling woman sitting in front of him played a part in that. She hadn't opened the envelope yet, but he was betting that she would soon. That curiosity would win out.

"Except you, of course." Jackson mumbled the comment but he got everyone's attention.

She asked, "Wait, you mean Carter really doesn't work for the family?"

"Technically, he doesn't right now." Jackson smiled.

Their back-and-forth about him without talking to him was more than a little annoying. "*He* is sitting right here."

"Well, my response is the same." Jackson shrugged. "I get not wanting to be manipulated by Eldrick but every day the envelope sits there you have to think about him."

She didn't even hesitate. "I made a vow months ago. No more letters from Eldrick."

"Then I'm out of options." Jackson pushed away from the bookcase and straightened. "Which means it's time for me to go."

Carter decided to interpret the remark for her just in case she didn't get it. "He plans to run back to my brothers and report that you're here."

Jackson walked over to his soggy coat, picked it up and slipped it on. "He's right."

The chair practically bounced against the floor as she stood up. "You can't."

"Because?" Jackson stopped buttoning the raincoat and waited a few seconds as he shot her a *well?* look. "See, if you can't answer that question, then I don't understand the need to keep the secret."

"I don't want Eldrick to know I'm here." Her voice vibrated as she spoke.

Carter got it and took pity on her. "Then you're safe."

"The one thing you'll figure out about the Jameson brothers, if you don't already know it—they stick together." When she started to talk, Jackson talked louder and finished. "And the thing they're the best at doing is creating a united front against their father."

She didn't say anything. Just stared at him. Carter waited for a sharp response but she looked lost in thought, not angry. All signs of yesterday's frustration had disappeared. He wasn't sure what that meant but it gave him hope.

"I'll be off." Jackson waved to Carter before smiling at Hanna. "Nice to meet you. We'll see each other soon."

Her mouth opened and closed a few times before she spoke. "Will we?"

He winked at her as he walked out of the room and disappeared into the hallway. "I can almost guarantee it."

Once they were alone again, Hanna turned back to Carter. "I didn't mean to—"

"Here."

Carter didn't know if Jackson still hovered in the hall and he didn't care. This topic was too important. It had consumed his entire morning because he needed her to believe in him.

She shuffled the paperwork in her hands, paging through it but not spending much time on any one piece. "What am I looking at?"

"Proof. It represents my whereabouts around the time I saw your sister again. My calendar. Some receipts that show where I was and when." He'd collected and printed off all of it before Jackson came in.

She dropped her hands to her lap. The papers hung loose in her fingers as she stared at him.

He had no idea what that meant, so he kept pushing his case. "I was outside Charlottesville, where your sister lived, for what looks like seven days because I'm missing some verification, but the real answer is three." He pointed at the receipts resting on her knee. "You can see the plane ticket and the hotel receipts."

She looked at him for a few more seconds then glanced down. "You stayed in dive motels."

"What?"

She shook her head. "Nothing."

"The point is, this big love affair or whatever you think happened between me and Gena isn't real." The driving need for Hanna to see him as decent pushed him. "I can't provide proof that we agreed to hang out for a few days before I left for California because those were discussions without witnesses, but I can give you all of *that*."

She balanced the papers on the edge of the desk. Didn't rifle through them or demand more verification.

"Why did you do this?" Her voice stayed soft. No judgment or anger.

He could ignore the question or come up with some flippant answer. That's how he usually operated. Kept things shallow. But he needed her to know the truth.

"Because, believe it or not, I care what you think about me." His hand cramped. When he looked down he realized he had a death grip on the armrest of his desk chair. Easing up, he unwrapped his fingers and let the circulation return to his hand.

"Why?"

He rubbed his right palm. "I wish I knew."

Hanna visibly inhaled then exhaled. It was as if she were trying to slow her breathing. "She told me… She said you two were…"

Since he dreaded what word she might come up with he used one of his own. "Dating?"

"Something like that."

"It was nothing like that." Not even close. He enjoyed talking with Gena but a few hours of that gave way to something else. She moved in a way that was almost erratic. She'd start a conversation, then break it off and start talking about something else. The sentence fragments never connected. She operated in chaos. "Look, I don't want to tick you off again, but I do have to say your sister was struggling."

"Struggling how?"

"Operating without boundaries. Nothing seemed to be off-limits." When he realized he was fidgeting, he folded his hands together on top of the desk. "I was drinking heavily back then and felt the full impact the next morning. She could outdrink me. She would wake up, ready for the next party."

"She'd never been great with rules but she kind of lost her footing after Dad died." Hanna's voice went from eager to listen to sad, sort of resigned. It was as if it were painful for her to say the words.

"I can understand that."

"You can?" She didn't sound skeptical. The tone was more like one of genuine interest.

The tension running through him eased. The sense of being on the edge of saying the wrong thing subsided. He hated this subject and never talked about it, but he felt like he owed it to her to explain. "After losing my mom I got hit with this mix of grief and how-could-you-leave-me-here-with-Dad anger and I really didn't know what to do with it all. My brothers were in college and I hated everything."

He wondered if Hanna's reactions now were due to grief, as well. Cancer and suicide weren't the same but the end result—standing on the sidelines while a loved one died—led to the same grief-soaked place.

"If you think I'm difficult to deal with now, you should have seen how I acted in private back then." She would have hated him. No question.

"You're not, you know."

She completed one of those conversational left turns that put him a few steps behind. "Not what?"

"You're not *that* difficult." It looked as if she were trying to hide a smile but the amusement in her voice gave her away.

The rest of the weight pressing down on him vanished. They hadn't settled much but he felt as if they'd reached some sort of common ground. That his worries about her viewing him as a useless playboy jerk might not be true.

He decided to test that theory. "Ever since we saw each other again you've been—"

"Dealing with your family is difficult."

Carter continued to rub his palm even though the slicing pain was long gone. "I'm not my father, Hanna."

"I know."

He blew out a rough breath. "That might be the nicest thing anyone has ever said to me."

"He wouldn't spend hours or days or whatever you did, tracking down evidence to get me to trust him." She picked up the top piece of paper, then put it down again. "That's something."

Probably too much. Vast overkill and a statement on his difficulties with dealing with people on more than a super-ficial level. But he wanted deeper with her. He had no idea why, but he did. "It sounds like you might actually like me."

She laughed as she held up a hand. "Let's not get carried away."

In that moment she sounded so free. The light tone sent a shot of need spiraling through him. But wanting her when there was still so much unsaid between them struck him as dangerous. "Is there anything I can do to help with your quest?"

"That's an interesting word."

If he knew what she was looking for or what she wanted to prove or avoid he would have chosen his words more carefully. As it was he only knew *something* was up. He was not the guy people went to for help, but maybe he could give her this before they both moved on, because that was inevitable. "If you find something negative about my father, something you need help with, let me know. We'll take care of it."

"What about family loyalty?"

He couldn't blame her for asking. "That only extends to my brothers, Jackson and a few others."

"Really?"

When she'd asked a question like that a few days ago, even yesterday, it came with a slap of disbelief. He'd seen it in her eyes and heard it in her voice. But this time it sounded like she wanted confirmation. That he could do it. "Do you know how Derrick ended up at the head of the company?"

She shrugged. "I figured it was a birthright thing."

He was pretty sure that was a knock on the size of his bank account, but he let it go because they were finally talking. He rarely had a chance to reason through these things with anyone. Letting outsiders into his family dynamic wasn't an option when you were a part of a family that landed in the news too often.

"He saved the company from my father's mismanagement and questionable deals. Dad doesn't really have the ability to distinguish right from wrong." Which Carter was pretty sure qualified as the biggest understatement he'd ever uttered. "I can give you the details if you want them. Suffice to say, Derrick was ready to go public and burn it all down. Spence and I supported him."

"But you would have lost everything."

He got the sense that the state of her bank account didn't matter much to her except to know she could take care of herself. But her obsession with *his* money, in terms of believing that it somehow defined him, was a huge frustration for him.

"Not everything, but a lot. But stuff doesn't matter all that much in the face of right and wrong."

She shot him an are-you-serious glance. "You do know you're a Jameson, right?"

"I'm reminded quite often." By the gossip press. By people at the office. By the estate and now by her.

"Including by me."

At least she didn't deny it. He decided to consider that progress.

"So far, yes. I'm hoping to change that. When you look at me I'd like for you to see me and not my father." He didn't mean to say the words but he'd never been more serious in his life.

"Lunch would help."

The turn of topic had his brain misfiring for a second. Then he focused on the lilt in her voice and the half smile she'd worn throughout most of their conversation. Something had happened to change her mood. His had changed, as well. The question was if they could sustain it or if they'd slip back into arguing mode.

"Why, Ms. Wilde. Are you using me for my access to food?"

"I bet there's a really big kitchen in this house." She stood up and glanced at him with one eyebrow raised, as if in challenge.

"Wanna see my pots and pans?"

She shook her head. "That's a terrible line."

"I have others." This time when he turned on the charm he intended to show her who he really was. He was not that shallow guy and he was tired of having people think he was. "Come downstairs with me and I'll let you hear some."

He got up and came around the side of the desk until he stood in front of her. "Your lines keep getting better."

He guided her toward the door, ignoring the buzz that moved through him when he put his hand on her lower back. "You are not going to believe how charming I am."

"Impress me."

He intended to do just that.

Eight

For the next several days Carter mostly left her alone, except at mealtimes. He'd show up with food or text her and joke about luring her to the main house with roasted chicken or something equally delicious.

Lynette prepared most of the food. Hanna had met her when she had ventured over to the house and accidentally met Jackson, as well. Lynette was a woman in her sixties with a touch of a German accent. She sang Carter's praises and grew quiet at the mention of his father. Hanna loved her priorities.

Jackson provided a different challenge. He had been charming and clearly close to Carter, despite the sarcastic comments. But meeting him made her uncomfortable, thanks to her father's journal. Most of the entries centered on her father's workdays and the television programs he liked and didn't like. But every now and then there would be a more personal entry. Sometimes about Eldrick's secrets. The man's sins worried her father. She didn't know if the cryptic "Jack" references in the journal were actually about Jackson, but she felt compelled to find out…somehow.

But not now. No, tonight she intended to concentrate on Carter. He'd brought pot roast to her cottage on this cool night. It was steaming and savory and she might need to run around the estate's many acres to work off enough to be able to sleep.

She dumped the dirty dishes on the counter next to the sink and leaned against it to watch him. "I'm starting to think you really do plan on wooing me with food."

Carter shot her a sexy smile as he continued to wash the serving plate. "Of course not…unless it's working."

"My pants no longer fit."

He chuckled as he dried the dish, then his hands and turned to face her. "Is that code for something?"

"Yeah, the fact I can't get the zipper up."

He wiggled his eyebrows. "Sexy."

Exactly, and that was a bit of a problem for her. Him cleaning. Him bringing her food. Him not assuming he could barge in and always asking permission first. Now that was sexy. The charm combined with that face and those sleek muscles were a sucker punch to her control. The more time she spent with him, the more her anger fizzled out. And she wasn't sure she was ready to let it go. Not after she'd been so wrapped up and furious for months.

During the day she'd think about him. Memories of that sly smile and deep voice would pop into her head and she'd forget why she disliked him. Those old feelings from childhood of being dazzled by him and blinded to his faults would rise up. She had to work to remember he was the same man who hurt her sister…though that was no longer as clear as it once had been.

Even she couldn't deny that her sister had embellished her time with Carter. She'd turned the reality of three or so days into what sounded like long-term dating. Now Hanna wasn't sure what she thought or what any of it meant, so she held on to what she did know—Carter's father had tried to blackmail her to stay away from Carter. He wasn't his father, but it wasn't that easy to separate the two.

Carter hung the now damp towel on the handle to the stove. "Did you want wine or anything?"

"I got the impression you didn't drink anymore, or maybe you still do and I don't—"

"Hanna?" With a palm resting on the counter, he leaned in until his mouth hovered just above hers. "You're on the verge of babbling."

"I'm trying not to be a jerk." For some reason the comment came out as a breathy whisper.

"If that happens, I'll let you know." His gaze wandered over her face like a gentle caress. It landed on her mouth and stayed there for a few seconds until he blinked and stepped back again. "But no, I'm not drinking. I figured out I value control too much. Also, it's too easy for me to lean on it."

"That's honest." She couldn't imagine the younger version of Carter ever admitting to having a problem. All those magazine articles and gossip columns about the brothers and what a catch the bachelors were never mentioned anything except their strengths.

There had been references to their athletic promise and college years, but now that she thought about it, she couldn't remember ever reading a quote by any of the brothers themselves in all those posts. It was all photographs of them dating this woman or that one. About charity events and movie premieres. Nothing about who they really were, nothing like the real-life glimpse she'd been getting since she'd agreed to come to Virginia with Carter.

"I really don't want to test my ability to form an addiction." Carter moved around the kitchen, stacking and restacking dishes and cleaning the counters for a second time.

She knew nervous energy when it smacked into her, and

that was exactly what was happening right now. "Did someone help you with that?"

His head shot up. "Like who?"

"A therapist? I think most people can't see they have a problem without assistance."

"If it had gotten worse, I'd like to think I would have gone to meetings or gotten help." He rehung the kitchen towel on the bar. "I know who I am without alcohol. I sort of fear who I am with it."

He created the opening, so she walked right through. "So tell me who you are, Carter Jameson."

She leaned back against the counter and sized him up. The conclusion was clear: a pretty outward package and a seemingly decent internal one. But she wanted to be sure.

"Irresistible, right?" he asked.

She didn't bother to lie. "A little."

That got his attention because he stopped fidgeting. "Oh, really?"

"You can't be immune to the impact of your charm." And he had to own a mirror. She refused to believe beautiful people couldn't tell they looked different from most people.

She could look in the mirror and see someone imperfect but pretty. She wore a solid size twelve, not tiny like her sister. Not someone who could walk around without a bra and be comfortable. A woman locked in a constant battle to keep a sliver of space between her upper thighs for comfort's sake.

Society might judge her as chubby but she saw a healthy person in the mirror. She loved food, which she balanced with walking and other exercise. Her whole life was about stability, about trying to maintain a middle ground. But Carter kept her totally off balance. The way his appreciative gaze swept over her made her feel beautiful, stunning and powerful.

"You know what I mean." She continued because he was

staring at her right now with this silly, tempting grin. "You go through life looking like that, with money and resources and that voice. I'm betting women line up to meet you."

He balanced his hands on the counter on either side of his hips, mimicking her stance while standing across from her. "What if I told you a secret?"

Her heart rate kicked up. She could feel the blood race through her. "Do it."

"The charm, the whole guy-who-can-run-a-party thing, is an act."

Not what she expected. No, this was far more interesting than any tidbit of family or dating gossip. "You're faking it?"

"Not with you. I mean, it's not real out there." He nodded toward the window and the dark night beyond. "That's how I found my place in the family. Derrick is practical and grumpy, or he was until Ellie. Spencer is really smart and can always find the right angle to make something work. Me, I'm the one who entertains people. I put on an act so people can't see that I lack my brothers' talents. That, except for them, I don't like being a Jameson very much."

She searched her memories, all those informal football games the brothers played on the lawn and how they stopped to talk with her father, and she could see it. Carter kept things light. He beamed in like sunshine. To know that it was a facade, some act he created to survive in his family made her stomach churn. "I can't figure out if that's sweet or sad."

He shrugged. "Maybe a bit of both. Don't get me wrong. I know how lucky I am with the money part. Even after being cut off financially by my father, I had an account from my mom. Derrick insisted on paying me a salary. He still dumps money into it. I just ignore it because I'm fortunate enough to be able to. I don't have to worry about food or housing because my name is on the trust that owns this house, again thanks to my mom."

His body language said "no big deal" but something dark and clouded moved through his eyes. She noticed the dimming, the blink of pain, before he talked with that light tone.

"So, you turn on this charm offensive to get through events and—"

"Life."

A peek behind the curtain. That's what this felt like. A brief glimpse into the real Carter Jameson, though he made it sound like the real version was buried pretty deep. "You seem pretty genuine right now."

"I am. With you. I can't explain why, so don't ask." He pushed away from the counter and walked the few steps to stand in front of her. "Maybe it's because when I first saw you again I thought we were both a little lost. I viewed you as a kindred spirit. Or I did, until you kept kicking me out and walking away."

Yes. He got it. Behind the stability and the attempts to maintain equilibrium lurked a certain insecurity and a fear that running up against another Jameson would only make her life worse. "Sorry about that."

"It's good for me to have to work for it." He didn't touch her but he moved until he stood between her outstretched legs.

"You should keep working at it." This close, her breath caught in her throat. She felt it hitch. Felt her pulse thump in her ears until it sounded like banging.

He nodded. "I plan to."

Risking everything, forgetting the cons and the past, she lifted her hand and rested it on his chest. The heat from his skin seeped through his shirt into her palm. The touch reassured her, and when he covered her hand with his she felt grounded for the first time in a long time.

"The lost thing? I never thought of it that way, but it's probably true. I've spent my life being the dutiful daughter, the supportive sister, the one everyone could count on. With my whole family being gone, I'm not clear on what my role is anymore." She had to force every single word out, push them past this hard lump in her throat. She expected to get pummeled with a load of new guilt for having said what she actually felt. Instead, a weight she didn't even know sat on her chest eased. Not completely, but a bit.

His fingers threaded through hers. "You could try living for you."

"I wish it were that easy."

What she really wished was that he'd kiss her. Just swoop in and take away the doubts and give her a few minutes without thinking.

As if he could hear her thoughts, he leaned in until his mouth hovered right over hers. "Yes?"

She nodded as she shifted to meet him. "Please."

His mouth swept over hers, soft at first, almost searching. Then he lifted his head and stared down at her again. Whatever he saw there must have erased any concern, and it should have because she was all-in on the kissing. When his lips covered hers again there was nothing slow and gentle about it. His mouth captured hers in a scorching kiss. The world fell away. It was just her and him and the heat and the feel of his arms around her and his hands on her back.

He kissed her like he'd never see her again. The intensity of it shook her. Her skin felt warm as she pushed up on tiptoes and wrapped her arms around his neck. This was about wanting and abandon, and she had no intention of fighting it.

Her fingers slipped into his soft hair. She could taste him, smell the peppermint scent of his shampoo. Sensations bombarded her—the feel of his tongue, the press of his hard body against hers. His mouth and that tiny rumbling sound she heard at the back of his throat.

She'd dreamed about kissing him as a girl but her dreams

hadn't felt like this. This was the kiss of a man who wanted a woman. All hot and demanding, smooth and coaxing. It reeled her in.

She wanted more.

That reality hit her like a splash of icy water. It was too much, too soon while the trust between them still stood on shaky ground.

She broke it off and gulped in a huge breath. Let her arms move down to his forearms. "We should…"

He immediately lifted his head and stepped back. "Sorry."

"Don't apologize for that kiss." The heat on her cheeks refused to die down. "It went nuclear faster than I expected."

"Right." His chest lifted and fell in heavy breaths. "I'm going to go."

"Yeah, you should go." But her fingernails dug deeper into his shirt as she held him there.

"You need to let go of me for me to leave."

Her brain battled with her body. There were so many secrets sitting between them. So much she wasn't sure about. Things he might not know that could wreck him. But every time she tried to move away, her hands grabbed on harder. "I don't really want to."

"Good." Then his mouth was on hers again. His tongue slipped over hers as his hand eased just under the hem of her sweater.

He didn't venture higher. He didn't need to because the touch of skin against skin, no matter how innocent or light, had her mind spinning and her stomach dropping to her knees.

Forget the girl crush, she wanted him. Here and now.

That simmering attraction had never gone away.

As soon as she thought it, he lifted his head and rested his forehead against hers. She kept her eyes closed for fear he would see the desire she knew she could not bank. But she could feel his gaze. Feel his thumb as it rubbed against her arm in a soothing gesture that made her want to wrap her body around his and demand he stay.

He breathed in and his whole body moved. "Okay, now I need to go."

"My feelings haven't changed."

"Oh, Hanna." He made a strangled sound. "But you are torn. I can feel it."

He could see it or sense it, she wasn't sure. But in that moment, she was relieved he had more strength than she did.

She sighed. "Yeah."

"Then I have my answer." He kissed her forehead, letting his lips linger before pulling back and looking at her again. "When I stay the night, and I'm hoping that happens soon, it will be because you know you want me to."

"What about you?" Her fingers played with his top button and the sliver of soft skin she could touch at the base of his neck.

"I want to. Trust me." He lifted her hand and kissed the back of it. "Now, good night."

This time he separated their bodies and stepped out of the kitchen. She watched him circle the chair and pick up his jacket off the corner of the couch. She didn't stop him when he took those long confident strides to get to the front door.

"Carter?"

With his hand on the doorknob, he turned around to face her again. "Yeah?"

"Thank you for not being your father."

"You can always count on that to be true." He winked at her, then left.

She wanted to call him back, which was why she didn't. She had decisions to make. Things they needed to talk about.

But one thing was clear: *they* were going to happen soon.

* * *

The next afternoon, Carter ventured into the D.C. office. He'd planned to meet Spence at a restaurant for lunch, but Spence texted that he was running late and told Carter to come upstairs for a few minutes.

As soon as he walked into Spence's office, Carter knew he should have seen this coming. Jackson sat there with his feet up on the edge of Spence's desk. They both held files but they were joking about something that didn't sound work related.

"You guys are hard at work, I see." Carter closed the door behind him because these two could say anything.

Spence's smile was almost feral as he put the file down. "Well, well, well. Look who it is. The guy with the big secrets."

Exactly what he'd suspected. Jackson finding out proved to be a communication line right back to his brothers. "You told him about Hanna."

Spence's smile only grew wider. "Hanna?"

"No, but you just did." Jackson mumbled under his breath about Carter being a dumbass. "I can't believe you fell for that."

Neither could Carter. He must be off his game. He usually stayed ready when it came to his brothers. They were smart and a bit sneaky. If there was information they wanted to know, they were clear that they would use any means to get it out of Carter. In this case, Spence used Jackson.

Spence leaned forward with his hands clasped together. "So, Hanna?"

Jackson nodded. "It's *that* Hanna."

"Hey!" Now he had to fight off both of them. Carter didn't like his odds.

Jackson held up his hands as if in mock surrender. "You already blew it."

"You have Hanna Wilde squirreled away at the house in Virginia? Wait until I tell Derrick." Before Carter could say anything, Spence glanced at Jackson. "Are they having a thing?"

Jackson made that humming sound he always made. "On the verge of it, I'd say."

Since that struck a little too close to the truth, Carter tried to take back the conversation. He dropped into the chair next to Jackson and across from his brother. "She is staying at the cottage."

Spence frowned. "That's a nice nonanswer. Why?"

"Excellent question." Jackson laughed. "Go ahead, Carter. Try to explain this."

"What am I missing?" Spence looked back and forth between Carter and Jackson. "Is this related to Dad's letter?"

"She didn't want to open it." This time, Carter thought the explanation sounded strange when he said it out loud. When she'd first said it, he got it. He hated being manipulated by his father to do things he didn't want to do and he was related to the man. He couldn't imagine how not interested Hanna would have been in playing Eldrick's games.

"And?" Spence asked.

"She came to the cottage instead." She used the excuse about her father's things, but Carter remembered her mention of a baby. He still didn't know how or where that piece of information fit in and it nagged at him. He'd checked emails and family bank records and…nothing.

Spence opened his hands and shrugged. "Okay, I admit it. I don't get it."

"She needed some time to work out things in her head, things about our dad and hers, and to collect some property. I offered the cottage so she's there—"

"Working things out. Right." Spence broke eye contact with Carter and looked back at Jackson again. "But you think they're having a thing."

Carter missed a lot about hanging out with these two when he was in California, but not this. The ribbing worked great when he wasn't the brother in the firing line, but right now he was and he didn't see that changing any time soon. "I'm standing right here."

"Fine. Are you having a thing with Hanna?" Spence leaned back in his chair. "I'm not judging. I remember she was cute but quiet, and I really liked her dad."

Carter wondered when he'd asked for permission. "Lucky me."

"Hell, I'd like to see you putting down roots, dating, and generally acting like a normal person and not someone who is planning to bolt."

"I'm not going anywhere." Carter repeated the words without thinking. He'd said them so many times to his brothers over the last few months that he was starting to believe them.

"So, you are in a relationship with Hanna or no?" Spence asked the point-blank question without blinking.

Carter picked at the fraying leather seam on the armrest of the chair. "I don't know what we are."

Spence nodded. "So, yes."

"I think it's more of an *almost* thing," Jackson said.

Carter really wanted to ignore both of them but that wasn't easy to do. Neither of them tolerated that sort of thing. Not with all the staring and talking over him and generally making up facts to any questions he refused to answer head-on.

"She's only here on a temporary basis." And that was true. That's what they'd agreed on. But now, saying it, Carter didn't like it. The idea of her picking up and leaving, of not eating meals together. Of not walking the grounds with her, like he did early this morning. His mind rebelled at all of it.

Spence shot Carter a you're-never-going-to-hear-the-end-of-this smile. "Then you, my dear baby brother, need to use some of that charm to get her to stay."

"She has some unfinished business with Dad." Carter couldn't let himself forget that little fact.

Spence's smile faded. "Don't we all."

Nine

So many secrets swarmed in Hanna's head.

She needed to share at least one of them with Carter. Last night they'd had a close call. She wanted to put the past to the side, if only for a few hours. Being with him, kissing him, felt like the most natural thing ever. But now, in the stark light of day, she thought about his father and hers, her sister, their families, and the baby. That was a lot of baggage piled up around them. Unpacking it seemed like an impossible task.

She used to think Carter knew most of it. That he'd been this carefree playboy who didn't care if he got a woman pregnant. The kind of guy who would send in his rich daddy to clean up his mess. But none of those characteristics fit now.

She sat on the couch, so deep into self-reflection that she almost didn't hear the knock. She glanced at her cell, expecting to see a text from Carter asking if he could stop by. That's what he did. He checked with her first. But maybe after last night he felt more comfortable stopping by without warning. If so, good.

Their relationship had taken a step forward. The question was how big of a step.

Putting all that aside, she went to the door. She had it open before she remembered the peephole and a lifetime of precautions and generally being smart about her safety. The big fence made an impression, but she'd learned from experience that evil could creep into her life without warning.

All of those things ran through her head as she looked at the two women standing there. The obviously pregnant one with the long brown hair and a pretty round face wore a cute empire-waist dress and a big smile. She also carried a carton with a bakery's name on the side, which made Hanna like her immediately. The other woman, equally stunning in a trim black pantsuit, shifted her weight around, looking far less comfortable about being there.

For a second Hanna couldn't speak. Then she forced out a fumbling greeting. "Uh, hello?"

"I'm Ellie. This is Abby." The pregnant one pointed back and forth with her free hand.

Hanna knew Ellie's name and that she was engaged to Derrick and obviously close to her due date, but none of that explained why they were standing in front of her. "Okay."

Ellie shook the box. "We brought cookies."

Since Ellie was about to be a Jameson by marriage, she'd probably own at least part of the cottage they were standing in. And they looked friendly. Maybe a little sheepish but still welcoming. "You said the magic word. Come in."

Hanna stepped back and let the women move past her. They smelled as nice as they looked. All put together and perfect. Shiny hair, comfortable but stylish looking clothes. Suddenly, Hanna felt like a lump of dirty linen.

She rubbed her hands on the back of her jeans as she followed them to the sitting area. They sat next to each other on the couch. Hanna opted for the safety of the chair across from them because she had a feeling there might be some Carter questions ahead of her.

"So…" The rest of her words died in her throat. That's all she had.

Ellie laughed. "Let me start. I'm engaged to Derrick and clearly pregnant. Seven months, so I have swollen ankles and a permanent case of grumpiness. But the cookies help my mood."

"You hide the bad mood well." All Hanna could see was Ellie's perfect complexion and shiny smile. Nothing seemed forced. She practically radiated happiness. "I figured out from the pregnancy who you were."

Ellie wrestled with the tape that held the box of cookies closed. "Well, we're both pregnant and both engaged to Jameson men, so you get both of us this afternoon."

"You're with Spence?" she asked Abby. Hanna heard her stunned tone and rushed to apologize. "Sorry, I didn't mean to sound so surprised."

But Abby took it in stride. Without breaking eye contact or showing any sign of being upset, she reached over and snapped the tape Ellie had been picking at, then she smiled at Hanna. A warm, genuine smile. "I'm still trying to believe it, and by 'it' I mean the pregnancy and the engagement. I hadn't really expected either."

Carter had skipped the two future sisters-in-law thing… or had he? Hanna couldn't remember. Their conversations touched on a lot of topics during all those meals together. His upbringing and Eldrick's constantly changing rules. Trips with his brothers. Time with Jackson and his sister. Funny things they all said during the day or did in the past. His thoughts about turning the Virginia property into a business. She loved hearing him talk, having him open up, so she encouraged all of it.

She didn't realize how much she did know until right that second. Somehow, despite her efforts to stay detached, she'd done the opposite. She'd let her defenses drop despite her vows to reinforce them. With the secrets and now the kissing, her mind spun. Being this close to him, this enmeshed in his life, was never the plan. They were not dating. She didn't know what they were, yet this all felt very domestic…and that made her jumpy.

"I think I'm nervous." When Hanna realized she was twisting her hands together until her skin turned white, she grabbed onto the armrests instead.

Abby frowned. "Why?"

"You two are so…" Good grief. They owned mirrors, right? They knew who they were and the kind of family they were marrying into. All that money and power. The potential to get stung by Eldrick and his schemes.

Ellie grabbed a cookie from the now open box. "I'm excited for you to finish that sentence."

That made one of them. Hanna had to fight off the urge to run into the bathroom and throw up.

"We're here because Carter told Spence you were staying here." Abby glanced at Ellie. "Actually, I think Spence tricked him into it." Abby waved a hand in front of her face before continuing again. "Anyway, we know you don't live around here usually and thought you might be lonely, so here we are."

"With cookies." Ellie lifted the box and handed them to Hanna. "They are so good."

Abby winked. "Her favorite."

They had such an easy back-and-forth. The rapport made Hanna miss Gena, or at least miss the relationship she'd always wanted with her sister but never actually had. They were close but Gena could be volatile. Her judgment wasn't great. Carter had been right when he said Gena teetered on the edge of control. Hanna had left because she couldn't watch it…a decision she'd regret forever.

Hanna balanced the box on her lap and glanced up. Ellie

and Abby watched her. Ellie wore a soft smile while Abby seemed to be studying and assessing.

None of it made Hanna uncomfortable. The silence did, so she rushed to fill it. "Did you guys grow up with Spence and Derrick?"

Ellie snorted. "Ha! No. I was out of work and hating Derrick when we started dating."

"What?" Hanna tried to remember the gossip she'd read about the couple months ago but she couldn't recall the details. She could see the photos and the locations—expensive hotels and parties. It all fit with the way she'd wanted to see the Jameson brothers before she got to Virginia.

Abby reached over and took a cookie. "I work for Jameson Industries and was about to leave the business because Spence's dad is a piece of garbage."

Some of the tension running through Hanna eased. She didn't realize how stiff she'd been holding her shoulders until Abby made the comment. "Man, he really is."

"We also have an ulterior motive for our visit." Abby pointed at Hanna with her cookie. "We wanted to meet you."

Hanna couldn't imagine their lives. Probably filled with parties and business functions. The idea of them thinking about her, even for a second, confused her. "Why?"

"Because of Carter," Ellie said.

Abby nodded. "You guys are together and we love Carter—"

Just as she feared. "No."

"Excuse me?" Abby's eyebrow lifted and for a second she sounded like the tough businesswoman Hanna imagined her to be.

Carter. Talk about a tough conversation. She'd been thinking about him nonstop. About that kiss, about how good his hands felt on her. She wished she could write him off; she needed to because being with him meant spilling so many secrets and trusting him. A voice in her head screamed a warning at the thought of doing either. "There's not… We're not… I mean, there was kissing and…ugh."

A huge smile broke over Abby's face. "That sounds so familiar."

"Right?" Ellie shook her head as she took a bite of her cookie. "Those Jameson men."

They lost her. Hanna had no idea what they were talking about. "What do you mean?"

Abby sighed as she put down the cookie she'd been holding but not eating. "The Jameson men have the power to get the most stable woman turned around and babbling."

Exactly. That description totally made sense to Hanna. She'd been off balance and stumbling ever since Carter showed up at her door. It was nice to know she wasn't alone. Sounded as if this was a regular affliction. "Have you met Carter's other girlfriends?"

"I like that you used the word *other*." Abby flashed a smile.

Hanna couldn't imagine Spence having any defense to that look. Hanna couldn't find one. "I didn't mean—"

"But no. He's charming and very sweet and funny, but also very private." Ellie's head tilted to the side. "Hence, our curiosity about you."

The women had been there fifteen minutes and Hanna already liked them. They were open and friendly. They searched for information but didn't try to hide their snooping with games. Hanna got the very real sense the visit came out of a love for Carter and a need to see where she fit into his life.

She guessed Jackson was to blame for planting that wrong seed…and it was wrong. It had to be because with their families and their pasts their lives couldn't intersect like that.

Disappointment slammed into her. Her chest ached and

she had to ball her hands into fists to keep from rubbing the spot. For a few seconds—a flash only—she wondered what it would be like to be with Carter, to be the one he built a life with. She blinked out the thought as soon as it formed in her head.

"I don't want to disappoint you, but we're really not *to-gether* together."

Silence buzzed through the room. Both Ellie and Abby stayed quiet. They watched her, but Hanna didn't sense pity or anger. After a few beats of quiet, Ellie looked at Abby and nodded.

Ellie turned back to Hanna. "But you still need company...or would you rather we leave?"

Now that they were here, she didn't want them to go. Hanna couldn't really explain it. She didn't have a lot of friends. Over the last year, she'd been mourning her sister and the baby, she'd been avoiding Eldrick, and hadn't had the time or emotional strength to be a great friend to anyone. She hadn't realized how much she missed the comfort of friends until now.

She shrugged. "I kind of want to hear why Abby hates Eldrick Jameson."

"Done." Abby stood up. "Let's get some drinks and napkins to go with the cookies, then I'll tell you all about how he made a pass at me in an effort to derail my relationship with Spence."

Hanna started to stand up, then fell back into her chair as Abby talked. "Are you kidding?"

Ellie snorted. "Oh, Hanna. We have so many Eldrick stories. The lies. The things he's making his sons do so that Derrick can officially run the company he already runs. You don't even have to share yours. You can just enjoy ours."

"He really is awful." Normally, Hanna wouldn't be so quick to share her true feelings, but she felt perfectly safe making that statement with this audience.

Abby stood in the middle of the kitchen. "Help me with those napkins and we'll fill you in on our experiences."

Hanna wasn't about to say no to that offer.

Later that night, Carter stood in Hanna's kitchen, holding a cup of decaf. He stopped in the middle of drinking when Hanna dropped her big news. "Wait, you had cookies with Ellie and Abby today?"

She slid onto the bar stool across from him with a warm smile. "Weird, right?"

Carter waited for the blood to rush back to his head. The women he considered family had rushed over to talk to Hanna. He assumed he could thank Spence for that, but later, because right now a million questions filled his head.

"Not really. I guess." While he was skeptical about the visit, he didn't want Hanna to think anything but good things about Ellie and Abby. He loved them and couldn't imagine either one of his brothers getting through the rest of their lives without them. But he barely knew his place in the family. The idea of bringing Hanna into the mess didn't make sense to him, especially when he wasn't sure what they meant to each other, if anything. "They likely came out because they were worried you'd meet Derrick and Spence first and then take off."

Hanna played with the fringe on the edge of the place mat, slipping the material through her fingers with precision. "I don't remember them being that scary."

Her nonanswer stopped him. Of course she would leave. They technically weren't dating. Hell, he didn't even know if he planned on sticking around much past Ellie giving birth. But they'd originally talked about her staying a few days and they'd blown by that deadline. The usual pressing need to move on hadn't hit him. He didn't want to think that was due to her, but he started to wonder. "Are you going to?"

She shrugged. "There's much we need to talk about."

The contents of the envelope. The mention of the baby. The secrets were starting to pile up. Still, he didn't want to push because he didn't want to push her away. "You have to stick around for that."

"So do you, which sounds like it could be a problem." She flipped the material around a few more times, then flattened it against the counter under her palm. "Your future sisters-in-law think you're going to bolt once Ellie's baby is born. They didn't say they worried about it, but I could tell they want you here. In fact, I think Ellie would be happier if you lived with them, like Spence did."

That must have been a hell of a talk. He'd been trying for days, and Ellie and Abby came in, offering cookies, and got more than he had. He didn't like that feeling of once more being on the outside looking in. "She's in nesting mode."

"It's more than that. She said she didn't want to freak you out, but she hated the idea of you moving on once Eldrick turned the business over to Derrick."

"Yes, I'll go, and Spence will work there. I'd get the benefit of their hard labor." He thought about how crappy that sounded. It was one thing to be the brother who schmoozed people. It was another not to contribute. "That was my original plan."

"But now?" She stared at him, head-on and no flinching.

He met her stare for stare. He decided not to answer the unspoken question about them because he didn't know what they were or even if they were a "they." "Nothing is as clear as it was a few weeks ago."

"We met a few weeks ago."

She was pushing and his usual reaction would be to pull away. He clamped down on that instinct and stepped closer to the counter. Reached across until his hand covered hers. "That's kind of my point."

For a few seconds, they stood there with music softly

playing in the background. He caressed the back of her hand with his thumb. Felt a burst of energy arc between them.

Her second hand joined her first until she cradled his fingers in all of hers. "What would you say if I asked you to stay here tonight?"

His heartbeat thundered in his ears until he could barely hear. "I'd force myself to stop and try to figure out if you're still conflicted."

"Not about this part. Not anymore."

That sounded so good but he still needed to be sure. "The other stuff, the things that are worrying you, can they wait?"

"They've already waited a long time."

He wasn't convinced that was the right answer. Everything between them felt…unsettled. Hot and full of need but a little off, as if they should just get to it and deal with the consequences. His father, Gena. That stupid envelope.

Before he could launch into the first topic, she walked around the counter. Never broke eye contact with him. Held his hand as she stepped in front of him with the other hand resting on his hip. "Hi, there."

"Hi."

"You going to run on me, Carter?"

The risks were high but right then, in that moment, none of them mattered. "I couldn't, even if I wanted to."

Need pounded through him. Everything about her intrigued him. Her voice, her body, that smile. He loved to listen to her, talk with her, share things. None of that matched with the guy he thought he was, the one who ran instead of staying to take the heat. He liked certainty and clarity and very few ties. He liked to breeze through without getting involved. The comfort that came with keeping things easy and shallow. But she blurred every part of his life. Shook it up and left him fighting for balance.

And that was without touching him.

But she touched him now. She slid her hand up his side

and every nerve ending ignited. Muscles strained at the soft brush of her fingers.

His arm slipped around her and he tugged her closer. His lips brushed her cheek and he felt a shiver run through her. So sexy and it only spurred him on.

His mouth skimmed the side of her face to her ear. He licked around the outside and her body fell harder against his.

"Yes." Her breath blew across his neck.

It was his turn to tremble. He couldn't hide the small shake in his hands as he held her. A voice in his head screamed *now*.

So much had happened, so many questions and half answers that he needed them to be clear on this. "Tell me to stop if you want me to stop. No questions asked. I'll go back to the main—"

"Carter?"

He watched her, waiting. "Yeah?"

"Stop talking." Her hand slipped lower, right to the top of his butt.

She couldn't be clearer than that. "Yes, ma'am."

He shut his mind off and kissed her. Poured all his desire and need into it. Let her feel how much he wanted to be with her, to touch her. He didn't hold back or play games because he didn't want to. Not with her.

Any hope of staying detached fizzled. His mouth covered hers and the heat sparked between them. Her hands slipped into his hair and his hands roamed over her back.

They touched everywhere.

He could smell her and hear her. Feel her. It was better than the dreams he'd been having about her, and those had been pretty great except for the part where he woke up alone and sweating.

He pulled her in until their bodies rubbed against each other. The friction had his brain misfiring but he managed to walk them out of the kitchen. He eased her back, guiding her through the living room, around the coffee table and chair, to the bedroom door. With every step he kissed her. Their mouths met in a series of breathtaking kisses that nearly knocked the knees out from under him.

Through it all he held her, cradled her against his chest as his mouth skimmed over her sexy neck. He didn't bother to look around. He spied the bed out of the corner of his eye and that was good enough.

He kept moving, spinning them around until the backs of his knees hit the mattress. Sliding down, he opened his legs and pulled her to stand between them. The position put his mouth even with her stomach. He leaned in and pressed a kiss against her shirt. Felt the muscles underneath jump in response.

Being this close to her, wanting her, humbled him. He didn't race or throw her down. Not when he wanted to savor every second. Wanted to unwrap her like she was a present he never thought he'd get. When she reached down and again tangled her fingers in his hair he couldn't help but lean into the touch.

His control hovered right at the edge. It blinked out on him a few times when he pressed his cheek against her stomach. He smoothed his hand up and down the backs of her thighs. "You feel so good."

Her breathing kicked up under his ear. Those hands, soft yet strong, trailed down his back. He lifted her then. Scooped her up and dragged her around him. He didn't let go until her back hit the bed and then he crawled over her. Slipped up her body, loving the feel of how they fit together.

When he reached into his back pocket and took out the condom he'd put there in the hope he might need it tonight, she nodded. Balancing on his elbows with an arm on each side of her head, he looked down. Ran his fingertips over her bottom lip as he thought about how good it felt to kiss her. Then he did. He bent down and pressed his mouth against hers. This kiss was slow and deliberate, a promise of what was to come.

When they broke apart she lifted her hand and caressed his cheek. "The answer is still yes."

He couldn't help but laugh at that. "Thank goodness."

Her fingers traveled down his chest, undoing each button as she went. She had his shirt open and slid her hands inside, tunneling under his white T-shirt to bare skin. The touch was electric. It made his heart pound and his mouth go dry. Every ounce of common sense abandoned him.

His head dipped again and this time he didn't stop. His mouth followed his hands as he pushed her sweater up. With a lift of her upper body, she helped him shove it off and onto the floor. Something he'd worry about tomorrow morning. Right now, he had other things on his mind, like enjoying the touch of his lips against her skin.

He kissed and caressed her. Slipped his palms over her breasts, loving the shape of her. He kissed her through her bra. Licked her until her back arched and she whispered his name. He'd never heard anything so sexy. Never been so ready.

Sitting up, he tore off his shirt and his hands went to his jeans. But she beat him there. Her fingers worked on the button and his zipper. The sound of it coming down screeched through the room but he blocked it out. This was about them and her breathing and the way the light hit her bare skin. He'd stripped off her top and unhooked her bra. Now he slipped it off her shoulders, letting it fall until she grabbed it in front of her and ripped it off.

He wanted to reach down and touch her again but his brain wouldn't send out the signal, not when Hanna slipped her hand inside his jeans. But who could blame him? She cupped him, caressed him with an expert hand. Her fingers danced over him, making his hips tip forward, then she tightened her hold.

Every brush of her fingers and the heavy breaths escaping her made him ache. He wanted to touch her, press his body against hers. When she put her hands on his hips and brought him against her again, he didn't fight it. He let her coax him closer. Enjoyed the way her hand slid over his length. Counting to ten while she did it over and over again.

But he couldn't wait any longer.

Pressing her back into the mattress, he stood up long enough to strip off his jeans and briefs. Then he was back. He sat between her legs, unzipping her pants and sliding them down. Slowly peeling them off her and taking the lacy black bikini bottoms with them.

When there was nothing between them, he kissed her again. He licked her bottom lip, nipped at the top. Felt his stomach flip over when she dragged him in for a kiss that blew out any doubt he ever had that they would end up like this.

He swept his hand down her body, loving the curve of her stomach and the softness of her thigh. Without him saying a word, she bent her leg and dropped it to the side. The shift gave him the access he wanted. His finger slipped over her, inside her. And when her head fell back, he took advantage of the position and skimmed his mouth down her neck to the inviting dip at the base of her throat.

With each pass of his hand, her body opened for him, readied for him until he didn't think he could wait one more second. Once again, she was there, dragging the condom from where he'd dropped it and handing it to him. Not saying a word as she trailed her fingers over his bottom lip.

He lifted his hips, separating from her only long enough to roll the condom on. Then he was back, easing inside her. Her internal muscles tightened around him, pulsed against him. He dragged in a hard breath, trying to regain his balance from the sensations pummeling him. But she wouldn't let him stop. She lifted her hips and he was done.

His body took over. The steady in and out. The way her body held him, wrapped around him. He couldn't think and gasped as he tried to drag in enough air. Their breaths mixed and echoed throughout the room. He pushed in and pulled out. Let her set the rhythm.

When her fingers clamped on his waist, he moved faster. One hand eased between their damp bodies. He touched her then and her mouth dropped open. She tensed under him and he knew she was close.

He whispered her name.

With a rough gulp of breath, she reached for him. Brought his mouth down for one more kiss. Broke it off as her mouth opened and her head tilted back. He watched, fascinated, as the orgasm moved through her. Her body shook and her legs clenched against his hips. She was strong and beautiful, so hot that she stole his breath.

Then it was his turn. He tried to hold it off, to savor every second, but his body had other ideas. His eyes slipped shut as his hips bucked. His body moved and shifted as the last of the pulses moved through him.

The orgasm zapped his strength and his arms gave out. He caught his weight in time, before he crushed her. Managed to slide slightly to the side.

Lying half on her, half next to her, he slid his arm over her stomach and pulled her close as he tried to calm his heart. It thumped so hard he half expected to see it move in his chest.

"Wow." She said the word without opening her eyes.

His smile was automatic. "You get all the credit."

She turned her head and looked at him then. "We were pretty fantastic together."

Whatever she wanted to say, fine, but he knew the truth.

She got the credit here. He found the energy to place a soft kiss on her shoulder. "And you are my inspiration."

"I like that." She fully rolled on to her side. "I like you."

Any chance at sleep vanished. All he wanted was to lie there, looking at her. "You're stunning."

"And you, Carter Jameson, need to rest." She smiled when he groaned. "I hope you brought another condom."

He held up two fingers. "That's it."

She pushed him to his back and slid over him. "After that we'll have to get creative."

He was wide-awake now. For the first in a long time, running was the last thing on his mind. "Lucky for you, I'm very creative."

"I'm counting on that."

Ten

Three days later, Hanna looked around the rectangular table in the Virginia estate's dining room. The fancy glittering chandelier hanging over the centerpiece likely cost more than most homes, and that was saying something in the D.C. metro area. Gold wallpaper gave the room a bright, sunny look despite the gray day outside. Glasses clanked together and bowls and plates of food traveled around from one person to the next.

The steady hum of conversation echoed in her head. She'd formally met everyone here before this big family dinner, except Spence and Derrick, but she knew them from when they were all much younger. Despite being the new person in the room, they treated her like an old friend. Jackson and Spence joked with her. Ellie coddled Hanna with an overprotective mothering instinct. Abby spent most of her time shaking her head at all of the antics.

Hanna really identified with Abby.

When Jackson brought up some story about a lie Spence told as a kid to hide the fact he crashed a car, Derrick almost spit out his food laughing. Even Ellie lost it when hearing about those days.

Hanna leaned closer to Carter. "How did you talk me into this?"

"Blame Ellie and Abby. They are relentless."

Jackson leaned across Carter to talk with Hanna. "Are you trying to hide something?"

That earned him a tap on the side of the head from Carter. "Go away."

Hanna knew it could not have hurt but the fake stunned expression Jackson wore made her laugh. "Be nice to Jackson."

He winked at her. "Listen to your woman."

The table conversation picked that moment to stop. Everyone looked at her. There were smiles all around, the annoying kind that made her want to kick Carter for getting her into this. They had fallen into some sort of relationship but a big family dinner made what they had seem important. She couldn't think about that, not when Carter had emphasized his lifetime of keeping things shallow.

The clinking sound reminded Hanna of a wedding. She felt the rush of a headache a second later.

Derrick changed the subject by clearing his throat. "We wanted to make sure Carter was feeding you. That's why we're all here, at this house I despise."

Ellie slipped her hand over Derrick's. "And we wanted you to know we'd like to spend time with you."

"Yeah, Carter. We want to see her, too." Spence toasted Carter, then took a long sip of water.

Carter glared back. "You can shut up any time now."

With that, the conversation kicked up again. The brothers talked across the table to each other. Ellie rolled her eyes. The scene didn't amount to a food fight, or even veer out of control, because Hanna doubted Ellie would tolerate that, but it did steer close to the edge. So much noise and talking.

Memories plowed into her. The days filled with talking to Carter and walking the estate grounds. The nights spent cuddled together, touching and learning each other's bodies. The whispers, the joking. The way he kissed her... everywhere.

Then her mind traveled back to those dinners with her dad when he tried so hard to fix the things his young daughters would eat. How he would talk with Gena for what felt like hours to calm her down when she got so upset over unimportant things she viewed as slights. It all came flooding back to Hanna and she waited for the guilt to hit her. She was with the people who she'd believed made her family miserable, but in that moment all she felt was a sadness that her family couldn't be there, too.

She knew from Carter that Eldrick had never allowed talking at the table, not from his sons. Hanna assumed the thunderous noise now was a reaction to that past. It struck her as a right time to ask the question that had been poking at her since they all arrived. "Is Jackson a family name?"

Carter stopped talking to Spence and smiled at her. "Nice pivot. It's always a good idea to throw the attention on to someone else."

"I just wondered." Anxiety shot through her. She had a reason to ask. Those notes in her father's journal.

The suggestion that Eldrick kept the ultimate secret.

Jackson swallowed the chicken he was eating and put his fork down on the side of his plate. "My mom's name is Jackie. She didn't want a mini-me, so my twin sister—"

"Who is awesome," Spence slipped in.

Jackson nodded but never broke eye contact with Hanna. "Her name is Zoe. I got the version of Jackie."

Carter stared at Jackson. "I didn't know that."

"Wait." Derrick lowered his water glass to the table. "You're sharing family secrets now, after we've asked for years. That and the fact Hanna has gotten Carter to settle down for five minutes makes me think she has super-powers."

Jackson shrugged. "Not all of us have colorful families like you guys."

The conversation stayed light. And then Ellie looked straight at Hanna. "How is the cottage?"

"You're not staying at the main house?" Spence jumped in his seat, then glared at Abby next to him. "Ouch! What was that for?"

"Be decent," she said at a near whisper.

"Is it a secret they're sleeping together?" Jackson asked.

Hanna felt the tension now. It ratcheted up inside her. Not that she was embarrassed. The fear was about the lack of boundaries. If this topic was okay for the table, she hated to think what might be next.

She shot Carter a side look. "Are all of your family dinners like this?"

Carter nodded. "Yes."

"Unfortunately," Jackson said at the same time.

Carter slipped an arm over the back of her chair. His fingers slid into her hair. "If you want to go or—"

"It's fine." Being with him anchored her just as panic started to rise in her belly. The touch should have had the opposite effect, made her more tense and worried, but it didn't.

After a lifetime of quiet and calm dinners, this rowdy one actually invigorated her. But a wave of guilt hit her, too. They were nice and friendly and she knew things… things she didn't think they knew. Things she *knew* Carter had never learned. She didn't know when or even how to spill them. It really wasn't her place, but she knew and being with him, even temporarily, meant she had some responsibility for him.

"Maybe if you weren't sitting on top of her," Spence said before he popped a green bean in his mouth.

Derrick frowned at Carter. "Yeah, do you need a bigger chair?"

"For goodness' sake." Ellie sighed. "Don't you start."

Jackson laughed. "You heard the pregnant woman. Be nice to your brother."

"We have a lot of pregnant women at the table." Spence jerked in his chair a second time before he glared at Abby. "Again? I meant you and Ellie. I don't know if—" This time he shifted to the side. "Do not kick me again."

"Then stop talking," Abby said through clenched teeth.

The conversation continued to unravel. They talked for a few minutes about the habits of pregnant women, then moved on to how much of an emotional wreck Derrick had been when he found out Ellie's pregnancy was high risk because it had happened while she had an IUD.

The topics swirled around Hanna. She heard bits and pieces. Even as they moved on to something that happened at work and a discussion about the best kind of cheesecake, the truth weighed down on her and her mind stayed on babies. On pregnancy. On all the things she hadn't told Carter.

His fingers slipped through her hair, then massaged the back of her neck, as if he could sense her growing anxiety. The move, so sweet, felt comfortable and intimate. Something a boyfriend might do, like bringing her to a family dinner.

The dizziness hit her out of nowhere. The room began to spin and her stomach flipped with it. The voices blurred in her head as the guilt crushed her into the chair.

She'd never asked to be pulled into this family's drama. Carter had offered her a chance to search for her dad's journal. She thought she could look for answers and be left alone. Somewhere along the line, all of that changed.

A lump formed in her throat. She clutched her napkin on her lap with both hands. She could hear her breathing.

It sounded so loud in her ears. The rush in and out. She didn't know how they couldn't hear it. She thought someone called her name. Carter's fingers stilled. The ramp-up of noise turned to a scream in her head.

She had to get up.

She stumbled, trying to find her footing and unable to make her legs move. "I can't do this."

After balancing her hands on the table, she stood. Took a part of the tablecloth with her, rattling all the dishes.

Carter's voice cut off in the middle of whatever conversation he was having. "Hey."

She couldn't answer him. Not now. She had to get out of that room, maybe the state. When her balance faltered, Carter stood up next to her, keeping her on her feet.

His arm wrapped around her. "Are you okay?"

"No."

"What's wrong?" Concern vibrated in his voice and showed in every line of his face.

His tone—all that worry was genuine and sweet…and sent a new wave of guilt crashing over her. She couldn't look around the table out of fear of what she'd see. "All of them. You."

Carter made an odd noise. "I know it's a lot of people, but they mean well."

"It's not that." She shook her head, trying to force the words back. This was not the time or place. Talking now would be unfair to Carter. He might be close to his brothers, but he deserved privacy.

"Hanna, talk to me."

The truth was right there. She bit her bottom lip to hold the words in. But a quick look at Jackson's face told her she needed to say something. He looked half ready to lunge across the table and comfort her. They all did.

She turned to Carter, tried to face only him. Her fingers dug into his arm but he didn't make a sound.

"I… You weren't supposed to be this guy."

Along with all her other mistakes, believing the worst about him had been one of her biggest. Without that, none of this would have happened. She would have gone to him with the truth, been on his side against his father. Not expected him to be a version of Eldrick. "You were supposed to be a jerk. Rich and entitled. Someone who did awful things, then moved on and let other people fix everything for you."

He frowned. "I thought we already went through this."

"Gena." It's the only word Hanna could get out.

Carter's mouth opened and closed a few times before he started talking again. "Hanna, I promise you that was a fling. Short. It meant nothing to either of us."

"Wait, Gena?" Spence asked.

Carter ignored his brother, put his hands on her arms in a loose hold and stared at her. The look was intense and desperate, as if he needed her to listen. "I've been honest with you about Gena and—"

Not again. She put her hand over his mouth. "I haven't."

"What?"

She couldn't lie to him for one more second. The words spilled out on a rush of pain and regret as she dropped her hand. "She was pregnant, Carter."

His head snapped back. "What are you talking about?"

"The two of you. Gena. After that weekend together."

She heard a male voice. Someone swore, but none of them moved.

Carter shook his head. "Not possible. We used protection."

"I was there. She was definitely pregnant." There were so many details. Hanna wasn't sure what mattered right now. "She didn't know at first, not for many months, but then she got sick and kept getting sick. Then the weight gain."

"I don't…" Carter continued to shake his head as his gaze switched to Derrick, then Spence. "No."

She knew he needed to talk with the people he loved, get their support, but she had to tell him this one last part. Make him understand why she'd made the choices she'd made.

"Your father showed up and threatened her. Made it clear she wasn't getting into the Jameson family that way."

"He didn't know about Gena. He couldn't…" Carter just stopped talking.

Hanna took that as a sign to continue even though her stomach ached and her head pounded. "Maybe he had you followed. Honestly, she may have called him and begged for money. I really don't know anymore, except that it's clear you didn't send him to keep me quiet like I once believed."

"Is that when she killed herself?" Jackson asked in a soft voice.

He knew. Of course he knew. Hanna realized for the first time that Jackson was likely the person in the office who had investigated her for Carter after that first night in New York. "A month later."

Carter shook his head. "While she was still pregnant."

It wasn't a question, so she didn't answer out loud except to nod.

Derrick closed his eyes. "Damn."

"What did Dad want?" Spence asked.

She answered him but kept her focus on Carter. She could feel his fingers loosen on her arms and guessed he'd gone numb. "For her to go away."

"The baby…" Carter looked away from her, then back again. "Hanna, I didn't—"

"He came to me after she died. Threatened me not to find you or say anything. Gave me a check to stay quiet." She hadn't taken it, but she doubted that mattered right now. "I'm sorry."

Spence snorted. "Why are you sorry?"

"That's Dad's screwup, not yours," Jackson said.

The support sent a rush of relief through her, but she couldn't enjoy it. She wasn't ready for forgiveness or understanding. And she noticed Carter wasn't the one offering it.

She wanted him to know her side. "I didn't tell you because I thought you knew and didn't care. It's why I pushed you away when you first found me. Why I didn't want to open that envelope."

"I had no idea about any of this."

She touched his cheek. "I know that now."

A chair screeched against the hardwood floor as Derrick stood up. "You're saying Dad threatened Gena and then he threatened you."

"He talked about saving the family name and not allowing some maid to ruin everything." She looked at the rest of them then. "That's what I do. I'm sure you know, but in case you don't, I clean houses. I'm not a business executive."

Ellie shot her an odd look. "Do you think we care about that?"

That's just it, she didn't think they cared. Now that she knew them, spent time with them, saw them as adults separate from Eldrick, she saw them as warm and welcoming. Just like Carter. So, she didn't hold back. She tried to put it all out there.

"Hanna." Carter's voice stayed low and sounded a bit unsteady.

He would lose it now. Yell at her. She deserved it for holding back for weeks, but she couldn't stand there and listen to his anger. Having him be mad at her made something inside her shrink.

"I'm sorry." She shook her head, silently begging him to believe her. "I know you're not your father, Carter. You're a little lost and fighting to figure out who you are in this family. From what I see, you fit here. You're loved and respected."

Spence scoffed. "Of course he is."

She couldn't continue to stand there, looking at Carter's broken expression. She turned to the rest of the table. Forced her chin to stay up and forced herself to meet their eyes. "I didn't mean to lie to you guys or…" Her gaze stopped on Ellie. "You're all so nice. I keep waiting for you to be something else but it doesn't happen."

Derrick exhaled as he put a hand on the back of Ellie's chair. "Hanna, go ahead and sit down."

Ellie gave her a smile. "Yes, this is Eldrick's mess, not yours."

"And mine." Carter's voice dipped even lower. The despair lingered in every word.

Derrick winced. "Carter, come on."

"Gena was pregnant by me. She killed herself after Dad threatened her." He looked at Hanna. "No wonder you hated me."

But that was excatly wrong. All that anger hid the wanting she'd ignored for so long. They spent time together and what she felt for him, that blinding attraction, changed and swelled. It grew until it overtook everything else. Until the last of her control snapped and she tumbled and fell.

She could see it now. The truth rushed in on her, threatening to bowl her over.

"I wanted to but couldn't. Now I look at you and I see so much more than even you see. I want to be with you. Spend time with you. I think I'm falling for you. Love, Carter. Not sex. Not temporary." That truth slipped out right as it formed in her head.

She'd been fighting and making excuses, but the reality was she didn't need to be in Virginia. She stayed because of him. She wrestled with secrets and ran the risk of being on Eldrick's stomping grounds for Carter. He was worth it.

Jackson's eyes widened. "That's new information."

"What did you just say?" Carter's hand slipped to her chin as he forced her to return his gaze. "Hanna?"

She couldn't stay there one more second. It was all too soon, too much. She'd barely been able to process her feelings before broadcasting them. "I'm sorry."

Then she ran out of the room.

Eleven

Carter reached for Hanna as she rushed out of the room. He missed her and his hand knocked against the sideboard. He didn't even feel it. He didn't feel anything. His mind raced, unable to hold on to any thought for more than a second.

But then Jackson was at his side. "Hey, take a breath."

"She said love." Carter doubled over, unable to finish. "And there was a baby."

Love. Responsibility. A pregnancy he never knew about. It all clashed together in his head. He'd felt a pull toward Hanna from the minute he saw her in New York. He knew she was hiding things from him. That ticked him off and made him want to know more. Now that he did he felt sick. He lost a baby without ever knowing it. He played a role, however small, in Hanna's loss of her sister.

He and his father.

"I know. I got it," Derrick said. "We all did."

Carter dropped into the nearest chair. "Everything is upside down."

Spence shook his head. "Not you. You're still rock-solid."

Carter appreciated the support but right now all he

wanted to do was leave. Old instincts kicked in and shouted at him to get out. Only this time he could block them, tone them down. For now. "I don't feel that way."

Jackson sat down next to Carter and rested his hand on the back of his chair. "What would you have done if you'd known?"

Carter could barely think and Jackson was giving him a quiz. "What?"

"If Gena had told you. What would you have done?" Jackson held up a hand. "Don't think about it. Just answer."

Carter's brain scrambled. It was as if he'd been thrown back in time and confronted with the problem. "Convince her to move back here. Try to get to know her better. Make sure she got care and ask you guys to help me make her feel welcome."

Derrick came around the table to stand on the other side of Carter. "Okay, let's—"

"We barely knew each other. It was a weekend fling. Not like what I feel for Hanna." The words echoed inside him. Settled in. Everything was different with Hanna. Part of him knew it but now the reality beat inside his brain until he couldn't think of anything else.

Derrick nodded. "Then you have your answer."

Carter had lost the trail of the conversation. "What does that mean?"

"You wouldn't have pushed Gena away or ignored your responsibilities. You would not have run." Jackson leaned in. "And now you know that you get the difference between doing what's right and being in love."

"You're giving me too much credit."

Jackson took a deep breath. "As an outsider—"

Spence jumped in. "You're not that."

"Fine. As a non-Jameson, let me suggest a few things." Jackson looked around the room. "First, you're all too fertile and should think about different birth control."

Abby sighed. "I wish I could argue with that."

"And, you're also the best men I know despite being the offspring of one of the worst."

"Also true," Ellie agreed, leaning back in her chair.

"You have a lot of guilt and other crap to wade through, Carter," Derrick added, "but there is a woman at that cottage who loves you and is hurting as much as you are. If I were you, I'd go to her."

Yes, he needed to go to her. But he wasn't sure he was ready.

She'd held back information. But could he blame her? Thinking he was like Eldrick, that Carter had orchestrated his father's maneuvering, wasn't really a stretch. He and his father both acted one way in public and another in private. Carter could understand how she might have twisted that around to think he *was* his dad. Add in Gena's tendency to exaggerate and it was a miracle he'd convinced Hanna to come to Virginia.

Unbelievable that Hanna had trusted him enough to sleep with him.

"How could she not blame me?" He wasn't searching for an answer. He just needed to ask the question out loud.

Jackson grimaced and looked to Spence.

He nodded and then started talking. "I'm guessing she did, but now she knows better. Eventually, you will, as well."

Ellie made a grumbling noise before she stood up and walked around the table. She gave Jackson a gentle shove to move him out of the way. Then she sat down next to Carter, ignoring everyone else in the room. "Carter, you know I love you, right?"

"Is there a *but* coming?"

"But right now, Hanna needs you. The two of you can figure this out together, but you need to talk." She reached over and squeezed his hand. "Go do that."

Jackson laughed. "Listen to the wise pregnant woman."

"You should always listen to the women in the family." Then Ellie looked around, as if challenging the men to question her.

Abby nodded. "Exactly."

"And while you're doing that we'll plot how to make Dad pay for this." There was no amusement in Derrick's voice. The flat line of his mouth suggested he wasn't kidding.

The thought of them all ganging up on their father was the one light moment in this conversation. The mental image would fuel him for a long time.

"I want a part in that, so don't start without me."

She should pack.

The thought ran through Hanna's head as she sat down on the edge of the couch. She'd told the truth, delivered the bad news. She was nothing more than a messenger, but she would pay for this.

The way she'd told him, right in front of everyone. Not in the quiet of the bedroom after they'd had sex or during one of the many times they'd sat and talked together as they ate. Nope, she'd blurted it out. Made a spectacle of an already difficult situation.

How could she ever trust him? She'd likely killed any feelings or attraction he ever felt for her, and that possibility made her stomach roll. She wrapped her arms around her middle and tried to fight her way through the painful darkness falling over her.

"Hanna."

She looked up to see Carter standing in the doorway to the cottage. She'd been so lost in thought she didn't hear him come in. Even now, he only hovered without coming in.

Pain and confusion thrummed off him. She'd done that to him. She tried to think of a way to make some part of this better but nothing came to her except the obvious. "I'm sorry."

"My father…"

"Is not you." That point was so clear in her head now. She wished she'd understood it earlier. "You didn't do anything except go to California, and that had been your plan all along. You weren't running."

"I was running from him, from the family name." He shook his head. "Not from her and the baby."

"I swear to you I do know that now." The air in the room nearly choked Hanna. It felt thick as it passed through her raw throat. She half wished she could yell and cry and get it all out. That losing it would bring her some strange measure of control. "Do you want me to go?"

She hadn't found the strength to stand up, but she'd walk out, find another place to wait out the suffocating sadness that threatened to swamp her. She had her father's journal. She could copy it and send it to Carter. Maybe that would explain a little more about why she was so skeptical of his family.

His mouth twisted in a frown. "Why would I?"

"I kept this from you, and other things, then I told you this heartbreaking thing in the least private way possible."

And it *was* heartbreaking to Carter. She could see it in the paleness of his face and the way his eyes had dimmed. It was as if the life had run right out of him when he'd found out he'd almost been a father and never known.

Some guys would celebrate the near miss. Write Gena off as a bad decision and be more careful next time. But Carter seemed to feel the gravity of what had happened in every muscle. It confirmed what she already knew—what he seemed to not get—that he was one of the good guys.

Despite his father and the cold upbringing and feeling like the "extra" son, he was a good man.

"Hanna." He finally stepped inside and shut the cottage door behind him. He'd left his coat up at the main house and the wind had blown his hair until it stuck up in places. "You're not Gena."

"What?"

"You're not a stand-in for her. My feelings for you have nothing to do with that weekend with her. And you weren't responsible for her decisions. Knowing you, you tried to save her and are kicking yourself because you didn't do enough."

"She drove that car off a bridge." Hanna choked back a sob. "And I wasn't there to stop her."

"If you had stopped her then, there probably would have been a next time." He walked over and sat on the couch beside her. "Her decision wasn't about you. Hell, it might not even have been about Eldrick, though I'm sure he played a role in it."

Hanna stared down at her lap, at her folded hands as she dug her nails into her skin. The pinch didn't even register in her brain. All she heard was the sound of his soothing voice, sad but clear, as the coolness of the outside thrummed off him.

He put his hand under her chin and forced her to look at him. "We're—the two of us and what's been happening there—not about her. Not at all."

The distance between them, though small, proved to be too much. She wrapped her arms around him and held on. She'd admitted something so big, so overwhelming and seemingly impossible as her love for him. She didn't expect him to say it back, not with all the confusion swirling around them. But he held on to her. He didn't shove her away and move on, and right now that's all that mattered to her.

She wasn't sure how long they sat there. She didn't want to let him go. The vulnerability she felt… She focused on her breathing, on the feel of his warm skin beneath her hand, the sound of his heartbeat.

When she opened her eyes again, they were lying on the couch on their sides, with his chest against her back and his arm anchoring them in place.

She almost laughed at how right it felt.

In the silence, she matched her breathing to his. Brushed her fingers over the back of his hand, loving the feel of his lean muscles. Her skin tingled from the puffs of air blowing across the back of her neck.

Suddenly, she was very aware of him. Of every single part of him.

"I want to be close to you."

His lips lingered at her ear. "Me, too."

He exhaled and she felt the move through her body.

They touched everywhere. Tangled legs and arms resting on each other, holding each other.

"I've made a lot of mistakes." He pushed her hair off her face. "Serious ones. Ones that hurt people."

"I've made mistakes, too." Sometimes there were no good answers.

"I've watched my father's manipulations, and I haven't always stepped in."

"I came here because of your dad and to get answers and…" Now was not the time to unload every last detail. They needed some peace. "I need you to know that I've stayed for you."

"Because you love me."

"Yes." She debated not responding but she couldn't hide this from him. She had fallen. Quickly and unexpectedly. Hard and against every defense she'd set up to keep him at a distance. What she felt for him was bigger than she thought possible and so scary because she still didn't know how much he could handle. Well, she did, but she didn't think he knew.

He shifted their position until he balanced on an elbow above her. "Then you should know that I made the offer for you to come here because I wanted you here. Because I found your attitude sexy. Every part of you sexy."

She tucked one of her hands between his side and the couch cushion. The other fell on the pillow by her head. "Oh, really?"

"Like this part." He unbuttoned the top of her dress. Opened each one so slowly, until he moved the sides away and unveiled her skin. He ran a finger over the top of her right breast, right where it plumped out over her bra. "And definitely this part." That finger traveled, sweeping over her breast and down toward the bit of bare stomach he'd revealed.

He lowered his head and licked his tongue over her bottom lip, taking it into his mouth before he kissed her. The touch lasted for a few seconds before he lifted up again. "Should we move—"

"No. Here." The kiss, so warm and inviting, had her breathless.

He glanced at the couch around them. "I like your style."

"And I'd like this better off." Her fingers went to work on his shirt and he raced to help her. In a few minutes they had it off and then it fell to the floor. The T under it followed.

Then his hand slipped under the edge of her skirt. It was the type that hung full and swingy but it had caught on her upper thigh. He pushed it even higher. "Your skin is so soft." His thumb trailed up her inner thigh, right to the junction between her legs. "Next time you can skip the underwear."

"At a family dinner?" She managed to get the question out over the sensations bombarding her. That thumb rubbed over her, tracing circles on her underwear, over her heat.

"Is that weird?"

She wanted to punch him for sounding so in control. "A little, but I like weird."

"Do you like this?" One of his fingers slipped under

the elastic band of her underwear. Slid over her bare skin, then inside her.

She grabbed onto his shoulder. "Carter."

"I'll take that as a yes." He bent down again and kissed her through her bra.

The combination of touching and kissing sent her temperature spiking. The need to rip off the rest of her clothes swamped her. She didn't want anything between them except the one thing they needed.

"Any chance you brought more condoms?"

He lifted his head just long enough to answer. "I left some in the nightstand drawer a while ago."

His finger pressed in and out of her in time with the sweep of his tongue. A few more minutes of this and she wouldn't be able to move. She struggled to keep her mind focused. "Go get one and I'll show you."

She had no idea how she was going to walk. "Me?"

"I want to watch you." He leaned back, giving her enough room to slide out from under him.

If he wanted to play, they could play. But she did not intend to be the only one losing control. Being breathless and needy was a two-person game. That's why she didn't waste any time. She grabbed two condoms and returned to the living room. Took her sweet time walking back to him, swaying her hips. Letting the front of her dress fall open just a bit more.

His gaze never left her. He shifted around on the couch until he lay on his back. Took his time looking up and down, inspecting every inch of her with that sly smile on his face.

She hitched up the skirt of her dress and kneeled on the floor beside the couch. He watched in silence as she unbuckled his belt and lowered his zipper. His breathing grew faster. This close, she could see the labored rise and fall of his chest as she ran her fingers over the front of his briefs.

"Hanna." He made her name sound like a plea.

His breath hitched when she slipped the material off him, freeing him. Then she lowered her head. Her tongue swirled over his tip as her hand pumped up and down. She licked him, squeezed him, brought him into her mouth. She kept it up when his fingers curled into her hair and his hips arched off the couch.

"Hanna, now."

He was begging. She could hear it in his voice and she lifted her head to see his face. The color had returned. His mouth dropped open and he fought for breath. She could feel the slight tremble in his muscles.

Having the ability to snap his control and give him so much pleasure made her feel powerful. Sexy.

"So bossy," she teased.

Ready now, she stood up and slipped off her underwear. Shimmied her hips, putting on a little show for him as he raced to get the condom on. Wedging one leg into the couch cushions, she straddled his hips but she wasn't quite ready to put him out of his misery. She bent her head and dragged her tongue up his chest. Let her hair brush over his bare skin.

She heard his hiccup of breath and felt his hands squeeze her hips and knew it was time. Lowering her body down ever so slowly, she slid over him. Those tiny inner muscles protested at first, then tightened around him. He filled her as she pressed down, making her fight to pull in enough air to breathe.

She felt full and hot and ready. And when she started to move, pleasure crashed over her. She controlled every plunge. He guided her body over his, but he let her take the lead. Her hands balanced on his chest and her fingernails curled into his skin. If he minded the tiny bites, he didn't show it. He was too busy panting.

A sheen of sweat appeared on his forehead as he held back, adjusting to her rhythm. It didn't take her long to feel the pull inside her. A few well-placed touches from him and her body had been primed and ready. The stretching sensation, the way she could move until he hit just the right spot, it all had her tumbling over the edge.

The orgasm ripped through her before she could slow it down. Her hips shifted forward and her head fell back. She felt hot and sensitive and when the pulses started she rode them out, grinding her body against his. She bit back a smile when he groaned.

The next few minutes were a blur of sensation. She felt him move under her and those hands tighten against her. His legs tensed and his back rose off the bed. By the time they were done, they lay in a panting heap on the couch. Her hair swept over him and his hand rubbed up and down her back.

She blinked and the room came into view. It took a few more seconds for her voice to return. "For the record, I love this position."

"Consider me a fan."

His laugh rumbled through her. Every part of her that touched him, which was most of her, shifted as his chest moved. She loved being this close, feeling what he felt. "We should probably get up."

"Later." He kissed her forehead. "Much later."

She dreaded later. That's when she would have to tell him the rest.

Twelve

Carter almost dreaded seeing Spence and Jackson pull up the long drive to the estate the next morning. So much for the idea of alone time with Hanna. He watched from the library window as they got out of the black sedan and walked up to the front door, shaking their heads and talking.

He could tell from their expressions, this was not going to be good.

Hanna looked up from her seat at his desk where they had been having coffee and enjoying the slow morning while he talked with her about his idea for the estate. The one only Jackson knew. "What's wrong?"

Funny how she knew there was a problem just by looking at him. Carter couldn't remember anyone ever being able to read him that well. She had said she loved him and he believed her. He toyed with the idea of saying it back but once he did that was it. There would be no room for him to maneuver, and he wasn't sure he was ready for that. Not when he sensed she still kept something big from him.

"We have company," he said, trying to take his mind off

her and how right it felt to have her in his space and prepare for whatever was about to happen.

Putting aside the rough draft of the plans he'd been writing to restructure the estate, she frowned. "Is that a bad thing?"

He almost laughed because a few days ago she would have balked at the idea of anyone stopping by. She also wouldn't have been sitting with him, helping him work, being a sounding board for the ideas he intended to bring to Spence and Derrick for consideration. "In this case, I think so."

It took a few more minutes for Spence and Jackson to join them. They walked in, nodding a welcome to Hanna but not making a smart comment about her being there. That, alone, was unlike them.

Spence wore an unreadable expression as he leaned against one of the many bookcases outlining the room. "I have some bad news."

Carter had barely recovered from the last news he received. He wasn't sure he ever would. It had been one day. One very long day. "More?"

"I know you're still reeling from..." Spence's gaze shot to Hanna, then back to Carter. "You know."

Jackson rolled his eyes. "Subtle."

Hanna must have thought so, too. She closed the folder in front of her and untucked the leg she was sitting on. "I was there, Spence. You don't have to tread carefully."

But Spence was already shaking his head. "Don't be so sure."

"Okay." That was enough for Carter. "What's going on?"

"Dad is coming to town. Like, now." Spence focused on Carter. "He's on the way."

Carter's mind refused to grasp the concept. "Excuse me?"

"What?" Hanna practically screamed her response.

Jackson sighed as he sat down on the chair in front of Hanna. "Her tone sounded more appropriate under the circumstances."

The unexpected news also happened to be unwelcome. Carter had figured he'd have more time before his father blew back into town. The man couldn't even enjoy the beach the right way.

Carter didn't move from the window as he stared at his brother. "Talk."

"So yesterday, after dinner…" Spence winced as he glanced at Jackson. "Wanna help me out here?"

Jackson shook his head. "Not really."

This wasn't an easy topic. They all hated the idea of more time with Dad. Carter got that, but still. He needed to know what they were dealing with here. "Spence."

"I was furious on your behalf." Spence looked at Hanna. "Not at you. At the idea of Dad threatening you and your sister, possibly—"

"She gets it." Carter did not want to rehash the story again.

Spence nodded. "Anyway, the idea that he bribed you—"

"Tried to," Hanna said, breaking in to Spence's story before he could even get started.

They all stared at her. Only Jackson said what the other men were thinking. "Meaning what exactly?"

"I didn't take the money."

Jackson snorted. "Why not?"

"Good question," Spence said right after.

Her mouth dropped open as her gaze moved around the room. Whatever she saw had her scowling. "You all think I should have grabbed the hush money?"

That one was easy. Carter didn't have to think about it. "Yes."

"And ran. Fast and far." Jackson shook his head. "Honestly, I'm still confused that this is a question."

"The man has plenty. He deserves to lose some," Spence pointed out.

The men-are-idiots look on her face suggested she disagreed. "We all know it would have backfired on me. He could have made up anything. Said I blackmailed him. No way was I taking that risk."

"Let's get back to the reason we're here." Jackson leaned back in the fragile antique chair, ignoring the groaning of the wood beneath him. "And I'm happy to see you guys seem to have made up, by the way."

Spence glared at Jackson. "Really? You lectured me about their privacy the whole way here."

Jackson shrugged. "I'm not problematic like you are."

"Gentlemen." Hanna's voice managed to rise above the arguing. "Say what you came to say."

"I got ticked off and called Dad. Completely unloaded on him. Might have pointed out that none of us trust him." Spence rushed through the explanation, then stopped.

Silence settled in the library. For a few seconds, the only sound came from the ticking of the grandfather clock in the corner. Carter didn't realize how loud it was until just then.

"Did you specifically reference me and Gena?" Hanna asked.

Spence didn't avoid eye contact. "I called him about what happened with both of you, Hanna."

Hanna shot Spence a murderous look.

"Spence's interference came from a good place." Jackson's smile faltered when Hanna turned her focus to him. "Oh."

She just sat there, not saying anything. Carter didn't know how to make this better. He couldn't exactly blame his brother for doing what he had debated doing all night. At one point, he'd slipped out of the bed, forced himself to leave Hanna's side and picked up his cell. He'd toyed with the idea of calling Tortola but stopped when he heard Hanna moving around beneath the covers.

Her breathing seemed to slow now as she blew out a long breath. "So, your father knows I'm here."

Spence nodded. "Yes."

"And now he's coming."

Spence looked a little less sure. "Still yes."

She shook her head. "I can't see him."

"He's going to see me." This was a fight Carter intended to have the minute his father showed up. Eldrick could disown him again for all Carter cared.

Spence nodded. "All of us. He should expect a wall of anger when he lands."

"You're going to challenge him?" Hanna asked in a voice that was less stern than a second ago.

"Derrick suggested we insist Dad sign over the company and go away or we start talking in public." Spence smiled but it quickly faded when he looked at Hanna. "Not about you. About all the other things he's done."

She dropped her head in her hands. Carter had no idea how to read that or guess what reaction would come next.

When she lifted her head again, some of the fight had run out of her. She looked tired. Maybe still a bit annoyed. "You can't…he's your father. There's probably some business agreement in place. Confidentiality or something. That seems like a thing rich people would do."

Jackson made a humming sound. "Right? So paranoid."

"Carter, I don't want to come between—"

"Do not finish that sentence." Now his anger rose to meet hers. He refused to go another round of them competing to see who felt guiltier. Enough of that. "The man scared a pregnant woman. He hid the reality of my own kid from me. And he tried to bribe you. He scared you. Enough that you moved to New York. That you had to beg to get your deceased father's property back."

She clenched her hands together in front of her. "He's a terrible man and apparently an appalling father. I'm not denying that."

"Which is why I called and yelled at him."

She turned on Spence. Pointed right at him. "You're not forgiven yet."

"Hey." Carter moved forward then. He stood in front of her with his hands resting on the edge of the desk. "You don't have to be there, Hanna, but we need to draw the line. If there's more, we need to know it. He needs to come clean."

Her shoulders fell. "I'm sorry."

"For what?"

She bit her bottom lip. She looked like she was about to say something then shook her head. It took another few seconds for her to speak. "That you're related to him. That he's caused so much damage. I don't know. For everything?"

"Well, that all ends now. We're going to confront him and let him know we're tired of him playing games and pretending to be in charge."

"You could lose everything." Her voice had a pleading quality to it.

But on this point, she didn't need to feel any guilt. He smiled at her. "Not possible."

"The house and trust funds are out of his control," Spence said.

For a second the news didn't seem to settle. Then her eyes widened. "How did he let that happen?"

"He's actually a terrible businessman." Jackson leaned back a bit too far in the chair. A cracking sound had him jerking forward again. "His schemes worked back when things were done by a handshake. He couldn't function in the modern world. Derrick is the brains behind the operation."

Spence smiled. "And, the reality is, he couldn't screw everyone."

She still looked confused. Not that anyone could blame her. "What does that mean?"

Carter loved this part. "He was trying to hide assets when he started playing around with the company accounts and got caught. The only way to hide them was to move some items to our mom's name. He thought they had an agreement to switch things back. He believed she trusted him, but she was smarter than he gave her credit for. She put almost everything in our names instead."

"He doesn't own this estate anymore and while he can take most of the money away and shut down or sell the business as majority stakeholder, he can't take what we already got from Mom," Spence explained.

"And what's left over from her is more than most people will see in a lifetime." Jackson held up a hand as if to apologize for jumping into the middle of the talk. "Just saying."

She looked at all of them one more time. "You'll be out of a job. You all will."

Jackson made a noise that sounded like *nah*. "I'll be fine."

"You guys sound so sure." But hope lingered in her voice. It was tough to miss the sound.

Carter got it. In some ways, Eldrick seemed untouchable. Even Derrick had covered for some of the schemes a few years ago so the company could be rebuilt. "After a lifetime of dealing with his garbage, we are sure of this one thing. It needs to be over."

Spence nodded. "Trust us."

It took a few more seconds but she finally smiled. "I do."

The sun felt good on her face as she stood by the fence on the state lawn.

Hanna counted back, thinking about the overcast days

and the rain. She hadn't been outside for more than a walk between buildings or in and out of the car in three days. This morning, the sun streamed over the lawn, highlighting the bright red and orange of the leaves on the ground.

Fall would settle in soon. Under her original plan she would have been gone already, but she had no intention of moving on. Not yet. Carter hadn't formally asked her to stay or really even responded to her admission of being in love with him, not with words anyway. But he'd made it clear he wanted her around.

For now, that was good enough. The days with him, the nights… She wouldn't trade those for anything.

She let her head drop back and her hair fall down her shoulders. Closing her eyes, she soaked in the layer of warmth just above the cool breeze.

"We had a deal."

His voice. It snapped her out of her good mood. Out of everything.

She turned to see Eldrick Jameson standing in front of her. He was in his sixties and handsome, though she didn't see it. Other people mentioned it. He had a regal air about him, like he'd just stepped out of a country club magazine. Today he wore a navy blazer. She actually looked for a crest because he seemed like a guy who would have one of those.

If life were fair, he'd be ugly and have fangs, but no. He still had a trim figure with his salt-and-pepper gray hair. He'd aged well, which blew apart all those sayings about living hard…and karma.

"You're here." Like in every nightmare she'd had since he'd tried to bribe her.

He crossed his arms in front of him. "It's my house."

A strange lightness filled her. She almost smiled. "That's not what I heard."

"That trust?" He shook his head. "I can break that."

He sounded so sure. It was as if the rules didn't apply to

him. From the stories she heard and what she read in her father's journal, they kind of didn't.

She wasn't the type who wanted to be rescued by a man, but the idea of having reinforcements right now sounded good. "Carter is—"

"Weak."

Eldrick hadn't seen him yet, but Carter walked across the lawn now with a woman beside him. Hanna knew she should whisper or at least change the topic because Carter deserved better, but she couldn't let that comment slide.

"What is wrong with you?" What kind of man spoke about his children that way? She didn't get it.

The footsteps stopped and Carter sighed as he waited behind his father. "I've been wondering that for years."

Before Eldrick could respond, the woman stepped forward. Hanna had a hard time with ages but she looked way younger than Eldrick, but not nearly as young as Hanna expected his fourth wife to be. With her billowy wide-legged pants, slim sweater jacket and shoulder-length auburn hair, she looked maybe forty, and carefree. Like she belonged on an island. The fake smile plastered on her face suggested she'd prefer to be there right now.

"You said you were going into the office."

The woman didn't have an accent. Her expensive clothes and the sparkly diamond rings she wore on most of her fingers spoke for her.

"Soon, my love." Eldrick had the nerve to sound sweet, maybe even a little charming.

Hanna hated that.

Carter stared at his father. "She called me to ask where you were. I told her you weren't really welcome at the office."

Hanna loved hearing the strength in Carter's voice. She'd never seen him back down and he wasn't doing it with his father either. For the first time she felt like she had support.

That Carter would back her. That he really would fight for her. That security, that sense of being believed and protected gave her the mental push she needed. She'd tell him the rest and somehow it would all be okay.

But they had to get through this messy confrontation first.

"I own the business. I built it and—"

Carter held up a hand, seemingly not caring that he was taking on his father. "Enough with that."

"Do not interrupt me." There was an angry edge to Eldrick's voice now. That smarmy smile disappeared, revealing the slimy guy underneath.

"I'm Beth." The other woman held her hand out to Hanna.

"Technically, she's Jacqueline Annabeth Winslow Jameson," Carter added.

The smile Beth sent Carter looked genuine, even affectionate, as if she actually considered him family. "I go by Beth."

Hanna was still trying to recover from that name. It was quite a mouthful. "Why the nickname?"

Beth gave Hanna's hand a firm shake. "Eldrick isn't fond of the name Jacqueline."

A memory screeched to a halt in Hanna's head. Those journal entries about women Eldrick had slept with. About her father's conclusions.

The biggest one centered on the name Jack.

Eldrick broke through her mental gymnastics with his stern voice. "You and I need to have a talk about the rumors you're spreading."

There was no way Hanna would cower or run off. She might have given him the satisfaction last time. Not now. "You know what you did."

Beth took a step forward to stand by Hanna's side. "What?"

"It's nothing, Beth." Eldrick reached for his wife.

She waved him off, keeping her attention on Hanna. "Is it nothing?"

Hanna was torn between spilling the whole tale and trying to figure out which side this woman was on. She sounded so sincere and concerned, but Hanna had been reeled in by fake people before. It was one of the reasons she was so careful now.

"I'll let you decide."

Eldrick pointed at her. "Don't say another word."

Carter moved until he was beside Hanna, with his body inches ahead of hers as if he were ready to throw up a shield, if needed. "Do not get in her face. Ever."

After a nod from Carter, Hanna got to the spilling part. "He bribed me not to tell Carter that my sister had been pregnant with Carter's baby when she died."

Beth's eyes widened and her hand went to Hanna's arm. "Died? I'm so sorry."

"She killed herself after Dad threatened her," Carter said, not backing down either.

"That is not what happened." This time Eldrick grabbed his wife's hand and pulled her over to stand with him. "I told you these boys exaggerate. Ignore him."

Beth looked at Carter. "When?"

He didn't pretend to be confused. Didn't hesitate. "About six months ago."

"After we were married."

"Now, Beth." Eldrick patted his wife's arm while he scowled at Hanna. "Why are you even here?" Then he switched to Carter. "Don't you get it? This woman's goal is to cause trouble. She burst in here, making these claims."

Carter shook his head. "I went to see her as part of *your* requirements."

"What does that mean?" Beth asked.

Eldrick tried to answer, but Carter talked over him. "The things my brothers and I have to do before he'll consider turning the everyday operations over to Derrick. Each brother got an assignment. Finding Hanna and handing her an envelope was mine."

"I bet you cashed that check."

Now it made sense. The envelope was Eldrick's last effort to pay her off. He likely thought sending Carter would intimidate her in some way. The man did not know his son at all.

"This is all so confusing. Check?" Beth rubbed her forehead as she looked at Carter. "And Derrick already runs the business."

A stiff wind blew over the lawn. Hanna shivered but she thought it might be a reaction to the confidence pulsing off Carter rather than the cold. He looked so sure, so in control. So perfect...for her. No wonder she loved him.

Carter continued, "Eldrick needs to officially retire and step out or he can come back anytime."

Beth turned on her husband. "That's not what you told me."

"We're talking about Ms. Wilde right now."

Eldrick's tone was so soft.

Such garbage. "So condescending."

The sound of Hanna's voice seemed to tick Eldrick off. This time he went after Carter. "This was all your fault. You weren't careful. Dropping your pants and not using protection. What kind of man are you?"

"A real one who doesn't threaten women." Carter's voice stayed even. He never lost control. Standing tall and sure, he looked ready to take on any battle.

Eldrick shook his head as he continued to spew. "You made the mess and, as usual, I had to clean it up."

Anger lit up the inside of Hanna's head until she thought it might explode. "Gena was not a mess."

"I did you a favor," Eldrick said, still talking to Carter.

"Eldrick, the woman is dead." Beth's voice was sharp and biting now. Whatever tolerance she'd had, it vanished.

"Which is a shame but not my fault, and I don't appreciate the suggestion otherwise." Eldrick kept talking at Carter, who stood there looking bored, as if the words bounced off him. "You never learn your lesson. I got you out of one entanglement and then you shack up with the other sister?"

Hanna didn't know how Carter could stand to listen to the man. She sure couldn't. "Gena wasn't an entanglement either."

"I think it's time you leave the property." Eldrick pointed in the general direction of the street. "Whatever you're searching for, you're not going to find it here. You have your check. Now run along."

When that didn't work he took a step forward, reaching for her. Carter blocked the move. He stood right in front of her.

"She is with me. You aren't to go near her again." This time Carter's voice seethed with anger.

Eldrick tried to look around his son's impressive shoulders at Hanna. "He's ungrateful. And unemployed. Did he tell you that? Never held a real job. Never contributed."

It was now or never. Eldrick's usual hold on the conversation faltered. The concern on Beth's face was tough to miss. Carter looked ready to go into battle for her. But this Hanna needed to do.

She stepped around Carter, facing Eldrick head-on. "How did my father really die?"

The question seemed to flatten him. He took a step back as his eyes darted to the side. "What?"

She didn't hold back. "We both know he didn't fall off a ladder. The man built houses. He wasn't sloppy."

"He made a mistake and paid a steep price."

She felt a hand on her lower back. She knew it was Carter and it meant he supported her. He didn't even need to say the words to get her to keep going. "Taking a job from you, yes. But you didn't answer my question."

Beth shook her head. "I don't understand."

"He worked for us and died on the job. That's all I know. You've seen the reports. You know the truth. It was an unfortunate workplace accident," he said, showing he knew far more than he pretended to now. "Your mother already tried for a bigger payday and failed."

He could launch any accusation he wanted. Hanna intended to stand there and take it. "Did you push him?"

"Of course not." Eldrick looked over her head at Carter. "Usher her off the grounds or I will."

"What did you do, Dad?" Carter asked.

"Nothing. The lawyers already—"

"Eldrick?" Beth put her hand on his arm and looked up at him. "Just say it."

At the sound of her voice, Eldrick's resolve seemed to crumble. He didn't stand quite as tall and his words sputtered a bit as he spoke. "This has been resolved."

Beth's perfectly manicured eyebrow lifted. "Apparently not."

"This is your last chance." Carter's hand flattened on Hanna's back. He wasn't doing anything to hide the fact they were together and she had his support. "You answer her or I'll open an investigation. We'll go through every report and all the findings. Bring in people who worked here. Do recreations if we need to. Blow this wide and make it public."

Hanna loved him for who he was and she loved him for those words. It was a promise to her as much as a threat against his father.

"It's not anything," Eldrick said.

Carter swore under his breath. "The man is dead."

"Fine." Eldrick brushed a hand down the front of his blazer. "There was a piece of equipment. It malfunctioned. End of story."

Hanna had been holding her breath and now it rushed out of her. The knot in her stomach that had been there since the day her father died eased. For a second, she could breathe without being hit with the weight of unfinished business. "I knew it."

"He was working on it and there was a burst of hot air that blew him off." Eldrick waved his hand in the air as if the conversation were done. "That's it."

"Why not tell the truth back then?" she asked. The secrecy only created more doubt.

"It was an accident."

But not the same accident she'd heard all her life. "One your machinery caused."

"He fudged the story because it would have cost him otherwise." Carter sounded tired and frustrated and two seconds from losing his control. "Right? You knew the machine was a problem. Maybe Hanna's dad warned you, and you didn't bother to get it fixed."

Beth tugged on Eldrick's arm. "You put that man in a position to be hurt?"

"That's not what happened."

But it was. Hanna understood now.

This was about liability. Whatever feelings he'd had for her father, and she doubted Eldrick had many since he only cared about himself and maybe a little about Beth, those feelings didn't outweigh the fact that her father's death was a nuisance to him.

The realization made her want to scream and pound on his chest. That he could forfeit a life because it was cheaper than fixing equipment. Her mind couldn't grasp that at all. She leaned into Carter's side because she wasn't sure her legs would hold her much longer.

"We're leaving." Beth dropped her hand from Eldrick's arm. Nothing about her tone suggested she wanted to hear an argument.

Of course, Eldrick tried anyway. "I need—"

"To come with me right now." Beth started walking.

Carter shook his head. "I'd listen to her."

"I'll be back." Eldrick waited until his wife's back was turned to glare at Hanna again. "You need to be gone."

Carter slipped an arm around her. Put it on her shoulder and pulled her in even closer to his side. "She's staying."

"Don't fight me on this, Carter."

"From now on, expect a fight on everything."

Eldrick hesitated before walking away. In a few long strides, he caught up with Beth. They headed along the side of the house without saying a word.

Hanna expected to hate Eldrick's newest wife. She'd pictured one type of woman, a sort of female version of Eldrick. Once again, her preconceived notions had been wrong.

"So, your stepmom…"

"She's turned out to be a surprise. Most of the women he married went along with his schemes, at least in front of us. They all left shortly after finding out some new horrible thing he did in the past. She's sticking around, holding him accountable."

Hanna broached the one open question. "The name thing?"

Carter scoffed. "That's odd even for my dad. What kind of man makes a woman use a different name?"

"Do you think it means something?" Because Hanna did. She thought it was about Eldrick and his secrets. She wished she could be sure because once she exposed this last one she would turn all of their lives upside down. Before she took that step and launched one more emotional grenade at Carter, she'd think it through.

Carter shrugged. "My father has to control everything."

"Not anymore."

This time Carter laughed. "No, not anymore."

Thirteen

Later that night, Carter sprawled on the couch in the television room with Hanna leaning on his chest. By silent agreement they had started spending their nights in the main house. He'd insisted the furniture was more comfortable and she just rolled her eyes and went along with the excuse.

Today had been long and trying. Finding out his father had contributed to her father's death had not been an easy afternoon. Carter was starting to wonder if he'd ever have an easy one again. But this part he enjoyed, having her back rest against his chest. Listening to her laugh at some dumb joke in this lame buddy heist movie.

Somehow, she'd eased the harsh news into the rest of the day. After an hour of being alone, walking the grounds while he watched helpless and in desperation from the window, she'd bounced back. It was as if hearing the news had freed her to move on.

That made one of them. It knocked him down. He mentally struggled to understand why she didn't pack her bag and run as far away from the Jamesons as possible.

He slipped his fingers through her hair. "I love that you're here with me. Despite all the bad memories, this house has always been special to me. With you it's even more so."

"Sweet talker."

But he didn't want her to think it was a line. He'd never expected her to love him. It was a gift. And with each day his feelings for her became clearer. She'd been so unexpected that he was still trying to get his emotional footing. She deserved more and not just when it came to them.

"I feel like I should apologize for everything that happened to your family." He kissed the side of her hair, inhaling the scent of her floral shampoo. "I don't even know where to start."

She shifted, turning to look up at him. "I kept the baby information from you."

"Do you know if it was a boy or a girl?" He hadn't meant to ask that. He wasn't even sure where the question came from since he'd been blocking out any thoughts of the baby all day.

She slipped her hand over his knee. "A little girl."

An image flashed in his mind and he pushed it out again. "Was she healthy?"

"Yes." Hanna flipped around. Her legs balanced over his as she sat sideways, facing him. "I can't explain what happened that day. What one thing pushed her over the edge. I wish I could."

"Me, too."

She leaned her head against the back cushion of the couch. "The doctors I talked to explained that it's like darkness. Not just a lack of light. It's more like a weight and it shoves you down and spins tales in your head and convinces you there is no way out. Nothing, not sunshine or trying to be happy or any of the other things people talk about as possible ways through it really work. The darkness is relentless, joyless. It presses and presses until you break."

He brushed a hand over her hair. The silky strands slipped through his fingers. "Have you ever experienced it?"

"I used to think depression equaled extreme sadness, but now I know that's wrong. It's a much bigger, soul-sucking thing." She slid her fingers through his and brought their joined hands to her mouth.

"Is it weird for you that we're together after I spent that weekend with her?" He had been avoiding that question from the start. For him, the sisters were so different that he didn't even connect them in his mind.

"I try not to think about that part."

"I don't compare you." He stressed each word because he needed her to believe him. "You're distinctly Hanna. Not a substitute. Not the 'other' sister. Just Hanna."

She kissed the back of his hand. "Thank you."

"You knew that, right?"

"I think I needed to hear it since I'd spent so much of my life in my sister's shadow."

There was more. Feelings he hadn't expected. New priorities he'd tried to ignore but they refused to be pushed aside. "I'm not a guy who sticks around and fights through things."

She smiled. "I've heard."

"From?"

"You." She dropped their joined hands to her lap. "You've been pretty honest that settling in is not your thing."

Not before. Now he wasn't so sure.

He looked at the long stretch of life in front of him and he no longer saw travel and moving and switching houses and being alone. He thought about his brothers and the estate. About her.

Maybe this was how it happened. He'd made fun of his brothers for falling so fast. For acting like they'd lost all sense. He kind of understood it now.

"I think putting down roots could be the new me."

When she didn't laugh or run out of the room, he kept going. "The idea of making the estate into something new, an event space, a place for parties. Something other than a home. A place that employs lots of people and offers opportunities. That sounds good to me."

"And you would run it."

"Yeah. I'd build it and expand it and live here." But when he envisioned the plans, he saw her. Them eating dinner and lounging around like they were doing now. "You still married to the idea of living in New York?"

She lifted her head just long enough to tuck her hair behind her ear. "Why, do you need someone to clean this place?"

He laughed. "Yeah, a team of people, but what I'm really saying is I don't want you to go."

Her fingers tightened on his. "That's a big statement."

The biggest, because what he was really saying was he wanted her here, for a long time. Forever.

"What I feel for you is big." They sounded so serious as they sat there whispering. He couldn't help but lighten the mood. "Admittedly, maybe not preteen crush big."

"Ugh." She buried her face in her hands. "You knew about that?"

The embarrassment and mumbling were endearing. She could be hot and sexy and sweet and charming. The combination blew his control to pieces.

"The teen me might have ignored you. The grown-up me is so much smarter."

She lifted her head and started frowning. "What is that sound?"

The buzzing didn't let up. Carter reached for the remote and clicked on the number to show the security feed. "The box at the entry gate out front."

"Isn't that fancy?" Then she leaned forward to study the screen. "Wait, is that your stepmom?"

The image didn't lie. Beth stood there, without Eldrick or anything but a purse and stared at the house. "That can't be good."

"At least she's alone."

Carter lifted Hanna's legs off his lap and stood up. "That's what I mean. We're all doomed if she left him."

"Why do you say that?"

"She's the reason he lives in Tortola."

He went downstairs to retrieve Beth and ushered her into the television room about ten minutes later. Her usual put-together style seemed to be failing. A lock of her hair fell across her forehead and she kept playing with the metal band of her very expensive watch.

She stepped into the room, saw Hanna and the last of her blank expression fell. Beth's attitude morphed from *I'm fine* to *I'm barely holding it together* in a few seconds. "I'm sorry to disturb you."

"Come inside." Hanna stood up and gestured for Beth to sit on the couch. "Are you okay?"

"She left my Dad."

Carter knew because he heard the terrible news on the walk up the stairs. He nearly tripped in response. He could hardly wait to hear Jackson's and his brothers' reactions when he sent them a group text.

"Oh." Hanna shot him a grimace over the top of Beth's head as she helped the older woman sit down. Not that Beth needed an assist but her hands did shake and Hanna seemed concerned.

The watchband clasp snapped as Beth opened and closed it. "He lied about everything."

"It's what he does."

Hanna shot Carter a look that said he should be quiet. He just shrugged in return.

Beth didn't appear to hear him anyway. She sat there,

shaking her head as she stared at her lap. "All those promises that he was a new man. How loving me changed things."

"I actually think it did." That got her attention. Carter didn't say the words just to comfort her. He really did mean them. "The father I grew up with would never step away from the business, even temporarily, and move to an island to make someone else happy. You mean something to him."

"How am I supposed to trust him?"

He had to look at Hanna because the pleading in Beth's eyes proved to be too much after today's events. "You've got me there."

"Carter." Hanna stared at the empty space on the other side of Beth on the couch. "Sit down."

That much closeness struck him as unnecessary. He doubted Beth wanted his company but Hanna's glare didn't exactly give him a choice.

"I just wasn't sure where to go. We were here this afternoon, so I remembered this address."

"It's fine." Carter wasn't sure what else to say, so he went with that.

"Do you have a bag?" Hanna asked.

Carter did not like where this was going. He could sense his world turning upside down. Again.

Beth shook her head. "I left it at the condo."

"What condo?"

"Dad kept a place here," Carter said, answering Hanna's question.

"You rich guys have a thing for property."

Leave it to Hanna to take a second out of consoling to land a shot. "Is now the time?"

"You should stay here," Hanna said, ignoring him. "I'm sure we can find you what you need. I don't have much, but I'm happy to share."

Beth smiled at Hanna. "You're very sweet."

Carter still hadn't recovered from that move when Hanna

shot him a do-something look over the top of Beth's head. He knew he'd get sucked into this. "Make a list and I'll go grab what you need."

Beth shrugged. "A new husband."

"That may take me more than fifteen minutes." Carter jumped up and looked around for his phone. "I'll call Lynette to make up a room."

"Don't bother her. I'll do it."

Again with this. "Hanna, you don't work for me."

Beth put her hand on Hanna's knee. "I don't want to be in the way."

"There are a ridiculous number of bedrooms in this place. You can have one. Right, Carter?" Hanna looked up at Carter with an expression that suggested he better get the answer correct.

"Sure." Who wouldn't want the stepmother he barely knew to stay over when she was fighting with the father he hated? "Top of the stairs, first door on the right. It's a guest suite and all yours."

Beth nodded. "Just for tonight."

Carter doubted that would be true. "For as long as you need it."

He felt obligated to say that as he watched her leave the room and head for the hall. He waited until she disappeared to turn back to Hanna.

"Now what?" she asked.

They should relocate to another state. Somewhere like Utah. That was the only option here, though Carter knew Hanna would say no. That left him without a Plan B for dealing with his father's inevitable return.

"I have no idea."

Fourteen

So much yelling.

Not at each other, just in general. Those thoughts kept moving through Hanna's mind as she listened to the brothers and Jackson argue about what to do about their father. He demanded to see his wife and was coming over to make that happen. Hanna sent out an emergency call and Ellie swooped in and grabbed Beth to prevent the confrontation.

That left only the men and Hanna at the estate. Even the people who worked there had scattered. As she watched Derrick pace from one side of the library to the other, she wondered if she should have headed out with Ellie and Beth. Carter had told her to go so she could avoid another meeting with his dad. The offer had been tempting but a voice in her head nagged at her to stay.

He couldn't hurt her anymore. That was a fact. Eldrick no longer scared her. He blustered and threatened and probably could make her life miserable, but she felt like part of a united front now. Everyone in this room, plus the women who weren't here, had committed to standing up to Eldrick and his manipulations. She'd turned down not one but two checks. He had no hold over her.

But he did have a hold on Carter.

He'd never admit it, but hearing his father discount him had to hurt. He might be an adult now, but the words, the constant barrage that continued even now, the loss of faith, that had to bash a person's self-esteem. She vowed not to let Eldrick take one more slice out of Carter. She loved Carter and her mind had started spinning with ideas about a future with him. That meant she did not want Carter near his father very often.

And then there was Jackson. She watched him now as he walked to the window, peeking out, trying to stay out of the fray. If she was right, he'd experienced the worst slight of all.

At ten after three, Hanna decided Eldrick wasn't coming. Maybe he'd figured out his sons had conspired against him. Worse, he might have gone looking for Beth. Not wanting to worry anyone with that thought, Hanna reached for her phone. Ellie and Derrick had security. She wanted to remind Ellie to use it.

"Where is she?" Eldrick's voice boomed through the room.

Hanna spun around, expecting him to look like a man on the verge of losing his wife. Nope. He wore an expensive blazer and polished shoes. If this was his version of heartbroken, she didn't see how it was any different from his usual entitled look.

"She's not here," Derrick said.

Eldrick barely gave his sons eye contact. "I'll go find her."

Spence stepped in front of him, blocking his path to the door. "We want to talk to you."

Eldrick's expression did not disappoint. His gaze swept across the room. "You will never get the business this way."

Carter shook his head. "This is about you."

"You should be at work," Eldrick said as he looked at Derrick. Never mind that it was Saturday. Then his gaze landed on her. "And you should be out of town. Somewhere with a mop in your hand."

She knew the words were calculated to hurt. Only in his world would pointing out what she did for a living be a slight.

"Stop talking." The order came from Carter.

"You think you can take me on, son?"

Carter shook his head. "I don't think you're worth it."

She loved that response. She almost cheered.

"I've had enough." Eldrick smiled as he looked at them. "I'll see you at work on Monday." He glanced at Derrick. "I'll expect you to vacate my office."

Rage swept through her as he issued threats. She thought about letting him walk out the door and then helping the men sift through the aftermath, but then she looked at Jackson. Looked at all of them. They deserved to know the truth.

She knew Carter believed all the secrets had been exposed. Dropping this one was a risk, but he needed to know the truth. Once he did she was confident he would help the others. And then, finally, there wouldn't be any more baggage left stacked between them. They'd have issues to handle but no secrets.

She stepped up next to the desk. "Tell them the truth."

Eldrick rolled his eyes. "Is this about your father again? I'm done talking about the accident."

She let that word slide right by her. She refused to be derailed. That's what he wanted. He thought he could land a few well-chosen words and send them all spiraling. He didn't know his audience. The Jameson men weren't like that and neither was she.

"It's about Jackson."

Jackson frowned. "Me?"

"I don't have to listen to you." But Eldrick no longer looked as smug.

That's when she knew she was right. All the connections she'd made in her head, all the pieces that were right there but everyone else had been too close to see.

"He deserves to know. They all do."

Carter appeared at her side. "What are you talking about?"

She had to ignore him and the confusion in his voice. Not look at his face. No, she needed to push through for Carter. Eldrick could not squirm his way out of this lie like he'd tried to with so many others.

"She's just like her sister." Eldrick glared at Carter. "When will you learn?"

"Hanna?" Derrick held up his hands as if hoping she would continue and explain.

"My father kept a journal."

Eldrick jumped right in, spoke almost before she finished her sentence. "A book of some man's fantasies. It's irrelevant."

He was unraveling. She could see him falling apart in front of her. "You know that's not what it was. He wrote about you. The things you said to him. Side comments. Details about your exploits."

That was the tame version. Apparently, Eldrick liked to brag. Her father wrote it all down, along with comments about how upsetting he found it because he really liked Carter's mother.

"That's man talk. Nothing more."

No way was she letting that stand as his excuse. "Tell him or I will."

"You don't know anything."

Jackson's gaze switched from Eldrick back to her. "What does this have to do with me?"

"Everything." She ached for him. Seeing Carter's confusion only made the moment worse.

She was about to take a wrecking ball to his world. But he had to know. They all did. Jackson had a birthright and a connection. Carter had more family, and she'd come to understand that as much as he might deny it, he was all about family. A man who returned to help his brothers was not disconnected, which only made her love him more.

"Shut up." Eldrick practically spit out the words as he took a few steps forward.

Carter blocked his path. "Don't talk to her like that."

"She is about to ruin everything."

Spence cleared his throat. "Then she better speak."

"You don't even know." Eldrick looked at Carter and started to laugh. The evil sound filled the room. "That's rich. You're sleeping with her and she's sneaking behind your back, finding journals."

Carter didn't seem all that impressed with his father's act. But he did frown at her. "Hanna, tell me."

"No!" Some of Eldrick's calm faded then. He switched from laughing to explaining. The words rushed out of him. "I did this to protect you. Why do you think I sent you away? I couldn't let you date Zoe. She was off-limits."

There it was. Hanna closed her eyes, hoping to get hit by a wave of relief but all she felt was sadness. This man had actually disowned one of his kids to protect his secrets.

"How is my sister involved in this?" Jackson was standing up straight now, fully engaged.

"Zoe is your sister," Eldrick said to Carter. "Jackson is your brother." The words held all the emotion of a weather report. Purely factual, as if it were no big deal. "A mistake I made—"

"What?" All the color drained from Jackson's face.

"Your mother was a woman I knew. Worked in the office next door. It meant nothing, but you can't trust women when it comes to birth control. Not when we're dealing with this kind of money."

"Oh, my God." Spence's voice sounded small and stunned. "You think you're giving a fatherly lecture right now?"

"That's what I was doing with Gena. Making sure this didn't happen to you." Eldrick looked at Carter.

"Jackson and Zoe are our siblings." Carter said the words as if they'd just crystallized in his head.

"Half," Eldrick corrected.

Derrick scoffed. "As if that matters."

"Of course it does," Eldrick said. "They're not Jamesons. It's as simple as that."

He was unbelievable. He used words as a weapon and Hanna was sick of it. "Because of you. Because you made the decision not to tell."

Eldrick looked her up and down. "You're worse than that piece of trash sister of yours."

Carter lunged then, but Derrick caught him just in time. But that didn't stop Carter from staring at his father. "Get out."

"You can't order me to leave."

Carter shook his head. "Your name is not on the title to this house. You're not on the trust. You have no right to be here."

"Yeah, family only." Spence walked to the door and gestured for Eldrick to go.

"You're all going to regret this." But he didn't stay and say more.

His footsteps echoed on the elaborate staircase. No one said a word as the fighting continued to vibrate off the walls.

Hanna knew they couldn't take the risk of Eldrick getting to Beth or Ellie. "I'll call to warn—"

"You knew." Carter turned on her. "All of it."

A lump formed in her throat as she looked around. Saw

the mix of pain, confusion and anger in their gazes. "I guessed."

"But you didn't tell me?"

Because she needed to be sure and they needed to have this conversation alone. She didn't plan to unload. She'd wanted to do this the right way, without an audience. Not put Carter in a terrible position…again. "It's not that simple."

"It is." He stepped closer. "You know how I feel about Jackson. I might not have said that I considered him family, but you could tell. You read people. We talked about so many things."

Derrick winced. "Carter, maybe now isn't—"

"You didn't say anything. All those nights, all that talking. You held back secret after secret. I forgave it all."

She didn't have to guess his mood now. There was no pretending or trying to hide it. With every word the fury built inside him and he aimed it right at her. She didn't even try to duck.

"The journal didn't spell it out. I put it together through Beth's real name and…there was this notation."

"When?" When she didn't immediately answer, he continued his interrogation. "It's an easy question, Hanna. When?"

Part of her wanted to shrivel under the rapid-fire questioning, but she forced her shoulders back. She didn't do anything wrong. Another case of bad timing, maybe. But she was not the guilty party here.

"I found the journal right after I got here. When Beth said her full name and how Eldrick hated her real first name. It was a different spelling, but so close to Jackson's." She said his name and turned to him. "I'm sorry."

He just shook his head. "I don't get this."

Spence grabbed Carter's arm. "Stop and think for a second."

She silently begged for Carter to listen. Eldrick made the mess and she got stuck with the cleanup. She'd tried to stay away in the safety of New York. She'd put her teen crush behind her. She never expected to have her life tangled up with Carter's again. To ache to be with him. To love him until she couldn't think straight. "I know you're blaming me, but this was your dad. It's always about him."

"I don't expect anything from him, Hanna." Carter swallowed hard enough for her to see it. "I trusted you, or I tried to."

"Carter, please…"

But he just shook his head.

The tension in the room closed in on her. She tried to breathe but the suffocating pressure nearly choked her. She could feel Carter's anger, knew it was aimed at her. It pulsed off him and crashed right into her. She tried to hold on to her balance, to think of the right thing to say, but she could see he'd shut down. His mouth fell into a flat line and a coldness she'd never expected to see moved into his eyes.

She needed the cottage…no, she needed to go. He was the one who spent his life running and she got it now. Sometimes the crushing pain, the slip into the abyss as one more thing was lost, proved too much.

She rushed across the room, right past him. He didn't make a move to stop her, sending a slicing pain through her. It was Spence who touched her arm. "Don't leave."

"I can't stay."

Spence called out to his brother. "Carter, come on."

She didn't even need to see his face to know he'd given up on her. She'd betrayed him one time too many. Maybe it was a good thing he never told her he loved her. The weight of all she lost pummeled her, but at least she didn't lose his love.

She'd never had it.

* * *

Carter heard her go. Listened to her mumbling and knew his brothers were staring. Still, he couldn't move. He stood in the middle of the library, the one room in the house that gave him peace, and his world crumbled around him.

"That was a bloodbath." Derrick's voice sounded softer than usual. "Jackson?"

"I might throw up."

Carter looked at his friend, now brother. Jackson's shoulders curled in and he held on to the bookcase as if it were the only thing keeping him upright. "Don't blame you."

Jackson sat down hard in the desk chair. "I spend half of my day being grateful he's not my father, but he is."

"Did your mom ever give you any clue?" Spence asked.

Jackson shook his head. "None."

She'd died a few years ago. It seemed like she'd thought it was better her children never know. There was a part of Carter that understood that. Eldrick was a hard man, even to his children. "She was likely protecting you."

Carter rubbed his stomach. He tried to focus on the carnage in front of him, not let his mind wander to Hanna and the look on her face as she walked out.

"Zoe is going to lose it." Jackson looked up. His expression flipped from blank to concerned and back again. "Now you know why your dad pushed you away, disowned you. He was trying to keep you away from Zoe."

The logic made no sense to Carter. "Shows how much he knows about me. We were only ever friends."

"What were you thinking?" Jackson sounded confused now. "The way you unloaded on Hanna."

The words pounded into Carter. He had been expecting… well, anything else. "She lied to me."

Spence made a strangled sound. "How was she supposed to tell that story?"

"What if her theory hád been wrong and she said it and caused a bigger mess?" Derrick asked.

Carter had no idea what was happening. They should be furious with her and with him for inviting her back into their lives.

"You guys are ganging up on me now?" He barely knew what to think and now he didn't have anywhere to turn.

"We tried to stop you a few minutes ago and that didn't work." Jackson pointed in Derrick's general direction. "Well, they did. I was too busy trying not to pass out or throw Eldrick out a window."

"You should have done the latter, but the former would have been funny." Spence actually laughed but then stopped when no one else made a sound. "But back to you."

For the first time in his life, Carter didn't know what to say. The speechless thing never happened to him, yet here he was. Stumped. "What?"

Spence shook his head. "You have to stop her."

What were they even talking about? "From?"

Jackson sighed. "If my guess is right, leaving."

"You didn't exactly support her." Derrick's look… Was that disappointed?

Maybe they didn't understand. Carter decided to try again. "She knew—"

Spence held up a finger. "Thought she knew."

That wasn't the point. Not the one he was trying to make. "She didn't tell me."

Jackson frowned. "Since she was still dealing with her sister's death and just learned that our father played a role in her father's death, maybe cut her some slack."

"Look, I've been there." Derrick continued as if he were telling a story. "You fall in love and become vulnerable, then you say and do dumb things."

They'd all lost their minds. Yes, the news about her father's death…maybe he wasn't taking that enough into account. Carter felt a slap of guilt about that. But the rest?

Jackson did his usual humming sound. "He's not saying no to the love thing."

Love.

The word sat heavy on Carter's chest. He'd thought about a life with her, but love still seemed out of reach. "It's too early."

Both Spence and Derrick laughed but Derrick was the one who responded. "Right. Because love works that way. It has a time limit."

Spence took his turn. "You and Hanna have a lot to talk about and work through but, personally, I'm hoping you fix this."

"And stay." Derrick shrugged. "There, I said it."

"Carter has a business proposal for you guys concerning this estate," Jackson said.

The guy's world had been turned upside down and he managed to keep up with the conversation and offer insights. Carter had no idea how. He'd been shaken by the news he had more siblings and body slammed by the idea of being in love and spun up with anger about Hanna not talking to him…and now he wondered if his vulnerability on one front might have had something to do with his reaction to the other.

He could not find his footing at all.

"Good. If he fixes things with Hanna, we'll listen." Derrick ended the comment with a wink.

Carter was still reeling. But now that he'd had a moment to recover, he realized he'd made a misstep. His behavior hadn't risen to Eldrick levels, but he hadn't exactly been subtle or private in his condemnation. And he hadn't fought to keep Hanna here, with him. He'd made it so easy for her to leave him before he could leave her.

Thinking about all he needed to figure out and put back in order made his chest ache. "It's not that easy."

"Oh, it's not going to be easy." Derrick laughed at the thought. "But it will be worth it."

Jackson had gone quiet. He sat in the chair, looking into the distance.

"You okay?" Carter asked.

"No. It's unlikely I'll ever be okay again, but go."

Derrick nodded. "We'll babysit him."

Jackson let out what sounded like a groan. "Lucky me."

But there was one bright spot. Jackson might not see it, but Carter did. "We're family now."

The groan only grew louder.

Fifteen

Hanna stood over her duffel bag, knowing it was time. She'd opened it and thrown it on the bed. Next came the packing, and she had to do it. Despite all the flowery words and talk about her sticking around, she'd outstayed her welcome.

That scene at the house...

The information had needed to come out—for Carter, for Jackson, for everyone—but her delivery sucked. This seemed to be her thing. Have information and stumble into getting it to the people who needed it. She could still see their stunned expressions. The looks of shock and pain. And Carter's anger.

"Put the bag away unless you're packing to officially move in to the main house, which you need to do."

At the sound of Carter's voice, she turned around to find him lounging in the bedroom doorway. She'd seen that so many times over the last few weeks. He fit here. Always looked so comfortable in his skin, so sure.

But he'd told her that underneath it all he wasn't always so confident. The confession had sent her heart into a tailspin.

Looking at him now, it flipped right over.

That vulnerability and the way he expressed it softened her anger toward him. His words had been genuine. She was sure of that.

But right now, even though she loved him, she wanted to punch him.

"I'm leaving." She turned back to the bed. Her heartbeat raced and she quietly inhaled, trying to settle it down.

"No."

He walked around her and grabbed the duffel. "I can have Lynette or someone grab your stuff."

"What are you talking about?"

He hitched his finger in the direction of the living room. "Get that pretty butt of yours back up to the main house."

Pretty butt?

The ups and downs of being with him were killing her. "You've got to be kidding."

"I am done fighting with you, Hanna."

From the snap in his tone, she doubted that. Sounded like he had lots of fury he still needed to burn off. Well, no thank you.

"That would be nice."

He held up both hands as he walked across the room to the end of the bed. "My reaction to the bomb you dropped wasn't great. I'm sorry for that. I'll do better, but you have to meet me partway."

His presence filled the room. Everywhere she looked held a memory of him. Now she had the live version staring her down. "Meaning?"

"You weren't completely honest with me, and I get to be pissed off about that." He sat on the end of the bed and watched her. "It won't last long. You'll probably say something funny in an hour or two and the edge will fade. I predict by tonight, I'll be fine."

"You'll be fine?" She repeated the words but they still didn't make sense to her.

What is happening?

Here she was, packing and halfway out the door, and he was talking about their usual movie night. It was as if the last hour hadn't happened.

He stared at her. "You have spent this entire relationship holding things back—"

"I didn't—"

"And I let you get away with that. I admit, I have to take part of the responsibility here. But enough. When you do stuff like this, I get to be angry. That's how relationships work."

This sounded like a lecture. He'd morphed from angry to professor. She refused to find that sexy. The in control thing…okay, that was a bit sexy. But still. "We are not in a relationship."

He rested his palms on the mattress and leaned back. "Since I'm in love with you, we sure as hell better be."

"What?" Her brain stopped working.

His words, that sly smile. With every minute, a bit more of the Carter she was used to came back to her.

"Yeah, it stunned me, too." He sat up straight again. "Do you know how much grief I'm going to take from my brothers after all the jokes I made about them being sad and pathetic? From all three of them. Wow… I am never going to get used to that."

In the confusion and with the touch of excitement at seeing him walking through the door, she forgot about Jackson. "How is he?"

"Floundering. Horrified to be related to us, which is understandable."

Giving up on the packing and trying to follow the conversation, she sat down next to him. If this was it, she needed to be clear about one thing. "I really didn't know."

He shot her one of *those* looks. "Don't engage in verbal gymnastics. You should have told me what you guessed and I think you know that."

She wanted to argue, but he wasn't exactly wrong. Not telling had felt safer. Everything had been going well and unloading one more thing on Carter had seemed like too much. "Would you have performed a secret DNA test?"

"Maybe." Then he reached for her. Snagged her around the waist and settled her on his lap. "This okay?"

She winced as she wrapped her arms around his neck and held on. She didn't want to let go.

Ten minutes ago, she'd felt hollow and empty and thought she'd never have this again, and she wasn't about to miss it this time. "I didn't want to hurt him."

"He knows that. We all know that," he said as he rubbed a hand up and down her arm.

Okay, enough of that topic for now. "You said something about love?"

He held her a little tighter. "First, you need to know I'm still angry."

She nodded, but she couldn't fight the hope building inside her. She'd been slammed from one end of the spectrum to the other, ever since he'd shown up at her door weeks ago. Now her heartbeat kicked up again.

"Got it."

"But yes. I'm about two steps away from being irretrievably in love with you. Right now I'm *mostly* irretrievably in love with you."

She tried to swallow her smile. Tried and failed. "Two steps, huh?"

"If you keep things from me, it's going to take longer to get there."

She rolled her eyes at him because…really. "Okay, you made your point."

"Then get this." He kissed her cheek, then her chin. "You wind me up and spin me around. I love verbally sparring with you. I love the quiet times. I really love the bedroom stuff." He stopped and took a long breath. "But, mostly, I love you."

Her fingers slipped into his hair. She couldn't get close enough. "That's ridiculously romantic."

"I want you to stay here. Build the estate with me and help me win over my brothers."

That sounded so permanent. So much like a relationship, a commitment. She'd never dared to hope she'd find that with anyone. With Carter she'd been so careful to guard her heart. He'd talked about running in the past, but this sounded very different.

"What about your dad?"

Carter frowned. "We'll hope he reconciles with Beth and leaves the country."

"Poor Beth."

"I have a feeling we're going to be saying that a lot." His hand slipped up and under the hem of her shirt. "You make me want to set down roots, to be better."

"Carter."

"But there's one thing." His smile faded and he grew more serious. "I know there's a load of baggage between us that neither of us put there. We need to take some time and unpack it. I'm just asking that we do it together."

The last few minutes had been perfect. He'd opened up, confessed his feelings for her when he wasn't totally sure he'd intended to stick around. He took a risk; now she could, too.

He was stubborn and exasperating and so hot and as good as it got. So many amazing characteristics rolled into one. "I love you."

His eyebrow lifted. "You sure? I've been told I can be difficult."

"It doesn't seem to be something I can stop, no matter how grumpy you get."

He nodded as his hand continued to skim over her bare skin. "Ditto."

"What now?" She asked, but the fact that his fingers had started roaming gave her a clue.

"We make up."

She couldn't help but tease him since he looked so determined. "Didn't we just do that?"

"Formally."

"Oh, I see." She turned in his lap until she straddled his thighs. "This involves the bed, I presume."

He shrugged. "Those are the rules."

But one more thing.

When he leaned in to kiss her, she put her fingers over his lips. She wanted to be clear one last time. "I am sorry for not sharing more. I promise I'll work on it."

"We'll take our time."

"But you still want me to move in to the main house?" She'd live in a shoe, if he wanted to, but the main house was pretty spectacular. She still couldn't walk into a room without wanting to dust it, but she was pretty sure that sensation would go away at some point.

"Right after we formally make up."

There was that phrase again. She was a fan of the idea. "I like your priorities."

He shot her a sexy smile. "Well, I am the same guy you had a crush on as a teenager."

With a groan she dropped her forehead on his shoulder. "Am I ever going to live that down?"

"I plan to tease you for the next forty years."

Through the joking and the touching and all the talking, she heard the promise in his voice. With other men that might not mean much. With Carter, it meant everything.

She kissed him instead of answering. Let him feel her love and her commitment before lifting her head again. "I'm going to hold you to that."

"Forever."

Yeah, forever.

* * * * *

PLAYING
MR RIGHT

KAT CANTRELL

One

The building housing LeBlanc Charities felt the same as every other time Xavier had set foot in it—like he'd been banished. Despite sharing a last name with the founder, this was the last place he'd choose to be, which was too bad considering he'd been forced to walk through the door nearly every day for the last three months.

And would continue to do so for the next three months until this hell of an inheritance test drew to its conclusion. Xavier's father had devised a diabolical way to ensure his sons danced to his tune long after he'd died: Xavier and his brother, Val, had been required to switch places in order to receive their inheritances.

So the ten years Xavier had spent learning the ins and outs of LeBlanc Jewelers, plus the five years since he'd taken over the CEO chair and broken his back to please his father…none of that mattered. In order to get the five hundred million dollars he'd have sworn he'd already earned, Xavier had to pass one final test. But instead of being required to do something that made *sense*, the will stipulated that Xavier would become a fundraiser in Val's place at LeBlanc Charities and his brother would assume the reins of LeBlanc Jewelers.

Even three months after the fact, Xavier still foamed at the mouth if he let himself dwell on how unfair and impossible the terms were. His father had betrayed him, bottom line. While Xavier had been putting enormous energy into connecting with his dad and basking in the glow of being the favored son in blissful ignorance, Edward had been plotting to posthumously show his sons how much he really hated both of them.

In that, Xavier and Val were alike. It had been a surprisingly effective bonding experience for the brothers who shared similar faces and not much else. Though twins, they'd never been close, even choosing completely different paths as adults. Val had followed their mother into LeBlanc Charities and thrived. Xavier had gladly shucked off anything remotely resembling charity work in favor of the powerful CEO's office at one of the world's largest and most profitable diamond companies.

All for nothing.

The terms of the will had sliced off a huge piece of Xavier's soul and he'd yet to recover it.

Bitter did not begin to describe his feelings toward his father. But he used that bitterness as fuel. He would not fail at this test. Success was the best revenge, after all.

Xavier had swept into his new role at LBC with gusto…and despite his fierce need to ace his task, he still hadn't gotten his feet under him. It was like his father had stacked the deck against him, somehow. The problem was that the will stipulated Xavier had to raise ten million dollars in donations while doing Val's job. No easy feat. But he hadn't given up yet, nor would he.

Even at 6:00 a.m., LeBlanc Charities teemed with life. The food pantry operated seven days a week, fifteen hours a day. It was ludicrous. A huge waste of capital. Oftentimes, the volunteers reported that no guests had darkened the door of LBC during the early morning hours, yet they always kept the light on.

Changing the operational hours of the food pantry had been one of the first of many executive orders Xavier had come to regret. He'd changed them back, but Marjorie Lewis, the tiny general of a woman who had been a surprisingly effective services manager, had still quit. Sure, she'd told Val—her *real* boss, as she'd informed Xavier—that her mother had fallen ill with a long-term condition. But Xavier knew the truth.

She hated him.

Nearly everyone at LBC did, so that was at least consistent. The staff who reported to him at LeBlanc Jewelers—his *real* job, as he'd informed Marjorie—respected him. Did they like him? Who knew? And Xavier didn't care as long as they increased profits month over month.

LBC was *not* the diamond industry. No one here *owned* any diamonds, except for him, and he'd stopped wearing his Yacht-Master watch after the first day. Marjorie had pointed out, rather unkindly, that the people LBC helped would either assume it was fake, try to steal it or paint him with the ugly brush of insensitivity. Or all three.

Therefore, a five-hundred-thousand-dollar watch now sat in his jewelry box, unworn. Talk about a waste. But he'd left it there in hopes of garnering some of that mythical respect. Instead, he'd met brick wall after brick wall in the form of Marjorie, who had rallied the troops to hate him as much as she did. And then she'd quit, leaving Xavier holding the bag. Literally.

Yesterday, he'd worked in the food pantry, stocking shopping bags the hungry people LBC served could grab and go. The families took prepacked boxes. Once a day, LBC served a meal, but Xavier stayed out of the kitchen. Jennifer Sanders, the meal services manager, had that well under control and also agreed with the popular opinion that Val walked on water, so anything Xavier did paled in comparison.

Like he did every morning, Xavier retreated to his office. Val's office, really, but Xavier had redecorated. He'd ordered the walls painted and new furniture installed because if this was going to be his domain, it shouldn't remind him every second that Val had been here first—and done it better.

Xavier pushed around the enormous amount of paperwork that a charity generated until his brother popped through the door. Thank God. Xavier had started to wonder if Val would actually show up for their planned meeting about the missing services manager. After Marjorie stormed out, the majority of the day-to-day operations management fell to Xavier and that left precious little time to plan fundraisers that he desperately needed to organize.

Val had offered to help with the interview process, which had been a lifeline Xavier had gladly snagged, without telling his brother how much he needed that help. If the terms of his father's will had taught him anything, it was not to trust a soul, not even family.

"Sorry I'm late." Val strolled into his former office and made a face at the walls, flipping his too-long hair out of his eyes. "If you were going to paint, at least you could have picked a color other than puke green."

"It's sage. Which is soothing."

It was nothing of the sort and did not resemble the color swatch the decorator had showed him in the slightest. But Xavier had to live with it, apparently, because LBC didn't have a lot of extra money for frivolous things like painting. When he'd tried to use his own money, Marjorie had flipped out and cited a hundred and forty-seven reasons that was a bad idea. Mostly what he'd gotten out of her diatribe was that LBC had a negative audit in their rearview and thus had multiple microscopes pointed at their books.

Meaning Xavier needed to watch his step.

"Who do we have on tap today?" Val asked pleasantly as he sprawled in one of the chairs ringing the director's desk that Xavier sat behind.

No one was fooled by the desk. Xavier didn't direct much of anything. He would have claimed to be a smart man prior to this inheritance test, but LBC had slowly stripped away his confidence. At his normal job, he ran a billion-dollar company that was one of the most highly respected jewelry operations in the world. LeBlanc was synonymous with diamonds. He could point to triumph after triumph in his old world. This new one? Still Val's baby even though Xavier's brother was currently helming LeBlanc Jewelers with flair.

Xavier stopped his internal whining and picked up the single résumé on his desk. "After you ruled out the others, this is the only one. The candidate has experience similar to Marjorie's but with a women's shelter. So probably she's a no-go. I want someone with food-pantry experience."

"Well, that's your call." Val's tone held a tinge of disapproval, as if wanting someone with experience was the height of craziness. "Do you mind if I look at it?"

He handed the résumé to Val, who glanced over it, his lips pursed.

"This Laurel Dixon is the only new résumé you've got?" Val asked.

"From people who are remotely qualified, yeah. So far. I posted the job to the usual sites but we've had very little response."

Val pinched the bridge of his nose. "That's not good. I wonder if our little inheritance experiment has made the rounds. I would have expected more applicants, but if you've scared off all the candidates, I'm going to be in a world of hurt when I step back into my position here."

That stung, but Xavier didn't let it show. He never did. He'd learned to school his emotions at Edward LeBlanc's knee from an early age. CEOs didn't wear their hearts on their sleeves or they lost the respect of their workers. That lesson had served him well—until his father had upended everything in one fell swoop.

"This is not my fault," Xavier responded evenly, though Val's point wasn't lost on him. *Marjorie.* Again. He wouldn't put it past her to have poisoned the well of potential applicants, but there was no way to fix that now. "If you're going to blame anyone, blame Dad."

Val's expression didn't change as he waved the résumé. "We should interview this candidate. What other choice do you have? No one says you have to keep her if she doesn't work out."

"Fine."

Xavier picked up the phone and left a message at the number listed on the résumé. He didn't have time to argue the point or let his feelings get in a twist because Val was throwing his weight around. This was all temporary, and as Val had so eloquently pointed out, he'd be back in the saddle again soon, anyway. Little that Xavier did would make a difference in the long run.

Since they didn't have much regarding Marjorie's replacement to meet about, after all, Val apparently thought that was a license to ask a few barbed questions about how things were going operationally at LBC. They were interrupted by a brisk knock on the door.

Adelaide, the admin who had been a disciple of Marjorie's, poked her head into the office with a sweet smile for Val. If he hadn't seen it himself, Xavier wouldn't have believed she knew *how* to smile.

"There's a Laurel Dixon here to see you," she said. "About the position."

Xavier had called her less than thirty minutes ago and he'd said nothing about coming by. Only that he'd like to schedule an interview.

"No notice," he said quietly to Val. "That's a little bold, don't you think?"

It tripped his sixth sense and not in a good way. Downtown Chicago was not known for having great traffic patterns, so either she lived really close by or had already been on her way here.

Val raised his brows in challenge. "I'm already impressed. That's the kind of go-getting I like."

Of course he'd say that and manage to make it sound like Xavier was in the wrong at the same time. "I'd rather send her away and schedule a real interview. After I've had time to go over her qualifications."

"She's here." Val shrugged. "What's there to go over? If you're unsure, I'll do the talking."

"I can talk," Xavier fairly growled. "I just don't like surprises."

Or anyone stepping on his toes, which was what he got for stupidly mentioning to his brother that Marjorie's exodus had caught him sideways. Val had taken full advantage of that show of weakness, too, storming in here like a victorious hero and earning adoring glances from his staff.

Val just grinned and flipped hair out of his face in true slacker fashion. "I'm aware. Don't sweat it. I came by to handle this problem. Let me handle it."

When hell froze over. "We'll both interview her. Adelaide, show her in."

Val didn't even bother to move to another chair like a normal person would. You positioned yourself behind the desk as a show of authority. Val probably didn't even know how to spell authority. That's why his staff loved him, because he treated them all like equals. Except everyone was not equal. Someone had to be in charge, make the hard decisions.

And that person was Xavier, for better or worse. Val could step aside. This was still Xavier's office for three more months.

Laurel Dixon walked into the room and Xavier forgot about Val, LBC…his own name. Everything else in the world went dim. Except for her.

The woman following Adelaide looked nothing like Marjorie, that was for sure. She looked nothing like any woman Xavier had ever met. Long, lush sable-colored hair hung down her back, but that only held his attention for a split second. Her face was arresting, with piercing silvery-gray eyes that locked onto his and wouldn't let go.

Something otherworldly passed between them and it was so fanciful a feeling that Xavier shook it off instantly. He didn't do *otherworldly*, whatever the hell that even meant. Never had he used such a term in his life to describe anything. But nothing else fit, and that made the whole encounter suspect. Besides, it was ridiculous to have any sort of reaction to a woman outside of desire, and even that was rarely strong enough for Xavier to note. Most, if not all, of his encounters with females could be described as mildly pleasurable, at best.

This woman had *trouble* written all over her if she could elicit such a response by merely walking into a room.

Coupled with the fact that she'd shown up without an appointment—Laurel Dixon raised his hackles about ten degrees past uncomfortable.

"Ms. Dixon." Val stood and offered his hand. "I'm Valentino LeBlanc, the director of LBC."

"Mr. LeBlanc. Very nice to meet you," she said, her clean voice vibrating across Xavier's skin with a force he couldn't shake.

He'd have said he preferred sultry voices. Sexy ones that purred when aroused. Laurel Dixon's voice could never be described as carnal, but that didn't seem to matter. He instantly wanted to hear it again. It was the kind of voice he could listen to for an hour and never get bored.

This was supposed to be an interview. Not a seduction. Actually, he'd never been seduced before, at least, not that he could recall. Usually he was the one making all the moves and he wasn't all that keen to be on the receiving end with a woman who wasn't even supposed to be here.

"Xavier LeBlanc," he announced and cleared his inexplicably ragged throat. "Current director of LBC. Val is just passing through."

She flicked her attention from Val to Xavier. This was the part where he had to stand and stick his hand out. Laurel Dixon clasped it, and when no lightning bolts forked between them, he relaxed an iota. That's when he made the mistake of letting his gaze rest on her lips. They curved up into a smile and *that* kicked him in the gut so hard, he felt it in his toes. Yanking his hand free, he sank back into his chair, wondering when, exactly, he'd lost his marbles.

"Two for the price of one," she said with a laugh that was just as arresting as her face. "I applaud the fact that you have such different hairstyles. Makes it easier to tell you apart."

Automatically he ran a hand over his closely cropped hair. He wore it that way because it looked professional. The style suited him and the fact that Val's too-long hair marked him as the rebel twin only worked in Xavier's favor. "Val gets lost on the way to the barber."

Despite the fact that he hadn't meant it as a joke, that made her laugh again, which pretty much solidified his resolve to stop talking. The less she laughed like that, the better.

"We weren't expecting you," Val said conversationally and indicated the seat next to him, then waited until Laurel slid into it before taking his own. "Though we're impressed with your enthusiasm. Right, Xavier?"

Figured that the second after he'd vowed to shut his mouth, Val dragged him right back into the conversation.

"That's one way to put it," he muttered. "I would have liked to schedule an interview."

"Oh, well, of course that would have been the appropriate thing to do," she admitted with an eye roll that shouldn't have been as appealing as it was. "But I'm so very interested in the job that I didn't want to leave anything to chance. So I thought, why wait?"

Why, indeed? "What about directing a food pantry excites you so much?"

"Oh, all of it," she answered quickly. "I love to help people in need and what better way than through one of the most basic fundamentals? Food is a necessity. I want to feed people."

"Well said," Val murmured.

Since his brother could have written that speech word for word, Xavier wasn't surprised he'd been moved by her passion. It sounded a little too memorized to Xavier's ear, and his gut had been screaming at him from the moment he'd first handed Val Laurel Dixon's résumé.

Something about her was off. He didn't like her. Nor did he like the way she unsettled him. If he had to constantly brace himself to be in her presence, how could they work together?

"Your experience is on the sparse side," Xavier said and tapped the résumé between them. "What did you do at the women's shelter that will segue into a services manager at a food pantry?"

Laurel launched into a well-rehearsed spiel about her role, highlighting her project management skills, and wrapped it up by getting into a spirited back-and-forth with Val about some of her ideas for new outreach.

His brother was sold on Laurel Dixon. Xavier could tell. Val had smiled through the entire exchange. Sure enough, after the candidate left, Val crossed his arms and said, "She's the one."

"She is so not the one."

"What? Why not?" Val dismissed that with a wave without waiting for an answer. "She's perfect."

"Then you hire her. In three months. I'm still in charge here and I say I want a different candidate."

"You're being stubborn for no reason," Val shot back, and some of the goodwill that had sprung up between them as they navigated the Great Inheritance Switch—

as Xavier had been calling it in his head—began to slide away.

His caution had nothing to do with stubbornness and he had plenty of reasons. "She's got no experience."

"Are you kidding? Everything she did at the women's shelter translates. Maybe not as elegantly as you might like, but you only have to deal with her for three months. After that, I'll be the one stuck with her if she's the wrong candidate. Humor me."

Xavier crossed his arms. "There's something not quite right about Laurel Dixon. I can't put my finger on it. You didn't sense that, too?"

"No. She's articulate and enthusiastic." The look Val shot him was part sarcasm and part pity. "Are you sure you're not picking up on the fact that she's not an emotionless robot like you?"

Ha. As if he hadn't heard that one before. But obviously Val had no clue about what really went on beneath Xavier's skin. Xavier just had a lot of practice at hiding what was going on inside. Edward LeBlanc had frowned on weakness, and in his mind, emotions and weakness went hand in hand.

"Yeah, that must be it."

Val rolled his eyes at Xavier's refusal to engage. "This is not the corporate world. We don't hire people based on how well they rip apart their prey here in nonprofit land. You need someone to replace Marjorie, like, yesterday. Unless you have a line of other options hidden away in the potato closet, you've got your new hire."

The damage was done. Now Xavier couldn't readily discount Laurel Dixon as a candidate, though the barb had hit its mark in a wholly different way than Val probably even realized. No, this wasn't the corporate world and his raging uncertainty might well be rearing its ugly head here.

His father had done a serious number on him with this switcheroo. Xavier was only just coming to realize how many chunks of his confidence were missing as a result. How much of his inability to take an applicant at face value had to do with that?

Everything was suspect as a result.

"I'll deal with Laurel Dixon if that pleases your majesty," he told Val. "But I'm telling you up front. I don't trust her. She's hiding something and if it comes back to bite you, I'm going to remind you of this conversation."

Odds were good it was going to come back to bite Xavier long before it affected Val, who would leave to go back to the world of sane, logical, corporate politics in a few minutes. Xavier, on the other hand, would be working side by side for the next three months with a new services manager who made his skin hum when he looked at her.

He had a feeling he'd be spending a lot of time avoiding Laurel Dixon in order to protect himself, because that was what he did. No one was allowed to get under his skin and no one got an automatic place on Xavier's list of people he trusted.

Hopefully she liked hard work and thrived on opportunities to prove herself. Xavier was going to give her both.

Two

When Laurel Dixon had decided to go undercover at the LeBlanc Charities food pantry to investigate claims of fraud, she maybe should have picked a different position than services manager. Who would have thought they'd actually hire her, though?

They were supposed to admire her enthusiasm and give her a lesser position. One that gave her plenty of access to the people she needed to interview on the down low and plenty of time to do it. Instead, she'd been handed the keys to the kingdom—which should have put her in a great place to dig into LBC's books. Donors needed to know that LBC wasn't on the up-and-up, that they were only pretending to help people in need while the thieves lined their own pockets.

Except thus far she'd had zero time to even think about how to expose the charity's fraudulent practices.

Of course, a lot of that had to do with one infuriating man named Xavier LeBlanc.

Just because he arrived at LBC at the ungodly hour of 6:00 a.m. and worked through lunch didn't mean the rest of the world had to do the same. But they'd all done it, Laurel included, though she didn't suffer from the same sense of anxiety the other staffers seemed to feel around their interim boss.

But what was she supposed to do, stroll in at nine and draw attention to herself? She'd taken this job under false pretenses. And she couldn't back out now.

Ugh. This was what she got for trying a whole different approach to investigative reporting. This was supposed to be her big breakthrough story. The one that would fix her reputation in the industry while appealing to her sense of fair play and her drive to help people at the same time. If she went undercover, surely she could get the facts for the exposé, and this time, there would be no embarrassing counter-story exposing the lack of foundation for her accusations.

Embarrassing and nearly career killing. Thanks to social media shares and the eternal stores of video, her blunder would never be forgotten. But she could give her audience something else to play with. As long as she didn't make a single mistake with this investigation. When she blew the whistle on LBC, it would be career *making.* A triumph that would erase the mistakes of her last investigation.

Or so she'd laid out in a foolproof mental plan that ended up having a remarkable number of holes.

Instead, she'd spent her first few hours on the job following Adelaide around as the admin explained how Xavier envisioned things working around LBC—and how fast he expected Laurel to get it that way. Apparently, the old manager, Marjorie, had left operations in a bit of disarray when she'd left, but Mr. LeBlanc couldn't be bothered to tell her his expectations himself.

At one o'clock, she'd had enough.

Feigning hunger and fatigue, she begged off from Adelaide's cheerful tour of the facility and bearded the lion in his den. She didn't mind hard work, but only if there was a distinct payoff, and so far, she hadn't seen one. It was time to shake things up.

Xavier LeBlanc glanced up at her sharp knock, his deep blue eyes registering not one iota of surprise or curiosity—nothing. It was a great trick, one she wished she knew how to replicate. It would come in handy as she pretended she knew what the hell she was doing at this new gig.

In lieu of that, she'd settle for a mentor who could give her the insight she needed.

"Got a minute?" she asked and didn't wait for the answer. He would see her whether he liked it or not. How was she supposed to figure out who was responsible for the fraud inside these walls if she didn't keep the man in charge very, very close?

His gaze tracked her as she waltzed right into his office with confidence. He seemed like the type who wouldn't appreciate a mousey approach.

"What can I do for you?" he asked, his sinfully sexy voice rumbling in his chest.

She missed a step. His sexiness quotient really shouldn't be something she noticed. At all. Xavier LeBlanc wasn't allowed to be sexy. He was her boss and she'd been hired based on a lie. One she'd told with good reason, and all of the experience on her résumé was real. But still.

None of that equaled free rein to be attracted to the man behind the desk. And none of that stopped her insides from quivering as his gaze slid down her face to her mouth. He'd done that in the interview more than once and she'd blown it off then. She thought she'd been mistaken. That they'd been stray looks that didn't mean anything. She'd imagined it.

Today? Punch in the girl parts.

She could no more pretend it hadn't happened than she could ignore it. Did Xavier have any clue how unsettling it was to have a man who looked like him slide his gaze to your mouth as if he couldn't decide how to kiss you? Not if. *How.* Because it was happening and he wanted you to anticipate it.

Okay, she had to ignore that. She had a job. Two jobs. Neither were going to go well if she didn't pull it together. Besides, he hadn't done or said anything inappropriate. Likely she was still imagining it.

"Adelaide is a sweet lady," Laurel began. "But I don't get the impression she's fully communicating your vision as well as I would hope. Would it be possible for you to be a little more hands-on?"

In a totally nonpervy way, of course, she added silently as the atmosphere in the room went dead still. Totally could have phrased that better. More professional. Less *I want you on this desk right now.*

Xavier's eyebrows lifted a fraction. "What, exactly, are you asking me to do?"

Oh, man. Surely he didn't mean for that to sound as leading as it did. But then, she'd started it. Was he expecting her to finish it?

Her mind immediately filled in those blanks with several things she could ask him to do. Curiosity was both her strength and her biggest weakness, and she almost never hesitated to investigate things she was dying to know, like whether Xavier's shoulders felt as strong and broad as they looked and how he planned to kiss her.

Of course, she'd never say that out loud. She couldn't. Well, okay, she totally *could* and she had a feeling Xavier would deliver. But she wouldn't. It was highly unethical, for more reasons than one.

But she couldn't get the sudden and sharp images out of her head of what might happen if she did take the hint in his voice and really laid out what she might like. Nothing wrong with a little harmless fantasizing about a sexy man, was there?

"I, um…" *Voice too husky. Not professional. Focus.* She cleared her throat. "It's my first day. I was hoping you and I might talk about your expectations."

Good. That didn't sound like the lead-in to a seduction scene at all.

"I expect you to manage the operations of this charity," he said succinctly. "Nothing more, nothing less."

"I got that part." Sexy, but either Xavier was obtuse or he had way more confidence in her than he had a right to. "But this is your vision I'm executing. I don't know anything about you or your ideas for how things should work. Tell me what my typical day should look like."

Xavier lifted his hands from the keyboard of his laptop and laced them together in a deliberately precise gesture that had the mark of a man demonstrating his patience. His hands were strong and capable, with long lean fingers that she had to stop envisioning on her body.

"That's what I asked Adelaide to do. If she's failing to—"

"No, no." *God*, no. The last thing she'd intended to do was put a spotlight on Adelaide. The poor woman probably had nightmares about Xavier as it was. "She's great. Very helpful. But I want to hear it straight from you. We're going to be working very closely together, after all."

"We're doing nothing of the kind. I hired you to be invisible and ensure that I never have to think about the operations of this place."

Oh. That was not going to work. Laurel leaned forward and laced her own hands together near the edge of the desk, mirroring his pose. "See, that's exactly that sort of thing that Adelaide could never convey. She showed me where departments are and introduced me to people. But I need the mind of Xavier LeBlanc to mesh with mine so we're in sync. Tell me what you'd do. That's the best way to ensure you don't have to think about things, because I will instantly know how you'd want something handled."

And that philosophy had the added bonus of filling in the gaps of her skill set, not to mention allowing her to grill him on how much he knew about the fraud. Her sources had been volunteers in the food pantry and they had given her several credible tips about substitutions that didn't make it into the books, among other things. What she already knew was likely the tip of the iceberg. In her line of work, there was always more to discover.

But she needed to know how high up it went, if Xavier knew about it or if this strange and unexplained switch between the brothers had removed the real culprit from LBC.

Maybe the mysterious switch had its roots in the fraud. She had to know.

At the same time, she couldn't make mistakes. If Xavier's brother had spearheaded or approved the fraud, she had to find proof. Of course, it could have started with Xavier's reign, which added to the complexity of the in-

vestigation. It was a wrinkle she hadn't seen coming but
adhering to Xavier's directive to be "invisible" wasn't
going to reveal even a tiny slice of what she needed to
uncover.

Xavier's gaze skittered over hers again and she had the
distinct impression he didn't quite know what to do with
her. Good. An off-kilter man spilled secrets he meant to
keep close to the vest. She relaxed a smidgen. This undercover business couldn't be too hard. Or, rather, she
couldn't allow it to be. This story was too important to
the people LBC should be serving instead of cheating.
The story was too important to her career.

"Here's what I want, Ms. Dixon." His low voice snaked
through her and she tried really hard not to react, but she
didn't have his ability to be stone-faced. Neither did he
miss her reaction, absorbing it with a long, slow pause
laden with things unsaid. "I want you to ensure LBC op-
erates smoothly enough that I can focus on fundraising.
Outside of that, I don't care what you do."

She blinked. "Sure you do. You're in charge. Everything flows uphill, right?"

That was the core of an investigative reporter's philosophy, the one they taught in Digging for Facts 101.
Follow the money. The guy in the corner office was always the place to start because he made all the decisions.
If anything illegal was going on, it usually went all the
way to the top.

Of course, this situation had the added layer of the
guy at the top not being the normal guy. All at once, she
hoped Xavier would be in the clear and she'd instead be
taking down his brother. Which would be a shame, because she'd genuinely liked Val.

She couldn't let her personal feelings compromise the

investigation, as they had in her last story. She couldn't afford to *like* anyone in this situation.

"Indeed it does," Xavier finally said.

His gaze still hadn't left hers, and if she hadn't known better, she'd have thought he might be fighting some of the same attraction she was. Surely he had his pick of women. He wasn't trying to be sexy as a come-on; it was just a natural part of who he was and she didn't for a second think he'd turned it on specifically for her.

"Great, then we're on the same page. You're in charge and I'm here to execute your orders. What would you like me to do first?"

"Explain why it seems like you're flirting with me."

Laurel's lungs seized and she choked on a breath. Tears leaked from her eyes as she coughed, and if she was really lucky, mascara streaks were even now forming below her lashes.

"What?" she asked when she recovered. "I'm not flirting with you."

If anything, he was the one exuding all the come-hither vibes. At times, it was so strong, she was barely hanging on by the fingernails.

His implacable expression didn't change. "Good. It would be a bad idea to get involved."

Oh, well, *that* was a telling statement. Not "You're not my type." Not "You've mistaken me for a heterosexual." *Bad idea to get involved.* That meant he felt all the sizzle, too.

Interesting.

How much closer could she get to Xavier LeBlanc and would that benefit her story? Or simply benefit *her*? The man knew his way around an orgasm—she could tell. And while this exposé lay at the pinnacle of her personal goals, she couldn't help but want to investigate her reaction to Xavier as a man.

She had a core-deep desire to *know* things, and at this moment, Xavier topped the list.

"A bad, bad idea," she repeated and crossed her fingers behind her back. "I solemnly swear that I will refrain from all double entendres, loaded statements and anything that could be construed as flirting while you and I are working so closely together."

"I didn't say we'd be working closely together," he corrected, and all at once she wondered what it would take to get him well and truly rattled to the point of revealing something unintended.

If she hoped to dig up enough dirt for an exposé, she'd have to figure it out. Everyone had their tipping point and people had spilled secrets to her in the past, often before realizing it. Usually that happened after she'd gained a measure of their trust, though.

How ethical was it to seduce it out of someone? She'd never tried that particular method before and there was no way to deny the idea excited her. Which meant it really was a bad idea. But still viable. She needed more information before fully committing.

"Oh, come on. We just hashed that out. You're in charge, I'm here to do exactly what you say but not sexually and we're both going to ignore the chemistry. Where, exactly, did I lose you, Mr. LeBlanc?"

At that, he actually laughed, and the heavy, rich sound did flippy things to her insides. His deep blue eyes speared her and she got all caught up in him in a very nonprofessional way. Yeah, there might not be a whole lot of choice in the matter and she might not be the one doing the seducing. It was delicious to contemplate, either way.

"I'm not lost. Just…reassessing," he said.

"That sounds promising. Why don't you share your vision with me, at least, and we'll take it from there?"

"Vision for what?"

He'd leaned into the space between them and she was having a hard time concentrating. Xavier had a very potent presence that had latched onto her skin in a wholly disturbing way. "For, um, LBC. As a charity. What's the vision? Mission statement? That kind of thing."

"Feed people," he stated bluntly. "What more is there?"

"A lot. At the shelter, our goal was to give women back some control in their lives. Provide them with choices. The shelter part was just one of the mechanisms we employed."

That had been satisfying work, even as a means to an end as she put herself through college. Sure, she'd had to fudge the dates a little on her résumé and leave off the last few years of employment so no one knew she'd worked for a news channel—which had subsequently fired her. But her drive to help people through knowledge hadn't changed. She still believed in the value of nonprofit organizations, particularly those that served people at the poverty line.

That's why it was so important to expose the fraud here. The money funneling through this organization should go to the people who came through the doors in need, not toward lining someone's pocket because they saw an easy way to skim profits.

Xavier's face turned to granite, which was his default more often than not. "You seem to forget I'm just filling in. This is not my normal world."

All at once, the information she craved had nothing to do with LBC and everything to do with Xavier LeBlanc himself. He was such a fascinating puzzle who gave very little away. She wanted to unlock him in the worst way. "But your brother mentioned that your mother started this charity fifteen years ago. Surely you've been involved to some degree."

"What you see is the sole extent of my involvement." He waved at the desk. "This is where I'll sit for three more months, and in that time I need to hold the best fundraiser this place has ever had. Mission statements are not my concern."

She blinked, but his expression didn't change. He was serious. Okay, wow.

"You're going to have a very big problem, then. People don't give money to fundraisers. They give to a cause they believe in. Your job is to make them believe in it. Don't you think that in a city like Chicago there are a hundred—a *thousand*—places for people to donate? How do they decide? You help them decide by passionately pitching your mission statement to them."

"I'll take that under advisement." In the long pause, they stared at each other without blinking. "You've done fundraising before. Did you apply for the wrong position here?"

Yes. Yes, she had.

That was all the opening she needed to segue this potential disaster into something more her speed. "Perhaps, but only because you posted a job opening for the wrong position. Sounds like you need someone in your back pocket to tell you what to do, not the other way around. Were you not aware that you have serious deficiencies in your operating philosophy?"

Xavier leaned back in his chair as his gaze narrowed. "Can I be honest with you, Ms. Dixon?"

Oh, God, yes. Please spill all your secrets, Mr. LeBlanc.

"Only if you call me Laurel."

His lips lifted into a brief smile that she fully expected meant he was about to argue with her. But he didn't. "Laurel, then. You need to understand what's happening here and I'm choosing to trust you, which is not something I do lightly."

His tone or his smile or her own conscience tripped something inside. Guilt plowed through her stomach out of nowhere. It was one thing to dig deep enough to learn someone's secrets when they were scamming, but she had no evidence Xavier was even involved in the fraud. What if her investigation caused problems for him?

Ugh, she was getting way ahead of herself. Her sources were credible and if there was something to uncover, Xavier would likely be happy that she'd done so. It was a public service, really. Surely he'd respect that.

"I'll do my best to be worthy of that trust."

He nodded once. "Then I have a confession. I am not well versed in how to run a charity. I do need help."

She very nearly rolled her eyes. This was him being honest? "I already figured that out."

"I'm doing my best to keep that nugget of truth from the rest of the staff," he said wryly. "Which is why I try to stay out of their areas of expertise. That's where you come in."

"I hear you. You want to hide out here in the office while everyone else does the dirty work." She stared him down as his eyebrows came together. "Too bad. You signed up to run LBC. Now do it. I'll help. We'll be partners."

She stuck out her hand and waited. She needed him, whether she liked it or not. Whether *he* liked it or not. And the reverse was also clearly true. They would do this together or not at all. If she had a partner, the less chance she had of screwing up.

Xavier let her sweat it for about thirty seconds and then reluctantly reached out to clasp her hand for a very long beat that neither of them mistook for a simple handshake. There was too much electricity, too much unsaid for that.

The less she let him focus on that, the better.

Three

Partners.

That was a concept Xavier liked a whole lot, given his distinct impression that Laurel Dixon was hiding something. He liked it even better that she'd been the one to suggest working together. The closer he kept her, the easier it would be to keep an eye on her.

He trusted her about as much as he'd trust a convicted car thief with the keys to his Aston Martin.

But he also understood that his lack of trust wasn't specific to Laurel. If he really wanted to get honest about it, his inability to stop being both suspicious and cautious had probably been at least half of Marjorie's problem with him. That's why he'd thought a hands-off approach with the new services manager might work best. Not to mention the fact that he couldn't shake that weird, misty feeling that sprang up inside whenever he was in the same room with Laurel Dixon. He'd hoped to avoid examining that by staying away from her.

Ms. Dixon had blown that plan to smithereens.

Jury was still out on how much wreckage he'd have to step over. Especially given the instant and volatile chemistry between them, which he'd been wholly prepared to pretend didn't exist until she'd so eloquently refused to let him. So that was a thing. The next three months should be incredibly taxing and exceedingly painful, then.

"Partners. What happens next?" Xavier asked Laurel once he'd dropped her hand, though the severed contact didn't eliminate the buzzing awareness arcing between them at all.

Not that he'd expected it to. Regardless of what he called the vibe between them, it wasn't going away. The trick was managing it. Which meant it would be a bad idea to touch her again, and of course, that was all he could think about.

"Follow me."

She slid from the seat she'd perched in when she first came into his office and glanced over her shoulder, perhaps to ensure he was doing as she commanded. As if he'd miss a second of whatever she had up her sleeve. Not likely.

Xavier trailed her to the receptionist's desk. Adelaide's eyes widened behind her bifocals as they approached and taut lines appeared around the woman's mouth. He nearly growled at her just to see if she'd actually come out of her skin. What good was it to have people afraid of him if he couldn't have fun with it occasionally?

Before he could try it, Laurel flipped a lock of her long sable-colored hair behind her back. "Today is your lucky day, Addy. You're in charge from now on. Mr. LeBlanc has given you a promotion."

"I did not. *Oof.*" Laurel's elbow glanced off his ribs,

leaving a sharp, smarting circle of *shut up* below his heart. "I mean…yeah. What Laurel said."

Adelaide's wide-eyed gaze flitted back and forth between the two of them as if she couldn't quite get her bearings. He knew the feeling.

"That's very generous, Mr. LeBlanc," she squeaked. "But I don't understand. A promotion?"

"Exactly." Laurel beamed so brightly, Xavier could see the rays from his position behind her. "To Services Manager. You're going to take Marjorie's place."

Wait, what? That was going a little far. If Adelaide had been remotely qualified or interested in the position, she would have applied for it the second the job posting had gone up. What, exactly, was Laurel up to?

"Are you sure about this?" he muttered in Laurel's ear and caught her elbow a hairbreadth from his ribs, holding it tight just in case she was stronger than she looked.

Clearly she had a plan and intended for Xavier to follow it. The elbow to the ribs indicated that if he wanted to have a conversation about her tactics, she'd indulge him later.

"You know everything about this place, Adelaide. Tell Mr. LeBlanc," Laurel instructed with a nauseating amount of cheer. "You gave me such a thorough tour of the place that I thought it would never end. There's not a nook or cranny at LBC that you don't have some sort of insight into. Is there?"

Obediently, Adelaide shook her head. "No, ma'am. I've been here seven years and started in the kitchen as a volunteer. I love every last board and nail in this place."

"I could tell." Laurel jerked her head at Xavier. "Mr. LeBlanc was just bemoaning the fact that he didn't have anyone to help organize a fundraiser that LBC so desperately needs."

Oh, dear God. That was not what he'd said. *At all*. But before he could correct the grievous misrepresentation that gave everyone the impression he was being a big baby about the tasks laid out for him, Laurel rushed on.

"I figured, this is Addy's opportunity to really make a difference. Step up and show us all what she's made of. You just do what Marjorie did and that'll leave me free to help Mr. LeBlanc get some money flowing in. Are you good with that?"

When Adelaide smiled and clapped her hands like she'd just been given the biggest Christmas present, Xavier's mouth fell open. Hastily, he closed it before anyone figured out that Laurel Dixon had just shocked the hell out of him. He didn't shock easily, and it was even harder to remember the last time he'd been unable to control his expression.

The two women went back and forth on the logistics for a furious couple of minutes until Xavier couldn't take it any longer.

"So, that's it?" he interrupted. "Adelaide, you can do what Marjorie did and everyone's good with that?"

Both women swiveled to stare at him. Laurel raised a brow. "Sorry, did we lose you again? Yes. Adelaide is in charge. She'll do a fantastic job."

Xavier should have asked more questions back in his office, like whether *partner* meant something different where Laurel had come from. When she'd thrown out the idea that they'd be working closely together, he'd reassessed his idea of how their interaction might go. And he'd come to the conclusion that perhaps she *could* come to him for approval on the budget, or maybe to get his help vetting new volunteers. That sort of thing.

He had not once suggested that she sign herself up to take over his inheritance test. That was *his*. He needed to prove to his father—and himself—that he could and would handle anything the old man threw at him. Ten million dollars was a cheap price to pay in order to get back on even ground, regain his confidence and lose the edge of vulnerability he'd been carrying since the reading of the will.

No one was allowed to get in the way of that.

"Excuse us, please," he said to Adelaide through gritted teeth.

Pulling Laurel back into his office, he shut the door and leaned on it, half afraid she'd find a way to open it again despite the hundred and seventy-five pounds of man holding it shut.

Instantly, he realized his mistake.

Laurel's presence filled the room, blanketing him with that otherworldly, mystical nonsense that he couldn't think through.

"What the hell was all that about?" he demanded and couldn't find a shred of remorse at how rough it came out. "You shuffled off all your duties to Adelaide—without asking, by the way. What, exactly, are you going to be doing?"

"Helping you, of course." She patted his arm and the contact sang through his flesh clear to the bone. "We have a fundraiser to organize. Which I'm pretty sure is what I just said."

The trap had been laid so neatly that he still hadn't quite registered whether the teeth had closed around his ankle or not. "You don't have enough experience fundraising."

She shrugged. "I do have *some*. What's your hang-up about experience? Adelaide doesn't have any experience." She accompanied that statement with air quotes. "But she's been learning on the job for years by following Marjorie around. She'll do great."

"Running a charity takes an iron fist," he shot back instantly. "Not an owl face and a lot of head nodding."

Laurel just laughed. "Owl face? Better not let her hear that. Women who wear glasses don't take kindly to name-calling."

"I didn't mean—" The headache brewing behind his eyes spread to his temples. "I called her an owl because she just stands there and looks wise. Instead of telling people what to do. I— Never mind."

Laurel Dixon had officially driven him around the bend. And now Adelaide had just been given a promotion that she seemed super pleased with. He couldn't take it away, though likely he'd have to spend a lot of time following *her* around to make sure she didn't drive operations into the ground. Hiring Laurel had been one thing, because at least he could blame that on Val if it didn't work out, but this was a whole other mess.

One he had no graceful way of undoing without upsetting the admin. Or Laurel, who might do God knew what as her next trick.

"Okay. Fine," he ground out. "Adelaide is Marjorie. She's going to be great. You're going to help with fundraising. Are you going to be great, too?"

"Of course."

She flipped a lock of hair over her shoulder again, and he couldn't help but wonder why she wore it down when her hands were constantly fiddling with it. She should wear it up. Then he wouldn't be tempted to put his own hands through it just to see if it felt as satiny and lush as it looked.

He crossed his arms. No point in tempting fate. "Fantastic. What's the plan, General?"

"Nicknames already?" Her long eyelashes swept her cheeks as she treated him to a very long, pointed once-over that lingered in inappropriate places. "I thought that wouldn't happen until much later in our association. Under…different circumstances."

In bed, she meant. The implication was clear. And he definitely shouldn't be feeling the spark of her suggestion in those inappropriate places. "It fit. Can't help it."

"Don't worry. I like it." The atmosphere in the office got a whole lot heavier as she stared at him. "And I like that you've already clued in that I don't sit around and wait for things to happen to me."

"I knew that a half second after Adelaide told me you were here for an interview that I hadn't arranged," he told her bluntly. "You're an easy read."

Something flitted through her gaze. A shadow. He couldn't put his finger on what she had going on beneath the surface, but that gut-deep feeling told him again she had something to hide.

How many secrets might she spill if he did take her into his bed?

Once that thought formed, he couldn't stop thinking about it. He wasn't like that, not normally. But Laurel had barreled right through what he'd call his *normal* and redefined everything. Maybe he needed to return the favor.

"I'm pretty transparent," she agreed readily, but another layer dropped into place over her expression.

She was a terrible liar. Or perhaps he was just incredibly tuned in to her, which didn't seem to have a downside. Other than the one where he'd just been boxed into a corner and had no graceful way to avoid spending a lot of time in her company.

"I probably see more than you'd like," he told her, and she blinked. This was a fun game. "For example, I'm pretty sure that you just maneuvered yourself into a position as my fundraising assistant because you can't stay away from me."

He didn't believe that for a second, but he definitely wanted to hear what she'd say to counter it.

Her eyebrows inched up toward her hairline and she relaxed an iota. "Well, that's a provocative statement. What if I said it's true?"

Then she'd be lying again. She had a whole other agenda, one he hadn't figured out yet, but if she wanted to work it like the attraction between them got top billing, he could play along. "I'd say we have a problem, then. We can't get involved. It would be too…sticky."

Her lips curved at his choice of words, as intended. "That's a shame. I'm a fan of sticky."

"Stickiness is for candy." All at once, a very distinct image sprang into his head of her on his desk naked with a caramel melting on her tongue. His whole body went stiff. "I like it best when things are uncomplicated."

At that, she snorted, moving in to lay a hand on his arm in the exact opposite of what this back-off conversation had been intended to convey. He'd wanted to catch her off guard but so far she'd held her own.

Reluctant admiration for this woman warred with bone-deep desire and flat-out irritation.

"Please," she muttered with a sarcastic grin as she squeezed his forearm. "You're the least uncomplicated man I've ever met. At least do me the courtesy of being honest about the fact that you're not attracted to me, if that's what's going on."

Oh, nicely played. She'd put the ball firmly in his court. He could take the out and claim he didn't feel the heavy arousal that she could almost assuredly see for herself, giving her the opportunity to call him out as a liar.

Or he could admit that she made him hotter than asphalt in a heat wave and call a truce.

He went with option three: ensuring she fully understood he didn't dance to her tune.

"I don't think honesty is on the table here. Do you?"

The atmosphere splintered as she stiffened, but to her credit, she kept a smile on her face. "Touché. We'll go back to ignoring the chemistry, then."

"That's best." And not at all what he'd been talking about, but he also hadn't expected her to voluntarily blurt out her secrets. All in good time. "Now, about this fundraiser…"

"Oh, right." Her hand dropped away from his arm—finally—and she got a contemplative look as if she really had given away her job with the intent of diving into his hell with gusto. "We should attend someone else's fundraiser and take notes."

"That's—" he blinked "—a really good idea."

One he should have thought of. That's what he'd do in the diamond trenches. If another jewelry outlet had a strategy he liked, he'd study it. Why not apply the same to charity?

Laurel smiled, putting some sparkle in her silver-gray eyes. "I'll start researching some possibilities and then we'll take a field trip."

Fantastic. If he couldn't stay away from Laurel, then he'd settle for spending as much time in her company as he could until he figured out her agenda. If it was merely to indulge in their impossible-to-ignore chemistry, then he might find a way to be on board with that, as long as he could protect what was his at the same time.

Jury was still out on just how difficult she'd make it.

Four

By Friday, Adelaide had Xavier's vote of confidence. She really had been studying at Marjorie's side for quite some time, showing off a deep knowledge of all things LBC, and she made sound decisions without a lot of deliberation. The staff responded to her as if she'd always been in charge, and he liked her style.

Not that he'd tell her that. She managed to convey a fair amount of dislike for him with pretty much every word out of her mouth and sometimes without saying anything at all. It was impressive.

But it felt like LBC was running smoothly for the first time in forever. Since Marjorie had dropped her set of keys on his desk with a clank and turned on her heel. Maybe even before that. So he gave Adelaide a pass on the disdain. She didn't have to like him as long as she did her job so he could do his. Or, at least, pretend to do his until he figured out how to turn the tide in his favor.

Laurel poked her head through his partially opened office door, sable hair swinging. "Why am I not surprised to find you behind your desk?"

"Because this is where I work?" he offered blithely.

In the week since he and Laurel had become "partners," he'd learned that he had almost no shot at responding to a question like that to her satisfaction. He'd given up trying and went with the most obvious answer.

She made a noise with her tongue that could easily be mistaken for a ticking clock. "Because you're hiding now that Addy has it all under control, more likely."

He lifted a shoulder. "Must not be hiding well enough. You found me."

"I was looking for you." The rest of her body followed her head as she slid through the cracked door uninvited. "Probably I'm the only one who is, though."

"For a reason, one would hope," he shot back pointedly before she launched into yet another discussion about how he could do more to interact with the staff. Laurel's job had somehow morphed from Services Manager to Fundraising Assistant to Xavier's Keeper. He hadn't figured out yet how to veer her back into something a little less invasive. "I am actually doing paperwork."

If staring at paperwork counted, then it wasn't so much of a lie. Otherwise, he'd stopped doing paperwork an hour ago and instead had been stewing about the latest fundraising numbers.

He was short. A lot. He had less than three months to raise north of seven million dollars and the near impossibility of the task writhed in his stomach like a greasy eel. As a result, he'd spent a lot of time sorting through fundraising ideas on his own, which was something he'd outsource to Laurel over his dead body.

The trick was engaging her enough so that she *thought*

she'd snowed him into this partnership, when in reality, he only let her have enough rope to bind them very closely together—strictly so he didn't miss whatever she had up her sleeve. Sharing the actual work with Laurel wasn't happening.

Thus far, she hadn't seemed to clue in. She barged into his office at her leisure to discuss what had become her pet project. He'd bet a hundred K that she'd spotted a notice in the society pages about the Art for Autism Association fundraiser tonight and she'd come by to announce she was dragging him along to it, pretending it wasn't a date when, in reality, it was a great excuse to spend the evening together without admitting she wanted to.

He'd put up some empty protests and eventually let her think she'd talked him into it. Getting out from underneath the eyes at LBC sounded like an opportune way to dig a little deeper into Laurel Dixon and whatever it was about her that niggled at his suspicions.

She curled her lip at the printed pages under his fingers, eyeing the black type as if she could actually read it from that distance. "Good thing for you I have something much more exciting to put on your agenda. You're taking me on a hot date tonight."

Oh, God, yes. The scene spilled through his mind without an ounce of prompting. Laurel in a little black dress—backless, of course, designed to make a man's mouth water—and sky-high heels that did amazing things to her legs. Her voice would be lowered enough to keep their conversation private. Hair down and brushed to a high gleam. She'd take his breath away the moment he opened the door and he'd never quite get his equilibrium back until maybe the next day...

What was he *thinking*?

Xavier sat back in his chair and crossed his arms with

feigned nonchalance in case his initial—and so very inappropriate—response got too big to stay under his skin and started leaking out of his pores.

And this even though he'd *known* it was coming. It was just…she'd called it a date, after all, and in the process, uncovered his previously undiscovered craving to do it for real. What was he supposed to do with her?

Laurel was so much more dangerous than he'd credited.

"We're not dating." A token protest. It was only a matter of time before he figured out how to keep his wits about him as he seduced the truth out of her. Meanwhile, he had to play it like he still planned to keep her at arm's length. All the balls they had in the air should be exhausting. "We've covered this."

Instead, it was invigorating.

She waved it off. "Yeah, yeah. This isn't a real date. You're taking me on a field trip. I found a great foundation doing a unique fundraiser. Tonight."

Pretending it was not a real date he could do. In fact, it got a righteous *hallelujah*. Silently, of course, but still. His arms relaxed and dropped into his lap. "Fantastic. Where?"

"Art gallery." She glanced at her watch, her attention already galloping away from this conversation into whatever else was going on in her brain. "I called as your representative and they were more than happy to take your money. The lady even sent a courier over with the tickets. I have to leave now so I can pick up a dress and get my hair done. I have reservations at LaGrange at eight. Meet me there."

Like hell. He did things the right way when it came to taking a woman to dinner. Especially one he wanted to keep close for more reasons than one. "We'll need time to strategize. I'll be at your house at seven thirty to pick you up."

Her eyebrows lifted and he couldn't help the smug sense of satisfaction that crept through him. Laurel wasn't so easy to surprise. He'd have to repeat that a whole bunch more, simply because he liked the idea of knocking her off balance before she did it to him.

"Well, then, I have to say yes to *strategizing*."

Innuendo dripped from her voice and the suggestion pinged around inside him, doing interesting things down below. He let the charged moment drag out because it suited him and then smiled. "Wear black."

"Duh. You, too," she suggested with a once-over that clearly said she found his jeans and T-shirt lacking in some way.

"I've been to my share of society events. I think I'm good." Finally, he'd have a chance to slip back into his old self, the one that wore three-thousand-dollar suits to the office as a matter of course. He could even pull his Yacht-Master out of the box in his closet. "See you at seven thirty."

She lifted her chin in amused acknowledgment that he'd won that round and took off to do whatever female rituals she'd lined up to get herself ready for tonight.

Xavier was dressed in his favorite tux by seven, but forced himself to cool his heels. Laurel did not need any ammunition, and showing up early would clue her in as to how much he'd been anticipating this not-a-date—and not just because he had an agenda of his own for the evening. He wanted to see her.

Labels were simply a mechanism to drive them both toward what they wanted using acceptable parameters. They'd be spending the evening together in formal wear, eating dinner and attending an art show, all of which could lead to something very good. Sure, it was pitched as an opportunity to scout out how another charity did fundraising, but they were both adults who shared a sizzling attraction.

There was no reason he couldn't enjoy the results of seducing her, even if his motives weren't entirely pure. Women who hid things didn't get to be self-righteous about how their secrets came to light.

Besides, if she hadn't wanted to play with fire, she'd have picked a fundraising field trip with a lot fewer matches. Like the 5k run through Highland Park that the Chicago Children's Advocacy Center had on tap for tomorrow. No chance to get the slightest bit cozy in the middle of the day while sweating your butt off. Probably that's what they should have signed up for.

But he had to be honest and admit that he liked a good fire, himself. As long as he was the one controlling the flame.

The moment he rang Laurel's doorbell at 7:31, she swung it open as if she'd been standing there waiting. Clearly *she* had no qualms about letting him know she'd been eagerly anticipating his arrival. And then his brain registered the woman. Whatever illusion he'd cooked up that had given him the idea he might have the slightest iota of control vanished like smoke in a hurricane.

Holy hell. "Laurel…"

His brain couldn't form coherent sentences after that. She was so far past gorgeous that she bordered on ethereal. Angelic. Something a man with far more poetry in his soul than Xavier LeBlanc would have to immortalize because all he could think was *wow*.

Black was Laurel's color. There was something about it that paired with her skin and eyes to make both luminous. The dress was exactly the right length to be con-

sidered modest, but also to make a man wishful. And
her stilettos—sexy enough to make his teeth ache along
with the rest of his body.

"I got lucky," she said with a laugh, like everything
was fine and his entire world hadn't just been knocked
from its axis. "This was the first dress I tried on and the
price tag wasn't the equivalent of my mortgage."

"It's…" *Perfect*. But his tongue went numb. He swallowed. What the hell was wrong with him? It was just a
dress. With a woman inside it. He'd participated in hundreds of similar scenarios where he'd picked up a date
at her door.

But none of them had ever intrigued him as much
as this one. None of them had irritated him beyond the
point of reason. None of them had caught him off guard
as many times in a row as Laurel. None of them had
stirred something inside that he couldn't explain or even
fully acknowledge.

It was far past time to stop ignoring it and start figuring out how to deal with it.

Because he still didn't trust her. No matter what. He
couldn't think of her as a hot date or he'd never regain an
ounce of control—and he needed control to get through
the evening. She was his companion for a fundraising
research trip. Nothing more.

"You look great," he said and cleared his throat.
That husky quality in his voice would not do. "If you're
ready?"

He extended a hand toward the limousine at her curb
and waited as she locked the door behind her, then he
followed her down the sidewalk, trying to keep his eyes
off her extremely nice rear. The dress wasn't backless
but it did dip down into a V beneath her hair, which she
had worn down. She didn't seem to ever put it up, which

he appreciated. Hair like hers should never be hidden in a ponytail or bun.

And he'd veered right back into thinking of her as a woman instead of his partner in all things fundraising. The problem was that she wasn't really his partner and he didn't want her in that role. But he had to do *something* with her now that she'd shuffled off daily operations to Adelaide, if for no other reason than because Val liked her and had asked Xavier to keep her around. Dinner and an art show it was, then.

The atmosphere in the limo bordered on electric, and he cursed the fact that he'd specifically instructed his staff to skip the champagne because this wasn't a date. It would have been nice to have something to occupy his hands.

Come on. You're better than this.

"LaGrange is an interesting restaurant choice," he said more smoothly than his still-tingling tongue should have allowed. "A favorite?"

Laurel shrugged, drawing attention to her bare shoulders. They were creamy and flawless, like her long legs. This field trip was either the worst idea ever conceived or sheer brilliance. He couldn't decide which.

"I've never been able to score a table there, but oddly enough, when I throw your name around, people jump." She winked. "Don't judge, but I'm enjoying my ride on the Xavier LeBlanc train."

Hell on a horse. The train hadn't even left the station yet and she was already impressed? He bit back forty-seven provocative responses about what else might be in store for a woman on his arm and opted for what hopefully passed as a smile. "I know the owner of LaGrange. Not everyone jumps when I say jump."

"I don't believe that for a second," she murmured.

"You seem like the type who takes no prisoners. Tell me about running LeBlanc Jewelers. I bet you're magnificent in the boardroom."

As ego strokes went, that one could have done some damage, but he'd caught the slightly off-color tinge to her tone. She was fishing for something. That alone put an interesting spin on the conversation. He couldn't help but indulge her, mostly to see if he could trip her up enough to spill bits of her agenda.

"I'm magnificent in every room." He let that sink in, gratified by her instant half smile that said she caught the innuendo. "But in the boardroom, I do my job. Nothing more."

"So modest. I read up on LeBlanc Jewelers. It's almost a billion-dollar company, up nearly 20 percent since you took over five years ago. That's impressive."

The reminder tripped some not-so-pleasant internal stuff that he'd rather not dwell on tonight. "Again. That's my job. If I didn't do it well, the board wouldn't let me keep it. What about you? Once we organize a fundraiser for LBC and I go back to LeBlanc Jewelers, what do you envision yourself doing?"

Val wouldn't keep her in the role of fundraiser, or, at least, Xavier didn't think he would. Honestly, he didn't know what Val might do and that was at least half Xavier's problem. The inner workings of his brother's mind had interested him even less than LBC, and that had left him clueless when thrust into this new role. Xavier had helped Val through some sticky mining contracts, and Val had sat in on the interview with Laurel, but then they'd drifted back into their respective corners. Their relationship didn't feel any more cohesive. Maybe by design.

They'd never been close. But then Xavier had never been close to anyone except his father. That betrayal would likely always be fresh enough to serve as a reminder of what happened when you trusted people enough to let them in.

"I'm fine with seeing what happens," Laurel informed him without a lot of fanfare. "I'm not much of a five-year-plan kind of girl."

That piqued his interest. "So you'd describe yourself as spontaneous?"

What was he hoping to get out of a question like *that*? Nothing remotely professional or even anything in the realm of strategy could come out of something that sounded more like first-date small talk. She should shut him down.

But she nodded, treating him to a smile that had secrets laced through it. "I'm full of surprises. And I like them, too."

That made one of them. "I'll keep that in mind. Tell me about your fundraising experience. I never did hear what qualified you to be my strategy partner."

Good. That was exactly what they needed to be talking about. No more first-date type questions that made him to want to get to know her better, as if they had some kind of future.

"I worked in a women's shelter," she said. "The women who came in looking for help…you can't see them with their slumped shoulders and tired eyes without wanting to pour everything you've got into erasing all that defeat. I didn't have any of my own money to give, so that meant I had to be creative in how I ensured we never had to turn away a single one due to lack of funds."

He blinked away the miasma of Laurel that had fallen over him as she caught him up in her passion. It was easy to see her point about people donating to her cause simply because she believed in it enough to get them to open their checkbooks. And easy to see why he'd yet to turn a corner on his own donation task—because he had none of that passion. For anything. Let alone LBC.

"I had to succeed," she continued somewhat fiercely. "Failure meant there was a woman out there who couldn't leave a bad home where she and maybe her kids were being hurt. I couldn't have that on my conscience. So I didn't fail."

"Failure is never an option." *That* part he knew all about.

Her brief smile didn't reach her eyes. "Right. That's why I wanted to help you. We'll be a formidable team because we're exactly alike, you and I."

"We're...um, what?"

"Alike. Peas in a pod." She circled an index finger between them. "You need to succeed at this fundraiser so badly that you hired someone to take over operations so you could focus on it. Because you can't fail. I get that."

She wasn't supposed to be getting ideas about anything other than a fundraiser that would fill LBC's coffers. Her canny insight crawled through him in a way he didn't particularly like, mostly because he didn't enjoy being so transparent when his goal had been to uncover *her* vulnerabilities. "I hired you to replace someone who had resigned. Reading into the subtext is not in the job description."

Laughing, she shook her head. "Lucky for you, that skill came with the rest, so you got it for free. If I'm wrong, say so. Otherwise, let's be real with each other. That's the only way for a partnership to work."

She wasn't wrong. But that didn't mean he had to announce it. Her comment had been founded on the premise that he cared whether or not their partnership worked. Not so much. He liked depending on Xavier LeBlanc only.

"We're here."

Wisely, she didn't press him on it and chose to exit the limo. But the knowing look she shot him as he extended his arm to sweep her into the restaurant said she was still analyzing subtext and had likely concluded that he'd changed the subject on purpose.

And hell if he didn't admire a woman who could do all of that without breaking a sweat. He'd have to work extra hard to stop admiring her. Otherwise, he might end up liking Laurel Dixon, and that could not work out well when his sole goal for the evening was to seduce her into a false sense of security, then prove his suspicions about her.

Five

Laurel was in a lot of trouble.

The longer she stood at Xavier's side and covertly watched him contemplate the chocolate sculpture, the more she wanted to crawl all over him and have her wicked way. If he would unbend enough to let her. And if it wouldn't compromise everything she was trying to do with LBC.

But…

The things a tuxedo did to that man's body defied description. He wasn't just good-looking or handsome. Xavier was lip-licking, finger-smacking, eat-him-all-up *hot*. It took considerable effort to pretend she was focused on the edible art surrounding them at the gallery sponsoring the autism benefit.

Dinner had been hard enough, when she'd gotten a solid hour just to look at him. Now he was close enough to touch and holy hell did she want to indulge her piqued curiosity.

If he tried to kiss her, she feared she wouldn't be able to stop herself from a thorough investigation of how good that could get.

As a distraction, she let the video play in her head of her greatest nightmare—the rebuttal story proving that Laurel had falsely accused the mayor's office of collusion. A rival news channel produced evidence that Laurel's sources weren't credible. That story had been all over the place the morning after she'd broken hers. Honestly, she was lucky the mayor had agreed not to press slander charges even after she publicly apologized and posted a retraction.

The shame of having made a mistake of that magnitude would never fully go away.

But ensuring she had all the facts *this* time—that was happening. Xavier was the key.

Which meant she had to stop imagining what his bottom lip would feel like between her teeth.

"I think it's supposed to be the *Venus de Milo*," Xavier commented finally and glanced at Laurel. "Do you see it?"

Yes. Art. That was a much better distraction. They were at an art show, supposedly doing field research on fundraising. "Um…yeah, I can kind of see the resemblance. If you squint and pretend that blobby thing at the top is a head."

He let his mouth curve up into a half smile. "Actually, that's what I do when I look at the real *Venus de Milo*. I skipped art appreciation in college."

She had to laugh because art wasn't really her thing, either. "I skipped everything in college in favor of working my butt off to graduate with no debt."

"That's admirable," he said as they moved to the next

edible art contribution, a replica of Monet's *Water Lilies* made out of crushed hard candies.

So far, they'd seen the chocolate statue of questionable composition, a portrait of Homer Simpson formed from Rice Krispies cereal and a very good representation of a fish tank laid out in a cast iron skillet with whole sardines posed to look like they were swimming through sage seaweed.

"Life Savers," Xavier declared with certainty as he swirled his finger in the air around one of the lilies. "The candy, I mean."

"Jolly Ranchers," Laurel said just to be contrary, though what she'd hoped to get out of that, she had no idea. Xavier didn't get riled. Ever. That was one of his most maddening qualities. No matter what she did, he took it in stride, never raising his voice or really seeming to get emotional about much of anything.

She had a perverse need to find out what *would* get him riled. What he was passionate about. What might pull him out from behind his corporate facade. Or, at least, what might move him enough to throw caution to the wind and act on the sizzling chemistry between them.

Because, honestly, nothing could distract her from wanting to know what it would be like between them. She could guess. Fantasize—and had done that a lot. But nothing satisfied her itch for knowledge. If she'd been the one in the Garden of Eden, no snake would have been required to entice Laurel into eating that apple; she'd have been climbing a tree trunk the first day.

Which was a problem.

"You think?" Xavier responded mildly, true to form.

Laurel rolled her eyes with a laugh. "Of course. Jolly Ranchers shatter when they break, like ice or glass. Life

Savers crack into big chunks. See the long shards in the leaves? Definitely Jolly Ranchers."

He crossed his arms, the art completely forgotten as he contemplated her, intrigued. "Spoken like a woman with experience breaking things. Do you have a temper I should know about?"

"Maybe I get a little spirited on occasion, sure. But I only destroy candy for fun."

"I must know more about that."

She shrugged and opted for honesty. "I like to see what happens."

"To what?"

"To everything." She spread her hands wide. "Curiosity is the spice of life. What fun is it to just unwrap a Jolly Rancher and stick it in your mouth? I want to know what happens when you hit it with a hammer. When you light it on fire. When you drop it in an ant bed. How can you *not* want to know?"

"I absolutely do." His gaze dropping to her lips as if she'd been talking about an entirely different kind of knowledge, of the more carnal variety. "I want to know everything, too. Tell me."

She swallowed as the vibe between them picked up strength, humming through the heavy atmosphere. It was so electric it became increasingly apparent there would be only one way to discharge all that energy and it wasn't an art discussion.

The real question was—would they opt to act on it?

"Well, that's the thing," she said, leaning into the conversation almost automatically. Xavier had this powerful draw that made her want to be closer to him. "You can't *tell* someone what's going to happen. You have to want to jump into that void yourself. Go on a voyage of discovery because you can't stand being in the dark.

What's over the horizon? Best way to find out is to sail toward it yourself."

"Curiosity," he said with a lift of his chin. "Isn't that what killed the cat?"

"Because the cat used up all nine of his lives," she informed him loftily. "I'm only on, like, number five."

He laughed, and the rich sound pebbled her skin with goose bumps. When was the last time she'd noticed the way a man laughed? But Xavier didn't laugh very often— and wasn't that a shame? She liked what it did to her, liked being the one to entice him into it.

What more could she entice him to do?

"I'm a fan of your approach to life," he said.

The compliment spread through her like she'd just gulped the first sip of hot chocolate after playing in the snow. "More where that came from."

"Really? Like what?"

He'd uncrossed his arms at some point and somehow they'd drifted to a space between two exhibits where they weren't impeding the flow of traffic. Glitzy couples strolled past them in both directions but she had a hard time concentrating on anything other than him. She'd just noticed that his eyes turned this incredible shade of deep blue when he forgot to be impersonal and let his face reveal that she'd captured his interest.

"See? Now you're getting it. You have to ask questions, dive in. That's when you find out what happens."

Her voice had dropped in deference to their close proximity and she had to admit it was also partly because she didn't want to burst the bubble that had formed around them. Being inside this circle of two did fascinating things to her insides. She didn't want to stop discovering how deep this thing went.

"What if the thing that's going to happen turns out badly?"

The undercurrents sped up as he leaned against the wall, his gaze tuned in to hers with laser sharpness. They'd moved on from talking about approaches to life to something else entirely.

"Well, you don't actually know that's going to be the result. Right? Again, part of the discovery process. Maybe it'll be very, very good. There's really only one way to answer that question."

"I'm starting to see that point," he muttered and then cursed. "This attraction between us isn't going away, is it?"

Well, that was blunt. She might be a pretty big fan of his approach to life, as well. She couldn't help the smile that spread across her face. "God, I hope not. I like the way you make me feel."

"That makes one of us."

But he punctuated that potentially deflating statement by brushing a chunk of hair from her temple with the back of his hand, lingering along her cheekbone with absolutely no apology. His touch zinged through all her empty spaces inside, filling her instantly with heat and light.

"You don't like the crazy energy of being like this with someone?" she asked somewhat breathlessly, but there was no way to help it. The man gave her lungs amnesia and they totally forgot how to function.

He was going to kiss her. She could feel the anticipation climbing. It was in the weight of his hand as he turned it against her cheek and cupped the back of her head.

"Not especially. I'm not used to a lot of crazy going on inside," he admitted and seemed as surprised that he'd said it as she was. The comment was far too personal. But then he shrugged. "You have this unique ability to pull reactions from me that I don't know what to do with."

That sounded so promising that she leaned into his hand. "This is the part where you experiment until you figure out what to do with me."

Heat stole through his gaze as his fingers caressed her hairline. "I know exactly what to do with you. It's me I'm not so sure about."

"We're partners, remember? We'll figure it out together. Step this way, sir, and prepare to be amazed at what's just behind this curtain."

He smiled, as she'd intended, but didn't immediately pull her into the kiss she was aching for.

"Sure you want to pull that curtain back? Pandora's box is a real thing, you know. Once you open it, then it's too late. You can't stuff everything back inside."

Yeah. That was a thing. Her *worst* thing.

She'd jumped off a cliff plenty of times and only realized a half step too late that she'd lost her parachute. But she hadn't splatted on the ground nearly enough times to kill her curiosity. Besides, she'd scraped herself off the sidewalk every single time and managed to limp away from the scene on her own two legs, so…

She wrapped her fingers around his lapel and drew him into her body. Slowly. The anticipation was too good to rush. He let her extend the moment before their lips met and then he took over, claiming her mouth with such ferocious need that it robbed her of her balance.

Falling into Xavier LeBlanc was, bar none, the most exhilarating experience of her life.

He consumed her from the inside out, his mouth lighting every nerve on fire. Not a little flame like the kind that sprang up when you struck a match, but the blow-torch variety. Huge, encompassing and bright, spreading so fast that it got dangerous instantly.

She wanted his hands on her. His heat. His skin. She wanted to know what he looked like when she brought him pleasure, when he came. What color his eyes would be when he peeked up at her from between her thighs.

If she got him naked, would he finally break and show her something other than absolute control? That she'd like to see. Because, so far, he was missing the abandon she'd hoped for if they got up close and personal.

What would it take to make him lose control?

Seeming to sense she needed more, he deepened the kiss. His hot tongue slicked against hers, heightening her arousal to epic proportions. The kiss took her to another dimension where she could do nothing but feel and she never wanted to return to earth.

But then his mouth lifted from hers a fraction and he murmured, "Wanna get out of here?"

Laurel crashed into reality with a sickening thud. Of course she wanted to follow him into whatever bed, limo or hot tub he had in mind to continue this, especially if it meant figuring out his magic buttons.

But she couldn't.

How could she? She wasn't Laurel Dixon, charity director and future lover of Xavier LeBlanc. She was an investigative reporter who had a bad track record of screwing up when she let herself get distracted by a source.

And that was all this man could be to her right now—a source.

She couldn't afford to have her ethics compromised in her investigation, either. If—when—she found some-thing off in LBC's accounting, she did not want the fact that she was sleeping with the boss to shade what she did with the information.

Fine time for this realization to surface. *Before* she'd started kissing him would have been better.

Through some effort of will she'd never possessed before, she pulled free of his delicious embrace and stepped back, hoping like hell her face wasn't broadcasting how much she hated having to do so.

"Forgive me if I gave you the wrong impression," she said smoothly and tucked a lock of hair behind her ear with feigned casualness. "But that wasn't a precursor to jumping into bed. I was curious about what kissing you would feel like. My curiosity is satisfied and now we should continue our field research."

God, she sounded like a sanctimonious prig, as if she routinely kissed men for curiosity's sake and then walked away unaffected. So not true. Not only did she not recall her last kiss, she was pretty sure she'd been ruined for kissing other men ever again.

"No problem," Xavier said, his expression blank. "My mistake."

For once, Laurel was thrilled he'd maintained his cool. How crappy would that be, to finally rattle him with her backpedaling?

Her own hands were shaking from the influx of adrenaline that had nowhere to go and she'd have liked nothing more than to sweep him back into a passionate embrace. "I appreciate your graciousness."

He lifted an eyebrow. "Is that what it is? I heard a woman say she was done. There's no option B after that."

Laurel blinked. He wasn't going to remind her that he'd been the one to question whether taking this to the next level was a good idea? He'd even given her a chance to back out before he'd kissed her, which she should have taken and hadn't. But to refuse to call her on it? That was graciousness all day long and then some.

Underneath it all, Xavier was a gentleman, and dang it if that didn't just make her want him more.

Six

The next morning, Laurel swallowed her pride and tracked down Xavier in his office with the sole intent of finding out how badly she'd botched everything the night before.

It wasn't exactly bearding the lion in his den—Xavier was more of a lion statue. When he glanced up in response to her knock, his blank expression hadn't changed from last night.

Great. They were back to being at odds, then. She'd have to fix that or she'd never get the dirt she needed. Her problem was that she hadn't been prepared for how much kissing Xavier would affect her. Her plan to get him alone outside the office hadn't worked out quite like she'd hoped. If anything, they were *less* cozy than they'd been before.

"Did you need something?" he asked.

"I have to apologize for last night," she blurted out,

which had not been even number ten or twelve on the list of things she'd meant to say.

What did she have to apologize for? It was her right to back off if she wanted to. The problem was that she hadn't wanted to. She genuinely liked him, which might be her biggest stumbling block at the moment.

He lifted a brow with that maddening calm. "For what?"

"Because we never really talked strategy. We got… distracted."

"That we did." He leaned back in his chair and swept a hand at the empty chairs near his desk to indicate she should pick one. "Tell me what you thought of the exhibit."

Something pinged through Laurel's chest as she absorbed that he wasn't going to punish her for backing off last night. He'd even repeated "we" as if it was partially his fault, when in reality, Laurel had been the one to push him toward a cliff he hadn't seemed terribly eager to fling himself off of. At least, not until he'd jumped and then masterfully taken control of that kiss.

Bad thing to be thinking about. His lips pursed slightly as he waited for her response, and the memory of the way that man's mouth felt on hers sliced through her again with a muscle memory that centered in her core.

Her face flushed and she scrambled into one of the chairs, hopefully folding herself into it before he figured out how much that kiss was *still* affecting her.

"The exhibit was interesting," she began, praying her mojo would magically appear. "But I didn't like it as a fundraiser."

"Why not?"

She shrugged. "No one really wants edible art. To assume you'll sell pieces to wealthy patrons as the main means of generating donations is faulty logic."

"But the cost of admission was nothing to sneeze at." Xavier's dark blue eyes narrowed as calculations scrolled across his expression. "Surely ticket sales will bring up the total figure."

Yes, *this* was the conversation they should have had last night, but instead, she'd gotten all caught up in the vibe. "Doesn't work that way. The venue wasn't free unless the art gallery gave the autism group a block of time as a donation. Sometimes they do, but it's pretty rare, particularly if the event occurs during normal business hours. Because then the gallery is dealing with lost sales, as well, right?"

"Right. But they benefit from the publicity. So it can be a win-win situation to write off the loss."

God, the man was sexy when he was using his brain. She loved watching him think, loved how he woke up her blood with nothing more than a well-turned phrase. The best of both worlds—Xavier was smart *and* gorgeously built.

Why couldn't she have met him under different circumstances?

Shaking that off, she tapped the desk for emphasis. "There's still the cost of the buffet and bar. Again, possibly it was all donated, but that's even more unusual. Catering companies get requests for donations all the time, so they typically deny everyone in order to be fair. It's more common to pay event expenses out of donations."

"That seems counterintuitive," Xavier argued and leaned forward on the desk, folding his hands over the paperwork he'd been reviewing when she walked in. "The more money you spend, the less goes toward the cause. I don't like that at all."

She couldn't help but smile at his enthusiasm. Or what passed as such when it came to Xavier. Some people jumped around when excited. He leaned on his desk. But it was a victory nonetheless, since she had his absolute attention and she got to look at him as much as she wanted solely because they were talking.

The awkwardness from last night had completely vanished, thank God. Maybe she was finally getting it together.

"It's an age-old quandary, Xavier. That's why you hear so much about the percentage of a charity's funds that go to administrative costs versus how much is allocated to actual research or whatever. Do you want someone subpar running your charity who can't get a job anywhere else and is willing to work for a crappy salary? Or do you want someone of your caliber, with CEO experience, running it? You're not free, either."

His brows formed a line as he contemplated that. "Point taken. So our fundraiser needs to have low overhead and the probability of higher donation amounts."

"Pretty much."

She eyed him, trying to gauge how easily she could segue into the subject of fraud without tipping him off. The problem was, she didn't want to investigate that right now. The fundraiser discussion was much more fun and had fewer potential land mines.

Except that wasn't the sole reason she was here. Laurel squared her shoulders. Her career was at stake and so were the lives of the people being taken advantage of by a charity professing to be doing good.

That was the reason she was here.

"Sorry if this is stepping outside of bounds, but how do you not know all this?" she asked. "Isn't your last name the same as the woman who founded this place?"

"Yeah." It seemed as if he might clam up after that, but then he said, "It's not my world. It never was. I had to bury myself in diamonds to survive at LeBlanc. The jewelry business is not for the fainthearted."

"But these are basic principles," she said cautiously, feeling out how to proceed when she didn't want to be treading this ground in the first place. "Basic accounting. Surely you've glanced at LBC's books in the few months you've been here."

He shrugged. "Once or twice. Accounting is boring. I have people for that, here and at my real job."

The relief that poured through her shouldn't have been so swift and sharp. It didn't prove anything. He could be lying. But she didn't think he was. And if not, then he probably didn't have any idea about the fraud going on.

Alleged fraud—or, at least, it was until she found concrete evidence.

When she did, people would go to jail. People she'd likely spoken to and smiled at in the breakroom. The charity would probably be forced to close. If LBC somehow escaped that fate, donations would likely dry up and Val would be out of a job. He'd seemed like a good person in the interview, and whatever happened to LBC would affect Xavier, too, especially if whatever she found implicated his brother.

Xavier wouldn't have too many charitable thoughts toward the messenger, either.

That put a sickening swirl in her stomach she hadn't anticipated.

Why had she thought going undercover would be a good idea again? The sooner she found what she needed, the better.

She had to get out of here before she started caring about the people more than the story.

* * *

Laurel's discussion with Xavier ended up being cut short due to an emergency in the kitchen with a small fire that one of the volunteers had accidentally started. No one was hurt and the fire department arrived well after the flames had already been extinguished.

It was still a timely reminder that playing with fire wasn't a good plan.

In the name of her ethics, she should stay away from Xavier. Except that made it hard to do either of her jobs, which put her in a terrible quandary.

Once the fire department finished checking the immediate area to be sure the danger had passed, they left. Quite a few people, Xavier included, pitched in to clean up the mess from both the fire and the subsequent traffic in the area. It was the perfect time for Laurel to steal away so she could do a little sleuthing.

Adelaide kept her desk spotless, with a square box of tissues in the right-hand corner and a lone pen holder on the left, an unusual placement unless the owner of this configuration was left-handed like the new manager. Laurel had noted that the first day.

The odds of Laurel figuring out how to break into the woman's computer were about zero, and she didn't want to do that anyway, since any evidence she found would be inadmissible in court. Maybe the filing cabinet had something of value she could use in her story.

Laurel crossed to the squat, two-drawer beige stand-alone cabinet and pulled open the drawer. The loud screech of metal on metal crawled down her spine. Freezing, she waited to see if her presence in a place she wasn't supposed to be had just been announced. But no one materialized at the door. She gave her heart permission to start beating again and blew out a breath.

The covert part of the job she could do without. She liked the rush of knowing that she'd be the one to expose the truth. This sneaking around grated on her nerves, though. She'd compromise her position here if she got caught.

Laurel quickly flipped through the first few folders, pausing at one labeled Performance Reviews. That might be interesting. Someone could have received a bad review and decided to take it out on the charity by screwing around with the books.

She pulled the file and thumbed through it quickly, memorizing names and their scores. Since most of LBC's workforce came in the form of volunteers, there weren't that many and the file strictly held signed copies, not the full detail that was likely in digital form.

Nothing of value. Moving on. She pulled out a second file and that's when Adelaide strolled back into her office. Laurel's pulse skyrocketed.

The woman stopped short when she noticed Laurel and pushed her glasses back farther on her face. "Oh, I wondered where you were."

Casually, Laurel dropped the folder back into the drawer as if she had every right to be rifling through the woman's files. Sometimes faking that things were cool would fool other people even when they'd started out thinking something was amiss. "Is everything straightened up in the kitchen?"

"As well as can be. Jennifer is supervising the last of it and I was in the way. What are you looking for? I'll help you find it."

Busted. Laurel didn't have much room to act like she hadn't been looking for something, so she had to scramble. "That's generous. I was trying to find out what kind of fundraisers Val had done in the past. So I can find some ideas for Xavier to use. But you don't have to help. I'm fine on my own."

The lie sat awkwardly on Laurel's conscience, especially when Addy shook her head with a small *tsk* sound and gave her a smile. "Please. It's no trouble. I owe you big-time and I haven't repaid you."

"You don't owe me anything. What are you talking about?"

Instead of answering, Adelaide crossed the room and flung her arms around Laurel. Mystified, she hugged the shorter woman in return, and when Adelaide pulled away, she had genuine tears behind her glasses.

"I do! I'm not dumb. I know you were behind Mr. LeBlanc giving me this promotion. He never would have done that unless you'd prompted him and I'm just... I love this place so much and now I'm in charge. It's like a dream come true that never would have happened without you."

For some reason, that made Laurel feel worse, probably because she'd only pushed Xavier into the idea so she could get closer to him. But she wouldn't have done so if she hadn't thought Adelaide would shine in the role. "You're a natural. He just needed help seeing the forest for the trees. He's a man, isn't he?"

Adelaide nodded and rolled her eyes. "Very much so. He's not like his brother, that's for sure. Val cares about LBC and loves the people he serves. This isn't just a job, not for any of us. I don't think Mr. LeBlanc gets that."

"That's not true at all," Laurel corrected instantly. "Xavier and I went to a fundraiser last night to get ideas for LBC. He's more dedicated to this than you think."

What was she doing—*defending* him? And so quickly, too. But it didn't erase her absolute belief in what she'd claimed. Xavier did care.

When she'd last seen him, he'd been sweeping the floor alongside a few volunteers. She'd also spied him in the storeroom stacking boxes a few days ago. He didn't turn up his nose at any job, no matter how menial. That said a lot about his character.

Adelaide looked doubtful as she eased past Laurel to take her chair behind the desk as if they chatted like this every day and she always found Laurel with her hand in the filing cabinet.

"I'll have to take your word for it. Also, I don't think there's anything about fundraising in Marjorie's files. Maybe call Val? He's always got ideas."

The woman's devotion to her boss came through loud and clear, which boded well for her employment situation when Val returned to his normal position here at LBC and found that Laurel had passed her job to Adelaide. "I'm sure he does, but you're the manager. What would you do?"

Adelaide blinked so fast behind her glasses it was a wonder they didn't fly off. Had no one ever asked for her opinion before? The woman lived and breathed this place, which meant she had a vested interest in seeing it succeed. Her thoughts counted.

"I'd let the staff donate things they're good at making and auction them off," Adelaide said decisively, then glanced heavenward with a dramatic pause as if waiting for a burst of lightning from the ceiling that would fry her for being so forward. "I mean, everyone has a hobby. Like knitting or making patchwork quilts. There's a lot of downtime on some days, so we all bring our crafts to work and sit in the meal service area, so we get to see what other people can do. Some of the pieces are amazing."

The visual Adelaide had supplied unfurled in Laurel's

head and it was easy to envision the staff showing off crocheted afghans or beaded bracelets. The auction was a surprisingly good idea. She liked it instantly. The staff would be involved and thus help spread the word, plus they could advertise the wares as one of a kind.

Though the pieces would be made with love, they would not fetch high prices at an auction with donors who were used to the finer things in life. Regardless, the premise had potential, especially if Laurel goosed it a little. "It's a fantastic idea. I'll bring it up to Xavier. I'm so glad I ran into you."

Laurel edged toward the door, since that was a good segue to get her out before her guilty conscience made an appearance. The fundraiser had been on her mind but certainly wasn't the reason she'd sneaked into Adelaide's office.

"Oh, me, too," Adelaide said so enthusiastically that Laurel almost flinched. "You come by any time. I'm thrilled to have a confidante who listens to me. You're the best thing that's happened to LBC in a long time."

A *confidante*? Laurel's investigative journalist's ears perked up. "That's a huge compliment. Thank you. I am trying to help Xavier keep the wheels on. Speaking of which, would you mind if I stopped by, maybe tomorrow, to talk about some other areas for improvement?"

"Please do. My door is always open."

Laurel nodded at Adelaide, letting the other woman's infectious smile reflect in her own. The sweet lady would be a great partner in all things LBC. Much better than Xavier, whom she wouldn't have been able to stop undressing with her eyes even if someone offered her a million dollars.

Case in point: if she'd had half a brain, she could have found a friend in Adelaide much sooner, but no. She'd been too busy cozying up to the boss and letting herself get distracted.

"There you are."

Xavier's smooth, rich voice cut into her from behind and she whirled, only to get caught up in his deep gaze. He was so much closer than she'd anticipated and he reeked of masculinity, his biceps flaring out from beneath his T-shirt sleeves. She'd just seen him in his office a little while ago, but he'd been behind his desk. Now, there was nothing between them but raw need.

She breathed him in, losing herself in his potent presence as she unexpectedly relived that kiss from last night. She shouldn't be. She should…go somewhere. Or do something. What had she been about to do?

"Was I missing?" she asked and thankfully her voice didn't crack.

What was wrong with her? Why couldn't she remember that she wasn't supposed to be attracted to him?

Maybe because she'd worked so hard earlier to ease the tension, and here they were. No longer at odds.

She'd failed to consider the ramifications of being on the same side.

"I didn't see you after the fire," he said, his voice low, drawing her into his sphere where the rest of LBC didn't exist.

He'd noticed she'd ducked out? That was bad—how was she supposed to be covert if he had his eye on her?

And yet it pleased her enormously that her absence had been noted. "I was working on a fundraiser idea."

The lie flowed from her tongue far too easily. She didn't want to be good at lying to him.

"Tell me." Xavier crossed his arms and leaned against the wall, so casually sexy that her mouth went dry.

"It's Addy's idea actually. An auction."

His beautiful lips pursed. "Like where you put bachelors up on the block and little old ladies pay ten thousand dollars to have a hunky guy show up to bring them tea all afternoon?"

"Um, not exactly. But now that you mention it, that sounds intriguing." Her gaze slid down the length of his long, lean body almost automatically, and it was such a visual treat, she did it again, but this time more deliberately. "Would you volunteer?"

"Depends." One of his eyebrows quirked as he sized her up in kind, a decidedly wicked gleam climbing into his gaze. "Would you bid?"

Oh, man. This was not one of those times when honesty was in her best interests. The acrid scent of burned sheetrock and plastic still hung in the air, a pungent reminder of how easily a flame got out of control.

"Only on you."

Dang it.

That had slipped out. But it was the absolute truth, which seemed like her default around him, and it was dangerous times twelve. She couldn't keep letting herself get sucked into him, but what was she supposed to do about how he affected her—quit?

His long, slow smile spiked through her core. The vibe crackled between them, growing with intensity as the moment stretched out. It was so delicious that she forgot why she should cut it off.

She was *never* like this with men, so forward and flirty, mostly because she couldn't trust herself not to screw it up.

But with Xavier—she could be anyone she wanted. He didn't know she had the tendency to be awkward around men. With him, Laurel Dixon equaled sexy and fun.

"I thought I'd already satisfied your curiosity. Did

you come up with more questions that you have a burning desire for me to answer?" he asked, and the carnal thread running through his voice deepened.

Well, that was a leading question if she'd ever heard one.

"Maybe." God, she needed to reel it back, not vamp it up. This could not end well, but it felt as impossible to stop as it did to stuff a bullet back into the chamber once a gun fired. "The first one is—how good are you at making tea?"

He laughed, as she'd intended, and jerked his chin. "Sounds like you need to be the highest bidder in order to find out."

There were so many provocative things she could say in return and none of them were work appropriate. She *had* to back away from that cliff, the one she longed to fling herself from in order to soar right into his arms. This was just a conversation in the hallway about a fundraiser, nothing more. He wasn't serious; in reality, he'd done nothing but honor the fact that she'd been the one to cool things off last night. If she was smart, she'd keep things light, expectation free and, most important of all, impersonal.

"That's supposing that we're doing a bachelor auction when, in fact, we're not," she informed him, more disappointed than she had a right to be. "We would run out of bachelors too quickly."

"That's a shame." His blue eyes blazed with something she couldn't help but think might be disappointment. "I was really warming up to the idea."

She blinked. She had *no* business leading him on. None. It was unfair to him.

As much as she might want to pretend they were just having a conversation in the hall, there was entirely too much sizzling beneath the surface for that to be the case. Ignoring it wasn't helping and playing into it *really* wasn't helping.

She couldn't kiss him again or do anything else to act on the attraction swirling between them. If she'd been nothing more than a woman working at a charity, then all bets would have been off. Of course, if she had just been a woman working at a charity, she'd probably never have had the guts to speak to Xavier.

And she would have never willingly lied to a man she was interested in.

The entire thing made her sick to her stomach, but it was too late to backtrack now. And it was reprehensible to keep flirting with him when she hadn't told him the truth. She couldn't do that to someone she'd come to like more than she should.

"If you're on board with the idea of an auction, great," she said hoarsely, her throat tight with the realization that she couldn't have her cake and eat it, too. "You can help by talking to your friends and business associates about donating items. Instead of bachelors, the theme is One of a Kind. The more expensive, exclusive and special the items you talk them into donating, the better. Your crowd will love the idea of bidding on things they can't get anywhere else."

He nodded, seemingly unaware of the shift that had just occurred. Good. The less she had to talk about it, the better.

"I can do that. It's a good idea."

That small bit of praise meant more than just about anything else he'd said thus far. It might already be too late to avoid hurt feelings in this scenario—she just hadn't grasped that they'd be *hers*.

"Fantastic," she said as brightly as she could and

started edging away before she lost her mind. "I'll get started on it, then."

She fled in the direction of her small office and thankfully he didn't follow her.

Seven

Xavier gave Laurel breathing room, deliberately not seeking her out for several days. He'd come on too strong in the hallway after the fire. Obviously. She'd been flirty and fun for a few brief moments and then it was like he'd slammed headfirst into a brick wall.

Bam! She'd withdrawn, just like at the art gallery. It was maddening, but he'd finally figured out that the problem was his. Not hers.

He was screwing up the plan. Somehow. Thus far, he'd failed miserably at figuring out what she was hiding, and instead had discovered a woman he wanted to spend time with. A lot of time, and not just in bed. That was tripping him up.

So maybe the breathing room was for him, too.

He distracted himself by digging through business contacts and buddies from college to hit up for donations. The conversations came out stilted and too formal, so it wasn't surprising that the first few calls netted him exactly zero enthusiasm from the other end of the line. It was disastrous for more reasons than one, not the least of which was the looming deadline to earn his inheritance.

He could hear his father laughing from beyond the grave. It echoed in Xavier's mind, solidifying his grim determination to succeed. Edward LeBlanc could not be allowed to win at this chess game he'd posthumously organized, though it was easy to see that his father had set Xavier up to fail, for God knew what reason.

Xavier tried again with the next contact, but couldn't get his feet under him until all of sudden, in the middle of a sentence, Laurel's voice crowded into his head.

People don't give to fundraisers. They give to causes they believe in.

He wasn't selling anyone on the auction donations because he didn't believe in LBC's mission.

That was an unsettling realization. He didn't think of himself as a selfish person or one immune to the plight of those down on their luck. Hadn't he just helped restock the kitchen yesterday, carrying heavy bags of potatoes so Jennifer, the manager of that area, didn't have to?

Charity was in his blood. His mother had founded this place, pouring her time and effort into it. Honestly, he'd thought she'd done so out of boredom. Her husband had worked ninety hours a week; she'd needed something to do and had created a purpose for herself at the same time.

Then Val had followed her, taking up the cause when she'd retired. His brother had passion to spare, which Xavier had long dismissed as a personality flaw. Right at this moment, he might be close to admitting that his brother's inability to keep his heart off his sleeve was the reason Val ran LBC so well.

Xavier didn't have passion. He had interests. Things he enjoyed. Principles he lived by.

That obviously wasn't going to cut it here. If he wanted his five hundred million dollars, he had to be better than this, better than Val. He had to be like… Laurel.

She had passion. It had spilled over when she talked about her work at the women's shelter. Actually, she dripped conviction no matter the subject: Jolly Ranchers, the auction, Adelaide taking over management. Even her one-kiss-and-done speech had been firm, with no room for argument—the difference there being that he had a vested interest in changing her mind.

He pushed back from his desk and went in search of Ms. Dixon.

Her office was on the other side of the building, the only one that had been available once she'd given Marjorie's office to Adelaide. But she wasn't inside and her chair had been pushed up under the desk like she'd planned to be gone awhile, as opposed to having run to get coffee or something. Stymied, he scouted around for her and finally found her in one of the conference rooms.

She stood at the head of the long table talking to four extremely rapt audience members—volunteers from Northwestern University by the look of them. They were all young and wore expensive clothes that were deceptively casual. The university supplied a large number of LBC's volunteers, but this was the first time he'd realized that Laurel chipped in to help with their orientation.

Instead of interrupting her, he crossed his arms and leaned against the doorjamb to listen. And look. He wasn't blind; her sable hair hung down around her shoulders, so vibrant it was almost a living thing. He'd love nothing more than to be given an invitation to put his hands in her hair. Even brush it, something he'd never done in his life to a woman. But her hair begged to be explored.

Who could blame the newbie volunteers for hanging on her every word? The woman was gorgeous, articulate and so animated that his attention never wavered.

"So that's what we do here," she concluded. "Give people hope. The moment you start thinking that LBC is about food, that's when you lose sight of the person behind the mouth. Sure, food is important. Critical. But so is understanding what it represents. And for many of the guests, it's hope."

The four volunteers applauded and Xavier very nearly followed suit. But then she glanced up to see him standing there. A smile spread across her face that wiped all functional thought from his brain.

"A rare treat for you all today," she said and lifted a hand to indicate Xavier. "Mr. LeBlanc himself has come by to say hi."

The volunteers swiveled to take his measure, one immediately launching to his feet to cross the room and shake his hand enthusiastically. "I'm Liam Perry, sir. My father runs Metro Bank and has long been a customer of LeBlanc Jewelers. It's an honor to meet you."

"Simon Perry is your father?" Xavier asked needlessly, because of course he was. There was only one head of Metro Bank with the last name of Perry.

The kid nodded as if it was a perfectly reasonable question. "Yes, sir."

It was just that Xavier had always considered Simon Perry a peer and contemporary. Maybe not precisely the same age as Xavier, but close. And yet, the man had a college-aged son and probably other kids, too. A wife, most likely.

The concept of a family scared the mess out of him. Val's wife was pregnant and even that seemed like it had happened too soon, too fast. His brother seemed okay with it, but Xavier had never felt *ready* for something like that. And meeting Simon Perry's adult son brought it home in a different way. How did you get to a point where it didn't feel like you were signing up to get it wrong for the next two decades?

Parenting was a recipe for failure all day long. All at once, he wondered if Laurel worried about being a failure as a parent like he did. Even if she did, that did not make them alike, as she'd tried to insist was the case at the art gallery the other night.

Xavier shook off the weird revelations and made small talk with the Perry boy and the other volunteers for a minute. Then he hung out near the table while Laurel sent her charges off to Jennifer in the kitchen, where they'd be spending the afternoon prepping the evening meal.

Once they were finally alone, she contemplated him. "To what do I owe the pleasure?"

"I can't attend the orientation of new volunteers in my own charity if I want to?" Up close, she smelled like vanilla and citrus, which he would not have said went together. On her it became a magical blend that was downright erotic. "Speaking of which, when did you become the go-to for that?"

She lifted one shoulder. "I do whatever needs to be done. Marcy normally does orientations but she's taking her daughter to have her wisdom teeth extracted. So I volunteered."

These felt like things Xavier should know. It was Adelaide's job to manage the day-to-day operations, but he'd bet money Val knew who did orientations on a regular basis, plus the name of the woman's daughter. His brother would have already ordered flowers to be sent to the girl and no one would have ever introduced Val to volunteers as Mr. LeBlanc.

Yet that was the only part of this whole scenario that had felt natural to Xavier. Everyone called him Mr. LeBlanc. Xavier was too personal. Plus his name had a faintly exotic quality better suited to someone who frequented hookah lounges in Turkey and backpacked the Himalayas. Someone adventurous and irresponsible. Not the head of a near-billion-dollar corporation.

He wasn't dealing diamonds today, though. And he needed a shot of something to get him out of his fundraising slump—Laurel. How she'd become the answer, he didn't know, but he did trust his gut and it was screaming at him to embrace the idea of partnering with her.

Going it alone hadn't worked. Time for Plan B.

"Where did you get that speech?" He jerked his head toward the front of the room where she'd been standing when she told the volunteers not to forget the people behind the mouth. "Is that part of the orientation package and you were just reading it?"

"No. It's mine," she admitted freely with a sunny smile. "I just made it up. Because it makes sense. The volunteers don't necessarily want to be here in the first place, so I try to help them see what we do is more than slapping some food into a person's hand."

Slightly agape, he stared at her. "The volunteers don't want to be here? That's a new one on me. Isn't that the very definition of the term *volunteer*?"

"You would think. But a lot of times, they're fulfilling some type of requirement to get their degree or to earn a badge. Their place of employment encourages it, maybe. There are all sorts of reasons they end up here, and rarely is it because they have a burning desire to hang out with a bunch of homeless people."

All of this was so foreign, as if Laurel had started speaking in tongues. How had he never discovered this fact or thought to ask questions about the people who did the work at LBC? He'd been pretty focused on fundraising because that had been the stipulation in the will, but Laurel had just uncovered a whole new dimension to running this place that he'd left previously unexplored.

Probably his lack of engagement explained his lack of conviction about LBC's mission. If only he'd fully listened to Laurel's point about that from the beginning.

But he was here now. Listening. Absorbing.

"You're here hanging out with homeless people on purpose."

"I'm not a volunteer," she reminded him. "I choose to work here because it means something to me."

That was the line he needed to press. Deliberately, he shut the door to the conference room and leaned on it. Interruptions of any sort could wait. "What does it mean? Tell me why you believe in LBC."

"So you can write it down and repeat it?" She arched a brow that said she had his number and it was zero. "Tell me why *you* believe in LBC. What makes you walk through the doors every day?"

Money.

The word sprang to his lips but he couldn't spit it out. It was a cold, hard truth that money made the world go 'round. But he had money and Laurel asking the question forced him to reevaluate. What he wanted was his *due*. What he'd already thought he'd earned by running LeBlanc Jewelers the way he'd hoped would earn his father's approval.

Instead, upon his mentor's death, Xavier had been

handed a task that was nearly impossible because he lacked the fire needed to complete it. And the woman he'd hired to be his ace in the hole wasn't biting. She wanted *him* to figure it out.

So he would.

"I walk through the doors because I need to prove that I have what it takes," he told her with biting honesty. "I've been successful at everything I've tried, until now, and I cannot let this defeat me."

Her soft smile caught him sideways and he let it pour through him until he was filled to the brim.

"Exactly," she whispered. "Now imagine you're on the other side of the counter and think about what you just said from the perspective of someone who needs LBC's help."

Transfixed by her voice, he shut his eyes and did as she asked, letting the sheer helplessness of being unable to complete this fundraising task rush through him. He was no longer a CEO with all the privileges, headaches and responsibilities that came along with the role, or even a son whose father had forced him to confront his own weaknesses. He was a man who knew what it felt like to have odds stacked against him, to have no one to depend on but himself and no hope.

Laurel's soft touch nearly unglued him but he didn't open his eyes as she slid her hand into his and squeezed.

"It's okay that you're hungry and broken," she murmured, speaking to him as if he were one of the homeless masses. "I'm here. You don't have to figure this out all by yourself. Let me feed you. Then you'll have the strength to figure out where to go from here."

Yes. He held on to her hand like a lifeline, absorbing the truth she'd so eloquently revealed. He didn't have to do this alone. Neither did the hungry people of Chicago.

LBC cared enough to see the real need—and it wasn't food. It was the recovery of an individual's soul when all seemed lost. It was renewed belief in yourself.

He could sell that. Dear God, could he sell that.

His lids flew up and the look radiating from Laurel's silvery-gray eyes walloped him in places he didn't know existed. Did she fully get that she'd been talking him through his own demons as much as she'd been describing the plight of the people LBC served?

And did he really want to ask? The answer might open up dimensions to their relationship that he wasn't ready for. Neither did he care overly much for the idea of being knocked flat again if he tried to take things up a notch.

"Where did all of that come from?" he asked, his voice tight with emotion he couldn't control. "You've been here for five minutes. I've had a peripheral view of LBC for years and couldn't have articulated that so clearly."

"It came from here." She tapped her heart using her free hand without breaking their connection. "Because it's my story, too. I refuse to be defeated, but determination alone doesn't cut it."

Yesterday he would have argued with her, but today… "I'm starting to see that point."

Neither could he deny that she might have been spouting God's truth about how similar the two of them were. How else could she have verbalized the contents of his soul so easily?

"You know what hell is to me?" she asked him. "Having no one to count on. No one to support me when I've been kicked to the curb. Finding that helping hand is what gives me the strength to take the next step."

Okay, that part wasn't the same. But maybe it should be. That was the gist of this whole discussion. Determination was only the first step, and you could be determined all day long not to starve, but to prevent that, you had to take the hand of the person offering assistance.

Or in his case, he couldn't let go of the person already holding his hand.

Suddenly it all seemed so clear. Laurel had been stand-offish because she knew he had issues with trust. She could read him like a book, had proven that just now. How hard would it have been for her to pick up on the fact that he hadn't been totally up front about his interest?

God, he was a moron. Of course she sensed his reticence and it had fueled her own. That's probably what had tripped his suspicions in the first place. The woman had been nothing but an asset from day one and he'd bumbled around, ignoring the partnership she'd offered. The same one she'd *told him* he needed, and he'd blown it off like she couldn't possibly join him on his island of one.

His father had done a bigger number on him than he'd realized. He couldn't fully trust Laurel to work on his fundraiser, couldn't trust her enough to be all-in with his attraction to her, couldn't trust his gut.

But he could trust the sizzling chemistry between them. That had always felt exactly right.

So he reeled her in, slowly, giving her plenty of time to clue in to his intent in case she still wasn't on board with what he'd come to realize was inevitable between them. Her eyes flared as she got caught up in his gaze. Heat climbed between them, searing the air.

"Xavier," she murmured. "We can't."

"We can," he assured her but stopped just short of sweeping her deep into his embrace in deference to her protest, opting to brush the back of his hand down her cheekbone, instead. "Not here. But soon."

She shook her head, her cheek grazing his knuckles repeatedly, but she didn't pull away. "Then *I* can't. It's—"

"Shh. I get it. You're worried about the fact that we work together." Her skin felt like poetry and he wished he had the words to describe the way touching it made him feel. "Don't be. I'm only here for a blip and then Val will be back. Until then, we're going to do this fundraising task together. It only makes sense that we'll eventually give in to this *thing* we both feel. Why wait?"

"Because *I'm* not going to give in," she countered fiercely. "You're riding high on emotions, not logic. You've let yourself be swept up in the moment."

"Exactly!" Finally, everything had clicked into focus for him and this was the moment she picked to be obtuse? It actually made him laugh. "I've never been swept up by emotions. Never. This is a first for me. Don't kill it. Help me embrace it."

"Xavier—"

"No, Laurel, don't. I need you. Let me be passionate about this. Let me romance you while we're working on the fundraiser. I'm probably going to suck at all of the above, so you'll have to tell me when I'm screwing up." He smiled, pulling one from her, too. "What breathing woman would turn *that* down?"

Somehow, she managed to laugh and shoot him a dubious smirk at the same time. "If you'd let me get a word in edgewise, I—"

"Will say yes." He nodded once and tipped her head up to brush a thumb across her bottom lip. She didn't pull away, and in fact, leaned into his touch with a smile. It was enough.

Flying high on that small bit of acquiescence, he fused their mouths together, drawing her into an instantly deep kiss. Her squeak of protest died when she eagerly met his tongue in a hot clash of need. Her arms clamped around him, fingers sliding along the back of his neck as she held on, urging him forward.

He took the prompt and hefted her more solidly into his arms, reveling in the feel of her body snug against his. Yes, that was the theme of this kiss. *Feel*. He wanted to feel her skin, her hair, her hands racing down his body, but he settled for this fully clothed kiss in the conference room of LBC.

There was plenty to experience. Laurel tasted like the best combination of sweetness and heat as she kissed him. Apparently, he hadn't situated her properly enough for her liking because she burrowed deeper into his arms, her hips aligning with his so perfectly that it knocked all the air from his lungs. God, she was something. A live wire that electrified his whole body. If he didn't stop now, he feared his hair would end up singed.

He didn't stop. He tilted her head to find a new angle and it was so much better that he couldn't help letting his hands wander to her amazing backside. It was firm in his palms, promising that she would be spectacular naked. Not that he'd ever thought otherwise. But with that small preview, his need for her shot into the red.

"Laurel," he muttered huskily as he pulled back to rain nibbley kisses along her jaw. "Dinner. Me and you. Tomorrow night."

Her answering breathy sigh sounded like a yes to him. He nibbled on her earlobe, gratified to feel her sharp intake of breath as her chest expanded against his.

"Xavier, I—" She gasped as he sampled the skin below her ear, sucking on it probably a little too hard to leave it unmarked, but oh, well.

He liked the idea of Laurel wearing his lip marks. But it sounded even better to hide them beneath her clothing. It would be a secret that only the two of them knew. Carefully, he drew her blouse off one shoulder, following the line of her collarbone with open-mouthed kisses. Her body swayed toward him and he steadied her with one hand to the small of her back.

That creamy expanse of shoulder that he'd been dreaming about since the art gallery beckoned, and he abraded it with his mouth. Her hands came up to grip his T-shirt and then twisted, yanking him closer as more of those breathy sighs ruffled through his hair.

When he lifted his mouth, the red mark wasn't any bigger than a dime, but it gave him an enormous sense of satisfaction just the same. "After dinner, I want to put more of these marks on you. On your thighs. At the small of your back. The curve of your breast."

Her eyelids fluttered closed in an apparent quest for fortification. He hoped she didn't find it because he wanted her defenses down. He wanted her open and affected, wearing nothing but her enthusiasm for life.

"You can't say things like that," she whispered.

"Because it's inappropriate?"

"Because it makes me want that!" She blew out a frustrated breath. "This is all wrong. I'm not supposed to want you this much."

He couldn't help but grin. "I'm really not seeing the problem, then. Just let me take you to dinner. No pressure. I need a plus one. For a thing at Val's house. Very casual, other people there. No chance I'll drag you into a back bedroom and ravish you."

Or rather, there was a 100 percent chance he'd do exactly that if she gave him the slightest sign it was something she'd welcome, but she didn't have to know that. For some reason, she was holding back, probably because she still thought she sensed his hesitation. He couldn't let her think he continued to have suspicions about her when he was trying so hard to be different.

"Come on, Laurel," he pleaded, letting his expression convey what was going on in his head. "Just say yes. I promise I will keep my hands off you if that's what you want. We can just spend time together. I would enjoy that. If you would, too, I'll pick you up tomorrow night at seven."

"I should say no." But she shook her head with a laugh that didn't sound at all like a no. "You promise it's just dinner and nothing more?"

"Cross my heart." Xavier pressed his sudden advantage by dropping a quick kiss on her upturned cheek and then releasing her. "See? I can stop touching you if you tell me to."

She stepped back, her face flushed as she resituated her blouse. "I shouldn't go. But okay."

That was such a hard-won yes that he broke into a huge grin. There was no reason not to let her see how happy she'd just made him, so he didn't temper it.

He had thirty-six hours to figure out how to break down the remainder of her objections. Thirty-six hours to learn everything he could about how to romance a woman after he'd already been an idiot. Thirty-six hours to convince Val he'd love to host a dinner party for Xavier and his date because that was the only invitation she'd accept.

After the hurdles he'd just leaped over, all of that should be a piece of cake.

Eight

The next day, Xavier left LBC at noon to attend a seminar in uptown Chicago. The moment he walked out the door, Laurel sneaked into his office.

She had to find *something* she could use for her story. Anything. As long as it was concrete enough to submit her resignation before seven o'clock tonight. Then she could feasibly go on this date he'd tempted her into accepting. Otherwise, she *had* to cancel, as much as the thought of not spending the evening with Xavier made her eyes sting with unshed tears.

Yeah, she was a crappy, weak person who'd totally given into temptation. She should have stood her ground, refused to engage. Definitely she shouldn't have let him kiss her, but holy cow, how could she have stopped herself? The man had some kind of secret power that rendered her mute and stupid.

And she really wanted to go on the date. Like, a lot.

Men like Xavier didn't ask her out. They didn't notice her at all. But he had. And it was screwing with her head.

As she ducked through the door of his office, she noted he'd left his laptop, but it was shut and would require his credentials to unlock. That was fine. She'd find something in his filing cabinet. But as she flipped through the file folders, the worst sense of déjà vu slowed her fingers.

What if he caught her in here like Addy had done when Laurel had been snooping in her office? Telling him the truth under these circumstances would kill her, especially after everything that had happened yesterday when she'd forgotten that she was undercover. When he hadn't let her tell him the truth. She'd tried!

That scene in the conference room had been 100 percent Laurel, no holds barred, baring her true self and begging for Xavier to do so in kind. And he'd responded to that with something amazing. He'd been so deep and personal she'd hardly been able to keep her wits about her.

Kissing him had been a natural segue, just like his request to extend the vibe over dinner. Totally reasonable, assuming everyone in the room had been on the up-and-up. It had taken every ounce of will in her to say no and then he'd gone and done the one thing she could agree to—promising her it was just dinner and he'd keep his hands off. It was the only stipulation that would have passed her ethics test.

Well, that or calling off the investigation.

Her hands froze as she filtered the concept through her beleaguered senses.

What if she did that? What if she said forget it and gave up her investigative journalist hat in favor of Charity Worker Laurel? She had a legit job here at LBC. No one had to know she'd started her stint under false pretenses, only that she'd continued it for all the right reasons—to help people. She'd just be doing it in a slightly different way.

Then she could date Xavier without fear. What would that be like?

The thought of throwing away her entire professional career made her heart hurt, though. She couldn't stop digging. LBC had a bad apple somewhere. If she gave up, who would expose the fraud? It was even more unethical to abandon the fight strictly so she could sleep with Xavier and avoid a guilty conscience. Her investigation had merit and at the end of the day, he was just a man.

Except he wasn't.

Xavier was special—she could feel it when he held her hand, see it in his gaze when he looked at her. He made *her* feel special, like he'd been pulled into her orbit instead of the other way around. They could have something amazing and she'd never get to experience it because she'd boxed herself into a corner.

Blinking back the moisture that insisted on gathering at the edges of her eyes, she forced herself to flick through the file folder from front to back. Nothing jumped out. Thank God.

She shut the drawer as quietly as possible and went on to the next, then the next, pretending she was being as thorough as possible when deep down, she knew *haphazard* would be a better term for this investigation technique. What was wrong with her?

Really, the best strategy would be to find solid evidence, get out and never darken the door of LBC again. If she didn't see Xavier every day, she wouldn't want him so badly. The man even smelled like erotic suggestion. His aftershave had some kind of earthy note to it that made her think of sex. Or maybe that was just because *he* was that potent and pretty much any time she came in contact with him, images of the two of them twined together sprang to mind.

Oh, who was she kidding? She thought of that even when he wasn't in the room. She'd said yes to dinner because she'd secretly hoped some magical solution would present itself that would allow everything to work out.

Xavier's office had nothing she could use, no obvious hint of fraud lying around for her to find. Bummer. She had four hours to decide whether or not to stand him up for their date or go anyway while pretending that it was "just dinner." Instead of weighing that out, she ended up using those four hours to berate herself for letting her feelings for Xavier get to this point.

Bottom line—it was already too late. Her investigation had been irrevocably compromised.

Now what? Jump into Xavier with both feet and see how everything shook out? It was entirely possible that she'd never find evidence of fraud. Then she'd have given up this chance with Xavier for nothing.

While her conscience battled it out, Laurel got dressed for a casual dinner at Val's house because she'd already agreed to it. It would be bad form to cancel at this late hour, right? She could always invoke the hands-off rule; Xavier had said it was her call.

But when she opened the door at seven, the man on her doorstep took her breath. Xavier wore the hell out of a long-sleeved Henley the same color as his eyes and dark jeans that hugged the lines of his body so nicely she could almost feel the drool forming in her mouth.

"Just to be clear," she said, "if I say you have to keep your hands to yourself, do I have to follow the same rule?"

"Absolutely not," he replied instantaneously, a wicked gleam spreading through his gaze as if she made comments of that nature all the time and he liked it. "You don't have any rules. Not one. You feel free to touch me whenever and however you want."

"Noted. So, I guess we should stop all the make-believe and admit that this is not just dinner."

This was Xavier's inherent danger. She had no filter around him, because he made her brave. Every time he got within two feet of her, she forgot to be awkward and she could not possibly express how much she appreciated that.

"I don't know what you're talking about." Xavier spread both palms in the air in the classic hands-off gesture. "Val's having a get-together, and since he's going to be your boss at some point, it's a chance to socialize ahead of time. I was just invited because he's my brother. We'll eat and there will be some conversation. If you want to read into that solely because I'm imagining what you look like under that dress, I can't stop you."

Her smile shouldn't be so wide. In fact, she should take him to task for being so forward, but the time for that had long passed. "I've got on a matching pink panties and bra set that I bought to wear the next time I had a hot date. I figured it was time to pull it out since it's been sitting in the bag for something like six months."

The heated gleam in his gaze went thermonuclear. "I can envision it perfectly. Shame that's all I'm going to get to do, since this is just dinner."

Somehow, his insistence on maintaining their artificial distance despite her provocative comments put her in a daring mood. It was Friday night and she could separate her personal life from work. Plus, there was no guarantee she'd ever have to worry about the results of her investigation.

Especially if she kept up the half-hearted techniques

she'd used thus far. She'd really have to give herself a stern talking-to. Tomorrow.

Until there was something to worry about, there was no reason to keep refusing to explore what might be a really good thing with Xavier. Was it so bad to ignore the complications for a few hours?

She made an iron-clad deal with herself: if she did find anything, she'd bring it to him first and ask permission to report on it. If he was the kind of man she thought he was, he'd be glad she'd done so and agree to the story. She refused to believe he'd brush it under the carpet, but if he did, then she'd know he wasn't a man she could fall for, and she'd have every right to break the story without his consent. That was the best she could do under these circumstances.

As of right now, she wasn't an investigative reporter. She was Laurel Dixon, a woman with a great man on her doorstep who wanted to take her to a get-together at his brother's house.

Val lived in River Forest, which was so far from Laurel's tiny clapboard house it might as well be in Timbuktu. The gorgeous, sprawling home her future boss shared with his wife defied description. Laurel drank in the enormous trees and manicured lawns as Xavier wheeled his slick sports car up the drive.

So much for pretending this was a normal date with a nice guy she'd met at work. Of course, that had pretty much flown out the window the moment she slid into the buttery leather seat of the Aston Martin Xavier drove that probably cost double the amount of her college education.

"I'm guessing your house could give this one a run for its money," she commented wryly as the car slowed to a stop by the massive double front door.

Xavier glanced her. "I wasn't aware there was a contest. If it's age, then no, Val's house wins. It's historic. Not my thing, but he loves it."

Obtuse on purpose to steer the conversation away from the vast wealth of the LeBlanc family? Unnecessary. She knew they had a lot of money; after all, he'd picked her up for the art gallery gala in a limo—and she *could* read. Did he honestly think she'd never Googled him?

"No contest. It just occurs to me that I'm not in Kansas anymore."

"Does the money bother you?" he asked quietly as he switched off the car.

Silence fell inside the small, cockpit-like interior as she contemplated his face, made so much more intriguing by the landscape lighting that had thrown it into half shadows. "I just forget about it on occasion. At work, you wear casual clothes and it's hard to think of you as anything other than the guy I saw with a broom in his hand after a fire."

"That's the nicest thing anyone's ever said to me."

She rolled her eyes. "I'm being serious."

"So am I." He reached out and tipped her chin up to lay a brief kiss on her upturned lips, then immediately released her. "I'm not going to apologize for that. But I do promise to keep my hands off for the rest of the evening."

Her lips tingled as she stared at him, wishing he hadn't retreated so fast. "What if I don't want you to do either one?"

"Then you say the word," he murmured, his gaze catching hers in a tangle of heat and promise. "I'll give you a personal tour of my house. We'll start in the foyer, where I'll back you up against one of the marble columns as I strip you. I want to see your skin against it. Maybe next I'll introduce you to the couch in the library.

It's overstuffed, so plush you'd disappear into it, and it's a shame it never sees any action since it's wide enough for two. There's a skylight and I think it's perfectly positioned to spill moonlight all over you. I'd like to kiss every place it touches."

She shuddered as that image buried itself in her core and started simmering. "Stop. You had me at *then*."

He laughed, the low rich sound tumbling through her already-stimulated erogenous zones. "I've only just gotten started. I have a big house."

"I'll keep that in mind." That might take some effort when it was all she could think about. As he'd probably intended. The next few hours would be spent in extreme anticipation and she honestly couldn't remember a time when she'd been more enthralled by a man. "I didn't realize you were so poetic."

"I'm not." He contemplated her for a moment. "I'm only dictating what I see in my head when I think about you."

Geez. They hadn't even gotten to the really real date part of the evening and already he'd given her plenty of reasons to ditch the get-together. "How am I supposed to go hang out with actual people and make intelligent conversation when you say things like that to me?"

"The same way I've been functioning at LBC when I know you're across the building in an office where hardly anyone seeks you out," he told her flatly. "I have to stop myself at least once an hour from paying you a visit to see if your door would be strong enough to take what I've been thinking of doing to you up against it."

Well, then. Seemed like she'd given him the green light to share all his secret fantasies and she couldn't find a thing wrong with that. If this was how it was going to be between them now that she'd decided to treat this like a normal date, she was a fan.

"Maybe next time, don't stop yourself."

His gaze sharpened with hunger that thrilled through her. "I do believe you've officially blown my chances of concentrating at work on Monday."

She laughed, trying to decide if she should let herself be so charmed by him. "It's only fair. You blew my chances of concentrating at this shindig. I'm already thinking of a few excuses that can get us out of here early."

"I like the sound of that," he growled. "Maybe you can think of one that I can text to Val right now, and then we don't even have to go inside."

"That's…" She lost her train of thought as Xavier's hand settled into the hollow between her neck and shoulder, and his thumb brushed across her ear. "Um—we should at least make an appearance. They probably already know we're here."

He didn't release her. "Probably."

"We should go inside."

"We should."

And then he settled his mouth on hers in a long kiss that was clearly designed to untether her from her moorings, since that's what happened. She dropped into it, greedily sucking up every ounce of sensation. Their tongues clashed. The frissons of awareness and need that bloomed in her center sizzled along every nerve ending, and it was easily the most encompassing kiss she'd ever experienced in her life.

He palmed her jaw, one of his magic hands on each side, and angled her head to take her impossibly deeper still, as if he couldn't get enough. Good. She didn't want him to get enough. If he was never sated, he wouldn't stop. That *worked* for her.

He worked for her. He had something wholly unique that smoldered below the surface, something amazing and intense and profound. It called to her and she couldn't help but answer.

Far too soon, he backed off, his torso heaving with the effort. Or maybe that was hers. Hard to tell. There was a lot of touching and an inability to speak going on in Xavier's car.

"We should—" He nuzzled her ear and rained little butterfly kisses along her cheek. "Um…go—somewhere."

"Uh-huh." She tilted her head to give his questing mouth better access to her throat. "Like your house?"

He groaned, his lips vibrating against her skin. "I wish you hadn't said that. Because you really sold me on your point that we had to make an appearance. It would be crappy to just not go in. Right?"

"I guess. Maybe we can think of it as foreplay."

"Or we can have a prearranged signal. You caw like a bird and I'll meet you in the bathroom," he suggested hopefully.

"Gee, that's romantic for our first time." She elbowed him playfully and then laughed when he nipped at her shoulder. "Keep thinking."

"I'm thinking I have to get out of this car before I do something irreversible," he grumbled. "I never would have pegged you for a romantic."

Because she wasn't, and it pleased her enormously that he'd clued in to that, especially since she'd been totally kidding. But she didn't correct him. What would he come up with instead, now that she'd challenged him? She burned to find out.

Somehow they made it out of the car with all their clothing intact. Xavier held her hand as they stumbled up the front steps, whispering and giggling over secret jokes that had just become a thing between them. It thrilled her. Look what she would have missed out on if she'd stuck to her ethical guns. It would have been practically criminal to give up this breathless sense of anticipation and the grin she could not wipe off her face.

A uniformed woman with steel-gray hair ushered them inside the grand foyer and Laurel pulled her attention from the perfect curve of Xavier's earlobe so she could properly greet her soon-to-be boss if her investigation stretched out much further. Val introduced her to his wife, Sabrina, who had eyes for no one but her husband. It was sweet the way she shot him little loving looks when she thought no one was paying attention.

Laurel paid attention. Apparently, her investigative brain hadn't been completely saturated with Xavier. Somehow, there was enough heightened awareness flowing through her senses that she easily picked up on the vibes in the room. Val and Sabrina were clearly very much in love, and she had a glow about her that could create some extreme envy.

The uniformed woman passed out stemmed glasses of chardonnay but gave Val's wife a glass of deep red liquid—cranberry juice if Laurel didn't miss her guess. Laurel lifted her glass as Val made a lighthearted toast to crisp fall Friday nights. That was the kind of small moment she liked to celebrate, too. She and Val were going to get along famously.

If her investigation dragged out that long.

The thought set her back. She couldn't seem to stop wondering what it would be like if this was her real life. If she kept her job at LBC, where she could still make a difference, and kept dating Xavier until— Well, that was putting the cart before the horse.

Until what? They hadn't even slept together yet. Maybe he'd be a dud in bed.

That nearly sent her into a round of uncontrollable

laughter. Maybe the moon would turn into Swiss cheese, too. Her problem was that, so far, she liked being Laurel Dixon, charity worker, and she suspected that it was only going to get better.

"Sabrina's pregnant," Xavier said into her ear as Val's wife went to attend to a matter the caterer had brought to her attention while Val fiddled with the stereo system tucked into the entertainment center across the room.

"Oh?" It was such a personal thing to share. What was she supposed to do with that? "Should I congratulate her?"

"I'm not sure it's public knowledge."

She *really* didn't know what to do with the fact that Xavier didn't put her in the same category as *the public*. "Are you sure you should have told me, then?"

His brief smile tingled her toes. "I wanted to. It's kind of tripping me up."

"It is kind of a screwy thing," she said slowly, trying to parse out his intent. "Makes you think. I mean, not like, hey, I want one of those. But more about your own mortality."

His eyes flared with something she wished she could reach out and touch.

"Exactly," he murmured. "Though I don't know why I'm shocked that you read my mind. I guess we are a lot more alike than I had been willing to admit."

That's when it struck her that she'd finally gotten to the point where he was sharing his secrets with her—unsolicited. This kind of rapport couldn't be bought. It was gold for an investigative reporter. And it made her feel like crap that she was still lying to him about her identity.

There was a part of her that wanted nothing more than to stop the investigation cold. Right then and there. Make it vanish. It just didn't feel worth it in that moment.

Except, being undercover had been a convenient shield that allowed her to be much braver than she could credit herself with normally. Ever since her career had crashed and burned, her fear of failure was too ingrained to allow her to take chances with men. With that shield removed, would she shrivel up again, unable to have a conversation with a man who affected her as much as Xavier LeBlanc did?

Because that wasn't going to work at all.

She wanted to be this Laurel Dixon, the one Xavier shared things with because he trusted her, nuzzling her ear as he did it. She liked who she was with Xavier. She liked that he brought it out in her.

Was there a way to be both versions of herself without screwing it all up? Her track record didn't speak well for the possibility. But she couldn't stop walking down this path that had opened up to her in the span of a few glorious moments.

It was the worst dichotomy—she yearned to discover everything she could get her hands on, to turn over each rock and explore all the crannies, but she couldn't stop being afraid that very thing would cause her downfall.

She had no choice but to be *both* of those people.

Nine

Xavier had thought being around Sabrina again might be weird, since he'd dated her before Val had, but Laurel had taken up so much real estate beneath his skin, he forgot Val's wife was in the room the second she stopped talking.

Honestly, he'd never been all that into Sabrina in the first place and had moved on pretty easily after she'd dumped him. Sabrina was beautiful in the same way a frozen tundra dotted with snowy trees had appeal—the farther away you viewed it from, the better. That philosophy pretty well summed up how he'd always approached relationships. Maintaining distance came naturally as he worked ninety hours a week at LeBlanc Jewelers, and it also served to ensure women didn't get ideas about the longevity of their association with him.

He'd never thought twice about it, never missed a woman after she'd left, scarcely noticed if one never returned his calls.

Until Laurel.

She was so not his type. He'd have passed right by her as a potential lover if not for the fact that he'd been convinced she wasn't on the square. That suspicion had fueled their interaction from day one and he'd had a devil of a time letting it go, something he attributed to lingering bitterness over the way his father had forced him to jump through hoops.

But now he wasn't so sure. Seeing Sabrina again reminded him that he'd always kept women at arm's length, and not just because trust had become a scarce commodity in Xavier's world. He'd just never been that interested in diving deeper.

Until Laurel.

He had a feeling he'd be repeating that a lot over the course of the evening. Mostly because he wanted to do things differently, see how it felt to be fully engaged. To trust that things could only get better the more invested he became.

So…how did he do that?

After dinner was over, the couples moved to the casual living area off the kitchen. Laurel and Sabrina sat near each other on the long sofa near the fireplace, chatting up a storm. Val had set up camp near where Xavier stood by the double French doors leading to the covered patio that overlooked the pool. They'd been talking shop, mainly about the failing New England division under the LeBlanc Jewelers umbrella that Val had been struggling to correct. But that conversation had wound down and Xavier wasn't putting a whole lot of effort into starting a new one because watching Laurel was far more fun.

Somehow, he had to figure out how to stop automatically creating distance between himself and a woman. After the scene in the car, when it seemed he'd melted the last of her objections, he'd kind of thought everything would fall into place. Now he wasn't so sure.

"So," Val said, followed by such a long pause that Xavier glanced at him expectantly. "This is a thing, then. Between you and Laurel."

"Depends on your definition of a thing."

Xavier took a long, pointed pull from his beer. With his mouth busy, he couldn't say more and he didn't intend to. Mostly because he was still trying to work through his next steps. An audience wouldn't help.

Val didn't bother taking the hint to butt out. "A thing. As in you and Laurel are dating. Which I never saw coming, by the way. I wondered why you were so hot for me to invite you over tonight. Sabrina and I canceled our previous plans, you know."

"You shouldn't have," Xavier responded mildly. "And it's not a thing. It's…"

What was it? Complicated?

It shouldn't be. Tonight they'd turned a corner of sorts, and he couldn't wait to get Laurel alone. So why was he still here, still sorting through his strategy? This part should be a snap. He'd never had trouble getting a woman into his bed.

Except this one. It was still tripping him up. *She* tripped him up, had since day one.

Sometimes when he looked at her it felt like his brain had been sucked out of his head through his ear. What was he supposed to do about that? If he couldn't think, he couldn't maintain control, let alone ensure he could see what was coming. No surprises. No blindsides.

Of course, it didn't seem to matter how alert he tried to stay around her. She still managed to pull the carpet out from under him twice an hour.

Val's eyebrows quirked. "If it's caused you to be at

a loss for words, it's a thing. And that's why I canceled my plans. I had to see the lady firsthand who had prompted this round of finagling. Imagine my shock when you walked through the door with your new services manager."

"About that." Probably Xavier should have mentioned her role shift sooner, but it served multiple purposes to mention it now, not the least of which was a subject change. "Adelaide took over that position. Laurel is helping me with fundraising instead."

"It's like that, is it?" Val grinned, his dogged determination to stick with this subject apparent. "Keeping her close for some after-hours action?"

"No, it's not *like that*," Xavier countered fiercely and lowered his voice, one eye on Laurel in case she wasn't as involved in her conversation with Sabrina as he'd assumed. She didn't need any new excuses to throw up roadblocks. What would she think if she overheard their relationship being labeled something that she didn't agree with? "She's got a lot of great ideas and she's—I don't know. Inspiring. She makes me think about things a different way."

Wow. That had peeled off his tongue with literally no forethought, but it was pure truth. She was all of that and more. Five minutes ago, he'd have claimed that his sole focus with Laurel had to do with getting her into bed, but clearly there was more here than just sex. She did get him thinking in new directions when it came to his inheritance task. When it came to his approach to helming LBC as a whole. Was he supposed to feel so dazed to discover it, though?

"Yeah. That's what I meant. It's like that." In a totally unexpected move, Val socked him on the arm playfully, the way a brother who cared might. "She gets you fired

up. When's the last time you raised your voice? Over anything? Laurel is obviously special. Just do me a favor and
don't be yourself. I'd like to keep her at LBC."

"What the hell is that supposed to mean?" Xavier shot
back and had to lower his voice again. Twice in one conversation? Laurel did have him twisted around—and they
hadn't even slept together yet.

How much worse was all of this uncertainty going
to get by dawn if he did get her into his bed tonight as
he'd planned?

"Remember that she's a human being with feelings,"
Val said easily. "Women like it when you acknowledge
their existence and take them out on dates occasionally."

"I'm here, aren't I?" he growled.

Which had pretty much been Val's point, as indicated
by the look his brother gave him. "Yes, you are. Make
the most of it. She's obviously good for you. Let her continue that trend."

Val broke off as Sabrina called to him to ask his opinion about moving to the patio. But Xavier held up a hand
before his brother could answer.

"As much as we appreciate the invitation, Laurel and
I will take a rain check on the rest of the evening, if you
don't mind."

Hell if he couldn't take Val's hint. The reason he hadn't
figured out his next steps yet had just crystalized—it
was because he was supposed to do it *with Laurel*. This
wasn't a solo journey. Besides, she'd been in the driver's
seat since day one. Instead of wrestling back control, the
key had to be letting go. It wasn't so hard to determine
how this should work, after all. If he wanted to be different with a woman, he had to let the woman guide him.

Laurel met his gaze from across the room, and that
otherworldly sensation rocketed through him again, like

it had from the first. But this time, he recognized it as *connection*. She got him in ways he'd never wished for, never wanted.

It was too much. With nothing more than a look, she'd stripped him raw, exposing him, as if she could read the things written on his soul.

This was what he was supposed to embrace? It was madness.

Yet, he couldn't look away. She drew him into her chaos and he had zero desire to break free. Not when it felt like he was on the brink of something cataclysmic. The only thing he had to do was follow her.

Except he was the one who held the keys to their escape. It was on him to perform the extraction, so he said his goodbyes to his brother and Sabrina, then hustled Laurel into his car.

"That was the hastiest exit I've ever seen." Laurel's smile lit up the dark interior of the car as she let her fingers drift down his arm suggestively.

It was all he could do to grip the gearshift instead of sending his fingers on a quest of their own. "It was time to go. I have lots of evening left to fill and the things I have in mind can't be done at Val's house."

"I like the sound of that. Dare I hope that means you're taking me on a scenic drive along Lake Michigan?"

His mouth fell open a little wider than he'd have liked. "You're kidding, right?"

Her quick, sharp laugh loosened his lungs and had the odd effect of tightening everything else.

"I misspoke. What I meant to say was, where were we? I think your hand was under my dress, if I recall correctly," she said with a purr that vibrated through his erection, thickening it so hard and fast that he groaned.

His hand had been no such place, or they'd never have

gotten out of the car earlier. But who was he to argue?
"Like this?"

He slid a palm along her bare thigh and skimmed
under the hem of her dress, feathering her skin with his
thumb as he went. When she didn't stop his progress, he
kept going until his thumb brushed across the silk fabric between her legs. Pink, hopefully, as promised. He'd
been anticipating getting a peek at the matching bra and
panties set ever since she'd mentioned it earlier in the
best sort of tease.

She sucked in a breath. The moment snapped with
so much sexual tension that he was pretty sure his heart
stopped.

"Something like that," she warbled so brokenly that
he almost withdrew, but then she clamped her own palm
down on his, grinding his hand deeper into her core. "But
maybe more like this."

Yeah, that worked for him and then some. He circled
the heel of his palm hard against her heat, yanking a gasp
from Laurel that embedded itself in his nerve endings,
enlivening them beyond anything he could stand. He
wanted to touch her without the barrier of clothing in the
way, without the center console of his car obstructing him
from pulling her into his lap so he could do this properly.

"This is not the romance I promised you," he muttered. She deserved better, and he sure as hell could deliver something more fitting than a quick grope in the
front seat like a randy teenager who didn't know a thing
about a woman's body.

With a growl, he pulled his hand free and stabbed
the starter button, then slung the car into Reverse. "I'm
taking you to my house. If you'd prefer something else,
speak now or forever hold your peace."

"I'd rather hold something else. Care to guess what it

is?" she asked saucily and slid her hand up his thigh in much the same fashion as he'd done to her, except she hadn't been driving at the time.

The side of Laurel's finger stroked his erection. It was the barest hint of a touch, but it felt like she'd encased his entire length in her warm palm and squeezed. The speedometer shot past ninety as the car careened up the entrance ramp to the freeway.

He forced himself to slow down before he killed someone and then he forcibly removed Laurel's hand from his lap. "Save that. We'll be there in less than five minutes."

Wisely, she chose not to press him and folded her hands into her lap. "I like your brother and his wife."

"Good," he said shortly. "I have zero interest in talking about them. If you're in a chatty mood, maybe you could list your favorite positions. Surfaces you favor. Water, yes or no? That kind of thing."

Her laugh washed over him. He glanced at her as he changed lanes to go around a minivan driving sixty-five in the fast lane, as if there weren't people behind them with a raging hard-on.

Laurel tapped her bottom lip as if contemplating. "I'm a fan of spooning. I don't like carpet but couldn't say if I did like something besides a mattress because I've never tried anything besides the two, and please clarify the water question. Would we be having sex in it or would you be pouring it over me?"

"Yes," he said instantly.

Water splashing down Laurel's body, droplets clinging to her pert breasts just begging to be licked off. Definitely that.

An image of her lounging on a stone ledge in his hot tub became superimposed over the previous fantasy. Yes to that, too. His mouth went desert dry as he imagined her spreading her legs for him in invitation, her head tipped back as she waited. The clear water would magnify her secrets, beckoning him to explore.

Why did Val have to live all the way over in River Forest? Civilized people lived in the Lincoln Park area. When he finally turned into his drive on Orchard Street and managed to get through the porte cochere opening to the garage without hitting anything, he considered it a minor miracle.

He left his car in the drive because it would take entirely too long to open the garage door. Would it be bad form to lift Laurel bodily out of her seat? Fortunately, she seemed to pick up on his urgency as her feet had already hit the pavement before he'd rounded the car to open her door. He chose to skip the admonishment. Next time, he'd get there in time to do the gentlemanly thing. Grabbing her hand, he led her to the door nearest the garage and ushered her inside.

She glanced around the darkened living area expectantly. "I seem to recall there was some talk about a marble column?"

"That's all the way in the front of the house," he said with a dismissive *tsk* and hustled her to the back staircase off the kitchen. "Way too far away. Forget I mentioned it. We'll tour the upstairs first."

They'd also skip the part where he was a moron because he hadn't had the foresight to give his staff the night off. No telling who might wander through the foyer while he was busy worshiping the goddess he'd brought home.

Once he got her into his bedroom, he shut the door and backed her against it. "This is oak. Close enough."

And then he sank into her lush mouth with a groan, molding it to his as he kissed her with every iota of pent-up longing. The awareness and anticipation that had begun simmering in the car in front of Val's house exploded into a firestorm that radiated outward to consume his entire body.

This was not the kiss he'd been envisioning. It was more. So much more. Never had he *wanted* so badly.

But he couldn't reel it back, couldn't think, couldn't do anything but feel. And she was doing plenty of that herself, her hands flat on his back, skimming downward to dip under his shirt to explore his bare skin.

The kiss deepened almost automatically as he devoured her, pressing into her delicious form until he scarcely knew where she began and he ended. Laurel's little moans of pleasure sang through him, heightening the experience even further. If he didn't hang on, he'd soar clear to the ceiling on an upward spiral of need.

Her mouth worked against his, sucking him deeper into this swirl of heat. She filled him with so many things: sensations, emotions, needs. None of which he recognized and neither could he stop the flood.

Still he didn't have *enough* of her inside him.

What was she doing to him? He never got this invested. Never got this *hot* for a woman. It was, indeed, madness in every sense of the word, as if his brain had been possessed.

He couldn't stop. He needed her skin bared, his hands on it. His mouth craved a taste of the curve of her breast, of the dew between her legs that would broadcast her desires.

As he slicked his hands down the sides of her thighs to grab the dress's hem, it occurred to him that he wasn't letting her guide him at all, and neither was he following. This was all 100 percent urgency and heat and uncontrollable desire. And yet…he struggled to find a problem with that. If they were both so overcome with eagerness, then there wouldn't be any room for weird otherworldly crap to distract him from what this was—sex. Only.

That worked for him. A beautiful woman in his bed he could handle. Why did it have to be anything else?

With a meaty growl, he picked her up in his arms and carried her to the bed. "We'll work on some other surfaces later."

She was too busy laving her tongue across his ear to do more than mumble, "That's a deal."

More gently than he'd have said his violent need would allow, he set her on the edge of the bed and leaned into her to kiss his way down her throat until he hit her dress. It was in his way. Not going to work. He yanked on the hem until it came free, then whisked the checkered print over her head.

"Holy hell." The moan that tore from his throat didn't even sound human, but who could blame him? "Pink is my new favorite color."

She smiled and fingered one of her bra straps, then drew it down her shoulder provocatively. "Maybe I'd look better out of it."

"That's not even possible." But then again… "I should probably check to make sure."

Her heated gaze latched onto his, holding it tight as he knelt between her legs to reach around her back. His fingers trembled with the effort not to rip the clasp apart. He didn't want to ruin it. But it wouldn't come apart. He cursed and gave up.

With a guttural growl, he ripped the hooks from their sewn-in prisons, the thread giving with little pops. "I'll buy you the contents of a Victoria's Secret tomorrow."

What use was money if he couldn't spend it when it really counted? He slid the bra free and forgot everything he'd ever learned—his name, how to breathe, whether he was supposed to direct the blood pumping through his heart. The perfection of Laurel's breasts called to him and he could do nothing else except answer.

Leaning forward on his knees, he lifted one beautiful globe into his palm and raised it to his mouth, sucking her nipple between his lips to taste. It was glorious. Her flesh hardened against his tongue as he licked the pointed peak.

She moaned and arched her back, pushing her breast against his mouth. He opened wider to take in more. Gasping, she clasped the back of his head, holding him in place with talon-like fingers, as if he might be interested in stopping sometime soon. Not happening. He could stay here for hours.

Except there was a whole other unexplored breast just begging for his attention. He switched sides and the second one was even more luscious than the first. Her nipple rolled between his teeth and he nipped at it, making her moan. *Again.* Harder this time. She cried out and squirmed closer, a stream of encouragement pouring from her mouth. *Yes, Xavier, like that, oh, yes…*over and over.

Emboldened, he pushed her back against the mattress, determined to build on that. Those pink panties taunted him. They covered the spot where he most wanted to be. Hooking his thumbs under the waistband, he yanked them down her thighs, then threw them somewhere. Didn't matter where. She wouldn't need them anytime soon.

"Beautiful," he murmured as he bent one of her knees so he could look his fill. There was nothing on earth more exciting than Laurel spread out on his bed, her thighs open wide in invitation. Her arousal grew more and more evident as glistening dew gathered under his watchful gaze.

Bending, he mouthed up one thigh and then settled between her legs to discover what she'd been hiding underneath that pink fabric. The first lick wound through his senses as he registered both her reaction and his all at once. Breathy sighs. Her erotic scent. Hips rolling. *Delicious*. Heat. His own gut tightening with long pulls of need.

The act of pleasuring a woman had never gotten him this worked up this fast. Sure, he liked the satisfaction of knowing he'd made a woman feel good, but this was different. Her cries inflamed him, shooting through his erection to the point where it was almost painful. He wanted *more*.

More Laurel, more feeling, more everything.

"I need you to come," he mumbled hoarsely against her sex, then increased the pressure and speed of his tongue to hurry things along. If she didn't slide over the edge in about four seconds, he'd... Well, he didn't know what he'd do, but he couldn't stand to be inside his own skin for much longer than that. He needed her more than anything he'd ever needed in his life, more than oxygen, blood, water.

And then she cried out as she clamped down on his neck with her fingers, her core pulsing against his tongue. He helped her draw it out, suckling at her pleasure bud until she sobbed his name.

The sound of her voice in the throes—it drove him wild. He'd be hearing that in his sleep for days. Weeks. It was better than music.

Now he could take care of himself.

He shed the clothes that he'd almost forgotten he was wearing and climbed up the length of Laurel's body, kissing everything he could reach. She'd apparently recovered enough to do some exploration of her own, her hot hands stroking down his back, over his buttocks, between his legs.

She loosely gripped his erection, brushing her thumb over the tip, and hell if that didn't almost end the party in one fell swoop. The sweet sting of his arousal sharpened so fast that he had to lock it all down so he didn't come in her hand.

"Laurel." He extracted himself with a stellar force of will he hoped he would never have to replicate. "Wait."

Blindly he fumbled in the bedside table's drawer for the box of condoms he kept there and somehow got one on without tearing a huge hole in it with his trembling fingers. This was easily the most turned-on he'd ever been, and doing anything while in the midst of this much passion didn't work so well.

He settled back between Laurel's thighs. She smiled up at him, her eyes huge and full of wonderful, mystical things. Okay, *this* worked extremely well. So well that he couldn't wait a second longer. Taking her lips in a torrid kiss, he rolled her into his arms, snugging their bodies together so perfectly that it was hard to remember a time when he and Laurel weren't in this exact position.

Everything about this felt right. Exquisite. No way it could get better. And then she took him to the next level, wrapping her legs around his, opening herself up so wide that he could easily push inside with hardly any effort. So he did.

Her tight, wet heat welcomed him and she was so ready for him that he buried himself to the hilt instantly. Light pinwheeled behind his eyelids as she closed around him, squeezing him with enough pressure to pull a groan from deep in his chest.

He needed to move. She took his thrusts and then some, undulating with him until the heat and friction drove him into the heavens. He needed an anchor, something real and weighty to keep him earthbound. *Laurel*. She was the realest thing he'd ever touched, the sole tether that held him to this world.

But as he met her gaze, something inside him snapped and he soared away on wave of sensation and heat. Laurel flew right along with him, climaxing again while he was inside her, and it was everything he'd never had in a relationship before.

Everything he'd never realized making love could be.

She'd shown him the way, after all.

The fragmented pieces of this experience swirled together into one bright moment of connection and then he shattered, coming so hard that he saw stars.

He emptied himself and let her fill him back up.

When he could see again, Laurel was lying in his loose embrace, her hair mussed around her face. He couldn't think, couldn't speak. All he could do was clutch her tighter and hope like hell that she wasn't planning on going anywhere for the next month or so. He'd only just begun to explore his recently discovered passion and Laurel Dixon was it.

Ten

Laurel had to get out of this bedroom. Now. Before the huge thing inside her cracked open and let a bunch of emotions out that she shouldn't be having.

Sleeping with Xavier had been a mistake. A giant, life-altering mistake. He didn't seem too keen to let her go, though, and frankly, she wasn't sure her bones still worked. After treating her to the orgasm of the century courtesy of his talented mouth, he'd then turned around and introduced her to the orgasm of the millennium less than fifteen minutes later. The man was *amazing*.

And if she wasn't careful, she'd ruin everything.

That's what she did. Something great happened; Laurel screwed it up. It was the world's worst cause and effect. Only this time, she was in danger of losing a lot more than solely a fraud story. Her job at LBC hung in the balance, too, and she'd only just come to realize how much she valued it.

Then there was Xavier.

She didn't want to think about how quickly and easily she could mess up, especially given the flood of things happening inside. Really, she had no business being here. But how could she have refused? Especially when she'd kind of thought it was supposed to be a hookup. No fuss, everyone got some satisfaction and no one had to think about anything other than sex.

In fact, she'd tried really hard to get some car boinking going, talking dirtier to Xavier than she ever had to a man in her life. At points, she hadn't even believed the stuff coming out of her mouth.

His response? Bring her home. Like they were a couple. And he expected her to spend the night. It felt too real, too big, too much like something she'd leap tall buildings to continue.

This was not her life. Not her real life, anyway. Undercover Laurel, sure. That girl could do anything, especially since Xavier was the one who goosed her actions. That was the world's best cause and effect. Somehow, she'd find a way to mess it up, though.

The longer she lay there, spoon-style in his strong arms, the deeper the panic winnowed.

"I can feel you winding up to flee," Xavier murmured and rubbed his lips against her temple in something halfway between a kiss and a caress. "I'm not going to let you, by the way."

His mouth made her shudder. Dear God, how could the man get her so worked up with nothing more than the brush of his lips on her skin? And her temple wasn't even an erogenous zone. Or, at least, she'd never considered it one before. Right this minute, her whole body apparently fell into the category of erogenous zone as his mouth ignited something inside her.

"You can feel me thinking about leaving?" she asked,

since it seemed as if her voice still worked. A minor miracle. Nothing else did, including her brain, because she couldn't remember why it was so critical that she get dressed. Only that she had to. "I didn't come prepared for a sleepover. It's better that I go."

That way she could keep pretending this was only sex.

Except he'd have to drive her or she'd have to find her phone and order a ride, which would probably take a million years on a Friday night in Lincoln Park. She was stuck for at least a little while.

"That's a complete lie," he countered and moved down to the hollow of her throat, sending her lashes fluttering as the spike of pleasure deepened. "You have all this bare skin I haven't explored yet. What more do you need for a sleepover?"

"Toothbrush," she managed to mutter. Somehow. Her skin had pebbled with goose bumps the moment he'd started talking about it.

"I have several extras. Next objection?"

"Are you just going to knock them down?"

"Pretty much. So you can save us both a lot of time by quitting while you're behind."

For some reason, his change-up of the saying made her smile. "Aren't you the one behind?"

"Why, yes, yes, I am." He punctuated that point by nestling his hips against her buttocks, announcing the fact that he'd regained a hard-on without saying a word. He pressed into the crevice with tiny, firm strokes that had her gasping instantly.

When his fingers started toying with her breasts, she nearly crawled out of her skin. How did he know all of the best ways to touch her?

"Xavier," she breathed, and it turned into a plea instead of a warning.

"Right here, sweetheart," he rumbled into her ear, and his hands slicked downward to hold her hips in place as he ground against her from behind. "This is your favorite position, right? I didn't get to it first because I'm a bad boy. Let me make it up to you."

She couldn't do anything but warble a moan in response. How was she supposed to refuse that? Answer: she couldn't. Not when his fingers crept toward her center, dipped inside and set up a slow rhythm that promised to pull her apart at the seams.

"I can't help but touch you," he continued in that slumberous voice that drifted through her very soul. "You're so sexy and warm, and I sort of lost my mind earlier."

"Ha," she said, or tried to. It came out more as a long sigh. "You've never lost anything, least of all your mind. I don't think I've even seen you get overly excited."

"You obviously have no idea what you do to me. I was nearly insane over how much I wanted you." His fingers played with her flesh as if he planned to do the same to her. Turnabout was fair play and all that. "Now that I've taken the edge off, I can do this for hours."

She didn't get a chance to revel in the victory of pushing him into something other than calm detachment. He underlined his promise with a particularly deep twist of his fingers that sang through her entire body. She bucked against his hand, instinctively seeking more. His other hand joined the party, rubbing in circles at her nub as he plunged into her core again. Pleasure knifed through her, arching her back, which allowed him to grind deeper against her buttocks.

The triple punch of sensations pushed her over the edge and she exploded in an exhilarating tsunami of passion, clenching around his fingers over and over. He did something magical, furled them in a way that elongated the orgasm, and the intensity ratcheted up exponentially.

He wrung so much pleasure out of her body that tears leaked from her eyes.

And then, after the brief crinkle of a condom wrapper, he plunged into her from behind, filling her so tightly, so fast, that it set off another round of ripples. He groaned into her ear as she kept closing around him, and that might have been the most erotic sound she'd ever heard.

Then he half rolled her to the mattress and began to move inside her, whipping her scarcely cooled center into a firestorm instantly. The heat raged as he pushed her further, demanding even more from her body, and he got it. She cried out as another intense climax seized her, and she came so hard that her legs went numb.

He followed her a few strokes later, his lips in her hair and his heavy body collapsing to cover hers as he pulsed inside her. They lay like that for an eternity until she became convinced that she'd passed into another dimension where this kind of pleasure happened to her on a regular basis.

"That was unbelievable," he croaked against her neck and rolled to settle her into his arms. "Even more so than the first time, and that's saying something."

Sweet air rushed into her lungs as his weight redistributed. She missed his body on hers instantly. Breathing was overrated. "That's one word for it."

"Give me another one," he said almost as a challenge.

"Looking for compliments?" she teased. "It was cataclysmic. Earth-shattering. Miraculous. Shall I go on?"

His lips grazed her cheek and she felt them curve upward. "You sound like a thesaurus."

Her insides froze and the silk sheet beneath her body turned cold in a flash. Of course she had a command of the English language. That's what an investigative reporter did—found the right words to describe the current situation.

The reminder was ill-timed. And yet perhaps apt. The longer she let herself stay here, the deeper she dug her own grave. After all, he still didn't know she was Undercover Laurel, and removing that barrier meant she lost all of this. Even if he didn't care, she couldn't be bold, saucy Laurel without a shield against failure.

"I feel you thinking about leaving again." His arms tightened around her, cutting off the flow of air to her lungs.

This time, it wasn't okay. She pushed at his arms until he realized what she wanted and released her, his gaze following her as she sat up.

"If you want to leave, I won't stop you," he said quietly. "I won't like it, but you do what pleases you."

That only made it worse. "Stop being so understanding."

"Okay."

"That's being understanding!"

Frustrated beyond measure, she pulled the sheet up to cover her bare breasts. Not that it mattered. He'd seen them plenty already. That was the problem, the thing she couldn't undo. They'd flung open Pandora's box, all right, and as advertised, she couldn't stuff everything back inside again.

She wanted to stay.

He didn't know the truth.

But this wasn't supposed to be serious. Any decision felt wrong, like a recipe for failure.

"You weren't 100 percent on board with coming here tonight, were you?" he asked, his voice betraying none of his thoughts. Even in this, she hadn't ruffled his feathers in the slightest.

"I was! Completely." She could own that all day long, and it was important for him to understand that she had never once felt coerced. But how did she explain the real reason she was flipping out? "I make my own choices. It's just… I don't know."

"I know," he announced, refreezing her heart.

"You do?" As in *everything*?

That wasn't possible. If he knew she'd taken the job at LBC under false pretenses, surely he wouldn't have brought her home and treated her like his own personal smorgasbord. Yet there was a part of her that craved to hear him say exactly that.

It's okay, Laurel. I love that you care enough to expose bad people in my organization. Have another orgasm or two.

"I think so. You just wanted to see how it felt to make love to me and now you're done. Just like when you kissed me at the gallery." His wry smile twisted her heart something fierce. "It's fine. My ego might be a little bruised but I'll live, as long as I did a good job satisfying your curiosity."

He was so patient, so instantly forgiving that she couldn't stand for him to think any of that. "That is so not it. I have a history of screwing up things and I refuse to do that in this situation."

Maybe that was too blunt. She'd just laid out her vulnerabilities, baring herself far more than he had when he'd stripped her clothing off. That's why she couldn't do this two-personality tango; it was too hard to juggle the woman who jumped into research with both feet and the woman who couldn't be trusted to get it right.

It wasn't her strongest play of the night, but he just nodded, taking it in stride. "You forget that we're alike. I hate failing, too, so I get that."

Oh, God, what was she supposed to do with that? Or with the little tugs at her heart that had started with his smile and had only gotten stronger with the possibility that he might actually understand her? Her vocal cords froze as she stared him, totally stricken into silence. Definitely not her finest hour.

But he didn't seem fazed at all. Gently, he took her hand, contemplating their twined fingers. "Given all of that, I've got to ask, Laurel. What do you think is going on here? If I want you to stay, am I moving too fast for you? Because that's not my intent. We're adults. I enjoy spending time with you. That's all. Don't make it into a bigger deal than it is."

She blew out a breath she hadn't realized she'd been holding. The crash and burn of her career had totally paralyzed her and it was far past time to get her head screwed on straight.

"I'm sorry. I'm being an idiot. Of course this thing between us isn't far enough along for me to be such a basket case."

Good. She could breathe. Everything was smoothing out, including her pulse.

"Basket case is going a little far," he said with a smile. "You reacted to me being an idiot, not the other way around. I don't do this kind of thing well, where I like a woman and figure out how to see more of her. Because tonight was great. Far more so than I was expecting, and selfishly, I want more of that."

"I tend to be a little cautious," she admitted. It seemed they were at a place where it was okay to confess a few things and no one had to run screaming from the room. "In the romance department. Strictly because of bad experiences."

He shook his head with a light snort. "Sweetheart,

you're the least cautious woman I've ever had the pleasure of getting naked in my bed. Whatever bad experience you had that caused you to believe such a lie, banish it from your mind."

She couldn't help but smile at that, even though the only reason she'd allowed herself to get naked in his bed had everything to do with trying not to be herself tonight. Look how that had turned out. She'd nearly botched the whole thing.

"Easier said than done," she said, well aware she was treading a fine line by trying to be this person Xavier saw—the person he helped her to be. She could easily lose her balance at any moment. "I'm probably going to need lots of reminding."

"Or I can just keep you naked and let you have your wicked way with me." His naughty smirk made her laugh. "No, no. I insist. We're partners. We'll do this together or not at all."

The promise of remaining Xavier's partner thrilled her. Especially when he'd extended it to the bedroom. He was basically saying he would continue to help her be that woman he saw, the one she could only be with his influence, and that it was okay. He got it. She didn't have to be afraid of screwing up because there was nothing to screw up since they weren't serious. They were just two people who enjoyed each other and wanted to continue doing so until one or both of them ended it.

She could do that.

"You're such a trouper," she teased. "Volunteering yourself like that. How did I get so lucky as to have a partner with such a selfless streak?"

"It's nothing, really. I do run a charity, obviously because I'm the kind of guy who likes to give back." Xavier shrugged good-naturedly and tugged on her hand until she lay back down, settling her head into the hollow of his shoulder. "Now that we've settled the subject of your untimely departure, there's something bothering me about this conversation."

Since they'd just decided she shouldn't be freaking out, she tried really hard to keep her voice level when she replied, "Oh?"

"At the gallery, you talked about jumping into voids and discovering what lay over the horizon. I was pretty moved by that speech."

"You were?" She didn't recall much of anything other than the feel of his mouth on hers. "You never said anything."

"I was trying to get a few things worked out in my head," he admitted. "I don't jump into stuff. It takes a certain kind of temperament to just blindly trust like that, and I've developed an inconvenient sense of caution lately. I'm trying to get past it. That's partially what tonight was about."

Oh, man. That spoke to her on so many levels. Emboldened, she smoothed a hand over his glorious pectoral muscle. "I'm glad I could be a part of your experimentation."

"You're not just a part of it. You inspire it."

Slowly, she absorbed that, trying to sort through what he was telling her. It sounded an awful lot like they'd just figured out yet another area they had in common. "I make you want to be bold?"

He shrugged, lifting her head a notch before letting it settle back into place. "To a degree, yeah. But I sense this hesitation in you and it's driving me nuts. I want to be all-in, Laurel, really experience what it's like to explore passion with someone. I hate this caution I've been feeling. I thought tonight would banish it, you know, if I jumped in, but then you started talking about your own caution, which doesn't jibe with the woman I've been getting to know. Maybe you're just saying that because you sense mine. I'm tripping you up."

Her eyelashes fluttered closed. Oh, God. No, that wasn't it at all. Her two-person tango was messing *him* up.

She'd never even considered that he'd pick up on all of her indecision and inability to just be herself. Of course he had. Xavier LeBlanc was not a stupid man. Yet, somehow, he'd decided that his limitations had caused hers.

"I'm sorry." What else could she say when confronted with the evidence that she'd managed to screw this up, after all?

"Don't be." He sat up, taking her with him. The covers puddled into their laps as he gripped her bare shoulders earnestly. "I'm saying I want that woman you let me glimpse at the gallery. Don't hesitate. Jump off a few cliffs in a row. I'll follow you. I want this crazy you make me feel inside. I'm sorry if the way I've held back thus far has contributed to your hesitation. Don't let it. That's all."

She stared at him, her insides a riot she could scarcely sort out. "Here's the thing. You're the one who makes me feel like I can jump. Like I can be courageous enough to put my fears behind me. Not the other way around."

A smile unfurled across his face, warming her instantly. "How about that? We're discovering how this works together. We really are a good team."

Something loosened in her chest. "I've been telling you that since day one."

Now she had to put her money where her mouth was. Xavier wanted her to be the bold, unapologetic woman she truly was inside, no fear. She had to trust that she wasn't going to mess up, trust that he was going to stick right by her side as she relearned how to be Laurel.

Because that was the best discovery of all—she wasn't two people. Just one who had forgotten how to be brave.

And brave Laurel took what she wanted.

Right now, that was Xavier.

Eleven

The weekend stretched into Monday morning and Laurel still hadn't left. That was fine by Xavier. He'd taken her shopping Saturday morning and spent an obscene amount of money ensuring she never had to leave if she didn't want to.

This was all new to him, but he liked where it was headed so far.

Especially when his alarm went off Monday morning at 5:00 a.m. and Laurel didn't stir. He'd tucked her into his embrace to fall asleep for the third night in a row, but at some point, she'd moved over to her own side, clutching her pillow like someone had tried to take it away from her. He watched her for a moment in the low light of the bedside lamp and opted not to disturb her as he went about his Monday morning routine.

Halfway through the middle of his workout, Laurel wandered into the gym. Her sable hair spilled down her back with mussed strands haloing her face, and she was easily the most beautiful woman he'd ever seen in his life. Even in sleep shorts and a tiny white tank top. Especially in that. In about four seconds, he was going to peel it off with his teeth.

"Good morning," she called with a sleepy smile. "This place is hard to find. I had to ask Greta where you were."

The immeasurable benefit of live-in staff. He rested the dumbbell in his hand on his thigh, which did nothing to free up his hands so he could pull her into his arms, but he *was* hot and sweaty. So he came up with a much better plan.

"I didn't want to wake you. But since you did that on your own, give me five minutes to finish my last set and we can take a shower together."

"Deal." She hesitated and just when he was about to remind her that he preferred it when she gave it to him no holds barred, she continued, "If you want to drop me off at home before work, that's fine."

"Why the hell would I want to do that?" He'd told her on multiple occasions that there was no expiration date to their affair and neither did he want to set one.

Sure, he was overly enthusiastic about continuing to sleep with Laurel on a regular basis. So? He had never been one to pull punches and he liked Laurel in his bed. When that changed, he'd let her know.

"Because, you know. The rest of LBC might not like it so much that I'm dating the boss."

"The rest of LBC can jump in Lake Michigan," he growled, but then had to concede that, while obviously Val knew he was seeing Laurel, the rest of the staff didn't necessarily hold the same views about dating in the workplace as Xavier did. Namely that it was none of their business.

Except he was supposed to be steering the ship until

Val's return. He couldn't do what he pleased without ramifications.

It was a tricky dynamic, one he'd never had to contemplate before. What would happen when they stopped seeing each other? Would things grow uncomfortable between them or would they remain friendly, working together easily despite the fact that they no longer had the right to get each other naked behind a shut office door?

The idea of not having the right to sleep with Laurel put him in a foul mood. That was not on the horizon anytime soon, not if he had anything to say about it. Part of the problem was the fact that it wasn't all up to him. Laurel could decide at any point that she was done and there was nothing he could do to stop her.

Was it too soon to bring up the idea of something a little more permanent than whatever it was they were doing right now?

Xavier shook his head. Hard.

Yes. It was way, *way* too soon. What was he even thinking, that he'd blurt out an invitation for Laurel to move in? She'd laugh in his face and she should.

He needed to take a huge step back before he did something irreversible solely due to phenomenal sex.

"You have a point," he conceded. "The staff needs to get used to the idea that we're dating, but that doesn't mean we have to throw it in their faces. I'll drop you at your house on the way into LBC."

It was an easy solution to multiple problems. He didn't like it.

She nodded as if that had been the outcome she'd hoped for, but he couldn't muster the same enthusiasm. What if she didn't want to come back here tonight? Maybe she wanted her space. He didn't like space.

Laurel had cracked something open inside him, something that wished for more substance than a weekend affair, and now it was being threatened.

All the more reason to let her do as she pleased. He blew out a breath. Space would be good for them both. In fact, he should probably take a shower alone. This house had five bathrooms. Surely he could find one that would be Laurel free and then he didn't have to contemplate what had taken over his brain since Friday night.

"Once I have my car, I can drive myself back and forth from your house to LBC," she said with a smile. "We'll do it on the sly for a little bit until we figure out how big of a deal this is going to be for people. Maybe, eventually, we can drop the pretense and I'll just ride with you into the office. Speaking of which, if we're taking a shower, we should get started because I've been standing here aching for you to put your hands on me for a million years and the things I want you to do to me will take a very long time. We don't want to be late for work."

He got so hard so fast that he almost couldn't breathe. But that didn't stop him from picking her up and carrying her into the closest shower off the gym. As the hot water sluiced over them both, he lost himself in her soapy, sexy body.

Space was overrated.

Of course she wasn't done with him. His trust issues were rearing their ugly heads again, that was all. Until he had something to worry about, he needed to relax and enjoy the benefits of seeing a great woman who was allowing him to discover all the things he'd missed thus far in a relationship.

Despite all of that, he still had a very difficult time letting her go later that morning. Finally, she sprang from the front seat of his car, wrenching away from his kiss with the promise that she'd come by his office later.

That at least made him smile as he drove to LBC in rush hour traffic with a raging hard-on. He'd have thought the shower sex would have sated him for the morning, but no. He wanted Laurel 24/7.

She let him cool his heels for an hour. His coffee had long grown cold, but every time he picked it up, he heard a noise outside his door that he hoped was Laurel, so he set it back down again, only to be disappointed.

Getting her naked behind closed doors had become his number one priority. The amount of work he'd accomplished since arriving—zero—attested to that more than he cared to contemplate.

He should be working on plans for the next fundraiser, not moping about like a lovesick teenager. When she finally blew through the door wearing a lime-green dress that ended just above her knees, everything but her drained from his head.

"About time," he growled. "That dress is the perfect color for what I have in mind to do to you."

She shut the door and leaned against it, her smile nothing short of naughty. "You want to make a margarita out of me?"

"More like suck the juice out," he said succinctly and pushed back from his desk, patting the space in front of him. "Up you go. Let's see if you taste as good as you look."

She didn't move but her gaze went heavy with arousal as she eyed the spot on his desk. "That sounds like a recipe for getting nothing accomplished today."

"Exactly. That was always going to happen."

"Then why did we bother to come in to the office?" she asked with maddening practicality. "We could have both taken a sick day and spent the entire morning in bed."

"Now you're talking." Why hadn't that occurred to him? "We'll do that tomorrow."

But she shook her head with an amused laugh. "We can't spend two days in a row doing nothing but boinking."

"Wanna bet?" *Boinking.* It was such a cute word for sex, especially the way they did it. Laurel had gotten him so hot a couple of times that he'd devolved into nothing but animalistic instinct. "We just spent the last two days in a row doing nothing but."

"That's not true—we went shopping. And I distinctly remember a movie. Maybe there was some eating."

Why was she still talking when he'd already told her he planned to pleasure her on his desk? Maybe he hadn't made it clear what he'd meant earlier. "Do you have some objection to me putting my mouth between your legs while we're at work?"

Her gaze went molten as she zeroed in on his lips. "Yeah, actually. I do."

Despite her protest, he'd watched her come enough times over the weekend that he could tell how turned on she was. It was doing a number on him imagining how wet she must be under that lime-green skirt. He crossed his arms over his chest and leaned back.

"Really? Because your face is telling me a different story."

"Wanting something is not the same as thinking it's a good idea." She crossed her own arms over her stomach, which tightened the fabric across her breasts, highlighting her hard nipples. "We have important work to do and I'm getting the distinct feeling you're using sex to avoid it."

That put enough of a hitch in his stride that his arousal fizzled a notch. As such, he couldn't let the comment go. "What's that supposed to mean?"

"The fundraiser. We've done nothing to plan it. We haven't even had one conversation outside of the initial one where I presented the idea of an auction. Why not?" The sensual vibe in the room vanished as they stared at each other. "Because it seems an awful lot like you want me in your bed but not your boardroom."

That stung. And put his back up at the same time. "You're being ridiculous. That's not true."

Even as he said it, he couldn't fully sell it to himself, though. With considerable effort, he took a figurative step back and examined her point.

She wasn't wrong.

He hadn't fully trusted her with details about his inheritance test. Actually, he hadn't trusted her at all. He'd maybe had a couple of discussions in the hallway once upon a time, but as a whole, he'd kept tight control over the fundraising aspect of his job. Because it was *his*. He needed to prove that he could do this task, despite having no idea why it had been thrust upon him.

And maybe that was the real reason he'd yet to share any of it with Laurel. If he didn't understand why his own father had turned on him, how would he recognize it when someone he didn't know as well did the same?

Someone like Laurel.

Keeping everyone at arm's length had become his coping mechanism. Passion hadn't even come all that easily, but he'd at least been able to quantify the benefits of that. His inheritance test? Whole other story.

Laurel was calling him on his crap and he'd never been more affected by a woman in his life.

She raised her brows. "If it's not true, then help me stop feeling like you're brushing me off when it comes to the partnership we've both agreed to."

Laurel deserved that explanation and probably a whole

lot more. He stood and pulled a chair around, setting it next to his, a pointed equal distance from his computer. "Let's talk."

Shooting him a smile that was far too forgiving, she skirted the desk and settled into her seat. "Did you talk to your friends about donating items?"

"A few. I got sidetracked."

A poor excuse, though he *had* been a little busy getting wound up with the woman in lime green. Before Laurel could call him on that, too, he held up a hand. "I had a hard time, okay? It didn't go very well. You helped me get my head on straight during our conversation in the conference room the other day after the orientation session, and then I never cycled back around to it. I absolutely should dive back in."

She glanced at his phone emphatically. "No time like the present."

That was fair. As a show of good faith, he picked up his phone and scrolled through the contacts. Under Laurel's watchful gaze, he dialed up Simon Perry, the head of Metro Bank and father to Liam from the orientation session. The man answered on the second ring. Odds were high Simon had Xavier in his contacts, and he took a moment to be grateful the LeBlanc name held enough weight to warrant such attention.

"Mr. Perry," Xavier began, struck all over again by how much further along in life his acquaintance was. "Xavier LeBlanc calling."

Unnecessary to identify himself, most likely, but this call justified formality.

"A welcome surprise," Simon said warmly. "My son mentioned that he'd met you the other day. Thank you for making him feel like he can make a difference in the world. It's an important concept I've tried to impart to him and I'm glad to hear he's finding similar influences in the business world."

"My pleasure," Xavier said and meant it. How about that? There was some actual emotional satisfaction in being the head of a place like LBC. Temporary head, though that qualification was coming a lot less quickly lately. Val had once mentioned that Xavier might be a better man for his time here. Perhaps this was what he'd meant.

"What can I do for you?" Simon asked.

Xavier launched into an unrehearsed spiel about the auction and within a few minutes, Simon had offered up a rare bottle of Macallan whiskey. While not a personal fan of the brand, Xavier knew the bottle would likely sell for upward of a hundred grand. It was a phenomenal donation and he told Simon so. They wrapped up the call after Simon tacked on a promise to send Xavier a few names of colleagues who might be willing to contribute.

"Well done," Laurel said softly when Xavier hung up.

"You don't even know how it went," he teased, even though he knew he wore a grin he couldn't quite control. Why should he, though? He'd taken her advice, done something he'd previously failed at and came out a winner this time. If that didn't warrant a smile, nothing did.

"Yes I do. I can see it in your face. It's breathtaking." Her quiet voice curled through him with warmth. Or maybe it was the content of her words that had such an unexpected effect.

"What is my face doing?" He couldn't help but ask.

"Everything. Your expression is typically very schooled. I like it better when you let me see what's going on inside you."

Since there was no point in trying to compose his features into something less revealing, he didn't bother trying. "Well, you're a limited audience of one who can actually read me with any degree of accuracy."

"I like that, too."

This whole conversation shouldn't be happening. It was far too intimate. But the real danger lay in how much more intimate he wanted to get, which should have been scaring the daylights out of him.

Instead of reeling it back, he leaned into her space and tipped up her chin to feather a kiss across her cheek that had nothing to do with getting her naked or even aroused; it was a small token of gratitude for the things he was feeling inside.

"You're good for me, apparently."

That pleased her immeasurably, judging by the light that dawned in her eyes. Maybe he was good for her, too. Wouldn't that be something?

For the first time in his adult life, he hadn't kicked a woman out of his bed and then promptly forgotten her. The uncharted waters he'd sailed into weren't as difficult to navigate as he would have guessed.

"Maybe you should make a few more phone calls while you're riding high," Laurel suggested wryly, intentionally moving out of his reach.

Yeah, yeah, it was getting too mushy in here for both of them. He got it. Plus she'd already called him out once for his avoidance tactics. Neither did he want to scare her away simply because he'd discovered something new and amazing.

He could wait to show her how much he appreciated her.

Twelve

Auction day started at five in the morning.

Xavier didn't typically get up this early on a Saturday, but he and Laurel had a to-do list a quadrillion items long. Even though they'd recruited as many volunteers from LBC as possible, the list never got shorter and Adelaide, who had turned out to be his second-greatest asset after Laurel, had to run the food pantry while they were off-site.

Xavier drove the truck they'd rented while Laurel rode shotgun, chattering a mile a minute about the changes she'd made to the catering menu. He listened with half an ear, not because her comments weren't important, but because he'd gotten more and more nerve-racked the closer they got to the venue.

This was it. The event they'd been planning for a solid two weeks. What if it didn't go as well as they'd projected?

Sure the appraised value of the donations had topped

three million dollars, but only for insurance purposes. Actual value might not even turn out to be half that. It all depended on whether the attendees opened their wallets. Scratch that—it all depended on how wide Xavier convinced them to open their wallets.

What if *he* was the reason it failed?

Worse, what if his father had set him up for exactly that? Instead of proving his father wrong, Xavier would be proving his father so very right.

The pressure mounted until his shoulders ached, as if the weight across them had real substance.

"I can feel you panicking," Laurel said into the silence, reading his mind.

"*Panic* is a strong word," he responded mildly.

"And when you start using your 'nothing's bothering me' tone, I have to believe *panic* is the right word." Her hand slid across his thigh and squeezed, imparting comfort and understanding. "Of course, if you don't want me to guess, you could always tell me what's going on."

The traffic light ahead of him turned red, but he waited until he'd come to a complete stop before answering her.

"I'm panicking, okay?" He scowled. Boy, he was really inspiring confidence here, in both of them. "I don't know why. I shouldn't be."

Her hand smoothed over his thigh again. "Because this is important to you. There's nothing wrong with that."

"But there is something wrong with letting it affect me. I can't fail today."

"You won't," she said fiercely enough to make him do a double take. "*We* won't. I'm here and we're going to do this thing together. Haven't you figured that out by now?"

Yeah. Maybe. Mostly, anyway.

After everything she'd said, all the conversations, the proof that she was aboveboard, there was still a part of him that automatically held back. He had to consciously loosen his grip on his worries, and sometimes that didn't go so well. It wasn't a crime. They were taking things slowly, or at least he was taking *that* part slowly. If she didn't like it, too bad.

"Why are you so invested in this, anyway? It's my deal," he grumbled, well aware that his nerves were causing him to be crabby.

He'd thrown that question in her direction strictly to change the subject, but now that it was out there, he realized it had been bothering him. They'd worked twelve hour days, even on the weekends. She had literally no skin in this game other than volunteering for the job.

"That's why, silly," she said with a smile, as if that should have been perfectly obvious. "You need me. Poof. Here I am."

He didn't deserve her loyalty, especially not when he was still deliberately holding back.

"But you don't even know why it's so critical," he blurted out and immediately wished he could recall the words. She was too sharp to let it pass.

His inheritance test was a can of worms he'd yet to open with her, and he'd just pulled into the lot of the hotel where they'd taken over one of the ballrooms. They had an enormous amount of work to do in order to get the venue decorated and ready for the auction, which would take place at eight o'clock sharp.

Not only did they have to transform the ballroom, they'd opted for black tie, which meant they both also had to change out of their T-shirts and jeans at some point. He didn't have time to get into the details of the inheritance test with her. And he really didn't want to have a conversation about why he hadn't told her about it already.

She cocked her head. "You mean, there's another objective besides the obvious?"

"Yeah." Now he had yet another reason not to go down this path—thus far, she'd apparently assumed he was fired up over fundraising strictly for altruistic reasons. And he didn't want to disappoint her. "Can we talk about it later?"

"Sure," she said immediately, and that made him feel even worse.

He had to tell her the truth. He owed it to her, if for no other reason than because she *did* have skin in the game: her time, her efforts, her faith in him. But also because this was where the rubber met the road. If he wanted to practice letting go of things and showing Laurel that he trusted her, this was what trust looked like. He had to lay out everything, even the ugly parts, and hope she didn't leap from the truck in disgust.

"Is this the part where I'm allowed to yell at you for being so understanding?" he asked. When her mouth quirked up, he returned the smile almost automatically. It was like a reflex; Laurel smiled and it made him happy. "My father's will…it's a little unconventional. Val and I had to switch places as a stipulation in order to get our inheritances."

"Oh." She drew the word out to about ten syllables. "*That's* why—"

"There's more." He hated interrupting, but he might not get this out if he had to wait. "I have to raise ten million dollars or I don't get a dime."

"That's ridiculous," Laurel returned immediately. "An inheritance shouldn't come with strings. What in the world did your father hope to accomplish by attaching fundraising to his will? It's not like he's around to see whether you succeed or not."

"Well…yeah. Exactly." Was he supposed to feel so relieved that she got it? That she'd latched onto the real culprit in all of this instead of lambasting Xavier for being so shallow? "I know diamonds. Not fundraising. It's been tripping me up to be so far out of my element."

"You listen to me, Xavier," she said sternly and slid her fingers through his hair to cup the back of his head, holding him in place so she could speak directly to him. "You're doing spectacular at fundraising. You're amazing and you've got this. We'll get your ten million dollars come hell or high water. If this auction doesn't do it, we'll keep going until we get there. I'm just mad enough on your behalf to dig my heels in."

"That's it?" he asked and couldn't even care that his incredulity was likely plastered across his face. Of all the possible reactions she could have had, that one was not even on his list. "You're all-in even knowing that I'm doing this for purely materialistic reasons?"

She flicked that question away with her hand as if it was a bothersome insect and shook her head. "You're not doing this for the money and there's not one single thing you can say to make me believe that you are. Your father insulted you, maybe even hurt you. You want to get back at him by succeeding. I get it."

"Uh, yeah, I guess you do." Dazed, he stared at her as something monumental shifted in his chest, making room for Laurel to settle inside as if she'd always been there. "Where did you *come* from?"

"Springfield," she said with a laugh. "Born and raised. I only came to Chicago to go to college and then I sort of stuck around."

He couldn't do anything else in that moment but grab her up in a fierce kiss, one she eagerly responded to. If they hadn't been in the cab of a panel truck, he'd have been stripping her at this very moment, determined to get to that place where she made him feel whole.

Hell, she was doing that right now, even dressed. For the first time, he fully believed he could complete this inheritance test. Laurel would stand by his side until he did. What more could he ask for?

The auction was a rousing success from the first moment to the last. Of course, it couldn't have been anything less given the involvement of LBC's staff, who had donated their own items handcrafted with love. As the master of ceremonies, Xavier had been magnificent. So much so, Laurel hadn't been able to peel her eyes from his gorgeous form all night.

Especially now, with his black tie unbound and hanging around his neck as he directed a couple of the volunteers who were removing the giant banner over the raised dais where the auctioneer had led the festivities.

Though dozens of people still milled through the ballroom, Xavier caught her watching him and slid her a secret grin that might mean any number of things, but she hoped it was an indicator of how thrilled he was with the outcome of the auction. As he should be.

Once the banner came down, he extracted himself from the volunteers and somehow managed to maneuver her into a private corner, where the foot traffic wasn't as heavy.

"The auction went far better than I had a right to expect," he said as he gathered her close in a celebratory hug that quickly grew into something more precious than air.

She let herself be swallowed by the enormous rush of emotions for about five seconds and then wormed out of his embrace. With regret. It was always hard to stop touching him, regardless of the location. But the longer she stayed in his arms, the more she wanted to whisper the things in her heart.

"There are way too many LBC staffers still here to be getting so cozy," she reminded him pointedly. They still hadn't announced to the world that they were dating.

Bold, brave Laurel had taken what she'd wanted and been richly rewarded over and over again for far longer than she would have expected. She kept waiting for everything to come to an immediate and abrupt halt when he told her he was through exploring.

"Then we should go home," he murmured, heat leaping into his gaze so fast that it made her dizzy.

Things *never* came to an abrupt halt because he kept saying stuff like that.

Home, as in his house. The place she'd started subconsciously calling home, as well. But it wasn't hers, no matter how hard he tried to make her comfortable there. Neither did she dare fall prey to the seductive idea that he might eventually ask her to stay permanently.

They weren't doing permanent. They were doing hot, uninhibited and adventurous. Nothing else, no matter how many times she found herself straying off in a fantasy that had a different end.

"Don't we still have work to do?" she countered breathlessly, as he treated her to a hungry once-over that affected her almost as strongly as it would have if he'd used his hands. Maybe more so because he wasn't touching her. They were in public and he couldn't. That somehow made it more delicious, more arousing.

"There's only one thing I want to do right now, and it has nothing to do with the auction," he told her. His low voice snaked through her, heating everything in its path. "We've been here almost all day. We have volunteers for a reason."

"I can't argue with that logic."

Before the entire sentence had left her mouth, he was steering her toward the door, murmuring wicked things in her ear until she shuddered. The valet had his Aston Martin waiting in the lane by the time they arrived at the curb, even though he'd driven the rental truck—a trick that she had no clue how he'd performed, but that she appreciated, especially when he threw the car into gear impatiently.

She'd learned to gauge exactly how turned on he was by the way he drove, and the screech of his tires around a corner said he was nearly thermonuclear.

Good. So was she.

They still hadn't explored the foyer, nor had he made good on his promise to back her up against a stone column, but she didn't mind. His bed worked for her. *He* worked for her.

Within seconds of hitting the threshold of his bedroom, he'd lifted the hem of her dress over her head and pulled her onto the mattress, twining their bodies together until she scarcely knew which way was up.

Then it didn't matter as he plunged her into a netherworld of sensation where only the two of them existed. Xavier drove her body to the heights of pleasure, wrung so much feeling from her very soul that she nearly sobbed with relief when she came. As he followed her, she clung tightly to his shoulders, anchoring herself lest she float away.

The longer she did this, the less certain she was about whether she'd walk away unscathed. But she'd agreed to help Xavier explore passion and she couldn't just stop cold turkey because she'd started assigning more importance to their relationship than she should.

This wasn't the precursor to something long term. It

couldn't be—she hadn't told him the truth about who she was and she didn't believe for a second that they were headed to a place where she needed to. They were sleeping together because they both enjoyed it and one day, that would stop being true. He'd even said they were helping each other be bold.

Plus, she'd pretty much decided that her story about the fraud was a no-go since she hadn't found any evidence. Besides, Xavier made her feel like she could focus on her flagging career and successfully find another story to break that would fix her mortifying gaff. She'd be better for her time with him and look back on it fondly.

But that's all there was to this.

It was just…when he snuggled her close and stroked his strong fingers through her hair, it didn't *feel* like they were winding down. She spent every night in his bed and they'd worked on the auction for hours upon hours outside of bed, yet she never got tired of being with him. Surely that meant something. But what, she couldn't wrap her head around.

"I still can't believe that Miro painting went for 1.4 million dollars," Xavier commented out of the blue as his lips toyed with her hair. "*One* piece fetched what I had braced myself to accept as the sum total of *all* the donations."

"You're the one who drove the price up," she reminded him, relieved to jump on something that would pull her away from the angst and drama in her own head. "It was like you'd been auctioneering your whole life when you got up on stage and announced to the audience that there were two collectors in the crowd, then got them bidding against each other."

He shrugged modestly, his muscles rippling against

her back and shoulders. "Helps that I knew so many people in attendance."

"Yes, it does. Whatever your father's posthumous game is with that will, it's not going to keep you from your inheritance."

Laurel could at least help give him that satisfaction before they ended this. At this point, she'd all but abandoned the idea of uncovering anything problematic at LBC. Not on purpose. She'd just been so busy with the auction that investigating had slipped in priority. Okay, maybe the slip had been a little more on purpose than she'd let herself admit. If she didn't investigate, she didn't have to worry about how to bring it up with Xavier, nor did she have to worry about making any mistakes.

"If all the money comes in from the auction as expected, I should be pretty close to the ten million," he said.

"If you want, I can meet with Addy and someone from accounting on Monday to get some solid numbers."

"Sure." Xavier mouthed down her neck to her shoulder, then lower, ratcheting up the intensity within seconds. Her body bowed beneath his talented lips as he worshipped one of her breasts, and she forgot all about the auction.

It wasn't until Monday morning, after she'd already taken a seat between Addy and Michelle from accounting, that it occurred to her that this was precisely the position she'd hoped to be in when she'd taken the job: trusted enough to be given access to LBC's books.

Her pulse drummed in her throat the entire time Addy and Michelle talked her through the numbers. Nothing calmed her ragged nerves, not even the news that Xavier was, indeed, very close to the ten-million-dollar mark. If he hosted another successful fundraiser, he'd hit his goal easily, as best she could tell from the preliminary figures.

That meant he might cut her loose soon and that hit her hard. She couldn't keep pretending that everything was going to work out fine, not when the thought of losing him hurt so deeply that she couldn't make it stop. It all seemed to be coming to a head but she couldn't see what the next steps were.

Laurel asked Michelle when she could check back to get final numbers and then scribbled out a few ideas Addy had for another fundraiser. The three women chatted and then Michelle and Addy segued into an entirely different conversation about a problem with the meal services area that apparently had been going on for some time.

Laurel listened with half an ear as she added her own notes to Addy's thoughts. The auction had been so successful because they'd heavily involved the staff and there was no reason to change that. In fact, Laurel wanted to take it a step further and involve the staff's families.

"Jennifer has been off with her estimates for so long, no one even thinks twice about it," Michelle said to Addy, flicking her fingers dismissively at the computer screen open in front her.

"Oh, I know." Addy rolled her eyes. "Marjorie used to complain about it twice a month, when Jennifer submitted her budget and then again when she submitted her expenses. I don't know why Jennifer bothers to come up with a budget at all."

"It's only because I make her," Michelle said with a laugh. "If I had to approve her expenditures, I'd go insane trying to match them to her budget. I'm more than happy to let Val handle that."

Laurel tried really, really hard to ignore the way her spine tingled. But it was no use. She'd heard every word and her vast experience with human nature told her there was more to this story than had been expressed thus far.

"Val approves all the invoices from the meal services area? Not someone in accounting?" Laurel asked.

"Yeah," Michelle offered readily. "Or he did. Xavier does now, because of the amount. LBC has a rule about who can approve over a certain dollar threshold."

Which wasn't uncommon. But it was somewhat irregular for no one to reconcile the budgeted amount to the actual spend, which didn't seem to be happening. Nor had anyone done anything about the discrepancy, if it extended as far back as when both Val and Marjorie had been involved.

Laurel tucked that information away, opting not to press Michelle on it since there was no evidence of any wrongdoing. Except, as the day wore on, Laurel couldn't quite dismiss the whole thing. Her original sources had mentioned discrepancies with accounting for items stocked in the supply closet, not with the meal services area, but who was to say there weren't issues in more than one area? Or it could be that there were no problems at all and all of this was unfounded suspicion that would be easily disproved.

That's what she'd come here to find out.

Either way, it was time to bring Xavier up to speed on what she'd heard. It was exactly what she'd promised herself she'd do if and when something like this came up. It would be a great test of his intentions toward her and definitely would reveal whether they were moving toward something better than what she'd braced for.

This whole matter would be decided, once and for all.

Thirteen

When Laurel appeared at the door of Xavier's office after a very long morning apart, the look on her face immediately eliminated the idea that she'd been thinking about him in a wholly non-work-related way. Which meant he couldn't boost her up on the desk and push her skirt to her waist like *he'd* been thinking about.

"Is this a business visit?" he asked, just in case he'd misread things.

She nodded and shut the door. Xavier closed his laptop and crossed his arms, though it was a sure bet neither would prevent him from angling for a way to get her onto the desk in a few minutes.

"I talked to Michelle in accounting a little while ago," she began and then hesitated.

His throat tightened as he recalled that Laurel had mentioned she'd ask for the fundraising numbers today. Surely he wasn't *that* far behind his ten-million-dollar goal. "Why doesn't your expression look like the news is good? I'm not that bad at math. I can't be more than a couple of million off."

"Oh, yeah, no, you're not." She waved that away, obviously startled that he'd mentioned it, as if fundraising hadn't even crossed her mind. "You're right on track. We just need one more good event like the auction and you're all set. Addy and I already hashed out some preliminary ideas that I'll run by you sometime."

"Okay, good. Why does that not make me feel better?"

She flashed a brief grin that warmed his insides, and that did make him feel better. As long as she kept smiling like that, nothing could go wrong.

"While I was talking to Michelle, some other stuff came up. About the accounting for the meal services area. I…" Laurel made a face. "Well, I hate to speculate, so I'm just going to tell you what she said and let you draw your own conclusions. Apparently there's a running joke that the manager of that area can't hit her budget. She's constantly over in her expenditures but no one has asked for an explanation."

A decade of monthly meetings where he'd scoured the balance sheet at LeBlanc rushed into his head in an instant and it was all he could do to remain calm. "You suspect fraud."

It wasn't a question, and the brief, bright flash in her gaze told him everything he needed to know. The calm he usually called up easily when dealing with the unexpected wouldn't surface.

"I don't know *anything*," she said simply, which didn't settle his stomach. "Only that Michelle mentioned that Val approves that area's expenses. And now you do."

"Okay." He had to start digging. Right now. "I hear you. This is my mess to clean up."

His stomach sloshed a bit more when she didn't immediately insist they were in this together or lean on the desk with fire in her eyes as she demanded that he let her be his clean-up partner. He couldn't focus on how much he wished she had, not when there was a potential issue festering beneath the surface of LeBlanc Charities.

If someone was stealing from LBC on Xavier's watch, there would be hell to pay. Then he could worry about why it felt like Laurel was slipping away.

Many long, grueling hours later, he and Michelle had run through enough of the numbers enough times to be convinced they'd only scratched the surface of the problem. The head of accounting had worn a sick expression on her face for the whole of the meeting. Xavier was pretty sure that same look had been etched on his.

"It's late," he told her and glanced at the clock, not at all shocked to see that it was past eight. "You should go home. I'll hire an independent audit firm in the morning to do a thorough excavation of the disarray our books are in."

And he meant "our" in every sense of the word. He'd signed off on some of the receipts and invoices, which appeared to have been inflated above their actual amounts. This was his to fix.

"Thank you for not firing me," she said quietly, her gratitude evident. "This should have been caught a long time ago."

"It's not all on you. Marjorie had a role in this, as does Val." Not to mention Jennifer Sanders, the manager of the meal services area who, it appeared, had been skimming off the top of LBC's operating capital for quite some time and rather blatantly, too. "I would ask that you keep this to yourself until we have enough evidence to bring up charges."

That was the real reason he hadn't fired anyone yet. He

needed facts before acting, and he couldn't trust the rage that seethed just under his skin. Until he had rock-solid proof from an unbiased third party about what had been happening, and for how long, he couldn't blame anyone 100 percent. Though Val topped his list at this moment.

His brother had some explaining to do.

Michelle slipped into a brown leather coat to brave Chicago's fall weather, then left without a backward glance. Xavier was too keyed up to go home, where Laurel was no doubt waiting for him, though he hadn't had a chance to really speak to her since she'd brought him the news that LBC wasn't being run as tightly as it could be.

He sent her a text message that was short and to the point: Don't wait on me for dinner.

Then he drove down by the lake, though the scenery wasn't all that pretty this time of year. Closer to New Year's, the trees would be bare of leaves and ice would form in large chunks on the shore. When the water froze, the lake looked like a giant sheet of glass, a testament to the power of an Illinois winter. That was his favorite. Tonight, the lake was choppy and dark and there was no moon to light the water.

He wanted to go home, despite how angry and heartsick he was over the suspected fraud. The problem was that he was even more heartsick over not understanding the reasons Laurel had basically dumped this in his lap and backed away. Was it because her role in his life was temporary and they were almost done? Maybe she wondered why she should get involved.

It wasn't that he wished for her to solve his problems. Only that he wished they were partners in this, too. That they could be partners in everything.

And he wished he could bring that up with her. It was too soon. He couldn't rush things.

Instead of heading for Val's house in River Forest, which was where he should be going, Xavier found himself on the North Shore. On a whim, he pulled up to the gate of his mother's neighborhood. The attendant nodded the moment he recognized Xavier and opened the gate to admit him, though he hadn't visited his mother since Thanksgiving last year. She wasn't expecting him.

If anyone would have some advice about how to handle this problem with LBC, it would be its founder. His mother answered the door of the palatial mansion herself, swinging one of the double doors wide as he came up the marble stairs. He hadn't even had a chance to knock.

"Xavier, what in the world are you doing here?" she asked, concern tightening her mouth. "Is everything okay?"

Patrice LeBlanc could pass for forty-five all day long and wore her ash-blond hair in a timeless style that women half her age envied. He studied his mother for a moment, struck all at once by the fact that that she'd run LBC by herself for a number of years until Val had joined her.

He hadn't fully appreciated the effort that had required until this moment. "Hi, Mom. I think we should talk."

She lifted her brows but didn't comment, ushering him into the salon she preferred. The sunny yellow always made her smile, as she'd gladly tell anyone who would listen. She didn't do so this evening, opting to take a seat on one of the brocade couches.

"You're scaring me, darling," his mom finally said as he settled into the leather chair at a right angle to the couch, though he knew she'd prefer it if he sat next to her.

They'd never been close. He'd been his father's son from an early age, while she'd favored Val, openly and unapologetically. Once upon a time, he'd been pretty jealous of the easy rapport she had with his brother, but he'd gotten over it, turning his slavish devotion to his father. Look where that had gotten him.

"Sorry, I didn't mean to drop in on you completely unannounced."

"Don't be silly. You're welcome here any time of day or night."

She meant it, too. How about that? He couldn't recall a time when he'd felt overly welcome at the house his parents shared before his father had died, but maybe that was on him. He hadn't tried to form any kind of bond with his mother, just retreated into his own misery over his father's will. Maybe it was time to change that.

"How are you doing, Mom?"

She laughed nervously. "Now you're really scaring me."

Because he didn't make a habit of asking after her health, emotional or physical, which shamed him more than he liked to admit. "It just occurred to me that I haven't given much regard to how lonely you must be with Dad gone."

The look on her face pretty well matched the confusion going on beneath his own skin. Where had that *come* from? But even as he asked that silent question, he answered it.

Laurel.

She'd opened up so many channels of emotion inside him, unlocking things he'd never considered before, things he didn't know existed or that he'd care about.

But he knew now.

"That's sweet of you to ask, darling. I'm doing okay, considering." She wagged her head back and forth. "Your father and I were married for nearly thirty-five years. It's hard to be alone. But I'm managing. Why did you really come by?"

He had to chuckle at her directness, which reminded him of his father for some odd reason. He'd have never said they were at all alike. But neither would he have claimed that about himself and Laurel. And he'd have been wrong.

"I uncovered some accounting issues at LBC. Looks like someone is stealing from us using fake invoices and receipts. I'm pretty upset."

"As you should be!"

Anger swept through his mother's expression, taking over her whole body, and she looked so much like Val in that moment that Xavier did a double take. That was the kind of passion he'd equate with his brother, all right, the same kind of all-in that Xavier had always avoided, with calculation. Hot heads didn't get results.

But he'd abandoned his emotion-free state in favor of a seductive lure in the form of Laurel Dixon. She'd enticed him to jump, holding her hand, as they soared into a free fall together. And as his reward? He would eventually be as alone as his mother, and he was suddenly very aware of how much he didn't want that.

"Tell me everything," his mother demanded, visibly bristling. "I might be retired, but my name is still LeBlanc."

Despite the somberness of the subject, that made him smile even as he laid out what he knew. Xavier concluded with the news that he'd already contacted an audit firm who specialized in nonprofit-sector accounting. His mother nodded and laid out a few of her own thoughts, namely that he needed to involve Val as soon as possible.

"I appreciate that you came to me first instead of Val," she told him. "It's a real testament to how far you've come since the reading of your father's will. I was against the idea of forcing you and your brother to switch places, at first, but Edward talked me into it."

"Why?" he blurted out, aching to understand once and for all why his father had hated him so much. "What possible good could have resulted from these ridiculous inheritance terms?"

"Darling." She shook her head, piercing him with a look that said he should have already figured this out. "If you hadn't been deep in the heart of LBC, would this theft have come to light? Would you have ever darkened my door? Your father worried that you were becoming too much like him and he didn't want you to get to the end of your life, only to have the same regrets he had."

Regrets? Over building an almost billion-dollar-a-year company? Something did not add up here. "Are you saying that Dad did this because *he* had regrets?"

But as she nodded, he couldn't summon a shred of anger. His mother was right; none of this would have happened if Xavier had stayed locked in his office at LeBlanc Jewelers.

Laurel wouldn't have happened.

And if he hadn't let her into his life, she might never have brought this theft to his attention. It had been the best combination of fate and design, but only by putting his trust in her had he gotten here.

"Sure. Regrets about not spending more time with Val, regrets about teaching you to be so hard, regrets about not traveling the world with me when he had the chance." His mother lifted a shoulder. "He had many."

Xavier would not have described himself as *hard*, at least, not prior to being propelled into LBC. LeBlanc Jewelers required a firm hand and, apparently, so did LBC, which he could provide. But he'd also learned that there were people at the cores of both enterprises that he'd overlooked—some of them, like Adelaide, to his detriment.

After standing at the helm of a charity for the last few months, he could at least take an objective step back and wonder if there was still more truth to uncover. Especially the one thing that still bothered him about all of this.

"If Dad did this to help me, where does Val fit into his master plan?"

His mother didn't miss a beat. "Val has his own challenges, namely that he cares too much. He needs to learn how mix objectivity with his tendency to lead with his heart. Your father thought both he and LeBlanc Jewelers would benefit from the switch. I think he was right."

Xavier ran a hand through his hair and tried to make some sense out of his reeling thoughts. The will *hadn't* been a blunt instrument designed to wreck both Val's and Xavier's carefully constructed lives, if his mom could be believed.

He believed her.

And that meant he no longer defaulted to not trusting anyone, up to and including his family.

If he took anything from this conversation, it was that nothing was as it seemed. Which meant he had some more thinking to do about *all* of his next steps, not just the ones associated with the accounting issues at LBC.

He couldn't keep holding Laurel at arm's length and neither could he let her go.

It was far past time to admit he'd fallen in love with her.

When Xavier blew through the door of his bedroom and snatched Laurel up in a fierce embrace, she scarcely had time to yelp before he'd swallowed her whole with the most mind-altering kiss she'd experienced from him yet.

His hands were everywhere, in her hair, slicking down her back, holding her so tightly that she couldn't imagine being separated.

And they were still dressed. She didn't have enough working brain cells to question him about his meeting with Michelle, whether he'd eaten or what occasion had prompted such a display of raw need. She just let herself be taken by the storm until he finally pulled back and rested his forehead on hers.

"Hi," he murmured with a small smile.

Dragging in great big quantities of air, she scratched out her own *"Hi"* in response.

He followed that with, "I missed you."

Oh, God. She'd missed him, too, pacing up and down the length of the study downstairs that smelled like him, the best combination of man and sandalwood. Eventually she'd wandered back to his bedroom to bury her face in his pillow.

It shouldn't have been such a big deal to miss one night together, especially not when he'd been contending with the accounting issue. But they'd spent 24/7 in each other's company for weeks. Without him around, she'd fallen into withdrawal, seeking out anything she could find to give her even a small hit of Xavier.

And here he was, rocking her from the inside out with nothing more than a few simple words.

"I gathered something of the sort," she managed to get out. "I hope it was okay that I waited here at your house—"

"I wanted you to. In fact, I want you here all the time." He cupped her jaw, feathering his thumb across her lips. "Move in. Tomorrow. Let's make this official."

Yes. Yes, yes, yes.

Yes to discovering what it felt like to love him wholly

and completely. Yes to exploring what they could mean to each other. Yes to—

Oh, no. *No.*

Her throat closed so fast that she saw stars. A monumental weight dropped down on her chest as she struggled to extract herself from his grip. This *could not* be happening before she'd had a chance to tell him the truth. He finally let her go, ruefully rubbing the back of his neck as he stared down at her.

"Too fast?" he asked with a half laugh. "I practiced what I was going to say on the way home from my mom's house. It kind of all rushed out, so I'm sorry if I messed it up."

"You, um…" He'd gone to his mother's house? Strictly to work out how to upend her entire world or for another reason entirely? Her head spun. "You didn't mess up. At least, I don't think you did. What exactly are you saying?"

"I'm saying I'm falling for you, Laurel."

And with that one single devastating phrase, everything came apart. Her soul. Her plans. Her sanity.

"You can't drop that on me," she whispered, even as her heart greedily latched onto the idea that Xavier LeBlanc had just admitted he was *falling for her.* "Not now."

"When, then?" Confusion marred his beautiful face, which made the swirl in her stomach worse. "I don't hear you saying you don't feel the same. What's holding us back?"

The truth.

"The fact that you don't know who I really am," she burst out, wishing with all her might that she'd already told him so she could admit she'd fallen for him, too.

This wasn't supposed to be happening, not like this.

He took a step back, his expression veering between

such a wide range of emotions that she couldn't sort them all. "What are *you* saying?"

"That's what I'm trying to explain! Give me a minute to get my feet under me."

She took a deep breath. It didn't help. She still had no clue how to approach this conversation other than to jump and hope he took her hand on the way down.

Please, God, let that be what happens.

She wanted Xavier more than she wanted to breathe and it was all within her grasp. Or it never was and she'd ruined everything prior to even walking through the door of LBC by choosing not to reveal her true profession.

"I'm an investigative reporter," she said bluntly and prayed he'd take it with the spirit she'd intended. "I took the job at LBC to uncover the fraud I suspected was going on. I'm sorry. I should have told you sooner."

"But you didn't," he said slowly. "Why not?"

"I tried to! In the conference room. You interrupted me at least four times—"

"And I've kept a muzzle over your mouth every minute since then?"

"I didn't think we were serious, Xavier. I never expected to have a reason to mention it after that. But then I got into this with you so much deeper than I planned. I wanted to tell you, but I never found solid evidence until today. And then you blew in here and things got all jumbled up."

In that respect, he *had* moved too fast. But it was too late and she couldn't blame him, not when it was all her fault.

"Let me get this straight." He pinched the bridge of his nose, his eyes closed in apparent disbelief. "You aren't a fundraising wizard and you've been toying with me this whole time."

"No! Oh, my God, no." Horrified, she reached out without thinking and then flinched when he jerked out of her grasp. "Why would you think I was toying with you? I have done fundraising in the past. That part is true, just like the way I feel about you. Everything between us is real."

"Nothing between us is real," he corrected harshly. "I don't trust a single word coming out of your mouth right now."

"Xavier." She bit back at least four different trite phrases, all designed to prove her innocence, which wasn't fair. She wasn't innocent. "You're right, and I'm sorry. I shouldn't have hidden my reasons for being at LBC. But you're missing the most important part of this. I'm not going to do the story on the accounting discrepancies. That's why I told you about it. I changed my mind."

"Thank you for your generosity," he said flatly. "I plan to press charges against the likely suspect as soon as I get the proper evidence. If you'd broken the story in advance of that, she might have had time to cover her tracks. So we'll call it even. I won't fire you for taking the job under false pretenses and you'll turn in your resignation to Adelaide first thing in the morning."

Oh, God. He wasn't going to give her a second chance. Her heart tore in two and lay there in pieces, bleeding.

"That's it, then?" she asked in disbelief.

She didn't have to wait for his nod. She'd screwed up again, even though she'd been trying to do the right thing.

"What would you like me to say? Apparently we weren't that serious and I misunderstood our relationship."

His voice had taken on that quality she hated, the one that he adopted to make sure everyone understood he was above the petty emotions swirling through the room. Nothing fazed him.

Except she knew better. "I *wanted* it to be serious. I just didn't…"

There wasn't a good way to end that sentence.

"You didn't what? Think I deserved the truth? Think I'd find out? Think I'd care?" His gaze bored into hers. "I did. To all three."

Past tense. She got the message loud and clear. He didn't care anymore. And he was done with her at the exact moment that she figured out what she wanted— Xavier.

"Okay. I get that you're angry—"

"I'm not angry. I'm ambivalent, at best," he said with a shrug. "You can clear all of your things out of my house at your convenience. I won't be here."

With that, he calmly walked out the door, leaving her trembling in the middle of his bedroom wondering how she could have been so colossally stupid as to lose both the story and the guy in one shot.

Fourteen

Xavier ended up driving to Val's house, after all. There was nowhere else to go and he'd developed this eerie calm that had started to scare him.

After weeks of consciously letting go, of allowing himself to roll around in sensations and experiences, he couldn't seem to feel anything at all.

A blessing, really. Laurel *had* been hiding something from him. A pretty big something. She was a liar—and a really good one, at that. All this time, he'd taken the fall for his suspicions, blaming his father's will for instilling this inconvenient sense of caution that he'd had to work on overcoming. In reality, Laurel had been undercover, scheming to break open a scandal starring LeBlanc Charities. *On Xavier's watch*, no less.

He wanted to hate her. To bask in his righteous indignation. To wallow in his justifications for walking away from her. But he couldn't feel anything other than numb.

When he got to Val's, it was well past midnight. Probably because he'd taken the long way around via Naperville. He shouldn't go inside Val's house. If there was a prize for least-fit company, Xavier would win it. Given his mood, the last person he should be speaking to was Val when they hadn't hashed out the Jennifer Sanders problem yet.

Just as he hit the start button to gun the engine so he could jet out of there, Val materialized at the car's driver's-side door and tapped on the glass.

Xavier slid down the window. "What?"

"Laurel called me," Val explained without fanfare.

Val hadn't found it necessary to take Xavier to task for his snippy tone, so Laurel must have told him everything. Xavier sighed. He was the one in his brother's driveway disturbing an entire household when everyone had to work tomorrow. The least he could do was have the courtesy to let Val explain how someone could have been robbing LBC blind for months without the director's knowledge.

Xavier peeled out of the car and slammed the door, which didn't help his mood, and followed Val into the dimly lit house.

"Sabrina's asleep," Val whispered. "I'd like to keep it that way, since she's sleeping for two."

"Yeah, yeah." Rub it in his face that Val had it all figured out in the romance department while Xavier had literally been sleeping with the enemy.

Or the potential enemy. If she'd broken the story. Which she hadn't because… He didn't know why. Not enough evidence or something. Maybe Laurel had hoped Xavier would spill the beans to her after sex one night, once she'd gotten him good and pliant.

She wasn't like that. He knew she wasn't. Except she'd lied to him. Repeatedly. Was any of it real?

Wearily, he sank into a chair and let his head fall into his hands. He had to move on and stop thinking about her. Massaging his forehead, he glanced up at Val from under his fingers. "Start talking."

"I know Jennifer's skimming. I've known for months," Val said with a nonchalant shrug that belied the bomb he'd just dropped. "Her husband is dying of stage-four colon cancer and they're struggling to pay the bills. You know how insurance is these days. High deductibles and such. She won't take money from me. I tried to give it to her. Tell me what you'd do in that situation."

"None of that," Xavier countered immediately. "Letting employees steal from you is not how you run a profitable business. I'd fire her and let her lie in the bed she made."

And that was likely the very reason his father had conceived the inheritance switch. His mother's words flooded his mind and he flinched. Maybe *hard* was a better word to describe him than he'd been willing to admit.

"That's a crap answer, Z." Val raised his eyebrows, likely in deference to the fact that he hadn't called Xavier by his childhood nickname in many years. "That's Dad talking. What would *you* do?"

"I don't know," he mumbled as he thought about his mother being alone now and how horrible it must be to have to watch your husband die, knowing there was nothing you could do to stop it. That's why it was better never to trust in something as fleeting and unreliable as another human being.

It was too late to stop the subtle and powerful internal shifts, though. He'd already started thinking with his heart and knew he wouldn't fire the woman, though it would be within his power to do so as the acting director of LBC.

"Until you have an answer, don't press charges," Val suggested quietly. "Marjorie had a back door where she handled the accounting discrepancies, so we're okay on the audit front. I can get you details."

Of course Marjorie had been in on it. She would have to be, since the accounting manager, Michelle, had known nothing of this. And he had a feeling the independent audit firm would find exactly what Val had just told him. They were totally in the clear from a legal standpoint. Ethically, maybe not. But he could make an argument that Jennifer's judgment was impaired and thus she was not worthy of discipline.

"I'll sleep on it." *Alone*, apparently. And for some reason, the sudden image of his empty bed crawled through him, opening doors that had been shut so far this evening. The most profound sense of sadness weighed down everything, and that was the only excuse he could come up with for the reason he blurted out, "Laurel and I broke up."

Val just nodded, his expression troubled. "I know, she told me that part, too."

Was nothing sacred around here? "All of it? Like how she lied about everything?"

"All of it, like how much she loves working for LBC and how she wants to walk away from reporting. She asked if I could possibly forgive her deception and see a way to keep her on board after you go back to LeBlanc Jewelers."

Oh. She'd called to beg Val for her job. Probably she had done so strictly to curry Val's favor, since he'd be the one she'd be working for in the long term.

"You said yes," Xavier guessed grimly. "I suppose

you also told her it was okay if she worked there in the interim, too."

Why not? It would be fun and games to continue working with Laurel, at least as far as Val was concerned. It had been his idea to hire her in the first place, against Xavier's better judgment. He deserved a medal for not throwing that back in Val's face.

"That's your call."

"I see. So I get to make the decision about whether to keep the best fundraising partner I could have dreamed up? Is that what you're saying? I'm the one who gets to decide if I'd like to feel as if I've been eviscerated every time I see her, day in and day out? I suppose it's all supposed to be easy, then. I should just decide to stop being in love with her, too." Xavier smirked at Val and then everything inside caught up with what he'd just unwittingly blurted out.

Oh, God, there came the hurt.

That's what he'd been so successfully avoiding thus far. He didn't like feeling so out of control, so raw inside. The same way he'd felt after the reading of the will, with all of the questions and lack of answers and overwhelming sense of betrayal.

Only this was worse. Laurel had tripped his radar from day one and he'd consciously forced himself to let go of his caution. He'd *purposefully* walked into her executioner's ax.

And what had she done? Smiled at him as she let her ax fall.

He'd *told* her how messed up he was about his father's will and she'd *understood*. Claimed to, anyway. How *dare* she say she got it when she'd been keeping secrets from him?

The rage spread, burning the raw places inside. Everything hurt. He hated it.

"I'm sorry, man," Val murmured. "I know how rough you must feel."

"What do you know about it?" he snapped back and then sighed. "Sorry. I'm messed up."

Val nodded and put a comforting hand on Xavier's shoulder. The warmth bled through his T-shirt, reminding him that he hadn't put a coat on when he'd walked out of the house.

"That's the part I know," his brother said. "I was in the opposite boat, though. Sabrina is the one who got hurt because of me and I had to fix it. I'm lucky she didn't think too hard about my flaws before accepting the ring I put on her finger, or I'd still be messed up."

"That's totally different." Also, whatever Val had done to Sabrina couldn't be nearly as bad as what Laurel had done. His brother was a saint, running a charity with flair and figuring out how to let a woman whose husband was dying pay for expensive medical treatments without losing her job or her dignity. "What did you do?"

"I hurt her." Val closed his eyes for a beat, as if the memory alone caused him pain. "We weren't serious, and then she got pregnant. I didn't shift the way I treated our relationship in time. I should have. But it happened so fast. I'd never been serious with a woman before and it was all new. I made mistakes. Fortunately, she forgave me, which, by the way, is the secret to marriage. You never stop making mistakes because it's all new, every day, if you're doing it right. As long as you go into it with forgiveness, it all works out."

"Who said anything about marriage?" Dazed, Xavier tried to take in all the things his brother had just said. "I barely even got to the point where I asked her to move in."

Val raised his brows. "Maybe that's part of your problem. You treated the entire relationship casually until *you* were ready to move forward and then didn't give Laurel enough warning to shift the way *she* thought about your relationship."

"Did she say that to you?"

What was *wrong* with him, greedily begging for scraps of information about Laurel? He should be banishing her from his mind. Except when he tried, all he could picture was her face as she pulled him down for a kiss, or her laugh, the way her voice always curled up in his gut. She'd been all-in from the beginning, charging ahead, partnering with him on a million small things that, added together, formed a woman who had given him a reason to change the core of how he dealt with relationships.

That was the thing he couldn't get over. She'd come to mean a great deal to him but he couldn't see much evidence showing she felt the same about him.

"No," Val said. "She told me that she'd screwed up the best thing that had ever happened to her and she didn't want to do that with the second-best thing. That's why she called me in hopes of salvaging her job at LBC since she'd already lost you."

"Me?" He blinked. "I'm the best thing that ever happened to her?"

"I know, it was a shock to me, as well," Val said with a smirk. "This is the part where you get back in your car and go find her so she can apologize to you directly instead of through me."

It was a testament to how befuddling this entire conversation was that Xavier almost nodded and did exactly that. But then he beat back that impulse with some heavy reminders of Laurel's treachery.

"It doesn't matter how she apologizes. There are some things that are unforgivable."

"Like stealing?" Val gave Xavier a minute to absorb that. "If you take a specific action out of context, sure. But I hope your exposure to the less fortunate has given you a different frame of mind. Motivation is complex. People make mistakes. You can seek out ways to rise above the things people do to hurt you or be alone. Your choice."

"When did you get so smart?" Xavier grumbled without any heat because, yeah, he got it.

Val just laughed. "Hey, when I sit at the head of the boardroom table at LeBlanc Jewelers, I feel like the stupidest person in the room some days. You manage that environment day in and day out with so much success that you make it look easy. So I guess I'm saying we each have our strengths, and when we put them together, we do all right. That's what Dad wanted us to figure out, you know."

If so, Xavier had played into his father's hands all along because Laurel had been the one to truly teach him that. That much had been real; he could feel the difference beneath his skin. She'd made him into a better person. And if that was true, then there might be room to reevaluate her reasons for not telling him the truth.

Xavier made a face at his brother. "I already knew that. I have no idea what took you so long."

"Then take my advice." Val punctuated that by shoving Xavier's arm until he stood up. "Go. Talk to Laurel. Don't let anything stand in the way of your happiness."

Xavier wasn't sure he could actually take that advice. Having an academic understanding that Val was probably right didn't magically make the big black bruise inside go away. Neither did he feel like he should be the one to make the effort. Laurel had been in the wrong. Not Xavier. He shouldn't have to hunt her down.

Apparently, she was of the same mind, because when he got home, she was still there, quietly sitting on his bed as if she'd been willing to patiently wait for him, even if it took all night.

"What are you doing here?" He questioned her gruffly, even as he drank in her troubled face and his soul soaked up her presence.

"Not making another mistake," she informed him, her voice doing that thing where it felt like she'd climbed inside him. "I screwed up by not telling you the truth soon enough and I'm not screwing up again."

"Then you should leave—"

"No." Slipping from the bed, she stood and faced him, her hands by her sides, though it seemed as if it took some effort to keep them there. "I need you to hear what I have to say."

He crossed his arms before he went insane and pulled her into his embrace, which was feeling more and more likely the longer she stood there within touching distance. All of this could have been avoided if he'd ensured that she'd really left the first time. Or if he'd resisted trusting her.

If she hadn't been so wonderful, so easy to be with, so amazing. Or a million other things that hadn't happened that way.

What had happened was Laurel.

She hadn't left. Apparently she wasn't going to unless he gave her the floor. "Fine. I'm listening."

Her silvery-gray eyes latched onto his, bleeding into his soul. "Xavier, I fell for you, too."

And with that, the last piece of his heart broke open and sucked him under.

* * *

Laurel's nails bit into her palms as she waited for Xavier to say something. Anything. But he just kept staring at the floor as if he'd discovered a pattern there that fascinated him. Or he couldn't bear to look at her a second longer. Either way, it meant her gamble hadn't paid off.

It was over.

She'd apologized. She'd admitted that she'd fallen in love with him, opening herself up to that single point of vulnerability, and it wasn't enough.

But then he finally glanced up, his eyes damp. That punched her in the gut. She'd hurt him and he was allowing her to witness exactly how much. What was she supposed to do with that, mourn the loss of what she could have had with him? She had been mourning it, for several long hours.

"Say that again," he demanded.

"I fell for you," she repeated succinctly, happy to have an excuse to admit it all over again. "I've never been in love before. I had no idea it would scare me so much. It made me do stupid things that I can't take back."

He nodded. "I get that. We're more alike than you might think."

Dampness sprang into her own eyes and she had to smile at what had become a running theme with them. He couldn't be too mad if he was telling jokes. There might be a thread of hope here. "Do tell."

"I've never been in love before, either, and it's making me do stupid things, too. I don't trust easily, and then you broke the fragile bit I was able to scrape together."

Oh, God, that stabbed her through the chest.

He'd *trusted* her and she'd shattered him by not telling him the truth sooner. Not breaking the story, deciding to take the evidence to him, all the small moments—none of that mattered in the end because she'd done the one thing he couldn't tolerate.

"Darling, no." She rushed it out before he could complete the last word. "Don't you dare take any of this on you. I'm the one to blame here, and it is not stupid of you to have trusted me. You have every reason to be angry and I—"

"The stupid thing I'm doing is forgiving you," he interrupted and she was so shocked, she shut up. "I'm not sure what tipped the scales but I'd rather practice getting this right with you than be alone with my self-righteousness."

Stunned, she stared at him. He was forgiving her? And wanted to be with her? None of this made a lick of sense.

"I don't understand."

"Let me spell it out, then. Laurel, I love you. Stop talking and come over here so I can show you."

Just like that. So simple and yet so complex. *I love you.*

The words penetrated into every fiber of her body until it felt like her skin would burst from the fullness inside.

Obediently, she fell into his embrace, scarcely able to credit how she was being wrapped up in Xavier LeBlanc's warm arms without having to perform seven years' penance for her sins.

"How can you just forgive me like that and not even care that I misled you?"

"I care, sweetheart," he said into her hair, his breath sensitizing her. "It's because I do care that I'm giving you another chance. If I didn't care, I'd let you go and move on easily. I've done it many times. But I don't want to not care anymore. I want to love someone enough that when they screw up, it hurts. So here's the thing I'd ask of you in exchange. Try not to screw up any more. But if you do, I'm pretty sure I can forgive that, too. Just as long as you're here being my partner at all things in life."

She laughed even as the tears started falling. "You're very gracious. You should teach a class."

"Noted. I'd rather take you to bed, if it's all the same to you."

She nodded and squealed when he picked her up, then threw her on the bed, following her down to wind her body up with his until she couldn't move. That was perfect. If he wanted to get right to the makeup sex, that worked for her and then some.

Except...

"There's just one thing I don't understand," she said instead of kissing him senseless, which was what she should have been doing—not opening more cans of worms. "What changed between earlier tonight and now?"

Surely not her phone call to Val. Had his brother talked him into giving her another chance? If so, she owed Val about a million handwritten notes of gratitude.

"I remembered how much grace you gave me when I told you about my father's will," he muttered, color staining his cheeks. "I'd kept it from you for my own reasons and you didn't even seem to notice, just jumped right on the Xavier bandwagon, supporting me in my fundraising tasks with no questions asked. I decided I was being a little high-handed to throw away what we had solely because you hadn't yet figured out the right timing to share your guilty secret. I'm sorry."

"Did you just apologize to *me*?" Laurel choked on the phrase and not all of it came out audibly. "I'm the one who screwed up—"

"Shh. You did and you apologized." He stroked his fingertips down her face, enlivening everything under his gentle touch. "For me, this is what trust looks like, and I have to spend a lot of time getting it right. It's a concerted effort that I'm still working on. So, for now, just know that I'm over it."

"How can you say that? What if I'm lying about forty-seven other things?" She wasn't. But how could he blindly accept that?

"You forget how well we can read each other." He kissed the tip of her nose, his heart spilling all over his face. "Because we're so much alike. I'm not worried. Plus, I'm sure you'll have to forgive me on occasion when I screw up the trust thing. We'll figure it out together."

Greedily, she soaked it all up. She loved it when he let her see how much she affected him. Loved that he trusted her enough to do so. Loved him. What had she done to get so lucky as to find a man like him?

"If you can read me so well, what am I thinking about right now?" she asked, letting her heart bloom through her expression.

"A drive down the shore of Lake Michigan?" he guessed and levered one of his knees between her legs to bind them even closer together.

She snorted. "Try again."

But, instead, he just kissed her and that was exactly right. He really could read her mind.

Miraculously, Xavier was giving her the second chance she'd always craved but had never been granted. She didn't have to worry about making mistakes with him because he'd be right there with her, holding her hand as they both jumped into the unknown. Together.

Epilogue

The charity fashion show Xavier and Laurel had put together with Val and Sabrina's help started off with a bang. Literally. A glitter cannon rained sparkles onto the stage as the first model strutted down the runway dripping with LeBlanc diamonds.

This time, Xavier wasn't a nervous wreck. Not about the fundraiser, anyway.

Not only was the fashion show designed to raise money for LBC, it was also a showcase for LeBlanc's new jewelry line. The buzz for it had grown to a fever pitch, which, in turn, put the spotlight on the charity. Who would have thought that Xavier and Val could combine forces in such a seamless way?

Laurel and Sabrina, that's who. Laurel and Val's wife had become fast friends, burning the midnight oil to help pull this thing together. Xavier couldn't believe how hard the two women had worked, but he showed Laurel how much he appreciated her every night when they finally rolled into bed together.

They did everything together now, including showers and shopping. Xavier had never been happier to have given someone a second chance. He had reaped enormous rewards for it. She felt the same. How did he know? Because her actions always spoke louder than her words. Though she had plenty of those, and she told him often that she loved him, which he wouldn't mind hearing daily for the next fifty years.

Tonight, he hoped to permanently etch that into stone. A diamond, to be precise.

"You have the ring, right?" Val said in his ear as they stood at the back of the venue monitoring the show. "I cannot tell you how many favors I had to call in to get that thing done in time."

As Xavier surveyed the crowd, he noted that several celebrities they'd invited had shown. Val had been schmoozing them in order to get signatures on the dotted line for a new LeBlanc advertising campaign and their presence here meant he'd sealed the deal.

In response to Val's question, Xavier patted his pocket, where the one-of-a-kind diamond engagement ring nestled inside a velvet box. "I would have slept with it, but I didn't want to ruin the surprise. Laurel loves surprises, you know."

His brother made a face. "You don't say. That's only the nine thousandth time you've told me."

The thought of proposing choked him up a little, but he didn't temper it. Why should he care if Val knew the subject of marriage tripped him up?

"So I'm a little excited to ask the woman I love to marry me. Sue me."

Saying it out loud didn't alter the swirl inside his gut

one bit. *Excited* was the wrong word. Nervous, exhilarated, emotional, sick to his stomach that he'd get it so wrong she'd say no. Any of the above might be more accurate.

Rolling his eyes, Val clapped him on the shoulder. "I would have thought you'd be more excited to hear that I got the preliminary numbers from Roger. LeBlanc Jewelers is going to hit the billion-dollar mark in revenue for the year by the end of this quarter."

Something bright bloomed in Xavier's chest and he grinned at his brother. "You did it!"

"We did it," Val corrected instantly. "You stacked the dominoes, I knocked them over. We're a team and that's why this fundraiser is going to put you over the figure for your goal, as well. Our inheritances are almost locked up."

Funny how the thought of having succeeded didn't make him as happy as catching sight of Laurel Dixon in the crowd did.

He watched her stop to speak to someone on her way to the dais, where she'd announce to the crowd how they could purchase the models' jewelry with all proceeds benefiting LBC. Edward LeBlanc's will had stated Xavier couldn't write a check to cover the ten-million-dollar fundraising goal, but it had not stipulated whether LeBlanc Jewelers could make a sizable donation—which had been Laurel's idea. Her passion for LBC had spilled over as she'd sold both brothers on the idea.

It was a no-brainer to also let her win over the crowd. It was also the perfect time to drop a surprise proposal on her.

She took the stage, which was his cue to move. But he was frozen, all at once. What if this was a mistake? What if she had no interest in getting married? What if—

"Stop freaking out and go propose," Val muttered from behind him as Laurel's brilliant and beautiful voice rang out through the loudspeaker. "She's going to love that ring you designed. I approved the workmanship personally."

"Yeah, yeah." Somehow Xavier got his body moving and he hit the floorboards of the stage.

Laurel glanced over at him expectantly as she smoothly finished her sentence despite the unplanned interruption. Her silvery-gray eyes caught him sideways, warming him, loving him. His ingrained sense of caution vanished in an instant as he strode across the stage to take her hand.

This was right, no question in his mind.

"Laurel." He cleared his throat as she smiled, totally as caught up as he was, her attention on him instead of the hundreds of people watching them. "Before I met you, I spent a lot of time shutting people out and blaming it on the need to be clearheaded in order to run a company. You taught me that no one can do much of anything by themselves, then helped me figure out that I didn't want to, anyway."

Tears splashed down her face but she didn't interrupt, even when he pulled out the box and flipped the lid, letting her get a glimpse of the ultrarare, smoky gray diamond that matched her eyes.

"This is me, down on one knee, asking you to take my hand and jump." When she arched an eyebrow, he realized he'd forgotten to kneel and hastily corrected that mistake by dropping to the platform with a loud thud. "Both knees, then."

The crowd laughed along with Laurel, who promptly got down on her knees, too. Of course she had. That's what she'd always done—ensured he knew they were a team beyond a shadow of a doubt.

And he had none.

"Yes," she said into the microphone attached to the neckline of her dress. "I'll marry you, but only if you buy me that Jada Ness necklace on the third model as an engagement present. Did you guys see that thing? Gorgeous!"

With that, she turned off her microphone and dove into his arms for a scorching kiss that got the entire crowd cheering and hooting.

"Driving up the price of LeBlanc's donations?" he murmured when they finally came up for air.

She shot him a misty smile. "You see right through me."

How could an inheritance compare with this woman? It couldn't. And that was the real lesson he suspected his father had intended for his sons to learn.

Nothing could replace the people you let into your life.

*****

COMING SOON!

We really hope you enjoyed reading this book. If you're looking for more romance, be sure to head to the shops when new books are available on

Thursday
6th September

MILLS & BOON

LET'S TALK
Romance

For exclusive extracts, competitions
and special offers, find us online:

Or get in touch on 0844 844 1351*

For all the latest titles coming soon, visit
millsandboon.co.uk/nextmonth